Across Torn Tides

Val E. Lane

Wave Song Publishing

ISBN 979-8-9874248-3-4

Cover Art: Stefanie Saw/Seventh Star Art
Header design: Etheric Designs

This work of fiction contains scenes and events set in an alternate 18th Century time period. Names and places may differ from actual historical names and locations, and it is not meant to depict historical events, myths, or figures accurately.

To the little seagull that flew into my life and sent me on my own adventure while I was writing this book.

PLAYLIST

Scan the code or click to listen. Each song corresponds to the chapters in order. You can also search for the playlist on Spotify by book title.

1. "heartbeats" by Hanniou
2. "30 purple birds" by why mona
3. "Through Me (The Flood)" by Hozier
4. "Throw Me in the Water" by WILD
5. "Deep Water" by Lyves
6. "Self Sabotage" by Ruelle

7. "In The Stars" by Benson Boone / "WHERE YOU BELONG" by Matt Hansen

8. "Hold On" by Will Church

9. "Amen" by Stereo Jane, James Gillespie

10. "My Mind & Me" by Selena Gomez / "Overthinking" by Zoe Wees

11. "Hurricane" by Josh Alexander

12. "Cómo Cuándo y Dónde" by Sofia Carson

13. "Truth Comes Out" by Willyecho

14. "Secrets" by Jay Denton, Hannah Parrott

15. "Will It Ever be the Same" by Young Summer

16. "Contigo" by Sebastian Yatra / "All Things End" by Hozier

17. "Sígueme y Te Sigo" by Daddy Yankee

18. "Stronger" by Thunderstorm Artis

19. "Look What You Made Me Do" by Taylor Swift / "Upside of Down" by SVRCINA

20. "Be Here For You" by Sam Tinnesz

21. "Ships + Tides" by OneRepublic

22. "Wave After Wave" by Sleeping At Last / "Wasteland" by NEEDTO-BREATHE

23. "Follow the Sun" by James Mclean, A. Void

24. "Don't Give Up" by Ursine Vulpine, Annaca

25. "I Feel Like I'm Drowning" by Two Feet

26. "MAYDAY" by Culture Code, Natalie Major

27. "Drown" by HANDS

28. "Wish That You Were Here" by Florence + The Machine

29. "Lost at Sea" by Rob Grant, Lana Del Rey

30. "Unsinkable" by Sail North

31. "Not Gonna Break Me" Jamie N Commons

32. "Can You Hear Me Now?" by Owsey / "Never Been Away" by ABBOTT, 2WEI

33. "Where Do We Go From Here" by Ruelle

34. "Leave Her Johnny" by Sean Dagher, Nils Brown / "Carry on Wayward Son" by Kansas

35. "What's Left of You" by Chord Overstreet

36. "I Don't Wanna Leave Just Yet" by Thomas Day

37. "Daylight" by David Kushner

38. "We Go Down Together" by Dove Cameron, Khalid

39. "Past Life" by Trevor Daniel, Selena Gomez

40. "Get Free" by Lana Del Rey

41. "Brother" by NEEDTOBREATHE

42. "Gracestone" by Phildel

43. "Can You Feel It Coming" by Steelfeather

44. "mirrorball" by Taylor Swift

45. "Way down We Go" by KALEO

46. "Live Like Legends" by Ruelle

47. "Black Water" by The People's Thieves

48. "Ripples" by Davis Naish

49. "Francesca" by Hozier / "Sunlit Grave" by Saint Mesa

50. "The Deep" by Phildel

51. "A Storm Is Coming" by Tommee Profitt, Liv Ash

52. "My Jolly Sailor Bold" by The Hound + The Fox

53. "Never Let Me Go" by Florence + The Machine

54. "Destiny (feat. Krigaré)" by Generdyn, Krigaré

55. "Brother – Acoustic" by Kodaline

56. "Witness the Masterpiece – Orchestral Version'" by Ganyos

57. "Take Me to Church" by Hozier / "Say Yes To Heaven" by Lana Del Rey

58. "If the World Falls to Pieces" by Young Summer

59. "Home Again" by UNSECRET, Aron Wright

CONTENTS

1

Sea Glass

Katrina

"What's that?" I squinted, focusing in on the glimmering fragment drifting ashore on the waves. I didn't wait for Bellamy's answer before I took off running, my bare feet treading the dense sand into the roiling surf.

I nearly stumbled over grasping at the shiny object as seawater swept through my fingers. A piece of glass. It was just a piece of sea glass. I walked back to Bellamy, straining to hide the crushing disappointment on my face.

"Not a clue then?" He asked, probably out of pity. I knew I was being absurdly hopeful. He had to be tired of it by now.

"No," I croaked, swallowing. "Just broken glass. But I *know* I saw that albatross yesterday. He's telling me he's out there." I knew I was delusional. But was I, really? After everything that had happened to me, could it really be so ludicrous to hope a message or letter, or *something* might drift in from the far reaches of wherever Milo was?

Captive to this hopeless optimism, I roamed the shores each morning, looking for whatever remnants the tide had washed in overnight, hoping for anything I could convince myself came from him. When I saw the bird, it only fueled my fantasy.

The semester had begun without me, like a whirlwind whisking past. Isabel's campus resumed its usual bustle, and students had returned to their dorms, readying themselves for classes to start in a few days. But I had withdrawn to give my heart some time to grieve losing Milo. And more importantly because I couldn't afford school getting in the way of rescuing him.

"Are you ready for this voyage?" Bellamy asked, likely trying to pull my attention from this useless piece of glass in my hand.

"Of course, I am. Tomorrow can't come soon enough," I tossed the piece of glass back into the water with all my strength. We'd be setting sail to find the pirate lord who had the Crown of the sea goddess who could hopefully bring Milo back, and I'd been counting down the hours. "And you're sure you're going to be able to pull off sailing Cordelia's yacht across the Atlantic?"

"Love, did you already forget what you saw me do back in 1720? I think I can handle a ship that doesn't even have sails to manage." Bellamy smirked.

"Just saying, you might be a little rusty," I teased as Bellamy rolled his eyes. I secretly wished we could just fly there. It would be faster. But that wasn't an option for Bellamy. He had no ID, no passport, nothing that would allow him access to board a plane. So, sailing there was the only option. And luckily my deceased mermaid great-grandmother's unused private harbor was the perfect place to snag a ship seaworthy enough for us to do it.

"It'll be fine, Katrina. Clearly, it's not that easy to kill us." He patted me on the back and walked toward the surf with his hands in his pockets. It was strange to finally see him in some fully normal clothes, but he still refused to lose the black jacket.

I took a filling breath of the salty air around me as I watched Bellamy's focus lock onto the seawater. How I wished he would let me know what he was thinking under that aloof exterior. He seemed to keep his thoughts under lock and key ever since the morning at the pier, except for whenever we discussed our plans to get to Cuba and find this Pirate Lord Bastian Drake. But I figured I probably wouldn't be the same after everything he'd been through either. I couldn't say I was doing much better.

"I'm going back to the dorm to get an early start on packing things." I used the silence as an opportunity to excuse myself, leaving out the part about how I wished I could stop by Milo's old loft just to sleep in his bed. But Bellamy was staying there now, so I couldn't.

Bellamy sent a nod my way and then resumed his pensive stare into the ocean. I walked back to my car, thinking about it all over again. I touched my face to feel the scar along my jaw and twisted the silver-blue scale I now wore on a string bracelet I'd made so that if I needed my song, I wouldn't have to be in my siren form to use it. It matched the ring on my finger. My souvenirs from the past, each reminding me of the moment I lost Milo. I wondered where he was, and what he was doing now, and I lived each day in anguish wishing I could know he was safe. I knew we'd do anything to get him back, and morning couldn't come soon enough. But a small part of me—maybe some sinister remnant of my siren side—wouldn't stop asking myself if we could really turn back time and save him.

2

Part of the Crew

Katrina

I stared at the green call icon on my screen. I just had to bring myself to tap the button...to call my parents like I told them I would last week. I needed to tell them everything was fine and I was ready for my classes to start tomorrow. I couldn't tell them I was headed to the Caribbean tomorrow evening. They'd flip and ask too many questions I couldn't answer. I didn't need them to worry and complicate things even more. If something happened, I'd figure out how to deal with it. I pressed the button and waited while my stomach sank further with each ring.

"Hija, hi!" My dad's voice came through excitedly through the phone, as he always sounded when I called.

"Hi, Dad," I said, forcing a smile that I hoped made me sound more alive than I felt. "I just wanted to call before the semester starts tomorrow and check in."

"Claro, Trina. We know you're busy. So it means a lot when you find time for us," he teased. "How is Milo and your roommate friend...McKinley?"

"McKenzie." I corrected with a weak chuckle. "She's great. She's really hyped for a new year. And Milo he's..." I swallowed the burning lump that suddenly appeared in my throat, "he's better than ever."

"That's so great to hear, Trina. I'm so proud of you. And your artwork is still selling like crazy in the store downtown, yeah?"

"For sure," I shrugged, knowing that part was a lie. I hadn't even checked on those few paintings since before we'd ended up setting sail for Nassau. "Money hasn't been an issue for a while, trust me." That part was true at least. Cordelia's money had been more than enough to keep me afloat, though I wondered what would happen to her resort and the rest of her assets once her death was discovered. But for now, I had more than enough to tie me over for the near future. I'm sure she wouldn't have minded her great-granddaughter borrowing a little extra from the bedroom drawer in her yacht.

"I knew you'd settle in eventually. You're doing it, hija, and I never doubted you would." I could hear the pride welling up in my father's voice. He might be even more proud if he knew I'd saved us all from a global disaster of oceanic proportion, but I was content to let him go on thinking my biggest accomplishment yet was my college scholarship. Even if I was about to risk losing it.

"Your mom wants to say goodnight while I have you," My dad's voice was suddenly cut short by the rustling sound of the phone being passed off. Before I could respond, Mom's voice chimed through like a bell. She sounded healthy, and I still couldn't get over how glad I was for that.

"Hey Trina, sweetie," she greeted. "I hear things are going well. You're all the rage in Ozark. You're all Scott ever talks about around here."

"I'm glad to know he's spreading the word." I laughed. "How are you, Mom?"

"Couldn't be better, honey. I mean that. In fact, I've been thinking." She paused, her words hanging in the air. "I've been thinking about coming down there to visit you soon. It could be a great way for us to finally spend some time together. You could show me your campus and the beach."

My stomach sank. She couldn't come now. No way. I'd be in Cuba in just a few days. And I didn't know when I'd be coming back.

"Yeah, that could be fun. Maybe during spring break sometime. I think that'd be good for us." I really did think it would be a good thing for us to make up for so much lost time together. Just...later.

"The sooner the better. You just let me know."

"I will, Mom. Can't wait," I said, smiling lightly, still feeling a pang of mistrust that I felt guilty for having.

"I'll talk to you soon, honey. Your dad's already wandered off back to the garage probably, so I guess I'll say goodnight for us both. Love you."

"I love you, too, Mom. G'night."

I placed the phone down on my bedside table, ready to sleep. Ironically enough, sleeping was my greatest escape these days. I didn't dream much anymore—or if I did, I didn't remember them. But that was better than living the nightmare I'd found myself in.

I hadn't closed my eyes for five minutes when McKenzie crept in, rapping her fingers lightly against my wall. "Hey, you awake?" She crept into the shadowy room.

"Yeah," I uttered.

"I just came to check on you," she walked closer, "I know classes start tomorrow and I wanted to see how you're holding up."

"I'm good. Just wondering how long it'll be before they notice I'm not attending and kick me out." I forced a weak chuckle, but I don't think my facial expression matched.

"I would do the same thing," McKenzie cooed. "It'll be worth it. You'll find him, Katrina." McKenzie's sweet smile flitted across her face as I leaned forward to hug her. "Which is actually the reason I came to talk to you," she started. I pulled back to look at her while she spoke. "I just can't let myself stay here while you and Bellamy go do this. Not after everything we've been through together. And Noah feels the same. We can't stay behind."

I pinched the bridge of my nose between my eyebrows. "McKenzie, we talked about this. I can't let you give up what you have here at ISA. I can't let you throw away your dreams for this...for me. Milo didn't want us to all make it back home just so you could throw it away helping me look for him."

"You don't understand, Katrina." McKenzie paused with a breath that she held for a moment that felt like forever. "Being here at ISA isn't my dream. Graduating with an art communications degree isn't my life goal. I'm just here because I didn't know what else to do with my life. And trust me, with my family's money, they'll let me reenroll anytime and pick up where I left off, I'm sure of it. And that's just the thing I'm saying. I've always gotten what I wanted, easily, not because of who *I* am, but because of who my mom and dad are. And now I want more. Something their money can't give me. Something I can only give myself. The past month has made me realize what's important. And it's not a degree from some stupid preppy art school. It's the people in my life who matter."

I stared at her in silence, blinking in the dark. I didn't know what to say to any of that. I'd never heard such an eloquent speech come from those perfectly glossed pink lips. And I certainly couldn't believe it was the same roommate who was all too obsessed with dragging me to college parties and ignoring my pleas not to.

"I've never thought of it that way," I said.

"Well now you will. Because I'm coming with you. And so is Noah. And this time, it's on purpose." She grinned mischievously.

"McKenzie—" I tried one more time, futilely, to persuade her otherwise, but she was always one step ahead of me.

"You can't stop me. If you don't let us sail with you, we'll fly there."

"Fine," I sighed, though secretly I was glad I wouldn't have to leave her behind. "But you have to be careful, and if things get weird, you stay back and remember it's mine and Bellamy's fight. I'd never forgive myself if you or Noah got hurt because of me."

McKenzie leaned forward close to my ear with a sly look in her eye. "Yeah, yeah. Technically, you'd never even be in this mess if it wasn't for me taking you to that Halloween party last year, so ya know, it's kinda my problem now, too."

"If that's what you want to tell yourself." I shook my head, but even all the weight I was carrying couldn't hold down the tiny smile that snuck its way across my lips.

With one more hug and a couple more laughs, we told each other goodnight, and McKenzie slipped back out the door to her side of the dorm. She made no effort to muffle the sound of her excitement as she made a phone call I should've seen coming.

"Hey, Noah! All confirmed. Pack your bags because tomorrow we're going to Cuba."

3

From North to West

Bellamy

This room was too empty. Too cold. Too lonely. But I didn't have the energy to take myself somewhere else. So I sat on the edge of the bed in Milo's old loft, staring at the floor like it would disappear if I blinked. My leg wouldn't stop shaking from the nerves. Was I fucking crazy?

Being alive—truly alive—certainly brought its own emotions to work through, and I couldn't shake the crushing weight of feeling like I didn't quite understand who I was anymore. I wasn't sure I'd felt that in a long time. It was easy, back in the time of my best days, knowing exactly who and what I sailed for. But now, the world was different, and the wonder was gone. And even if I brought Milo back, as I planned to do, where did that leave me? What was I here for?

A broken life without the only person I ever truly loved—Serena. Even when I was finally able to die, she wasn't there waiting for me like I hoped. So where was I supposed to put my faith? Why would I care what mark I left in this world, good or bad? I was just here to do what had to be done.

In a moment of tenderness, I smiled as I remembered her voice, so smooth and sweet. Too sweet as she'd tell me she loved me in that strange, special way of hers.

"I love you 18 times 66. As far as North to West." She'd said one night as we said goodbye.

"That doesn't make sense, love. What does that mean?" I laughed.

"I don't know," she giggled. "Just popped into my head."

So from then on, that became our thing. Eighteen times sixty-six. From North to West. It made about as much sense as her loving me. She was too much of a fearless dreamer for this world. Perhaps that's why she longed so much to be part of mine. If only I hadn't let her. If I had just listened to Milo and stayed out of her world, she might be alive. I killed her, and I hated that I was back here, forced to remember it each day. My father wasn't here to blame anymore. Just me. My smile quickly curved into a scowl.

I raked my fingers across my hair, my head feeling heavy in my hands. I needed to sleep. But instead, I stood up, my eyes burning with the need for rest. My boots echoed along the aluminum stairwell as I walked down to the ground floor of the garage.

Across the darkness of the shop, I made my way outside, where the briny bay water hit my nostrils like a breath of fresh air. I sauntered over to Milo's motorcycle, where it leaned parked and lifeless. When we were cursed, I always thought it was strange that he wasted his time learning to tinker with things like this. It seemed like a waste of effort for someone damned to hell and trapped in a time loop of dying over and over each night. But I guess it paid off for him. Turns out it was me who was the fool in the end. Maybe that's why he loved to toy around with these damn things. Machines and maps couldn't break his heart.

I shook my head, knowing I should get back inside and force myself to sleep. As I stifled a yawn, I felt some weird sense of hope that maybe I shouldn't be so cynical. Right then, I swore to myself that I'd make sure I was brought back with a purpose. I'd take Katrina to Cuba. I'd protect her and find a way to get Milo back. And I'd do everything I could to keep from being the reason another person I cared about lost their life.

This was all I had left.

4

Rogue Storm

Katrina

Today was the day we left for Cuba. I completed my morning ritual as efficiently as possible. I scurried to pull back my unruly hair into a loose ponytail and slip on my worn sneakers—the ones dried out from saltwater and gritty with sand that I could never quite get rid of completely.

I drove to the marina, but I parked a block over so as to keep suspicions down if there were any. Hustling my way to the docks, I scanned the area for Bellamy. He was knelt over a tie down knot mooring a large yacht to the dock.

"Everything good to go?" I asked, studying the way his deft fingers ran over the rope.

"Good morning to you, too," He scoffed softly.

"I'm sorry," I said, kicking a broken piece of seashell over into the water. "I'm just anxious."

"Don't be." Noah's voice startled me as he appeared from above leaning over the boat's edge. "You got plenty of backup."

I glanced up at him with heavy eyes, but a heart that lifted at the sight. "You didn't have to come, Noah. Milo wouldn't have wanted—"

"Good thing none of us care what Sandy wants. Besides, I'd much rather be doing this than dealing with my pissed-off uncle and his insurance over the 'stolen' motorsailer. Kinda hard to explain how I let that happen."

I rolled my eyes with a playful shift in my stance. "I should know by now that I can't get rid of you and McKenzie."

"You might be able to control water, but you can't control us."

"I wouldn't be so sure about that," Bellamy said. "Remember she's still a siren." He winked at me, but something about his words still bothered some strange space within me. I didn't like remembering my power. It was too dangerous.

"Speaking of McKenzie..." Noah looked around. "Where is she?"

"Still sleeping when I left. I heard at least four of her alarms go off, so I'm sure she was going to get up any minute. She shouldn't be far behind me." I shrugged.

Noah's expression shifted, his dark brows creating inquisitive creases on his forehead. "Last night she swore she'd be here early. I've called her twice already and no answer."

I checked my phone. Nothing from McKenzie, but I had a missed call from Mom. I'd call her back later. "Maybe I should check on her," I said, turning back to face the outskirts of the romantic little town of Constantine. "I'll go back."

With a reassuring nod from both of them, I headed back to my Jeep, the damp air of late morning settling into my skin as the sun's golden heat began to make itself known. I drove back to Isabel, silently hoping McKenzie had changed her mind. I wanted her to go. I really did. But I couldn't forgive myself if something happened to her. And a part of me still couldn't shake the guilty conscience from feeling like she was giving up too much to help me.

With a quick dash to our dorm door, I poked my head in to hear McKenzie talking to someone. She sounded nervous and was speaking even faster than usual, which is pretty hard to do. A voice I didn't expect made me gasp and my stomach dropped as I realized who she was talking to. My mom.

5

SIREN'S CALL

KATRINA

"Mom?" I stuttered, glancing at McKenzie who looked just as confused as I felt. "What're you doing here?"

My mother turned to me, a strange smoothness in her movements. She smoothed her shoulder-length hair back behind her ears with both hands. "I told you, sweetie, I wanted to come visit you and see this little coastal town of yours."

"B...but that wasn't supposed to be *now*! Did you drive here? Does Dad know you're gone?" My panic came out in a string of questions. I was screaming inside. She couldn't—wouldn't—ruin my plans to rescue Milo. I had to get her back home somehow.

"He knows," she said simply. "He actually decided to visit his family, too, so he's gone away for a few days. It was perfect timing. Your friend here was just showing me around the dorm. These are so nice! It's not often you get your own bedroom in a shared space like this."

I shot McKenzie a look meant to press her for an explanation, but she just shrugged with a wide-eyed panicked gesture. My dad gone to visit family? Why didn't he mention anything about that on the phone? It all seemed too random to believe, but I would've heard from him by now if he really didn't know about Mom being here.

"Yeah, it's really great, Mom. But listen, today is our first day of classes. You really should come back when we're not in school." I touched her shoulder, trying to gently usher her in the direction of the door.

"Now, Katrina, you wouldn't be trying to get rid of me? After I came all this way just to show you how proud of you I am." Something in her words hung in the air a bit too long. An eerie softness that reeked of familiar manipulation. Had she gone back to drinking? No, no, I didn't believe so. It sounded different than when she was drunk. It almost reminded me of...

A rush of icy chill spread through my body as I realized just what was off about the way she spoke. It sounded way too much like Cordelia at the dinner table, or worse—myself when I was under the influence of my siren.

As my heart accelerated, I took a deep breath to calm myself and think through what this meant.

"McKenzie," I looked at my friend, desperate for her to understand. "Do you want to go ahead and get that thing we were talking about earlier? I'll stay here with my mom and we'll catch up later."

My friend nodded with certainty. "No problem."

"Thanks," I muttered as she disappeared out the door, hoping she would think to go find Noah and Bellamy and inform them of the hold up.

"Mom," I said, wondering what she must've said to my dad for him not to mention her traveling here overnight with no questions asked. "You're sure you told Dad you were coming here and he was cool with it?"

My mom reached for my hand. "Of course, Trina. I told him I just couldn't wait to see you any longer. And I told him I wanted to see the ocean. And he was fine with it. Then I suggested he visit his family and he thought it was a great idea."

Probably because he was being controlled in a trance, I thought.

"But you always hated the ocean," I swallowed, choosing my words carefully, trying to get her to confirm the suspicions swirling in my head.

"Hated? Oh no, no...I guess I was a little scared of it, I'll admit, but recently something's changed." She drew in a breath through a blissful smile before continuing. "I just can't stop thinking about it. I even dreamed I was at the beach, just looking out at the ocean and just itching to know what it would feel like to get in. And when my only daughter lives right by the sea, well, I didn't see a reason to wait any longer."

Hearing my mom speaking this way about the beach gave me mental whiplash, and if I didn't know better, I wouldn't have been able to believe it was my mother, Grace Delmar, I was talking to. But I did know better, and I knew that something I'd secretly feared was finally happening. My mother's siren side was awakening.

I didn't know what to do. I was afraid to leave my mom alone in the dorm while I went to sort everything out with McKenzie and the others. Who knew what she'd do? She wasn't herself, and I knew all too much what kind of mischief our siren side could get us into. I might come back to find her standing naked in the middle of the surf for all I knew.

"Come on." I took her hand. "I think that's a great idea. I think we should go visit the beach right now."

"I thought you said you had class?" Mom asked innocently.

"I do...later...sort of. It's fine." I continued dragging us both through the dorm hallway and to my car. I saw Mom's car parked outside, and shook my head, still in disbelief that she'd driven all the way here overnight. McKenzie's car was gone, so I was hopeful that she had already made it to the docks to warn the guys.

I drove us to the marina, silently tickled by the way my mom admired the scenery outside her window like a wonderstruck child. We passed the usual cobblestone streets of old town St. Augustine and Constantine, flanked by the swaying palms waving to greet us. The morning sun glittered along the bay like liquid silver crystals, as a majestic crane spread his wings overhead searching for breakfast in the open water. I wished I could admire it longer, but I knew the gravity of the situation didn't quite warrant us lingering to sightsee.

I didn't know exactly what I planned to tell Mom once we got there. I wasn't sure how I'd explain Bellamy, Noah, and the boat we were so obviously readying to take out on the water. But I hoped maybe Mom was just siren-possessed enough that a rational explanation wasn't necessary.

Making it all up with each passing second, I leapt out of the vehicle when we parked in front of the harbor. I saw my three friends standing by the boat, Bellamy leaning against a taut rope that ran from the dock to the boat's hull. They whipped their gazes around at me and my mother in unison, and I could tell McKenzie had already gotten the news out.

"What's all this?" Mom asked. "Shouldn't you all be going to class?"

"Bellamy and Noah aren't students." I rushed to explain, but then I realized that made the situation seem even more suspicious.

"Right," McKenzie chimed, stepping over to us defensively. "They're our teachers."

"They are?" I sputtered, but then quickly composed myself. "I mean—they are. Yes."

"Professor...Bell. He teaches our Cultural Arts class. And Noah is his TA." McKenzie lied proudly. She gestured to the two. Bellamy stood looking stunned, and Noah appeared hesitant for a moment, but then I saw his face muscles relax.

"Yeah...I mean yes." He nodded with a grunt to clear his throat. "We're just readying everything for this semester's cross-cultural trip."

"Oh?" My mom raised an eyebrow, but she still seemed so out of it that I hoped it just might've somehow been making sense to her. "I don't think you mentioned this. How exciting." She spoke clearly, but with a dullness in her voice. I noticed her gaze was focused on the lapping water below. It was calling her.

"Yes, I'm sorry I didn't tell you and Dad. Really, it was sort of a last-minute decision." My eyes nervously darted to McKenzie, who urged me to continue making up something. "It was a sudden opportunity that I just couldn't turn down. The option to study in Cuba for a few weeks. We can get extra credits for foreign language and some other art stuff."

My mom nodded. "I don't blame you, sweetie..." She stepped closer to Bellamy, who was still reeling from being introduced as a professor. "This must be your first time leading the class trip? You're so young."

"I'm old enough," Bellamy said coolly. I stifled a laugh that threatened to bubble up at any moment, knowing Bellamy's true age. But I quickly regained my composure. My mom suddenly seemed to have snapped back to a mostly normal version of herself as well. Just for a moment.

"Then you don't mean to tell me you're taking a group of students across the ocean by boat? Do they just let people sail into Cuba?"

Bellamy's face drained of color, and he glanced to either side with a tilt of his jaw as if thinking of some response on the spot. Mom was right. We'd done the research. We wouldn't technically be allowed to make port in Cuba in a private yacht. Only commercial cruise ships could sail in legally. But since when did legality matter when a pirate was our captain?

"I assure you, Miss Delmar," Bellamy said suddenly, his crisp, sure gaze meeting mine. "I have it under control. This is a very exclusive opportunity for students."

"Right, in fact, do you think you could show me that...thing...again with all the information about the trip...Professor? Taking a step forward, I urged

Bellamy to respond in some way that would get us closer to speak with each other more privately. I didn't expect Bellamy to play the part so well, but I guess it made sense. He'd always been the one snooping around in the city and on campus during his nights as a ghost. He was a pro at blending in by now.

"Certainly. It's with my things. Come here and I'll see if I can find it for you." He motioned for me to come closer. I told Mom to wait with McKenzie for just a moment. She seemed too fixated on the water to notice otherwise.

With our backs to McKenzie and my mom as we stepped aside and pretended to search a lockbox by the boat, my whispers erupted frantically. "What are we gonna do? I don't know how to get rid of her! She's in siren mode and came here because she wanted to be near the water."

"So, just take her with us," Bellamy shrugged.

"What!?" I nearly screamed through my hoarse low tone.

"Your mom is part siren. She's going to figure that out one way or another. The safest way for that to happen is for you to be with her through it."

"Okay but she's still my mom. I can't just take her on an expedition across the ocean when I'm supposed to be in school without her asking questions," I grumbled

"I never said we keep her conscious through it." Bellamy glanced over his shoulder with confidence. "I've done it plenty of times."

"Oh my gosh, no!" I pressed a hand to my face and dragged it downward. "You can't be serious. We can't just—" I paused at a sudden wide-eyed expression on Bellamy's face that looked like an idea had just sprung into his head. "What are you thinking?".

"Can you use your siren song on her?" The corners of his lips curled ever so slightly. "To make her sleep through it or forget the trip altogether?"

I swallowed, thinking about the idea before I replied. "I...I don't know if my song works on another siren. Cordelia couldn't really control me like everyone else, but she did make me feel sort of...hypnotized...but that was before I knew how to use my own siren powers." My thoughts flickered back to dinner with Cordelia in her resort. She'd sung the lullaby to me, and some strange wave of entrancement was certainly threatening to break its way through then. But by the time she sang to Milo and me on Valdez's ship, I was immune. So, I wondered if my mom was still too underdeveloped as a siren to resist another's song.

"One way to find out, love" Bellamy uttered.

"But...I don't want to control people. Especially not my own mom. It feels so...wrong." My words escaped in a sigh. The thought of this task weighed heavy on my conscience. I didn't want to be another Cordelia. "I don't want to have power over others. I *shouldn't*."

"But you do," Bellamy stated firmly. "And it's saved our asses more times than I'd like to admit. And right now, your reluctance to use that power might be the only thing that stands between you and getting Milo back."

I looked down beneath dark lashes, then back towards my mom by the edge of the dock, who was muttering something to a nervous-looking McKenzie. "You're right," I said. "I hate it, but I have to try."

Bellamy reassured me with a solid nod and a flick of those ice-blue eyes. "Good lass. Then let's get on with it."

"I'll try." I breathed in, pulling humid, briny air into my lungs. "But no promises it's going to work."

We both turned around, pretending to walk back as casually as possible, as if we hadn't just discussed the best method for putting my mom into an unconscious trance. As we neared her and McKenzie, I noticed my mom leaning down, fingers outstretched toward the water, and my feet began to race back faster. "Mom!" I yelled. She couldn't touch the water. I couldn't let her feed that hungry siren in the slightest. And I had to put our plan into motion quickly, before my mom discovered a new side of herself that might just make her able to resist it.

6

Sing Me To Sleep

Katrina

"Mom!" I shouted once more, getting her attention. She glanced up, yanking her hand from the water and backing up from the edge.

Mom seemed to shake herself loose from the grip in which her siren side held her. I remembered all too well what it felt like to fade in and out like that, making decisions in a fog, only to regain my senses and question what I was doing. It was mental anguish, like a swirling cyclone of confusion and chaos. So I pitied Mom, knowing what she was experiencing. It had to be somewhat scary for her.

As the faraway look in her eye dwindled, I placed myself near her, rubbing the siren scale around my wrist with my thumb. "I know you wanted to see the ocean, but this old dock on the bay is nothing compared to the beaches here. You'll see," I said, stepping closer to her so that I was speaking softly enough for just her to hear "Do you remember that lullaby you used to hum to me when I was a kid? Did you know it's actually about the ocean?"

"Really? What a coincidence. I never knew there were words...." Mom's voice trickled off with a hint of suspicion.

"Yeah, it's actually a beautiful song. Want me to teach you?" With the last question, I felt my own siren flicker within. She relished at the thought of putting my mom under her spell, of controlling someone else entirely. And I felt a riling in my stomach that made me queasy. I had to stop taking my time before my conscience talked me out of it. I hoped my scale bracelet would help channel enough magic on its own to keep an appearance from my alter ego from taking place.

"Sure, Katrina," Mom chuckled uncomfortably, clearly aware that my question was somewhat out of place.

I opened my mouth to sing. The scale glowed faintly, but I still felt the shift in my mind and body; the siren within taking the reins of my inner being. Human Katrina faded into the background as her alter took charge. I wondered if my eyes were shining vivid blue yet, but by the way my mom tilted her head and pressed her brows, I knew some kind of change must've been visible.

Ignoring my friends watching a few yards away, I carefully formed each syllable and line, my voice rising and falling melodically in a way even I had never stopped to fully listen to before. It was hauntingly beautiful, like no earthly voice could compare. The tone of my voice rang with eerie hints of Cordelia, but my song was lighter; a bit more delicate than hers. Certainly a siren song all my own.

I focused my energy on Mom, each tone and lyric carrying a spritz of power that washed over her. As I sang, the words faded, and it was just my melody driving her on. I told her to step onto the boat, and she clumsily did so. Bellamy and Noah rushed to her to help her over the bobbing hull. Once she was on board, I commanded her to sleep deeply.

At first, she lingered, standing on the boat, mindless and entranced, and for a moment I feared I'd either lost my hold on her or that she was resistant. But a few seconds later her eyelids fluttered and she lost her balance, collapsing into the ready arms of Noah and Bellamy. I stopped singing.

"Get her to a bed," I ordered, more harshly than I meant to. I watched as they carried her into the cabin, disappearing down the small flight of steps where they'd take her to one of the two sleeping suites.

I had to take a minute to shake myself free of the siren in command of my own mind. I didn't like to let her have control for long, but I'd at least learned how to reel her in before she got too far—at least for now. When I looked at McKenzie, who watched on with a pale, concerned demeanor, I felt sick again.

"Was it that bad?" I winced, tucking my neck into my shoulders.

"No, no, not at all," McKenzie muttered, looking around as if trying to relax her expression. "It's just always kind of freaky to watch your best friend mind control people. I'm not gonna lie, it's kinda scary."

"It's not just scary for you," I mumbled. "I didn't know what else to do." I shuffled my feet nervously and looked down. "Come on, let's go check on her."

I made my way into the yacht's interior, checking the smallest bedroom suite on board. It was simple, with a twin-sized bed pressed to the back wall, an interior wall to the right and a window with an outside view of the sea on the left. My mom rested peacefully on the mattress, her soft breaths rising and falling like the lulling motion of the boat.

"How do we know she's gonna stay like that the entire trip?" Noah asked softly, as if trying not to wake her.

"I don't," I admitted, remembering when I lost my grip on the crewman on Cordelia's boat. "I guess I'll have to come in here every few hours and sing to her again, just to make sure she stays put under."

"And she's not going to remember any of this when she wakes up?" McKenzie raised an eyebrow.

"I can't say for sure, but back in Nassau when Milo was controlled by Cordelia—she made him attack me—he didn't remember any of it when he came to, so that's my anecdotal guess."

"Well, I *can* say for sure." I wasn't expecting Bellamy to chime in, but I was glad he offered his input. "When Cordelia would control enemy crews and captains for my father, they never remembered a thing. Quite the perk."

"Well, that's good, I guess," I sighed.

Bellamy hesitated, parting his lips to speak and then glancing down at my mother, who roused a bit in her sleep, turning her head in a way that made us all freeze in our spots. "Just keep her under and we shouldn't have any problems." Bellamy shrugged with a whisper. He turned to leave the suite, and we followed him out before locking the door behind us.

Disappointment made me shudder as the siren in me swelled with pride at the sight of putting my mother to sleep. The way her will relentlessly grappled with mine was wearing me down. She was getting hard to control.

7

Lilies and Coconut

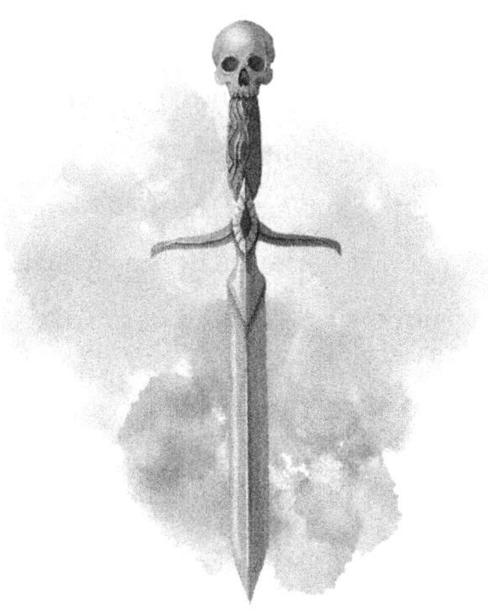

Bellamy

I made my way across the deck, striding toward the helm where I planted myself. With my back to Katrina and her friends, I gave the ship's wheel a firm tug. "Well looks like we're all set, crew. Any more last-minute interruptions I should know about?"

The trio stared at me, glancing back and forth between me and each other.

"I'll take the silence as a no," I lashed. "Then make sure your things are on board. Everything you need for a few days. Because once we're out there, we're not turning around."

"We should already be gone." Katrina stepped forward. "Let's go."

I smirked at the signature Katrina bossiness I'd come to know and love. She was right though. We needed to get going. Every passing hour in our time was who-knew-how-long in Milo's time.

The three scattered across the deck, scraping their belongings together and bringing them in from off the deck. I looked out at the sea ahead. Of course, this voyage would be different from those of my glory days as captain of a fleet ship. There were no canvas sails or wooden wheels. No twinge of ropes, scuffle of boots on the deck, or yelling overhead from the crow's nest. But I couldn't help but feel that something was still the same. That feel of the rush of the sea air on my face as the ship surged forward, mixed with the ever-constant roar of the ocean parting as we sliced through the water. There was no place like it. The sea was still my heart's desire, even though she'd broken it so many times. What was one more?

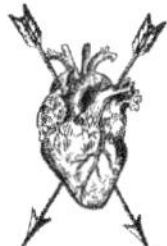

We'd been out on course for a few hours when Katrina appeared by my side at the helm. By the way she didn't say a word, I knew she wanted to talk.

"How's your mom?" I asked, keeping my gaze focused ahead at the hypnotizing blanket of blackish blue.

"She's still asleep," Katrina sighed. "I've had to sing to her twice now to keep her out."

"At least it's working."

"Yeah, for now," Katrina tossed her hands out in front of her expressively. "But what about when we get there? What am I supposed to do with her then? Do we have a plan?"

I leaned forward, propping my elbows over the helm as I stretched my shoulders. "One thing you'll learn soon enough, love, is that the plan always sorts itself out at the right time."

Katrina pressed her lips together. I didn't think she liked my answer.

"Don't worry," I reassured with a smile. "You'll see what I mean. The sea doesn't take kindly to plans. If she hears you trying to make them, more often than not she'll rearrange them for you."

"I thought you weren't superstitious." Katrina raised an eyebrow.

"I'm not. Just experienced." When she didn't respond, I glanced her way, just in time to see her watching the sky on the horizon, probably looking for that damn bird again.

The ocean certainly wasn't finished with her surprises. She never was. She'd given me the best and the worst of them. A life of adventure, a brotherhood on the sea, a curse worth dying to end, and a love lost in the same place I found it. Serena.

I ached to go back to that time, our first night together, like we'd known each other all our lives. I'd been out walking the shoreline, wasting another night in hell. I saw a girl, and I watched her diving from a distance. When she never surfaced, I ran to check on her. She came up for air effortlessly, easing my fears. But then she saw me, smiled and said hello. I wanted to run, because a ghost shouldn't be seen, but I was held prisoner by her beauty. And I'd been so deprived of a woman's touch for so long...

She told me to stay there on the shore and wait for her, and then walked out of the water to meet me. She kissed me, before I even knew her name. And then we fell to the sand, where I sat as she climbed onto me. With her legs locked around my sides, she tugged at my pants, wriggling them down just enough to free me. I was terrified and unsure, not even knowing if I was capable of feeling this fleshly pleasure in my damned state. But I pulled her tiny swimsuit down around her hips, my fingertips yearning to feel the heat of her skin. I couldn't, but I went on anyway. And there on that empty shore, astride me, she took me in her beautiful hands and made me fall apart, as if she'd known me all my life.

She went on teasing me with touches I would've given anything to fully experience. I groaned with both desire and frustration, but the faintest sensation alone was enough to keep me going. I knew I shouldn't have been doing this here with this mortal girl who had no idea I was dead. But I couldn't bring myself to stop her when she guided me right into her. It was like gulping from a fountain for a thirst I couldn't quench. Still, I let myself go, my only option to imagine the tightness and warmth as she moved. I kissed up and down her neck anyway, though I couldn't taste her sweat. I teased her through her swimsuit top, though I could only conjure up guesses in my mind of the sensation of her arousal. I couldn't feel any of it on my body, but I could feel the pain of wanting her so badly it hurt. And even that was enough to make me lose myself, coming undone beneath her while she sat with a satisfied smirk and bewitching look in her eyes that lured me in like the fresh scent of lilies and coconut.

She kissed me, her full lips toying with mine, as though to say thank you for those few fleeting moments of pleasure. Little did she know despite my body's physical reaction, I hadn't felt any of it beyond the reaches of my mind. If she'd known how my curse hindered me, would she have come to me like that? We were just two strangers on the beach, driven by some primal mutual instinct.

"What's your name?" I asked her, once I could catch my breath.

"Serena." She cooed, her own breaths still shaky. I can't forget the first time I heard her say her name. It fell on my ears like heaven. I thought we'd part ways and I'd never see her again. I told her goodbye, because I had to keep from hurting her. But I couldn't stay away, and I found her the next night. And the next...

"It always looks the same from up here." Katrina sighed, whisking me right out of my daydream. "But underneath it's so different, always changing, deep then shallow, vibrant then dark."

"It's not the view up here that makes it so special," I said. "It's the hope of what's just over the horizon."

She smiled at me with a soft nod before turning to go as if she'd grown bored. Not that I could blame her. We'd already been at sea for hours and there wasn't much to do besides mull over the reality of where we were headed and what that might mean. I listened as her footsteps faded on the deck floor, and I couldn't help but chuckle when I heard them coming right back seconds later.

"So... what's over the horizon then?" she chimed. "Do you know where this Bastian guy is? I mean I know he's in Cuba, but do we have a plan for *exactly* where we're going?"

"Sure do," I smirked. "La Isla. An old pirate haven about 60 miles from the mainland. It's had a collection of names over the years, but I think your most recent maps would show it as Isla de la Juventud."

"Isle of Youth," Katrina muttered under her breath. I watched her searching the place on her phone. I could tell she'd found it when she glanced up with a worried expression. "Doesn't look like there's much of anything there...just forest."

"Good to know it hasn't changed," I looked over her shoulder. "Should be easy to dig up old Drake's hideout."

"And what if he's not very welcoming?" Katrina leaned on the rail leading down the steps of the cockpit, her voice sly.

I released the wheel from my grasp, turning to face her. I placed both my hands on her shoulders and locked eyes with her. "If I didn't know any better, I'd think you don't trust me," I said lowly with a grin.

Katrina glanced down, her eyes falling to the space between our feet. "It's not that," She muttered, "I trust you. I'm just...it's just that...what if this doesn't work?"

I pulled in a breath, prepping my answer to keep from saying something sarcastic. "Well...I can't promise you that it will. And you're right that Bastian may or may not be a bit of a dick to deal with. But between the four of us, I think we stand a pretty good chance. Especially when one of us can control water and technically minds."

Katrina shifted uncomfortably at that last part. I knew she didn't like to embrace her power, but if we were going to do this, she needed to loosen up about using her siren song. Her mom was excellent practice, and for that, I was glad she'd shown up unannounced. Katrina would have to realize sooner or later it was our best shot.

"All I'm saying is, we'll figure it out, love." I pulled my hands back, but not before patting her on the cheek softly.

"I know we will," she said. "It's just that I'm still not over what happened with Cordelia." She glanced down at her hands, as though disgusted by them. "And I just hope I never have to do it again."

I nodded in understanding. "Fair enough, lass. I felt the same way after the first time I had to cut down a man—one of my father's hostages he picked up after looting a ship. He made me do it as a rite of passage. I was sick to my stomach, but I got over it." I knew that she'd kill again if she had to if it would bring Milo back. I had no doubt of it. Because we were strangely alike in some twisted way. And if it meant there was even the smallest chance I could find Serena again, I would kill without a second thought. So why wouldn't she do the same?

As Katrina turned away, I asked her if she could bring me something to snack on from the kitchen. As I waited for her to return, I refocused on the horizon in front of me. The ship's white bow nosing through the open blue, I couldn't help but wonder how Milo fared, stuck back in 1720. I thought back to how I saw him that day, after he realized he'd been left behind. He was feral; unhinged, and even still 300 years later I could vividly hear his screams of rage as he stabbed that enemy captain again and again and again. I'd never seen a man so broken. Except, I guess, when I'd been that man, too. When my father killed Serena...

I kicked the memory out of my head. I had to stop thinking. About everything. About anything. About Milo, Katrina, and even Serena. Every thought somehow redirected to her and what I'd lost. And I was beginning to feel like I might not have room for all of it at once.

8

Sailors and Swindlers

Milo

The chatter of the tavern nearly drowned out my own thoughts. But not enough. I'd just wanted one night unshackled from the weight in my mind. One night without bloodshed at the hands of my crew. One night to be free of the obligation of caring. But I couldn't seem to get drunk enough to escape the mental marathon my mind never seemed to stop running, replaying over and over each time I'd dashed my cutlass across another man's throat. There were too many to count.

"One more round, mate." I tapped my ale mug on the counter. I couldn't wait around in this cesspool forever. He had to show up sooner or later. But time was the one thing I didn't like wasting. Not that my men seemed to mind.

Tossing themselves at the rum and women, they would've been content to spend the whole of summer here. But I wasn't here for reveling and indulgence.

As I brought the freshly filled mug to my lips, I felt the coarse bristle of stubble that I hadn't bothered to groom in the months I'd been sailing these god-forsaken seas. Ten months building the trust of a crew I'd gained through force and fear. Ten months plundering ships and killing those that fought back. All leading to this moment to find a myth of a man who may not even have what I was looking for.

The cloaked figure in the corner may have assumed I didn't notice him, but I'd been watching him all night. If not for the small stature I might've thought he was the one I was looking for, but I knew Bastian better than that. He was a formidable figure with notable height. At least, that's what he looked like by the time I met him some years later in Valdez's crew the first time around. But that hadn't happened yet.

"Aye, you'd best cough up what you owe, ya cockless bastard!" A voice grated like cement across my ears, above all the noise and music. I turned to see the commotion.

"I'll not pay ye a cent more, you swindlin' dog!" I was ashamed to admit I knew that voice right away. I decided not to interfere. I'd leave Finlay to sort this one out on his own...again.

"Me? The swindling dog?" A man across the table from Finlay roared. "It's ye who keep coming to gamble without the means to take a loss!" He stood up, fists raised. "Looks like I'll be needing to teach ye what happens when you cheat one too many times at my table!"

I rolled my eyes. The last thing I needed was my men involved in some brawl that could mark us bad for business. I stood up, taking reluctant heavy steps to the gamblers' table.

"What's all this?" I asked, my gaze falling on Finlay.

"Cap'n," he stuttered, "He's lying. I ain't cheatin' here. He's the one trying to swindle me right from under our arses."

"Doesn't matter. You know all too well gambling's against the code. Especially when you're using the crew's funds to dig you out of the trouble you keep finding yourself in." I said sternly, looking over at the man in question. "What does he owe you?"

"Seventeen reales," he spat.

With a groan, I admonished Finlay. "If this happens again, I'm leaving you at the next port in whatever plight you find yourself." I had half the mind to leave him here in this pit in Madagascar. He wouldn't last a week on his own.

I reached into my concealed coin purse, noticing the cloaked figure still observing me as I counted out the amount. I slammed the money down in front of the man. "Here's what you want. Now find someone else to join your wagers."

The man scooped the money into his dirty hands. Looking up at me through bushy brows, spat on the floor in my direction.

"Is there a problem, lad?" I raised an eyebrow.

"Who you calling lad? You look far younger than me. And you're in my way." He did his best to bulk up and meet me at eye level. I stood aside to let him pass, refusing to say another word to him. He was too drunk to reason with, and I didn't want to waste my time. But just as he started to walk past me, he instead whipped around towards a nervous Finlay and sucker punched him across the cheek so hard that Finlay fell off his stool.

"Hey!" I shouted, my fingers balling up into fists. "You've been paid, bastard!"

"That I have, ya damned dog," the man sputtered. "But the principal is that he's a cheat, and I don't let cheaters get away without a proper lesson in courtesy."

"You'll leave my crew out of your shit-flinging tantrums when their debt has been settled."

"Maybe their captain is the one here who needs a lesson in manners." He grumbled, stomping toward me. I didn't want to cause a scene, but my patience was wearing thinner by the second. He threw a punch. I dodged him with a backward step, but he lunged at me again. This time, I propelled myself forward and swung back.

I struck his jaw, and he staggered into the table before finding his footing and lunging at me once more. I grappled him as we both tumbled to the creaking wooden floor below. He punched. I punched back. In a whirlwind of fists and slurred insults, the tavern soon lit up with jeers and shouts from all the sailors and swindlers flocking to the commotion.

I found my footing, standing just as he latched onto my ankle and tried to force me back to the floor. On the way down, I managed to grab hold of a metal tankard on the counter and slam it across his face. The tavern owner shouted at us and tossed a wooden stool our way, temporarily breaking up the brawl as it splintered into pieces over our bodies. But I managed to sneak in one last punch.

The man stayed down, groaning in pain as I eased myself back up. I rolled my shoulders to shake off the soreness in my knuckles and face, and without a word, made my way to the door, ignoring the riled men's hearty chuckles as they settled back into their seats. I was done with this foolishness for the night. I'd find Bastian another time.

It was raining. A sudden storm must've rolled in on the coast in the last two hours I'd been in there. As I stepped down the wooden planks for steps, my boots sunk deep into the thick mixture of wet sand and mud. I welcomed the calming sound of low thunder and rain patters as opposed to the never-ending commotion of the tavern.

But when I heard the door open behind me and the golden glow of light illuminated the ground below my shadow, I didn't hesitate to look back. The gambler I'd just fought came bounding out, desperate to continue our fistfight. He flung himself onto me, and I gripped both his arms as he came down, dragging him down to the mud. The rain beat down as we sloshed in the mire, adding to the challenge that much more. We rolled a few times, my grip slipping in the wet sand as we wrestled with strength closely matched. I was tired, and I knew I could reach for the hidden dagger at my side and end it all quickly, but I fought the urge to do that a bit longer as I pinned him down with my knees.

But in a split second, my left knee slipped, giving him just enough room to kick my stomach and knock me off him in a sudden motion. He reached over to hit me. I rolled out of the way, but he kept swinging.

I reached for the knife in my belt, more than ready to end this. Looks like we'd be marked bad for business after all. "One more move and you'll find this blade through your eye."

"You don't fight fair," he growled through his teeth.

"I'm a pirate," I hissed and then swung the knife at his face. But before my blade struck him, he went still, a sudden glazed look veiling his eyes. He swayed weakly, disoriented, and plopped forward like a bag of wet sand. Confused, I watched him roll his face into the mud, still breathing, but unconscious.

"Don't do some shite you'll regret later." A strange voice came from above me as a skinny pale hand reached down. I refused the help and steadied myself to my feet. The cloaked figure from the tavern stood facing me, not quite reaching my shoulder, with scarlet hair peeking out from each side of the hood. I was still feeling the sway of my own intoxication and the last few jabs, so I didn't trust my own senses when I heard the voice again. It was shrill and that of a woman.

"Yer welcome. Better than what you were about to do," she uttered in her heavy Irish accent, turning to leave. "Though he won't be out fer long."

"Wait," I stammered. "Who are you? How did you do that?"

The figure stopped and turned back to me. "Bit of nature and a good aim." She quickly flashed a flute-like tool in her hand.

"You shot him with a poison dart?"

"Aye, is that against your code, sailor? Or would ya rather keep smackin' each other senseless in the mud?" She tossed her head, shaking the hood loose from over her head to reveal ivory skin, peppered with flecks from the sun, framed by shoulder-length blood-red hair.

Her brashness surprised me, as well as intrigued me, so I stepped forward with piqued curiosity to follow her. "No...poison is...fair." I said, still shaking myself sober. "But why did you help me?"

"Cause Ranson's a feckin' idiot." She smiled, gesturing to the unconscious man at our feet. "And ya seem different from the rest of the scallywags wastin' air in that tavern. I been watchin' ya the past couple o' nights."

"I've noticed."

"Good," she repeated, circling me with curious eyes and a scoff. "Not bad for a man with one good eye. From a decent cap'n I'd expect nothin' less."

I tensed at the mention of my damaged eye. By now it had healed up enough to look almost normal, except for an unsightly scar. A scar that'd left me half-blind.

"What's a lass like you doing in a place like this anyway? You must have a reason to be lurking in that corner."

"Same as you, sailor," she nodded smugly with a stubborn grin. "I been waitin' round fer someone. And I think I've finally found him."

9

A Cap'n Worth His Salt

Milo

The girl stepped toward me, looking over her shoulder as she returned the cloak back over her head. "I need a cap'n," she said confidently.

"What for?" I asked.

She glanced around once more, the rain slowly lifting so that I could see her features more easily as the moonlight broke out from behind the crowds. Her eyes peered out from her hood, a striking green that nearly seemed to glow in the darkness. "What reason would I be lookin' for a cap'n than to join his crew?"

I shifted my shoulders, a bit taken aback by her unusual request. "Do you know what you're getting into? A pirate crew is no place for..."

"Fer who...a woman?" She spat. "Yeah, I don't need the likes of you remindin' me. I was marooned by my last crew when they discovered I don't quite have the same riggin' between my legs as them. Though no doubt I was as good as any of 'em. They never questioned my capability when I was swabbin' the deck with my chest bound and my hair tucked up under my hat. But I made the fool's mistake of tryna' bathe one night and they seen me fer all I was worth, they did."

I thought of my brief time sneaking around Nassau undercover. How difficult it must have been for her to portray this separate identity aboard a ship of stinking, rugged men, if it was true. I decided to press her. "And what makes you think I would let you aboard my ship?" I crossed my arms.

"Aye, there's the key, sailor. I been staking out in this tavern a few weeks now waitin' for a cap'n worth his salt to show himself. A cap'n who might'nt be afraid of lettin' a female on his ship. A cap'n less concerned with comparing the size of his dick and more with the wellbeing of his crew."

"And you think I'm that captain?" I raised an eyebrow.

"I dunnae. Are ye?" I glanced down at a light pressure just below my ribcage. She held a small dagger to my core. I grinned with a rumble of a chuckle and swiped the knife from her grip.

"Fair enough," I said, putting the knife back in her hand. "You've proved you can be useful. But I must warn you, I'm not just scouring the seas for wealth and gain as you might think. I'm hunting something...and maybe someone."

"Don't entice me further." She twirled her knife with a smirk. "So will ya be lettin' me aboard or not, Cap'n Harrington?"

I took pause at the mention of my name. I knew she would've heard it by now at the tavern, but it still took me by surprise. The leftover rain dripped from treetops in a rhythmic pattern all around, like the ticking of a clock waiting for me to make a decision. "What's your name and why is it you want so desperately to be part of a crew?"

"You only get one of those questions answered fer now." Her eyes bore into me as her brow hardened. "It's Clara. Clara Reid."

I drew in a breath, unsure of whether letting this flaming Irish girl join my crew was wise. But she *had* helped me during the brawl. And I was short a couple of deckhands since our last looting. She spoke with confidence unmatched in most men I'd recruited. Stuffing away my initial hesitation, I tossed a firm nod toward her. "Fine. Welcome aboard the *Falcon*, Clara Reid."

10

Raise the Topsails

Katrina

We'd been on the water a while, with fair weather on our side for most of it. One small storm had detoured us, but it didn't keep us from making good time. Every few hours I would check on Mom, feeling the pang of guilt hammering at me every time I looked at her. So when she inevitably woke up, while I sat beside her, I couldn't bring myself to put her back under.

Her eyes fluttered open. I watched her take in her surroundings, slowly and unsure as I expected anyone to be in this situation. I braced myself, running every possible explanation I could offer through my head. What would I tell her when she demanded answers? There was no way I could keep up this façade about a school cross cultural trip. Schools didn't take trips on yachts. And they certainly didn't kidnap students' mothers.

"Wh—where am I?" Mom asked weakly.

I thought fast, glancing around the room, as I fought to hide my own panic. "You're—you're on a boat, with me, sailing for an island off the coast of Cuba." The truth spilled out, and I chastised myself for being such a bad liar that I couldn't even come up with something remotely better than that.

"The school trip?" She sat up, rubbing her head and eyes.

"It's not actually a school trip. It's just a trip. It's hard to explain," I said, "But you have to believe me when I say this is something I have to do. And I couldn't leave you behind." I paused, fiddling with the thin ring on my finger as I fought back the nervous drop in my stomach. "Someone I care about needs my help."

"What about school? How did I get here anyway?" Mom's face went pale. "Oh no, have I been drinking again?"

I reached forward to reassure her with a soft touch on the arm. "No, no, Mom. You haven't. You're good." My voice eased out the words to calm her, but the wrinkle above her forehead only creased further.

"Then...what's happening? Why don't I remember getting here?" Her voice sounded more like herself, entirely different than the far away version it was back on the dock.

"What do you remember?" If I could probe her for what she knew or didn't know, it would determine how much I could get away without explaining.

"I was...I couldn't sleep. I kept wanting to see you—to see the ocean—and I drove here, well, to Florida. I told your father I was going. And he thought it was strange, and he started to ask me why, but I just suggested that he go visit his family up north, and he agreed. Just like that. It was very weird. But he didn't argue. He just...started packing."

Just as I thought. She was controlling him without realizing it.

"So you don't remember driving to Florida or coming to my dorm to find me?" I pressed.

She shook her head, appearing uncomfortable as though she had a pounding headache. "No...What's going on, Katrina?"

I hesitated, sitting back and blinking as I chose my next words carefully. Mom was currently out from under the siren's control for now. I didn't want to confuse her further. But I couldn't tell her everything here and now without sounding like a lunatic and sending her into a panic. So, I played the only card I knew to play.

"Mom," I breathed. "You know how you used to leave and disappear for a while, and you would tell me to trust what you were doing? You said you were trying to help. You were off doing something you thought you needed to do."

She didn't reply, but kept her shining, worried eyes pressed onto me, as if already knowing—and dreading—what I would say next.

"The fact is, I can't tell you everything right now, Mom. But you have to trust that I'm doing something I have to do. There's something in Cuba I need. And it won't make sense if I explain it now. You just need to know it wasn't safe for me to leave you behind."

She opened her mouth as if to question me further or argue. "Please, just trust me," I said. "I know it doesn't make sense, but it's what I need from you now."

She looked down, her brown hair rolling across her shoulder. Finally she looked back at me, her voice filled with something heavy. "I owe it to you to say okay," she uttered. "And your dad?"

"I've already called him. I told him you're here with me. In Constantine. On campus." I spoke firmly, thinking back to the phone call I'd made this morning. "He's perfectly fine, I promise."

My mom looked around, her breath short as she held back a reaction I could easily see brewing. Immediately, I felt my stomach turning in knots. Had I just made a huge mistake? Bellamy would've no doubt disapproved of telling her all that, but I couldn't just keep singing my mom to sleep this entire journey. Eventually—whether sooner or later—she was going to find out at least some part of the truth. But I just had to make sure she didn't find out too much at once. I couldn't foresee Mom handling it well. The sad truth was, I still didn't trust what she might do. I wondered if I ever would stop seeing her as someone on the brink of a mistake, so weak that I needed to protect, instead of my mother.

"Don't panic, please." I added. "My friends are with me. You've met them. Bellamy, McKenzie, and Noah. They're all coming with us and we're safe."

Mom nodded, her head movements growing faster and jerkier the more she processed. "I'll try to trust you. Because I know I've asked the same thing of you too many times not to."

"Thanks. It's the best thing for the both of us right now. I promise." I felt the water getting choppy. It was a subtle change that I could detect by a change in the boat's movement. I wouldn't have expected anyone else to notice.

"I'm going to go check to see how much longer we have to sail," I said, standing and making my way to the door. My mom nodded, her face still ridden with a look of worry. I hoped she'd stay put in the room at least long enough for me to get to Bellamy before she did.

On the way up to the helm, I ran into McKenzie, who was leaning on the hull, watching the never-ending landscape of water through her designer sunglasses.

"Your mom still good?" She asked.

"If by good you mean awake...then yes." I swallowed.

"What?" McKenzie exclaimed.

"She can't stay asleep forever," I said. "We're going to have to work together to keep her calm. I made her promise not to ask any questions."

"What are we gonna do with her when we reach land and actually have to go looking for this Pirate King dude?"

"I haven't thought that far yet." I grimaced a bit. "But I don't think it's safe for her to leave the ship."

"Then looks like we're drawing sticks for who gets to be her babysitter," Noah said, coming up behind us. "Because we'll be docking by the end of the day." We both glanced at McKenzie.

"Why do I have to do it?" She yanked off her sunglasses, her blue eyes narrowing at us.

"You were so good with her back at the marina," I pleaded. "I swear I'll never ask you for another favor ever."

Noah folded his arms. "It might not be so bad, Kenz. Besides, do you really want to go marching around a rainforest with no idea where we're going? In the heat, sweating, probably lost and getting eaten alive by insects? Remember how gross you said you felt in Nassau?"

There was a clear shift in McKenzie's face. Her eyes softened and her shoulders eased. "Well...that actually does sound like crap. But you have to put her back to sleep, Katrina. Just to buy me more time in case you guys are gone longer than you think you'll be."

I groaned inwardly at the thought of manipulating my mom again. But what could I say? I couldn't ask my friend this favor without being willing to help her through it.

"Allright," I said. "Whatever you need."

I turned away, burdened a bit by the plan, but my attention quickly shifted to other matters. Like what it would be like when we reached La Isla. Bellamy claimed to know exactly where Bastian would be, but I couldn't help but wonder if it'd still be the same as he remembered after all these years. And what would we say if we found him? What could we possibly offer him in exchange for this Crown of the Sea? What if he didn't even have it anymore?

No...I had to silence those fears. That's all they were...fears. And even if they were right, we'd just find another way to bring Milo back. There was always another way, I told myself, though I wasn't sure how much of it was convincing enough.

I imagined what Bastian might be like, painting him clearly in my head. I pictured him tall and stern, rigid and unyielding...maybe like Valdez, but less threatening, with a long beard and a flowing coat. As I dwelled on it, I took each step up to the helm with subconscious effort, barely paying attention as I ascended to the cockpit.

"Don't you ever get tired of being up here?" I asked, stepping up beside Bellamy. "I mean, you've only asked me or Noah to take the wheel like once each. Are you sure you don't need a break?"

Bellamy raised an eyebrow. "A break from what? Captaining a ship? My, my...it's like you don't know me at all."

"Well, I just wanted to make sure you're good."

"Never better, love," he smirked, those ice blue eyes sparkling, though I detected a hint of tiredness in them he tried to hide. "But if you don't mind, I'd be more than grateful if you could bring me another one of those...ah, what is it...Mr. Pepper drinks."

"You mean Dr. Pepper?" I laughed, eyeing the mound of empty, crushed cans at his feet. "Sure, I'll go get your third one today."

"Thanks." he winked. "Now if you could just find some rum to mix in..."

I rolled my eyes as Bellamy's laughter faded behind me. Walking to the kitchen, I reached into the cooler to collect another soda for Bellamy. But as I walked back up the helm, I saw my mom stepping out onto the deck from her room. And I immediately regretted what I promised McKenzie I would do. Because now I felt like I would have to do everything possible to keep from having to face her again and give her answers she wasn't ready for.

But I started singing.

11

EIGHTEEN SIXTY-SIX

BELLAMY

I breathed a sigh of exhaustion. Despite what I told Katrina, I *was* tired. But not from driving the ship. I was just tired of staring at nothing. Tired of thinking. Bastian was a slimy dog, with an eye always open for a bargain that benefited him. So I knew we'd have to be just as crafty at his game. I also wondered if he'd remember me. The cocky, proud son of Valdez who sniveled at the sight of him. As though we were any better than him.

For some reason, I eyed him with such disdain back then. As though he was somehow less worthy of his notoriety because he didn't ravage and plunder on the high seas as we did. As if his way of clawing his way to the top was somehow inferior to ours. Now I realize what a lead he had on us, if he really was still alive. We were the fools. Look at which one of us came out on top without a siren's curse damning him to hell. Well—I'm sure I'd see him in hell—but not for the same reasons. And with an easier way of getting there.

Whatever, I thought, refocusing my attention on the lush landmass in the distance. We'd be there soon. I wondered when the last time Bastian had a visitor. I doubt he'd had many from beyond the grave.

"I hope you're all ready. I don't know what kind of welcome we'll receive, but I doubt it'll be pleasant once he sees me." I left the helm long enough to call out down below deck. McKenzie, Noah, and Katrina peered up at me.

"You're sure he won't kill us?" Katrina called up, holding her hands over her eyes to block the bright sun.

I chuckled, "I never said that. Besides, it's your lad who sent us to him."

"Like you have a better plan!" Noah shouted up. I admired his boldness and constant desire to buck the system.

"I never claimed to have a plan at all!" I flashed a grin their way before spinning around back to the helm.

As I eased the ship near the island, I quickly remembered this coast. The shoreline was an illusion, appearing easy enough to sail straight into, but in reality, it was hiding sandbars and reefs jutting up from the sea floor, making a complex path for even the most skilled sailor. If I took this yacht in, we'd be run aground in no time. No one wanted to venture near this maze of sand and sea, making it Bastian's perfect hideout.

"Get the dinghy," I said, shutting off the ship's engine. I scurried to the windlass to drop anchor. "We're here."

"But we're miles out," McKenzie whined, "Look how far it is."

"Yes, well, unless you'd like to peel back the bottom of this boat like an onion, it's the only way to get to the island."

I waited as Noah left to ready the dinghy, glancing between McKenzie and Katrina who seemed oddly nervous. "What?" I asked.

"Nothing," they said in unison. I glared at them, suspicious, until my attention was captured by a fourth figure rounding the corner. Katrina's mother.

"What is she doing awake and walking about?" I shook my head, shooting a piercing gaze toward Katrina.

"I couldn't keep putting her under my spell, Bellamy. She deserves to know what's going on. At least some of it." Katrina's desperation drowned out my concern, but I still felt uneasy about the woman being loose on the ship.

"She stays here. On the ship. The whole time."

"Yes, that's fine," nodded Katrina. "McKenzie is going to stay with her."

"That works," I turned away, walking toward the back of the boat where Noah was lowering the dinghy into the water. "It's not ideal, but it works."

Katrina and I climbed down the ladder and joined Noah in the little inflatable gray raft. Its engine sputtered, hardly used to firing, it seemed, and we set off to the island.

"Careful," I warned, watching as we slowly drifted through the shallow dips and bars threatening to snag our inflatable vessel. Weaving through the trail of twists and corners proved more difficult than I remembered, especially when the dinghy seemed so delicate compared to our sturdy wooden jolly boats of old.

"This is breathtaking," Katrina uttered. "I'd love to paint this."

"Take it in. These are your roots, love. You said you were Cuban, aye?"

"Yeah," She looked away with a bashful nod. "Half Cuban. Half Mermaid."

"*Una sirena cubana*. Divine combination in my book." I winked.

Katrina and Noah both gaped in wonder as we entered the inlet surrounded by gray ragged rocks lining the entrance. Here the water became so clear you could see straight through to the bottom, and streams of greenery trickled down the rocky edges. We turned off the motor, using a paddle to navigate the horseshoe-shaped border of cliffs as we made our way to the sand.

We finally reached the shore after what might've been 20 minutes of rowing. As we dragged the little boat onto land, I welcomed the familiar feel of wild, unkempt island beneath my feet. No buildings or roads or modern amenities in sight. This secret cove of Cuba felt like home. Like the glory days of dragging our plunder ashore to some secret spot in the middle of nowhere. Then we'd celebrate with dancing and music and chugging rum and liquor till we passed out, waking up to the surf tickling our worn, calloused feet.

I noted Katrina glancing around, looking for our next destination, while Noah stood with arms crossed, as if waiting impatiently for the next move. I purposely took the time to take a long stretch, letting my open shirt drape down and the sun warm my bare chest.

"If I didn't know better, I'd say you were wasting our time," Noah grunted.

"Come on, mate, pull that head out of your ass. It's a wonder Milo gave you that compass to keep safe when you're so bullheaded."

Katrina nodded as Noah's expression turned to cold stone. "Well, all I'm saying is the quicker we find this guy, the better."

"I wouldn't be so sure of that. But come on then!" I clapped my hands together as I turned toward the mess of rainforest behind us. "Chop chop."

We plugged along, entering the grassy expanse of forest. The ground was damp with dark dirt that stayed sprinkled from the sea and humid rains. Vines and full branches of green arched over us, winding in every direction, with rocky terrain poking through the sandy dirt here and there. I chuckled as a brightly colored parrot swooped down past us and startled Noah with a squawk. It wasn't exactly the same as I remembered, but it was close.

Because there were no paths forged through this mangled mess of trees, we were left to fight through the foliage, and I was silently running through the directions to Bastian's hideout in my head. Fifty-seven paces through the forest. At the crab-shaped rock, take a left. Or was it a right? Was the rock even still here? I swear I didn't see it anywhere, but we'd gone far enough.

"Are you sure you know where you're going?" Noah asked.

"Is my answer going to determine whether or not you continue to follow me in an isolated, off-limits rainforest miles from civilization on an island you've never been to before?" I rambled off without even turning around, smugly waiting for the silence I figured would follow. "Right, as always, I'm your best chance here either way."

I saw Katrina roll her eyes, but I could tell she was fighting back a smile the way her lips twitched upward at the corner. "That rock looks just like a turtle!" She exclaimed, suddenly pointing at a gray stony mass protruding out from the bushes.

"Good eye, love," I winked, playing along, shocked at myself for my mistake. The crab rock was back in Madagascar. I couldn't believe I'd confused the two. "Now we go ten paces north. No, left."

I was sure now. It was definitely left. And as we marched along, past the turtle rock, and down a gradual slope, it all came back to me clearly. For a split second I was back in 1724, carrying a heavy chest laden with siren...relics...down this path alongside my father's crewmen. The heat was just as sweltering and suffocating now as it had been then. But the company was certainly different.

The two behind me followed carefully, as the path gave way to a small clearing that was barely a clearing anymore. The plants had become overgrown and shrouded the patch of dirt that should have been a subtle entrance to a cave below-ground. I pushed forward, wondering if it would still look the same, but the thick leaves and vines provided quite the challenge. A certain vine had crept over the cave doorway, hiding the singular clue that would have allowed us to enter the hideout.

I reached into my pocket for my knife, cutting away the vine that obscured the small empty space of chiseled-away rock that should've been visible to the trained eye. It was still there, though dirt and mud had filled its cracks solid. I plunged my knife in, hoping it would do the trick. Normally the tip of a short cutlass was used, or a broad dagger, but this modern knife would have to do. I missed the dagger my father gave me, with the golden skull hilt, and wished I had it then.

"What are you doing?" Katrina asked, looking over my shoulder.

"It's a key," I grunted, fighting with the dried sediment that hadn't been moved in ages.

I pried out the caked mud, then jammed the blade back into the opening, turning it to the right, then lifting it like a lever. I stepped back and waited for the door to open. A few seconds passed and both Noah and Katrina watched me with obvious uncertainty. Nothing happened.

I was almost ready to twist the blade again when the ground began to rumble, vibrating the loose pieces of sediment and broken shells at my boots. The cave entrance slowly came to life, as the stone that appeared to be nothing more than the underside of a ledge shook free, dust and roots falling loose above our heads. The rock slid back, groaning at the effort, just enough to reveal what I expected would be the dimly lit entryway down into Bastian's lair. But instead, I saw a cemented wall of solid rock, sealing up what would have been the entrance.

"Well...I didn't see that coming," I uttered, stepping closer.

"What does this mean?" Noah approached the spot, trying to get a closer look. "He's not here?"

"He's not here." I touched my hand to the stone wall, trying to suppress the anger and defeat I felt all at once. I knew this was the right spot. But Bastian was gone. And I wouldn't know where else to find him. Second by second, that sensation of helplessness creeped up in me, and I worried that just like I failed Serena, I would fail Katrina and Milo.

I stepped back, taking a breath to think through it all. Noah came forward, and I moved aside to let him examine the wall. He looked at it for a long minute before speaking. "Either one of you have a light?"

Katrina unzipped the backpack she carried and pulled out a flashlight as we closed in around Noah.

"Shine the light here," he said, running his fingers along the cemented entrance. "There's something..."

Katrina flicked on the light, illuminating it over the space where his fingers trailed. Now I could see it. Barely. There was some sort of engraved inscription, also caked with decades worth of rotting mud and remnants of insects. I squeezed myself in between them and used my sleeve to clean it off, just enough to make it legible. It was two numbers that sent chills through my bones.

18° 27'57" N, 66° 6'13" W

"Well, what does that mean?" Noah said. I held up a hand, unable to hear myself think. I trudged back to the top of the cave entrance, giving my surroundings one more glance before I said out loud what was stirring in my mind.

Drawing in a breath, I paced a bit, stewing on the numbers, taking them in with their chilling familiarity as her voice rang like a bell in my thoughts.

"I love you 18 times 66, as far as North to West."

Serena.

"They're coordinates," I finally said, my back still to a confused Katrina and Noah.

Katrina weaved her way up the fragments of stony, vine-covered ground and took up a position beside me. She held her eyes on me. When I finally looked up, those eyes burned into me beneath a tensed forehead, desperate for an explanation beyond my simple two words.

"Bastian must've left them as a clue to where he's gone. A clue only a pirate would understand."

"Hold up," Noah stepped alongside me. "You are not telling us this means we have to hunt him down somewhere else after we came all this way."

I raised an eyebrow. "I don't set the path, mate. I just follow it." I balked at my own words. Because given the chance to forge the path I wanted to be on...back to Serena...I didn't know how well I'd be able to stay on the current one. I'd try though. Because Milo needed us. Katrina needed me.

"So we sail on?" Katrina urged. "Where exactly do those coordinates take us?"

I glanced down, noticing at last the pressed stone we stood on. Ivy curled around it like snakes coiling through the mossy cracks. I nudged Katrina, asking her to step aside, revealing the remains of an intricate carving of a compass with mosaic tiles of shell and metallic stone.

"From here..." I uttered. "Oh forget it...Someone pull up a map on your phone."

Noah handed me his cellphone, a digital display of the world at my fingertips lighting up the screen. What we once worked so hard to memorize, chart, and track was now available at the press of a button. No longer drawings, but now photos of the real thing, as though we were larks overhead with a bird's eye view of the entire world. In some way, it saddened me. What was left to explore?

I studied the map, pinpointing where we stood, and followed the coordinates as they would lead. "Interesting." I grumbled under my breath.

"What? What is it?" Katrina was practically leaning over my shoulder to see what I saw.

"The good news is it's probably only a week away if the sea is on our side and the weather stays fair."

"The bad news?" Katrina pressed.

"The weather is never fair west to east through the Caribbean Sea. Rough waters and upwinds the whole way."

"What's east of here? Where are we heading next, then?" Noah asked. It was almost entertaining stringing them along like this. I looked at them both before answering, building the suspense just a bit longer.

"A little blip in San Juan, Puerto Rico."

12

Return of the Albatross

Katrina

"This is literally a building surrounded by souvenir shops and bars," Noah argued, staring at the phone after Bellamy returned it to his hand.

"And?" Bellamy shot Noah a glance with a furled brow and eyes that looked on the verge of rolling. "After everything you've seen you still think there may not be more than what you realize under the surface?"

"Fair enough," Noah clicked his tongue and looked away. I didn't blame him for his bitter attitude towards it all. A wave of frustration crested within me. We'd come all this way for nothing. And now we had to set out again. With my mom on board and with time running out.

"Do we have enough fuel for that?" I asked, trying to mask the worry in my voice.

"We should have enough using what's left in the tank and using some from the reserve we brought." Bellamy scratched his head, squinting as a ray of golden sun broke through the forest ceiling and hit his face.

"As long as we can refuel in Puerto Rico for the trip back," Noah uttered, kicking a crumbling rock across the stone.

"Right," Bellamy sighed. "But let's just worry about getting there first."

We all turned to head back to the dinghy and board our boat, silence falling over the three of us except for the sound of lush leaves and sand crunching beneath our shoes.

A sinking realization hit me and settled in my stomach, dropping like the weight of Titanic to the sea floor. Despite the thick air and sweat on my forehead from the intense heat, I suddenly felt cold. "Do we have another week?" My voice cracked as I choked back the thought.

"What do you mean?" Bellamy glanced towards me, confusion written on his face plainly. "Of course we have another week. There isn't exactly a deadline."

"I mean, when we traveled to the past, we were there for days, but when we got back here, it had only been a few hours. So that means that weeks here could mean..."

"Years there." Bellamy finished my sentence for me, a solemn shadow falling over his face as his steps slowed. "You're not wrong."

I fought back the hopelessness welling within me like a tide. What if too much time passed and we were too late? I wasn't so sure if it all really worked that way, but I sure didn't want to risk finding out.

"Time isn't on anyone's side now, then, is it?" Bellamy grumbled, helping me into the dinghy.

The short ride from the rocky shore to our moored yacht was silent as we all sat soaking in the dire reality of what we'd just discussed. I felt a tear threatening to trickle from my eye, longing for just a chance to talk to Milo just one more time. Just one more word. One more touch. One more kiss.

The thoughts continued creeping in, and the fear of not getting him back darkened my spirit. I blinked and the tear rolled down, plopping into the seawater below, and I suddenly remembered my unique abilities. It occurred to me that maybe they could give us just the boost we needed...literally. I decided to test it out.

With my fresh tear fallen, I summoned the water alongside the small boat as we charged toward the yacht. I painted the picture in my mind, clear as an image on canvas, of water roiling and rushing underneath us, propelling us forward with a lift as steady as a raft and quick-moving as a jet stream. Noah and Bellamy were thrown backwards from the force alone. Even the dinghy's engine paled in comparison to the thrust from the water. We rolled in close to our yacht, and I released my hold on the water. I watched the rolling current dissipate, returning to the calm waters from which it came.

"If you can push the big ship like that, lass, then we can cut our time in half." Bellamy said, his hand braced on his knee as he turned to look at me.

"I should be able to," I uttered. "I think I'm strong enough."

I was getting better at controlling the waves with just a single tear, sometimes even just the sensation of one. But I often wondered if I was really the only siren aside from Cordelia who'd ever realized this power. I guess I had to be...if mermaids truly didn't cry. I wondered if my mom would be able to access this ability if she had long enough to find out. And then I winced. I couldn't imagine what we were supposed to do with her for the rest of this journey.

As we climbed back aboard, I tried to think of what I would tell her, and I wondered what bits of information McKenzie had already let slip if she had woken up by now.

I took Bellamy's hand as he helped me up the ladder, realizing how adept I'd become at being at sea. Standing up in the floating dinghy felt as natural as walking across solid floor. I helped Noah bring the little boat up, securing it again until the next time we needed it. Then I braced as I heard McKenzie's voice and light, hurried footsteps closing in.

"That was fast!" She exclaimed.

"Because he wasn't there. He's moved. And now we have to track him down somewhere in Puerto Rico." Noah interjected before I could answer.

McKenzie's mouth stood agape as she listened to us explain what we'd encountered. I was relieved when she mentioned my mom still slept. But I knew sooner or later she'd wake up, and I was unable to cast out the guilt eating at me for leaving her in the dark all this time. She was just as much descended from a siren as I was. And though I was always afraid she couldn't handle the truth, she deserved to know it. It was only fair to that part of her. But how do you explain to your mom that she's a mermaid? I hoped I'd figure that part out when the time came.

"Allright, we can't waste time," Bellamy ordered, his voice loud and confident and reminding me of his 18th century self. "Let's get this ship moving." As he made his way to the helm, he glanced back at me. I watched him as he guided the yacht's bow to face our new direction.

"You're up, Katrina," he called to me with a nod.

I took a step towards the stern, but not before stopping to ask McKenzie another favor. "Will you be able to keep an eye on her while I control the currents from up here?"

"Sure can. Turns out babysitting an unconscious woman isn't all that hard." McKenzie's bubbly tone made me smile. It had been a strange while since I'd heard it.

"If...when she wakes up, can you come get me?" I asked.

McKenzie assured me with a nod, and I turned away to make my way to the stern. I could still feel my connection from the tear earlier, but it was fading quickly, so I had to grasp the power I still held over the sea before it left me. Fortunately, I didn't need much power to tell the water to carry our boat along. With one vivid image in my mind of the water swirling around us, foaming and writhing like silver spinning silk as it lifted our boat like air beneath a bird's wings. In combination with the strength of the propellers and my undertow flowing beneath, our yacht launched forward faster than I thought possible. I smiled as the sea sprayed up just high enough to mist my face. Perhaps there was hope yet.

I'd been holding the current all evening into the night. My outstretched hand throbbed with ache and my entire arm felt heavier than the anchor's chain. I'd moved to a sitting position on the hull, grasping a rope for security with my free hand, but my body groaned for a break from this position. Just for a moment. I didn't want to lose speed, but I couldn't continue like this for much longer.

Stepping off the hull sent a wave of relief flooding through my limbs, as the blood in my body had returned to flowing without restriction. I stretched, my tendons and muscles loosening as they'd been begging to do for the past few hours. A quick walk around the ship would do wonders. Then I'd get back to it.

I was steadily pacing around on the deck, chugging water from the bottle I'd grabbed from the cooler out on deck. My weary shadow danced on the deck floor, a lone silhouette outlined by the full moon above. When a greater shadow overtook mine, I gasped, nearly jumping back as I whipped around to see the culprit. I blinked in wonder at the sight of the great albatross soaring not even a foot overhead, circling me. It grazed me with a wing, the strong wind tugging my hair as it swept past me. When I looked back, it was gone. But there remained a feather in my hand. He was there. He was still there.

Recharged with a renewed sense of hope that it most certainly wasn't too late, I took one more swig of water and then rushed back to the stern. With my unexpected tears of joy, I called the ocean forth once more to carry us forward.

13

Only the Sea

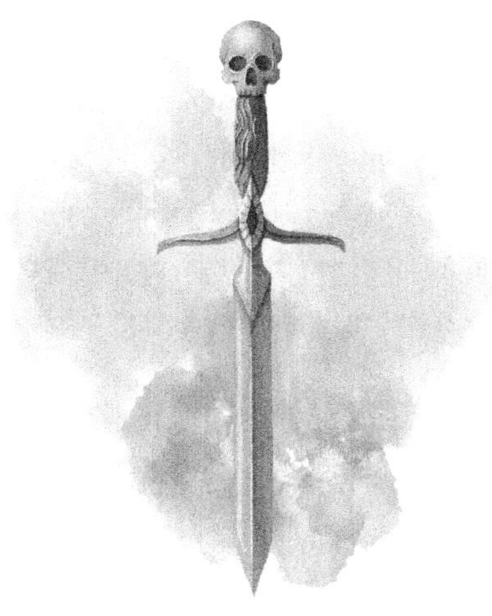

Bellamy

As the sun rose, I watched Katrina as she spent herself controlling the current. She'd been there all night, and wouldn't hear a word I had to say when I came to suggest that she should take a break. She didn't need or want my help steering, so I just sat there, lost in the sunrise as I thought of the last time I'd sailed this route. My father sent me to meet one of his "associates" in Puerto Rico, a powerful woman with a string of brothels across the island who'd made her fortune from the ground up as a mere pick-pocketing prostitute with a vendetta, and of course, a desire to live forever. I was always the middle man, negotiating with my hellish charm and making promises on my father's name. But dear old Dad had a thing about making the deliveries personally, so I usually had to abandon my own ship for a time to accompany him and be the face of his deals. I thought I enjoyed it. But then again, I don't think I realized I had any other choice.

As I stewed over the way my father controlled every aspect of my life back then, I thought how pissed it made me that Bastian was now doing the same. I refused to let him have the advantage. If he wanted to whisper sweet nothing bullshit in my ear all day and thought I'd listen, he was wrong. I'd resist him even if it killed me.

Noah's frazzled voice caught my attention from behind. I glanced over my shoulder to see him pacing the deck, phone pressed to his ear.

"You don't have any reason to be concerned about me. I didn't do anything, but even if I did, I can't believe you think you can just ignore me all these years and then suddenly act concerned over something that has nothing to do with you."

I couldn't curb my curiosity, so I went on eavesdropping as Noah argued with someone I couldn't identify. He finally hung up and shoved the phone in his pocket, taking notice of me watching. I didn't try to pretend otherwise.

"What's all this?" I asked, going over to where he stood with an irritated expression.

"It's none of your business, really," Noah snapped.

"You know you're right. I've got enough shit of my own to slog through right now." I walked away, tossing my hands up in a mocking gesture. I really didn't care about Noah's problems, but I was nosy as hell.

"It's my grandpa," Noah grumbled, earning a second look from me. I almost wished I hadn't asked. He went on without further prompting.

"He thinks I helped someone steal my uncle's boat—the one Milo took. Which, I guess I did. But my uncle outing my ass to my grandpa is just a whole new level. And now he keeps trying to call me, saying he's worried about me. I don't know. He's just never really been part of my life. Now out of the blue last year he starts trying to call me and talk. But man, when my parents split when I was younger, I needed someone, anyone. He was never there for me. So I don't understand who he thinks he is trying to waltz into my life and act like he gives a damn all of a sudden."

I don't know what I'd expected him to say but it sure as hell wasn't all that. And it sounded like a hell of a lot more than I felt like getting involved with.

"Sorry, mate, that sounds rough." I intended to walk away on that, but Noah trapped me with his next question.

"Yeah, it's just...sometimes I do wonder if maybe I'm being too hard on him. My dad told me he was never quite right in the head after his youngest daughter died. Said he'd spew all kinds of crap about her being kidnapped by pirates and..." Noah's voice shriveled away at the mention of pirates, his speech slowing with each word. He turned to look at me, eyes wide. "Oh my god. Maybe he wasn't crazy."

I had an inkling of suspicion that I didn't like, but the more he spoke, the more it made sense. "What's your grandpa's name?"

"Russell Loveday, why?"

"I can assure you, he definitely wasn't crazy." I pressed my tongue into my cheek as I squinted from the morning sun. What were the chances Noah was the grandson of the old man who hated my guts?

Noah's eyes narrowed at me, his voice hardening. "Did you have something to do with my aunt's death?"

How could I answer that truthfully? Of course I didn't kill Serena. But it was my fault she died. I could never deny that. My conscience ached at the truth, but I couldn't put the truth into words.

"No, but my father did." I finally said, hoping he wouldn't ask any more questions. "She was diving. He thought she was a mermaid. I tried to tell him."

"Damn." Noah groaned.

"Yeah." It hurt to think of her now. I almost even felt bad for the old geyser being so bitter all these years and his family thinking he'd lost his mind. It was a shame he'd let it ruin the rest of his life. But I guess I was no different. "Maybe you could cut him some slack. Losing someone is...difficult to say the least. Does things to the brain; makes you do strange things. Sounds like pushing you and everyone else away was the old man's way of handling it. But he learned the truth last year thanks to Katrina. Maybe that's why he's finally coming out of his shell to you. Grief is an ugly thing."

Noah was silent. "You ever lost someone like that? Sounds like you're speaking from experience."

I stared out to the horizon for a minute. There was no way I'd let Noah know about Serena. Only the sea knew my secrets. And that's how I planned to keep it. "No. I've just been around a while."

"Hm," Noah huffed, looking away and down at the water.

I glanced back over at Katrina, who was still working her magic on the water at the back of the boat. "Katrina's mom pretty much did the same to her. Turns out she had a decent excuse, but it doesn't change what she did. I don't think Katrina regrets giving her another chance, though." I paused as Noah gave me a skeptical look. "My father used to tie me to the masts with no food or water for two days if I left a knot too loose. In his own mind, that was his way of teaching me to do better. And then I found out he bartered his soul to try to save mine, even though he was the one that got me cursed in the first place. It took me a while to realize the bastard didn't deserve my loyalty. Point is mate, people try to love us as best they know how. It's up to us to decide if that's enough for us or not."

When Noah didn't say anything, I decided I'd spent long enough talking in circles. What did I care about his situation anyway? For all I knew Russell was an asshole who deserved it. Maybe Noah was, too. I couldn't afford to invest myself in anyone else. It wasn't worth the risk of seeing them suffer and actually caring.

I looked back once more to see Noah fiddling with his phone, staring at his screen. I hoped, for his own sake, he'd figure himself out sooner or later. But for now, he'd just better not let his personal problems jeopardize the bigger plan at play here. I was tired of finding myself mixed up in family dramas. But I thought I'd throw out one last piece of advice. "Maybe quit wasting the ship's Wi-Fi on these calls and figure it out later!"

Noah flipped me off, and I left the deck with a shrug.

14

Deal With the Devil

Milo

I waited another night at the tavern for Bastian, and Clara kept close to my men, who I'd commanded to accept her as a crew mate. No one had objected, probably because I'd threatened to keelhaul anyone who did. I observed the way she fit right in amongst them, drinking and slinging curses at one another in jest. I still didn't fully trust her or understand why she wanted this so badly, but she wasn't the greatest of my concerns for the time being.

When Bastian finally walked through the doors, I knew my chances of getting what I wanted were slim. But I hoped to bargain my way there with the riches I'd secured from pirating. It was a long shot, but one I couldn't afford not to take.

Brown roughened locks fell to prominent shoulders of a man likely twenty years my elder, matching his equally wily mustache and beard. His tall, sturdy figure loomed over the bar as he swiveled a coin between his fingers, rolling it along his knuckles and back again. I took a spot beside him, clearing my throat as I prepared to make my proposition.

"What do you want?" he asked, before I could even open my mouth. His voice was slow and careful, with a sly touch of mockery. "I'm not open for business right now."

"Except you're always open for business." I slammed down a handful of the known world's rarest diamonds and jewels I'd managed to swipe from a British ship. Right after I had my men execute those on board who wouldn't surrender and before I sunk their ship. "And I've heard that enough of this will get just about anything out of you. I've got whole trunks full. You could almost buy the British Empire yourself."

He examined the jewels in my hand, a subtle spark kindling in his eyes. "Almost. Perhaps I have some time to discuss it," he said, turning to face me on his barstool. "Any man walking around with those in his pocket might be worth talking to. What exactly is it that you hope to obtain from me with such a valuable collection?"

I paused. I knew the minute the next words left my mouth, things could get interesting, and I could very well appear a fool. But I had to know. "Just information."

Bastian shifted, crossing his legs and leaning back after a swig of his rum. "Ah yes. Information. Secrets. Rumors. The currency of the true elite." His voice drifted through the air like heavy smoke.

I took a breath and clenched my jaw, bracing for the question I had no choice but to ask. "Rumors say you have a map to the Fountain. The *real* Fountain."

A laugh erupted forth from him, as he slung his head back and slapped his leg, earning looks from eyes all across the tavern. This was what I was afraid of. "That's the problem with rumors, isn't it?" His gaze pierced me, a mischievous glimmer in his eye. "Can never be sure of what's true and what's not."

"What's your price for the truth? Because I'll pay it. I've treasures hidden that would overflow your frigate." I gritted my teeth, thinking of the fortune I'd gathered all for this moment. "And if I don't have what you want, I'll get it."

He thought for a moment, leaning forward as he stroked his beard with fingers laden with rings of bronze, gold, and silver. On the back of his palm, there was a marking—a black insignia of a serpent. "Let's suppose I do have the map...Perhaps I dug it up from Ponce myself." He paused with a grin. "And what if I told you it was unfinished? Useless. We all know De Leon never truly found it. What makes you think you will."

"Because I have the rest of my life to look for it, whether you tell me or not." I was growing impatient, eager, and nervous all at once. From the short encounter I'd seen of Bastian with Valdez, he seemed a bit of a showman who enjoyed making an ordinary situation dramatic. And I'd use his penchant for suspense to my advantage. I'd make it intriguing for him to help me. He would cave if I could make him think I was desperate enough.

"You really believe I know where it is, don't you?" His voice curled up, as though he was about to laugh again. I held my gaze on him, unwavering.

"If you don't, then tell me now and quit wasting my time. I'll find it another way if I need to," I stood up to leave, hoping it would pique his interest enough for him to reconsider.

"Wait a second," he cooed. "I never said we didn't have a deal."

"Then do we?"

"You tell me. I swear by the code I'm telling you God's good truth when I say I don't know where the Fountain truly is. Because it was never found."

I hesitated, considering his words for a moment before I said anything more. But as I pondered his words, it slowly began to make some bit of sense. If Bastian truly did know where the Fountain of Youth was, why would he have needed a siren heart from Valdez years later? He clearly hadn't gained eternal life from the Fountain. So perhaps he was telling the truth. In which case, I was now the one intrigued, which I was sure was his plan all along. But I didn't care. I needed information.

"So then what are you offering me?" I refused to sit back down, and instead I stood looming, waiting for his reply.

"There *is* a map, Captain. But it'll only take you part of the way. Ponce died before he could find the true location. I know, I've tried." He smiled with an almost feline look to his expression, and I began to feel unsure of what to trust or what to say next. It felt like a setup of some sort. But he went on. "So, what are you willing to do to lay eyes on this map?"

"I told you," I spat. "Name your price."

He pretended to think for a moment, the corners of his mouth twitching into a sly smile that reminded me of a snake about to strike. "I'll take that pocketful of diamonds and gold you have on you, just for fun. But don't worry about your 'frigates of treasure' and blood money. I'm not in want of that, I can assure you. But eternal youth...now that's a treasure even I can't manage to obtain. So consider this a commission from me. To do what I could not. Find the Fountain and come back to me when you have. You agree to that, I'll let you see the map."

I raised an eyebrow, skeptical of the ease with which he was willing to give up his map. There had to be something more he wasn't telling me. He was always careful with his wording.

"I want more than the chance to see the map. I want the map." I knew better. There was always a catch to everything.

"Well now, where's the fun in that? One good peek should more than suffice. You are a master navigator, after all," he snickered. Fair enough, for now. I'd come back to this somehow and ensure I got my hands on that map.

"And how would you ensure I'd return if I found it?" I asked.

"I'm quite the tracker when someone makes a deal with me, Captain." He rolled up the sleeve covering his forearm. It was nearly bare, except for two tattoos in random places. He flexed his muscle to suddenly reveal an intricate assortment of tattoos that took up the entire length of his forearm. I'd never seen magic like it, but the way the ink appeared on his bare skin before quickly fading away, sent me a step back.

"Every mark bears a deal. Only when the deal is done does the tattoo leave the flesh permanently. Both on me, and on he who makes the deal. You can see how often that happens." He looked up at me with the smirk of someone all too pleased with themselves. "And each tattoo binds the debtor to me until they fulfill their end of the bargain. So, I can *always* find them...if needed."

"How?" I stammered. "This is some kind of strange magic..."

"Magic indeed," Bastian spoke slow and smoothly, a taunting air in his voice. "Why do you think I want eternal life? My magic—my success on the seas—came at a cost like everything else."

"You sold your soul to Davy Jones for power," I uttered, looking again at the serpent tattoo on his hand. I never believed it was actually possible to make a deal with the sailor's devil.

"Don't worry, it's not all bad. The debtor at least gets to choose his tattoo mark. Though it's quite the painful process, so I'd advise something small." He chuckled as he leaned forward, his eyes darkening in the dim shadows of the tavern that now felt so cold and lonely. "So, make your choice, Captain. Do we have an agreement?"

I hesitated, my stomach churning at the thought of tying myself to this lunatic in any way. He was more dangerous than I thought. And now I realized the only clue I'd left Katrina with would lead her right to him. My heart dropped. And suddenly my mission became of greater importance than ever. But I knew my time was running out. I didn't have the luxury of thinking it over. I had to decide.

"On one condition," I said finally. Bastian's eyes illuminated with interest. "My tattoo will be the map to the Fountain of Youth."

God help me.

Bastian tilted his head with a hollow look in his eye, taking in the answer he hadn't expected.

"You must like pain," he laughed. "You've got yourself a deal, Captain."

I took his outstretched, ring-covered hand, shaking on the agreement as my blood swept through my veins like ice.

"Come on then, let's seal it in ink," he stood, motioning for me to follow. Everything in my body screamed against it, but I couldn't find the Fountain without it. I glanced back to see Clara watching me as I exited the tavern with Bastian. The concern was clear in her eyes, but there was no time to explain or get her involved.

I turned back around, following Bastian to a dark empty spot on the docks. With my heart racing and my mind flooding with a mix of fear, curses, and prayers, I held out my left arm as Bastian readied needles with black ink.

Clenching my jaw through the first mark, I thought of Katrina, and I wondered in that moment if I was too far gone for her now. I'd spilled so much blood out on the seas, and commanded my men to do the same. It was the only way to build the wealth I needed to buy my way to eternal youth—the only hope I had of seeing her again.

"Don't become like them."

I recalled the way she begged me after I'd killed Thane's men that attacked her. She would never want to see me like this, but this is what I had no choice but to become. I'd bought my ticket here with bloodshed, and now I was practically selling my soul for the rest of the way. And though the tattoo brought a searing pain unlike anything I'd ever felt, the fear that I may not be the man Katrina deserved stung so much worse.

I'm sorry.

15

Red Sky At Night, Sailors Delight

Katrina

Exhaustion washed over me like the dark waves we sliced across. The sun hung low behind the horizon, and we hadn't lost speed since we'd set out again. I'd never controlled water for this long, and I didn't know how much longer I could go. But I couldn't lose time, not when Milo's was running out. I focused with all my strength to keep from letting the water literally slip through my grasp.

I watched the crimson sunset tinge the rolling water below like blood. I remembered Bellamy saying something about the sky being red before nightfall. That it was a good sign for sailing. Conditions would be fair tomorrow hopefully. Maybe then I could get some rest and let the engine take over...If I could just hold out a bit longer...

But then something about the water looked so wonderful. I eyed the wake trailing behind us, rippling out into the sea like a spreading fan. I was so hot, so tired from standing in the relentless ocean wind. I could stop for a minute. Just a minute, and dive in for a quick swim...

A far, far swim. And never come back.

It was only when Bellamy appeared at my side that I dropped my guard. "You need to take a break, Katrina."

A breath trapped in my chest finally released, and my shoulders fell as I leaned forward to catch myself on the stern's railing. "I can't," I sputtered. "I have to...keep going." I stretched my hand forward towards the water once more, trying to keep the power from dissipating from me. Bellamy snatched my wrist firmly before I could even fully extend my arm.

"No." He stepped in front of me, "You know it's impossible for you to stand out here all night every night. And it won't matter how fast we get there if you kill yourself from exhaustion."

The piercing desperation in his icy blue eyes made me take pause. He was right, but some part of me wanted to slap him for telling me what to do. How dare he think he knew better than me? I was the only one with the power here.

Make him shut up. Cut him down to size.

Bellamy stepped back, his eyes staying on mine. "Blue doesn't suit you well, love."

I squeezed my eyes shut and shook my head in attempt to drown out the siren in me creeping back up. My desire to jump in the sea faded, and I silently praised myself for being able to shut her up so quickly.

"Sorry," I said, "You know how it is."

"Oh, I do," he chuckled, steadying me by my shoulders and turning me away from the sea so that I faced the deck. "All too well."

"I'm going to rest. But just for a couple of hours," I said as I took a step toward the cabins. Is my mom okay? Is she still sleeping?"

Bellamy nodded. “She’s still in her room.” He looked away from me and toward the cabin entrance.

“Okay, good.” I knew I should check on her. I knew she would be confused as hell when she woke up again. Honestly, I was surprised she still hadn’t woken up by now. I didn’t mean to put her under for so long. But I couldn’t bring myself to go to her yet, because I was terrified I might not be able to cover up reality the next time I spoke to her. I’d do it soon. Just not yet.

“I’m not the only one who needs to get some rest.” I shot a knowing glance at Bellamy, noting his bloodshot eyes and slouched shoulders.

“I don’t think my body remembers how,” he said with a smirk, but I could see right through it.

“I know better,” I said. “I think something’s bothering you.”

He pressed his lips together. “No more than what’s bothering you. Don’t worry, I’ll sleep when I have to.”

My mind was too clouded to argue with him. I put a hand to my throbbing head. I needed to sleep. I had to recharge before I lost myself in more ways than one.

I made my way to the room I’d been sharing with McKenzie for those rare occasions when I did sleep. She was there already, snug on her side of the bed, out cold. I’d always been envious of her ability to drift off so deeply and easily. But tonight, I didn’t have to be. Sleep wasn’t far from me tonight. The second I closed my eyes, I found myself fade into sleep’s comforting embrace, where I hoped I could ward off my siren side just a bit longer.

When I awoke, it was morning. The twilight of dawn cast just enough lowlight to brighten the tiny bedroom. Sitting up, I fixated on a little nautical lifesaver ornament hanging over the doorway until my eyes adjusted. I felt refreshed, though my arms ached with sore muscles from holding them outstretched toward the water for so long the day before. I looked over at McKenzie, who stirred just a bit, but didn't wake. I felt that familiar pang of guilt, knowing she should be back at the dorm oversleeping through her alarm right before class...if today was even a weekday. I'd lost track by now.

With a sigh, I accepted my fate. I needed to see Mom. I freshened up and changed into something clean before I trotted out the door to her room, energized by the much-needed night of sleep. As I neared her area of the cabin, I heard muffled thumps in between frustrated grunts and shouts. It almost sounded like my name, but I couldn't tell. After a few more cautious steps brought me closer, I realized it *was* my name. Mom was calling for me from her room. And she sounded frantic.

My pace quickened, and I rushed to her door, where I could hear her beating against it from the other side. I shook the doorknob and pushed, but it was locked from the outside. Thankfully, it only took a quick turn of the lock on the handle to loosen. "Hang on, Mom!" I pushed the door open to find my mom standing right on the other side, her hair a wild mess and her eyes framed above dark sleepless circles. "How long have you been up?" I asked.

"A few hours," she snapped. "I've been trapped in here! Katrina, what is going on? I can't pretend like this is fine anymore. What is happening?"

"I...I didn't lock—" Suddenly I remembered talking to Bellamy last night.

"She's still in her room."

He never said she was sleeping. He locked her in here.

Though it angered me to realize this was Bellamy's doing, I didn't have time to focus on that. All I could do was my best to contain the damage here with Mom. I had been worried about her siren side getting stronger, but I'd never accounted for mine doing the same while she was here. And I could feel mine bubbling to the surface even as I tried to talk her down right then.

"My phone is dead. I can't contact anyone. Your dad is probably panicking like crazy. Why are we still on this boat? Why do I keep passing out and waking up without any memory of what's going on? Tell me. Tell me what's going on!" My mom spoke faster and faster with each word. I glanced at her hands. They were trembling a bit.

Put her to sleep again. Shut her up now before she becomes uncontrollable.

My siren begged, and for a moment I listened. I felt my eyes shift, and then took a step toward her, parting my lips to start my song.

But then I clamped my hand over my mouth. This was exactly what I said I wasn't going to do. And if my siren side wanted me to do it, it *must* be wrong. I swallowed, fighting the urge in my head to silence my mother. I couldn't keep putting her through this.

And I couldn't resist my siren much longer, either. She was growing stronger. Using my powers so much seemed to draw her closer than I expected. So, I had to get rid of her for a while. I needed to be in the water. Soon.

"You want the truth?" I asked. "Come with me." I took her hand, my siren and my true self fighting for control every second. I was stronger against her now, but certainly not invincible. I had to get to the water fast. We were going to kill two birds with one stone.

I led her out to the railing on the starboard side. We were maintaining a steady speed I could easily keep up with. The water below looked divine, like soft navy satin flowing beneath the morning light. I couldn't wait to feel it encompass me, surround me, become me.

"Don't follow me whatever you do," I ordered, placing my bare feet onto the railing as I climbed over.

"Trina, stop!" My mom reached forward to pull me back, but my siren flashed before me and I swatted her hands away with my arm.

The sea whispered to me from below, pulling my soulless spirit toward it, drawing me to it like a thirst nothing else could quench. I closed my eyes, drowning out the sounds of my mom freaking out, and almost the sound of Noah and Bellamy screaming my name.

"Katrina! What are you doing?" Noah shrieked. The sound of footsteps approached from behind somewhere mixed in with the whipping sea wind.

I pushed out my breath, giving it to the breeze, and fell forward into the sea. As I hit the water, I felt her take over, and I drew in a deep inhale so that water would rush to fill my chest. There was barely ten seconds between the transition before I was staring back up at the sunlight through the surface from underneath, content and at peace, as though a burning itch in me had finally been scratched. I stayed suspended below by gentle sweeps with the fluke of my tail. A small pod of dolphins swept by, leaping and spinning along with me as we kept pace with the boat beside us until they finally moved on ahead without me.

I could see my friends back up on the boat, like rippling visions in a faraway dreamworld that was only a surface break away. My mom and Noah screamed my name, and Bellamy held my mother back from the edge of the ship. I swam alongside the length of the boat, keeping with its speed as Bellamy rushed away to the helm, leaving my mom with Noah. I noticed the propellers were losing speed and the bubbles left behind diminished as the boat began to slow.

I broke through the water, my thin top clinging to my body, though my shorts were long lost somewhere in the change. Mom watched me with a twisted look of disbelief, horror, and fascination all mixed into one. Noah held her steady as she leaned over the railing.

"This is it, Mom!" I called up boldly. "*This* is why we're on a boat in the middle of the ocean and why you're feeling strange. This is why we used to dream about drowning in the sea and only that necklace could stop it. It was a mermaid scale. This is what we're descended from. This is what we are."

I flicked my tail up, slapping the water to make sure she could see the silver-blue glimmer of the lower half of my body. Then I barrel-rolled back down into a dive to show off the entire length of it.

"I...I..." My mom stuttered.

"It's okay," I said. "I know you're freaking out, but you're not drunk. You haven't had a drink since Thanksgiving. Because I broke our curse."

More like just traded it for a new one, I thought.

I heard her mutter something to Noah. Bellamy was making his way back to them after stopping the engine. I figured I should get back up there and talk Mom through it a bit more directly. But I wanted to make sure she had no reason to doubt what she'd seen.

"Get back aboard," Bellamy commanded stoically, lowering a ladder down into the water.

I swam to the ladder and gripped the bars. My upper arms strained with soreness as the weight of my tail dropped when he began to raise the ladder.

He lifted me over the hull gently, but the look on his face was anything but gentle.

"You locked her in her room," I growled lowly as I looped my arm around his neck and shoulders for support.

"Clearly I should've locked you in yours too," he grumbled. "Why are you doing this?"

"She had to know eventually. This was the safest way for her to find out. I'm *not* going to keep using my power on her to keep you comfortable."

"You think this is about me? No, she's a liability."

"She's my mom," I snapped. "And maybe she's capable of more than we think." I couldn't believe how firmly I was defending her. But my sympathy for her had grown these past few days. And I couldn't help but think how screwed I'd be if I'd never been given a second chance to fix the things I'd broken. Shouldn't she deserve one, too?

Bellamy didn't respond, but the tension between us wasn't going anywhere. He set me down gently on a seat on the deck. Noah rushed to bring me a towel, and I dried my tail off, hoping I would regain my legs sooner rather than later. My mom watched on as the bottom of my tail left uncovered by the towel slowly split to become my two feet. I winced, still not entirely used to the pain, but much less surprised by it now.

"I heard screaming. What did I miss?" McKenzie came bouncing up from the steps leading down into the cabin, rubbing sleep from her eyes. I stood, keeping the towel wrapped around my otherwise bare lower half.

"They can catch you up," I said, nodding at Noah and Bellamy. "Right now, I've got to talk to my mom." I did my best to offer her reassurance in the way of a smile, but she didn't look convinced. I wondered if she knew about Bellamy locking my mom away.

I brought Mom back to her room, where she still looked at me like I had three heads—which I guess wasn't so much more different than a tail. She was so quiet, but I knew a million thoughts and questions must be racing through her mind. I motioned for her to sit on the bed, and she obliged reluctantly.

"Everything you just saw is the reason we're here." I tucked back damp strands of my hair behind my ear. I went on to explain the cursed pirates and Cordelia and how we'd stopped her from drowning away humanity. I explained the scar on my face from being kidnapped by Thane, the Sea Crown, and Bastian everything in between. "Milo's sacrifice left us stranded centuries apart. And finding this guy might be the only way to get him back."

She nodded, still visibly shaken. With stammering lips, she slowly reached down and placed her hands on her thighs. "Does this mean that I..." She couldn't finish the question.

"Yes." I put my hand over hers. It was weird, but I wouldn't let myself pull away. I had to help her through this. "And that's why you felt a sudden need to find me and come to the ocean. It's the mermaid part of you calling. And it'll be back."

She shook her head. "No, no. I don't want anything to do with that. Even if it's possible, I could never..."

"Neither did I," I said. "But eventually you'll have to answer the call, or it'll consume you from the inside out." I thought about whether I should mention that we didn't have souls, but I decided to save that damning news for another time. "Don't worry," I told her. "You don't have to do anything right now. It could be a long time before you feel it again." I really hoped it would.

"So none of it was my fault," she said, which I didn't quite expect. "None of it was my mother's fault. Or my grandmother." Her honey brown eyes shimmered as tears filled them. My chest ached a bit for her. She blamed herself all this time. Just like I did for the longest until I realized none of it was in our control.

"No, it wasn't. And I'm sorry for every time I blamed you." I gave her cold hands a light squeeze.

"Don't apologize, Trina. I wasn't there for you. I never protected you from anything. And no matter the reason, I will never get over that." She leaned forward, tears now streaming down her face in ribbons. "I'm here for you now, and I swear I'll spend every day making up for the mother I couldn't be when you were younger."

"Mom..."

"No." She sniffed, reaching for my scar and brushing it softly with her thumb. "You don't get to stop me."

"Okay, okay," I hugged her, whispering into her hair that smelled faintly of lavender and clean linen. I wanted to cherish the moment, but I couldn't stop worrying about how I'd keep my mermaid mom from diving overboard the next time her siren side returned.

16

Coral

Bellamy

It wasn't the end of the world, but Grace Delmar running loose on this ship made me uneasy. The last thing we needed was someone else getting in the way of this longer-than-anticipated journey. I couldn't forgive myself if something happened to Katrina's mom under my watch. Katrina would never forgive me, even though she'd say she would. But I couldn't live with myself if that happened.

But I was done fighting her for it. Let her unstable mom join us. Just as long as she didn't slow us down. Milo's fate depended on our timing, but I didn't need to remind Katrina of that. Still, I couldn't help but wonder if Milo wasn't the only one who could be saved. If this goddess could turn back time, maybe she could bring back Serena, too.

Maybe that's what the numbers meant. Perhaps Serena was leaving me a clue, too. Maybe she didn't realize it. Or maybe she was guiding me even in death. Maybe this was one last "I love you." The coordinate numbers flashed before my mind, conjuring up images of her looking up at me, her brown eyes shining as she wished me goodbye each morning when I had to return to my doomed ship.

I had to be crazy to think it wasn't just a coincidence. There was no way...

So I pushed the engine to speed up against the winds fighting against us. This was one last thing I could do for Serena. She would tell me to do everything I could to save Milo. After all, he tried to help me stop Valdez from killing her. He tried, and failed just like I did. But maybe her helping me save him was just her way of saying she forgave us. She had too much passion in her heart for bitterness.

"When I'm diving, it's like I'm home after being gone for far too long. Like I was meant to be underwater. There's nothing like it."

"I love hearing you talk about it," I said, kissing her forehead. "I love hearing you talk about anything." We lay in the sand together, secluded, letting the tide wash away the evidence of our time together. Serena sat up, making swirling motions with her finger on my shirtless chest, a plump smile forming on her dark lips that were swollen from kissing. "Now that we've had our fun, I can tell you the news."

"What is it?" I raised up as well, propping myself up on my elbow.

"I got the job. I'm going to be the mermaid at Buenavista! Mrs. Gutierrez said I was the best audition!" Her eyes lit up brighter than the moonlight as she spoke. I couldn't restrain my grin.

"I knew you would. The way you take to the water. You're as close to a real mermaid as they can hope to get." I winked. "So when will you start?"

"In a few days when my tail comes in. I wish I had a picture. It's gorgeous! She even let me pick the color."

"Let me guess," I breathed in her tropical scent—leaning closer to her, playing with a tight coil of curls at the end of one of her braids. "Orange."

"Coral, to be specific," she smirked.

I rolled my eyes with a grin. "Coral," I repeated. "It only makes sense. You'll look beautiful, as always."

"You have to come see my first show." Serena grabbed my arm teasingly, but I froze at her words. "You'll come, won't you?"

How could I tell her I couldn't? We'd been meeting like this under the night sky for weeks now, and I'd never told her the truth about me. About why I could only meet her at night. She'd never asked.

"The shows are...during the day?" I asked.

"Well, most of them. Sometimes they'll be in the evening. But the first one will be on opening day next Saturday. Please come."

I straightened, shaking the sand off my back and rubbing my face with a grunt.

"What? What's wrong?" Serena asked.

I really considered just diving in the water and becoming a ghost, fading with the sea foam and disappearing. And I might've done just that if I hadn't already tethered myself to this girl through unforgettable night after night.

"I have something to tell you," I said, taking her delicate face in my hands. She bore into me with those big, innocent eyes beneath perfect dark lashes. I hesitated, but I somehow managed to tell her that I'd been dead for centuries and was bound to the night. And true to that wild and fearless nature of hers, she didn't care.

I snapped back to the present as the ship smacked into a swell. I had to clear my head so I could focus on the open ocean in front of me. The waters were rough, and the winds weren't in our favor. I couldn't keep zoning out like that.

We were still two days at least from Puerto Rico, and maybe longer if we couldn't speed up. I needed Katrina back at the stern, propelling us forward with her power. I knew she was pissed off at me for locking her mom's door. But she'd have to swallow her pride and move past it, because from what I'd calculated in my lonely time at the wheel, in the time it was taking us, Milo had already been trapped in his time for almost a year.

I asked Noah to take the wheel for me as I hurried down to find Katrina. She was just leaving her mom's room, and the look on her face told me all that I needed to know.

"Don't be mad," I leaned on the wall in the tiny, cramped aisle way of the ship. "You'd think by now you'd come to expect this sort of thing from a pirate."

"You could have at least told me the truth when I asked you."

"I said she was in her room, didn't I? Omitting part of the truth isn't lying, lass. Not in this world. It's not all black and white. Sometimes it's the gray that saves your ass."

With a roll of her eyes, she turned to go, but I jumped in front of her to block her exit. "Did you forget you have a post on my ship?" I smirked.

"Okay now you're just being annoying," she scoffed.

"Am I?" I tilted my head. "Or am I just trying to help you get back your dear beloved? You're all rested up now, so I need you back there doing your magic water thing."

With a groan, she crossed her arms, accepting defeat. "I'm still mad at you for the time being."

"Good." I patted her on the shoulder as she slid past me. "Use that to fuel your energy."

Just seconds later I felt a violent jolt forward in the boat that knocked me off my feet, probably meant for me. I smiled, picking myself up off the floor. Now we were moving.

17

La Fuente

Bellamy

There she was. Puerto Rico. I remembered it as a wild coast of new discovery and lush beaches, but now it was infiltrated with sky-high buildings and resorts lining the shores. I asked Noah to take the wheel for a minute while I went to my room to prepare.

Walking over to the bedside table in my room, I opened the drawer and looked down. A loaded handgun rested there, nestled in an otherwise empty drawer. I'd noticed it here when we first boarded, but kept it to myself. But I certainly wasn't about to leave it behind when we were about to face Bastian. I picked it up, feeling its weight as I ran my thumb along the barrel. Not quite the same as the pistols I was used to using, but maybe that was a good thing. I tucked it away hidden in my belt beneath my shirt and turned to go back up on deck.

Before long, we reached the port of San Juan. The grand fort jutted out from the mainland, towering just as formidably as it did centuries ago. I moored our ship a half mile from shore, where we were least likely to be noticed. We didn't have time to sail around to the bay harbor and trek all the way back to the location of the coordinates. If they were correct, it wasn't far from the coast.

I called for Noah to drop anchor and help get the dinghy in the water. McKenzie and Katrina joined, untying ropes and securing our things on board. Grace followed in tow behind Katrina, still looking like a nervous wreck.

"So who's staying behind this time?" I propped an elbow on the hull.

"We're all coming," I couldn't believe my ears. I straightened to glance up at Katrina's mother, who had spoken. I waited for a response from Katrina as she swayed next to her.

"I won't leave her here alone. And it's not fair for McKenzie to stay on this boat any longer."

"Then one of you stay with her." I gestured to both Katrina and Noah.

Noah met me with a dead stare. "You think I want to be responsible if Katrina's mom jumps overboard and swims off like a fish? Absolutely not what I signed up for. You want me to trek through the jungle? Fine. Fight a horde of pirates? Sure. Steal an ancient relic from this pirate king guy? I'm there. But I'm not staying here alone with her."

"She'll stay with McKenzie and Noah on the mainland. It's just safer for her to be there than being on a ship surrounded by water on all sides. There's less...temptation...if her siren side comes back." Katrina explained, her mom nodding in agreement. "You and I will look for Bastian and if we need their help, then...then we'll deal with it then."

I clenched my jaw and rubbed the back of my neck. I didn't like this idea one damn bit. "I'd argue with you if I thought we had time," I groaned. "But where Milo is won't wait for us. Get in the boat."

"The dinghy only seats 4," Noah pressed his lips together.

"Of course it does," I smiled mockingly, "Then you four meet me ashore."

My eyes shifted to a jet ski that sat covered on the deck near the bow. Without another word I marched to it and tore away the tarp over it. Controlling the lever to direct the pulley it was attached to over the edge.

As it lowered into the water, I ignored the stares of everyone else. Sure, it would've made more sense for Katrina to just swim there, but I wasn't giving anyone else the option. I needed this for me, just a minute away from everyone to collect my thoughts. And to be honest, I just wanted a reason to do something fun for once. I was tired of the pressure.

I climbed over the bow, hanging from the railing on the hull and leapt down onto the jet ski. I didn't wait to hear anyone's objections, and if they said anything, I ignored them. They'd soon realize they needed to shut up and get to following me.

When I made it to the coastline, I anchored the jet ski a few meters from the beach, securing it behind some rock formations in hopes no one with authority over these waters would see it. It was a ridiculous thing to even have to worry about. No one owned the seas.

I hopped through the rocks the short distance to the edge of the shore where the rest of the crew soon appeared as well. Dragging our dinghy ashore, I studied the shallow beach on which we stood, my mind forming a memory of what once stood here in my past life. The stacked vibrant houses, well-worn by use and sea weather climbed upward, creating a cascade of color down the bluff shore. The last time I walked this coast, it was the start of a shantytown for the unfortunate poor and enslaved. The buildings weren't much different now than them, albeit much more festive, but the presence of cars and fences around the community was certainly a modern change.

I noticed a pair of men lingering by one of the houses, watching us, a sneer on both of their faces as they laughed at unspeakable profanities about the girls and Grace. "Let's make it through here quickly. Keep your heads down and walk fast."

"What? What is it?" Grace said, glancing around.

"Don't act nervous," I said, "Just stay behind me." I took the lead up front and Noah didn't hesitate to take a place at the back.

"Already on it," Noah said, walking past the girls, revealing an open pocketknife, down by his hip. "I noticed them too."

"Just be casual," I reminded them once more as we made our way to the main street that crossed through the neighborhood and led up to the rest of San Juan.

"Oye mami!" One of the men called to the girls, making kissing sounds and lewd gestures. When they didn't look at them, they got louder. "Oye, don't ignore me, bitches!" The men disappeared behind some houses as we moved, and my chest tightened as my pulse sped up. Something gave me the feeling they didn't just leave. We crossed a few more house fronts, mostly uneventful except for some old men chatting on their porch fronts as salsa music played through a fuzzy radio station. A weathered woman with a tender smile greeted us as she hung some sheets out to dry.

We were almost out of the neighborhood when the sound of something shuffling beside us made me glance, my body tense and ready to engage. The two guys from earlier stepped in our path, one of them reaching out to grab at the girls. Katrina side-stepped his swipe and he grinned. He smacked McKenzie on the ass, making her recoil.

"Mira' estas gatas," he hissed, licking his teeth, "Por qué andan con estos cabrones?"

"Porque I don't give a fuck if I have to put a bullet in your head, claro?" I growled, reaching for the gun I'd hidden tucked beneath my clothing, earning a terrified gasp from Grace and stunned looks from the others, even Noah who was already pointing his blade at the men.

"Dejalas," *Leave them.* I ordered, aiming the pistol at them, motioning for them to leave before I lost it. My blood ran hot, fuming under my skin.

As I expected, they were startled by my reaction, and while still hurling insults, they turned and disappeared into the alleyways between the last few houses lining the edge of the neighborhood. I quickly tucked the gun back away.

"How long have you been carrying that on you?" Katrina charged towards me, her voice shaky.

"Since cutlasses and flintlocks went out of fashion." I wasn't going to waste time going into detail of how I'd found it in the safe drawer of my stateroom on the yacht. "Come on, let's quit wasting time."

As we walked, Noah confirmed the coordinates once more, and we followed them through town, searching for the spot. The city had managed to keep some of its old charm. If I could learn to ignore the cars, cruise ship ports, and throngs of tourists, it would almost still remind me of the old Caribbean town it once was under Spain's control. Of course, it was never welcoming to pirates, but being Spanish myself made it easy for my father and I to sneak in and out of here easily.

We searched the old city, the sun still just as unforgivably hot as it was three-hundred years ago. The great fort stood mocking me in the distance with the irony of it all. Once a fortress to a lush, flourishing city, it was now a tourist attraction. And I, once the pirate it was built to keep out, now effortlessly walked past in through a sea of people oblivious to the echoes of the past around them.

"The coordinates lead right over there," Noah said, tracking the map on his phone and pointing to a cobblestone alleyway nestled between a line of two-story buildings. We followed his lead, and though I knew better, I held my breath waiting to see this location, to see if they would have some significance I would recognize from Serena.

We wove through the streets and people only to come to a little entrance of a white building with large, tinted glass doors, and an electric sign above in a seductive font that read "*La Fuente*." My hopes were dashed, and I reminded myself once more to stop believing in anything but coincidences.

"This is a night club. And it's closed till seven." McKenzie said, surveying the building front. "This doesn't seem right. This can't be what we're looking for."

I thought for a moment, just as perplexed as they were. But the more I pictured it, the more it made sense. Bastian Drake was exactly the type to hide in plain sight. And he was cocky enough to flaunt it. In fact, using a night club as a hideout didn't seem all that out of character for him. I was out of ideas to be honest, so I decided not to count it out, strange as it may seem. Breaking in would've drawn too much attention, so it'd be much easier to snoop around undetected in a crowd of dancing drunk people.

I clapped my hands together, drawing looks from the group. "Then I hope you're all in the mood to party, because when this thing opens up, it would seem we're going clubbing, mates."

18

Ghost From the Past

Bellamy

With twilight darkening the sky as the sun set, I realized it was much later than I thought. We'd be able to see just what lay within the club in less than an hour, but we scoped the area thoroughly while we waited. It would be a lie to say we didn't indulge a bit in some of what the streets of San Juan had to offer, filling our growling stomachs with paletas and alcapurrias. We took it as an opportunity to speak with the locals, who were more than welcoming and willing to answer mine and Katrina's questions about club *La Fuente*.

One man had told us it had been there as long as he could remember. Another girl told us she didn't even know it existed and had lived there all her life. Others knew a lot about it, but few people could recall details about what was inside.

I asked if anyone knew the owner, but everyone's answer to that was the same. No one knew his name or what he looked like.

But I did. Who else could it be but Bastian? So the moment the doors were open, Katrina and I were back in front of the building. Noah and McKenzie stayed outside, partially to keep a lookout for anything strange—or so I told them—but mostly to keep an eye on Grace, who wasn't very happy with the arrangement.

"Be careful in there." her voice was like steel as she gripped Katrina's arm. I understood she was her mother, but it felt a bit awkward to hear her sounding so concerned knowing what I knew about her. I couldn't wait for her to see how capable Katrina really was. She didn't have the slightest idea what her daughter could do.

We slipped into the club entrance, where muffled reggaeton pounded through the walls as the night closed in. I almost laughed when the man at the door asked me for ID to prove my age. Something told me he probably wouldn't believe me if I told him I was almost as old as the stone fort outside. I ushered Katrina on through the door. "Go on in," I said, "I'll get in."

Katrina's eyes lit up with confidence as she spun around to the doorman and leaned closer to his ear than I liked. "El esta conmigo," She whispered, her eyes flashing bright blue for a fraction of a second.

"Smart girl," I said just low enough for her to hear, looking away to divert the doorman's attention. We passed through together, disappearing into the crowd. Fog filled the air as lights danced to the rhythmic beat of reggaeton. The smell of alcohol and smoke was almost enough to tempt me to stay for a while. I'd be lying if I said Serena and I hadn't snuck out for a night of fun in places like this a few times.

"I thought you didn't like controlling people," I teased with a nudge to Katrina's side.

"Sometimes I make exceptions," she muttered with a grin I could tell she was trying to hold back. "Okay, what are we looking for exactly?"

We stared out into the ever-growing crowd taking over the floor. "Tall fellow with longish brown hair, freaky golden eyes, and a face stuck like he's always looking down on the rest of the world. But the last time I saw him was in 1725, so it's possible some things may have changed..."

Katrina wrinkled her nose. She was uncomfortable here.

"What, you don't like the smell of sweat and tequila?" I joked.

"It's just so loud and crowded," she squealed as people closed in around us. "I can't see anything."

"Come on, let's get through these people and we'll have a better view."

"I can't move..." Katrina complained as bodies began pressing against us, their energetic bobbing tossing her about like a boat in a storm.

"Dance through it," I told her. She didn't seem to think I was serious, until I pulled her to me and helped guide her body to the pulsing music. Ignoring her shocked expression, I encouraged her with my own movement, helping her to loosen enough to begin merging with the suffocating crowd of people at our backs. We weaseled our way through the dance floor, walking when we could, but dancing our way through most of it. When a guy began grinding against Katrina despite her discomfort, I didn't hesitate to shove him off with a few poetic words thrown in. He came back to lunge at me, and I grabbed the collar of his shirt, spinning as I swung his weight around. A gasping startled crowd parted the way as I forced him backwards into the bar counter.

"Back off her," I gritted my teeth, boring my eyes into him as he drunkenly attempted to push me away.

"Cuidate, cabrón," the bartender said firmly, calmly mixing a drink as he shifted to our spot at the counter. Katrina came rushing over, pushing her way through everyone, shooting me a stern look of warning. I remembered we couldn't get kicked out of here. I had to cool it.

I released the guy in my grasp, showing my open hands in a feigned sign of truce before pushing him back into the crowd. I stood beside Katrina, watching. He eyed me like a snake unsure whether to strike. Finally, he must've decided it wasn't worth getting removed from the club, and I held my eyes on him until he disappeared back into the color-lit mob.

Voices behind me at the bar caught my attention. The bartender was explaining to someone that their shipment of some certain rums hadn't come in yet and they were running low tonight. What a pity. But the reply froze my nerves.

"I've told you not to bother me with these details. That's what Hector is for. Wait till he comes in. I'm needed elsewhere, for far more important things." That strange, smooth curl in the man's voice only belonged to one very distinct person. Bastian Drake.

"Bueno, Señor. Sorry," the bartender ducked away like an injured dog, and I slowly turned my head to confirm what I was thinking. It was him.

"Katrina!" I called hoarsely, keeping my back to him, "There he is." I gestured with a tilt of my head. She glanced his way, and then looked away.

"He's walking off!" she gasped.

"Then we follow." I snuck forward, keeping Katrina close as the pounding music kept us undetected. He passed through the edge of the crowd, but it was easy to keep track of his movements thanks to his shimmering mustard suit shining like the last chest of gold I'd laid eyes on.

He headed toward the back of the building, toward a thick red velvet curtain separating the club from some type of private section. Before entering, he took a quick look over his shoulder and pushed the curtain aside.

Katrina and I hid behind the curtain, observing carefully as he stood at a blank wall. But with some invisible cue from him, a section of the wall retracted into the floor revealing a set of decorative double doors as he produced a set of keys from his suit jacket. A set of keys that certainly didn't belong in this century. On a brass ring, he counted out the rusted set before settling on a key with a golden skull for a handle, its eye the ringlet through which it hung.

He unlocked the doors, which opened to a carpeted stairway leading down. I really thought he'd be a bit more conspicuous. But I couldn't be too surprised. This was the same man who sailed in a ship inlaid with gold and sails stitched with silk for the hell of it.

I motioned for Katrina to follow. We left the blaring music and wild crowd behind, darting past the curtain and following Bastian down the steps as the doors closed automatically behind us. I could feel Katrina's nervous breaths and she trailed close behind me down the dark steps underground that finally became a wide cobblestone path. It was a short hallway, a stone tunnel with modern lighting lining the arches. At last, we reached a large, dimly lit room with expensive furniture and a wall displaying a vast collection of relics from the sea. I stood in wonder trying to figure out how all this managed to fit beneath a club. Katrina dragged her eyes over it all, just as curious as me as she took in the scene. A polished desk flanked by wine-colored leather chairs was the room's centerpiece, with nothing on it but a large glass jar containing a glimmering siren heart. I couldn't believe he'd just leave it out in the open like that. On the stone walls, portraits of Bastian hung, seemingly each of him in a different era. I rolled my eyes.

"A little obsessed with himself, isn't he?" Katrina whispered.

"You have no idea."

Finally, Bastian's footsteps slowed, and he stood silent in the middle of the room.

"You think I don't know you're here?" The question rolled from his voice slowly, echoing against the stone. I reached beneath my shirt, wrapping my fingers around the handle of the gun at my side. Bastian wouldn't hesitate to fight unfairly. And neither would I.

"Easy now. I didn't say you weren't welcome," he chimed, his back still to us, though his head was turned just enough that I could see the unmistakable profile of the man who'd double-crossed my father for a siren heart. "I'm always in the mood for a business proposition. And anyone willing to follow me down here either must have one, or they're a reckless fool unaware they won't make it back out alive without one."

My mouth tightened in annoyance. "Or they're a ghost from your past."

19

Eye for a Bargain

Katrina

"I hope this is important. I have a business meeting in 15 minutes." Bastian spoke without looking back at us, but when Bellamy was silent at his response, he turned around only to appear unfazed by the gun pointed at him.

"Ah, you do seem familiar." He grinned, lifting his ring-covered hands in a mocking manner of pretend surrender. Tattoos of every nature decorated him, but the black snake on his hand stood out to me the most. "Let me see...the Industrial Revolution? Wait, no... the Civil War? It all starts to blur together, you know."

"Let me jog your memory, then," Bellamy spat, still holding the gun. "Try a bit farther back. Isla de Juventud."

"Oh, now I remember." Bastian strode forward, moving toward the barrel of the pistol as though it was no more dangerous than a pool noodle. "The old glory days on the high seas. I made a bargain with you and your father...Oh for God's sake just put the gun down already." Bellamy complied with a lowered arm, to my surprise, but the weapon remained in his firm grip.

"Not with me. Just him. I never made a deal with you." Bellamy's words came out scathing and cold.

"Details, details. Yet here you are, a boy burdened with the sins of his father, still marked by the deal he never fulfilled. Though you certainly had no issue helping him bring the prize right to my doorstep."

"Did you expect some show of morality from a pirate? I do what the sea demands of me. Nothing more. Nothing less." Bellamy growled. "Besides, not like I had a choice."

I wondered what exactly he meant by that as my gaze wandered to the jar on the desk with the heart inside. It had to be the siren heart he'd conned out of Valdez. The heart keeping him alive.

"Fair enough," Bastian snickered, cocking his head to one side. He finally seemed to take notice of me at Bellamy's side, but he didn't address it. "I see you must've kept a siren heart for yourself for you to show up here after all these centuries. I suppose the temptation of immortality was a bit too much for you to resist."

"It's none of your concern how I'm still alive. All that matters is that you have something we want."

"Of course, I do. Otherwise, you wouldn't be here," Bastian grinned a slimy smile, and he looked over Bellamy's shoulder to make eye contact with me. Bellamy shifted to block his view. "And as your father well knew, I'm always in the mood for a good bargain."

"Except you don't uphold your end of them." I listened intently as Bellamy's voice tightened. Bastian stepped forward and I shuffled back without meaning to.

"Oh, dear boy, you've got it all wrong. I'm a man of my word. It was your father who breached the deal." Bastian closed in around us, like a vulture circling its prey. Bellamy kept an arm between us, a barrier between Bastian and me, but something told me it wouldn't do much good if this pirate lord-club boss really wanted to reach me. "You see…James misunderstood my conditions. He brought me the wrong thing. I asked for a siren heart…fully intact."

"And that's exactly what we brought you. Without it, you couldn't still be alive." Bellamy gestured toward the heart on the table. Our positions had shifted now, with Bellamy and I backed toward the desk in the center of the room and Bastian now blocking our exit. I glimpsed down at Bellamy's hand, just to reassure myself that he was still holding the gun.

"No, lad." Bastian's eyes narrowed. "You brought me a heart *cut* from the siren. Well-preserved, yes. But worthless. You see, when I said 'intact' I meant exactly that—a heart untouched, still beating, *within* a siren. I didn't get what was agreed to, so the deal was null and void, as was my right."

I made note of the way he twisted words and seemed to love the taste of trickery on his tongue. I could see Bellamy's jaw turning to stone, a vein tensing in his neck and forehead.

"You demanded a *live* siren? Something we never gave to anyone." he growled. "That's not what you said. You cheated."

"I didn't cheat. I simply chose my words very carefully. Something you should learn to do before you get that pretty lass with you into trouble."

I shuddered at the mention of me, suddenly aware of his gaze stuck on me, as though I was an item to be traded.

"This is why I prefer to let my weapons do the talking." Bellamy raised the gun, his finger over the trigger this time. "We came here for the Crown of the Sea. Where is it?"

Bastian released a cackle that echoed throughout the chamber. "If you kill me, you'll never find it. Assuming you could."

Bellamy put his finger on the trigger and began to pull. "Stop! Without him we can't find the crown!" I screamed. He fired and my ears rang. I trembled from the deafening gunshot and yelled in anger.

Bellamy stared at me with hollow eyes, not giving an answer. But he didn't have to. Because Bastian didn't fall. He stayed standing with a hole in his chest that blossomed red across his mustard jacket, and then closed up as if it never happened. Even the bloodstain vanished, retracting back into the threads of his clothes to leave a perfectly clean suit behind. Months ago this might have terrified me, but by now it almost felt normal. But my head spun at what Bastian said about the heart. I thought siren magic could only work if channeled through a living siren. So how could Bastian's dead siren heart actually keep him alive? The way mine kept Milo alive...

Bastian brushed off the arms of his jacket as if merely dusting away lint. "I can't fault you for trying. But you must know if your own father couldn't get it from me, what makes you think you could?"

"Because I'm not him. And that's all you get." Bellamy suddenly sucked in his words. "I won't keep talking so you can use whatever I say against me."

"Clever lad," Bastian uttered, stepping toward us and clapping Bellamy on the shoulder. "I tell you what. There's something I'm very much in need of and have yet to find someone who can accomplish it. You do the job, I give you the Crown."

"I know how your deals work well enough to know not to agree to them."

"Then I suppose you'll be leaving without your Crown," The words slithered from his mouth like spilled black ink. Bellamy had told me to let him do the talking, but I was growing frustrated with this douchebag.

Bellamy held his gaze for a moment, as if considering his options. "What is it you want done?"

"You could say it's an assassination of sorts. Of a sea beast of legend that few have encountered and lived to tell the tale. These past fifty years it has chosen to linger in the depths of the Mediterranean Sea. Some say it's a great dragon or sea beast. Others have called it 'Kraken.'"

"The Kraken? Really? You want us to kill the Kraken? What benefit could that possibly provide you now, far from the dangers of the sea, here in your cushy lair?" Bellamy raised an eyebrow.

"What benefit do you two seek from the Crown of the Sea?"

We both stared at him without reply, his hollow eyes sweeping over us in triumph. "Exactly," he muttered. "It seems we both have something to hide."

Bellamy shifted his weight around for a moment. He seemed to be gathering his thoughts as the weight of Bastian's words sunk deep. "Prove to us that you still have the Crown in your possession. Show us. I won't agree to anything without proof of it."

"Oh, come on, Bellamy. No need to be so melodramatic. You're just as demanding as your father was. But since you insist on making me prove myself..." He ducked his head and motioned for us to follow as he headed to the desk in the middle. I couldn't stop looking at the siren heart jar. If he showed us where the Crown was, we could just destroy the heart and take it. It felt too easy.

He waved a hand over the desk—the hand with the serpent. The desk slid back, revealing the entrance to a treasure trove of collected trinkets below. Some glittered like jewels and chests of rare metals. Some rotted with dust, like strange skulls and exotic talismans. There were items likely enchanted with sea magic or other dark powers, all things I assumed he'd accumulated over the centuries as a Dark Pirate Lord. A taxidermied mermaid fluke hung decoratively on the wall, making a bit of bile rise to my throat. And there, in the center of it all, meters from where we stood looking down, shone the glory of the Crown of the Sea, sparkling in the light reaching it. Seashells, pearls, and live starfish adorned its intricate golden frame as though designed by the gods themselves. I glanced at Bellamy to see if he felt the temptation to dive down into the pit to grab it as I did. His eyes were wide with wonder, but his scrutinizing and stoic expression remained the same otherwise.

I began to step forward, to climb down the cavern-like walls of this trove to see the Crown more closely. But an arm in a golden sleeve quickly put a stop to it. Bastian's voice snaked its way to my ears.

"Ah, ah. Look but don't touch. The Crown of Atargatis is a sacred thing."

"Atargatis?" I repeated.

"The first sea queen. The ancient mother of sirens. Myth says she was a divinely beautiful woman who fell in love with a mortal man. But she caused his death, and in her grief and guilt, threw herself into the sea. But she was too beautiful to die, and instead emerged transformed by her broken heart with the tail of a fish—and power of the seas—second only to Poseidon himself."

And somehow you managed to steal her crown?

Bastian went on. "A reward as hefty as her crown requires a task of equal proportion. A task no one has yet to survive accomplishing. Kill the Kraken and it's yours."

"You've sent others?" Bellamy asked, redirecting Bastian's attention to him.

"Plenty. You're a skilled sailor. You've heard the stories. You know none can kill the beast."

"Bellamy," I stepped forward, uttering my first word since we'd entered this place. "Is that true? Can it be killed?"

He hesitated for a moment, as Bastian wrung his hands excitedly, waiting for Bellamy's next words. Finally, he grumbled so low I was sure that only I could hear him. "It's true. It's an impossible mission."

"No, no. You've got to be wrong. We wouldn't just give up that easily. We won't. There's got to be a way."

"No...It's *impossible.*" He bit the inside of his cheek, as though biting back what he really wanted to say. I was careful not to argue too much to keep from accidentally giving away more information than Bastian should hear. But I was furious. And desperate. And I had an idea. Anything to save Milo. The heart on the desk tempted me beyond belief. But I couldn't bring myself to do it...to kill. I couldn't do it again.

I stepped forward, locking my focus on Bastian and his stupid arrogant expression. I opened my mouth and began to sing my song.

"What are you doing? Stop!" Bellamy growled. I commanded Bastian to shut up and bring us the crown. His eyes widened at the first notes of my song, and then he stood alert, under my control and ready to follow my orders.

He began walking to a corner of the room, his mind seemingly numbed by my enchantment. Bellamy watched, half horrified and mesmerized. And then, Bastian stopped, just as quickly as he'd fallen under my spell, and turned to look at me from across the room before bursting into a guttural laugh.

"You *really* thought you had me with that lovely song, didn't you?" He clapped his hands together like an entertained child and threw a nod to Bellamy. "So, sirens aren't extinct after all. You should've told me. Then at least maybe I could've warned you that their songs don't work on those under the mark of Davy Jones."

I stood planted, shaken and enraged at myself for being so stupid. I should have listened to Bellamy. I'd just dug us into a hole deeper than we ever intended to go. And I was clueless as to how we were going to wriggle out of it. I glanced at Bellamy, whose eyes had turned to stabbing glaciers jutting into me.

"I told you not to—"

"You told her not to what?" Bastian interrupted. "Prove what I already knew? I sensed her siren blood the moment you two stepped in here. And the fact that you're alive all these years Bellamy. It could only be because of her."

Bellamy seethed as frustration furrowed in his forehead.

"Don't worry. I can do nothing to her that we haven't agreed to," Bastian smiled. "But this certainly raises the stakes of our deal."

"We have no deal," Bellamy turned away, as if readying himself to leave, fists clenched at his sides.

I rushed to his side. "We can't leave without that crown," My voice cracked as I fought back the lump rising in my throat. "We can't give up after we came all this way."

Do it. Destroy the heart. Kill the man.

Bellamy's eyes softened, and in that moment, I realized how empty they truly were. He had given up long ago. Not just on this, but on everything. He had finally learned to be content with death, and yet was forced to live through his grief all over again. This was too much for even him. "Unfortunately, Katrina, sometimes you do everything in your power, and you still can't save them."

"Who are you?" I sputtered, nearly choking on the words. "The Bellamy I know wouldn't stop fighting. You're too stubborn."

He didn't respond, but something told me the Bellamy I knew might have been hiding behind more layers than I realized. And if this was all too much for him, that was fine. I understood. But it wasn't too much for me. There was nothing I wouldn't do to rescue Milo from the past. I spun around, facing a bored-looking Bastian, who watched us bickering just a few feet away.

I darted past him and grabbed the jar, raising it above my head and smashing it on the ground. The glass shattered and I swiftly grabbed a piece, slicing my own hand, and drove it into the glimmering heart. I looked at Bastian, longing to see him collapse so that I could rush down his trove and take the crown. But he stood there, smug, almost entertained.

"I was wondering when one of you would try that," he smirked. "Do you think if that heart was keeping me alive that I would really be so stupid as to keep it there?"

My mouth hung open in shock.

"How the hell are you still alive then?" Bellamy asked.

"Bellamy, you're adorable," Bastian laughed. "You both are, really. Thinking you can kill me that easily and that I'll just spill all my secrets. Why don't I just hand you the Crown and leave you the keys to my club?"

I was furious and sick. Sick of myself, for just trying to kill a man, but mostly at Bastian for his twisted games.

"I'll kill your Kraken." I straightened my spine and stood tall, speaking with all the authority I could muster. "I'll do it. For the damn crown."

A wicked curve slid over Bastian's lips, a shadow falling over his eyes. Bellamy whipped back around, pulling me to him. "No!" He covered my mouth. "She doesn't agree to anything. I'll do it. Your deal is with me. Always has been. I'll take the mark. Not her." I struggled against him, feeling guilty that he felt the need to jump in for me, and also wondering what mark I was meant to take. The idea of it made my skin crawl.

"She already agreed," Bastian approached us, stepping over the shattered glass and bleeding heart as he checked his watch. "And we really need to get this moving along. I'm expecting someone."

"No!" The tone in Bellamy's voice changed from anger to pleading. He lowered his face to mine, squeezing my shoulders so tightly I thought he'd bruise them. "No, Katrina, dammit! He'll always play the game in his favor. He's sending us to our graves. This wasn't part of the plan."

"Aren't you the one who told me the plan sorts itself out at the right time? You can't be afraid when it does!" I shouted, heaving as I thought of every second wasting.

"I'm not afraid for myself," Bellamy snarled back. "But I'm afraid of losing the last person I care about!" His words sliced through my heart like a cold steel cutlass. Bastian stepped between us, separating Bellamy from me.

"Such a touching moment, really, but we must get on with this. And don't worry, dear girl, I have no intention of sealing this deal like all the others. It does me no good to track the two of you with some tasteless tattoo. No, instead, let's bind our contract a different way...a more *effective* way given your nature."

"What do you want?" I blinked, afraid of the answer.

"Your voice. Your siren song."

"What?" I clutched a hand to my throat. "No..." I stammered. Bellamy pleaded with me, his voice dry and distressed.

"Don't worry. It's only a small deposit. A signature if you will—that you agree to my terms." Bastian coaxed. "You'll get your song back—and the crown—when you return...with the beast's head."

"Let's get on with it." I tried so hard to sound brave, but my confidence was wavering. I was doubting everything. The room melted around me like swirling paint and my head felt light. My palms were slick from sweat. Bellamy's voice faded out as he begged me—demanded me—not to do this. But I didn't see any other answer. I didn't know what else to do.

"Then sing your song," he commanded.

I opened my mouth. The first notes came out shaky and weak, but as I sang the haunting melody, my song strengthened into a powerful aria. Bastian raised his serpent hand, where he adjusted a ring on his finger. It was iron, with a black polished stone of some sort in the center. As he turned it, curling black smoke rose out of it. I was startled, but I kept singing.

The smoke coiled and writhed in the air like a snake made of shadow, slowly creeping its way across the air to me. It surrounded me, trickling down into my throat, where it wrapped its dark clutches around my song. I could feel it, choking me, but I was now powerless to stop my song. I gasped in horror as it pulled away, a glowing blue and white pulse of energy wrapped in its smoke-like grip. My song. It echoed as if distant, trapped in the glowing orb. Then as quickly as it appeared, it retreated back into Bastian's ring, now another part of his collection.

The room was silent. Even Bellamy was frozen in place and speechless. I opened my mouth to sing again. But my song was gone. It just sounded like an ordinary voice and an ordinary tune, one that no longer held a hint of magic or power.

Bastian grinned. "Well, a deal's a deal. As an added bonus for your compliance, I've thrown in a special tool to help you find the beastie." He crooned, looking to the door, before tossing me a spyglass that I barely caught. "Now get to Kraken hunting. Can't hold up my next appointment."

20

Spyglass

Bellamy

"How could you do that?" I stomped furiously after Katrina as we made our way out the door of the club the same way we came. Katrina ignored me as she pushed through the sweaty bodies in the booming crowd. "Katrina! Talk to me!" I shouted.

She finally whipped around once we made it to the outside past the bouncers, her long dark locks nearly smacking me in the face. "I did what I had to do. He wasn't going to let us go without that deal. You were the one who tried to kill him before we even knew where the Crown was!"

"But you completely ignored everything I said. Bastian is not someone to play around with."

"Aren't you the one who told me sometimes the gray is the only thing that can save us?" She spoke with such a strange calmness for someone who had just given up her voice to a dark pirate lord. "Just be glad he didn't ask for more. Speaking of, what did you mean when you said his deal has always been with you?"

I sighed with frustration and pulled down the collar of my shirt, pointing to a small sea serpent tattoo on my collarbone. "This came from Bastian when he made the deal with my father. *I* was the deposit." My thoughts glanced back to

"Bellamy, I'm so sorry." Katrina started, but I didn't let her finish.

"Don't be. My father didn't force me. I did it willingly. I was an idiot then, thinking Bastian would honor his deal. No one knew the dark magic he had then. But now I know. His power comes from Davy Jones himself, and that's nothing to underestimate."

"Why? Is this Davy Jones guy really so powerful?"

"Not a guy. Davy Jones is an entity, always looking for someone already dark-hearted enough to be under his control. The dark force of the seas that takes the souls of sailors to their eternal graves. And yes he really is that powerful and if Bastian's channeling his power... then I fear Bastian's got both of us at his mercy. He's marked me and stolen your voice, which was pretty fucking handy in a lot of situations."

"Well...yeah." Suddenly her voice softened. "But, you know, maybe that's what I'm scared of. I'm relying on it too much. Relying on my ability to control others...and I'm afraid if I keep doing it, one day I might not be able to rein it in."

It all made sense. Of course she gave up her voice. She was still afraid of her power. Furious as I was, my heart eased up a bit. There was more to this than she let on.

"Besides," she said. "There's nothing I wouldn't give up to get Milo back. I didn't have to think about it."

"Right." I clicked my tongue. I certainly understood that. I'd give my voice up too, if it could bring back Serena. "But we still have to do the impossible first."

"Don't forget you still have a siren on your side," Katrina's eyes flashed deep blue, like flaming sapphires glinting in the light.

"Technically two sirens." McKenzie's voice made me look to see her approaching with Noah and Grace flanking her. "What's this impossible mission you agreed to?" Her eyebrows pressed together tightly to spell worry clearly on her forehead.

Katrina and I explained to them in detail everything that happened with Bastian and his massive underground lair. I offered them the option to stay behind now, because once we found the Kraken, there would be no escape. And certainly no promise we'd live through it.

"We'll fight this thing with you. There are flares and maybe more guns back on the yacht." Noah straightened his shoulders, as if trying to prove his usefulness. Grace's eyes were wrought with worry, but she didn't say anything. I'd learned by now she wasn't one to speak up while processing. I almost cared to wonder what McKenzie was thinking, given that she was unusually quiet too.

No. The agreement was between myself and the both of you. Not your friends. They stay behind.

I gripped my head in my hands. The voice grated against my consciousness like knives raking my skin. Bastian's voice. It choked out my own thoughts like black smoke in a dark room. He was in my head. His mark had power over me after all.

Katrina and McKenzie rushed to steady me as my fingers dug into my hair. I was fine. I swear I was. But I was too livid to find the words to respond to them as they asked if I was okay. I tried my best to ignore the dreamlike command of Bastian, but it echoed within me until I admitted what I was hearing.

"He says you can't come." I fought to get the words out. "I think we reawakened this stupid tattoo. Bastian has a direct line to me. And he will until we do this. If we breach his terms of the deal, he'll be in my head forever."

"Bellamy." Katrina touched my shoulder softly. "I didn't know."

"Because you didn't listen to me. I told you he always takes more than he promises."

"I'm sorry. What was I supposed to do? Don't tell me you really would've walked out of there knowing you forfeited the only chance you have to help Milo. I know you. You wouldn't have done it. He's like a brother to you."

"Hmmm," I growled, turning away. I wasn't sure what I would've done anymore. Milo was my brother at sea, no doubt. But would I trade Katrina's life for his by pitting her against this beast? Either way I lose. I always lose. By the minute, I felt the pathetic scraps of faith I had left in everything and everyone around me slipping through my grasp. The never-ending battle of losing those closest to me was beginning to wear on me.

"You'll be fine here in Puerto Rico." I spoke firmly, leaving no room for argument to the trio watching me. If they tried, I'd shut them up quick and leave them stranded here without a choice. "We need someone to keep an eye on Bastian anyway. You can let us know if you see him trying to pull anything like relocating or running."

Suddenly, it seemed as though Grace found her bravery. "Trina, I can't just stay here and let you do this. I know you're used to doing things on your own, I do. But this...it's too dangerous."

"Mom," Katrina breathed. "This is something I have to do. If I don't, I'll never forgive myself. I can't leave Milo behind."

I almost wanted to roll my eyes as Katrina went on to reassure and plead with her mom. Grace wouldn't understand that fearless sacrifice Katrina talked about. She'd never been faced with anything of the sort. She was always the one being saved. She had no right to tell Katrina not to do this...Maybe I didn't either. I didn't know anymore.

"Please, Katrina. What if I feel the siren's pull again? What if I can't resist it without you?" Grace sounded more desperate than I'd ever heard her. I didn't believe she wasn't really worried about that. She was just reaching for whatever she hoped might anchor Katrina here.

"Katrina," I muttered, interrupting Grace's pleas. "Every second matters now."

Katrina switched her gaze to me, Grace glancing between the both of us. Noah stepped in to reassure her mother, because he must've known I wasn't going to do it. "Mrs. Delmar, if anyone can do this, it's Katrina. McKenzie and I will be right here with you, waiting for her when she gets back. She *will* come back."

Grace blinked, swallowing nervously as she shook her head. "I know I can't stop you," she said, her voice quivering and tearful. "But just remember you have to come back to me. No one else can show me how to be a mermaid." I caught a glimpse of Katrina's brief smile.

"I will." Katrina lifted her chin high. "I will." Grace leaned into her for a hug, one that looked clumsy from the start, but gradually softened into some semblance of what a mother-daughter embrace should look like. I looked away, fighting the feeling of awkwardness that hung in the atmosphere.

"At least let me help you prepare." Noah spoke to me, his tone somber. "You can't go empty-handed. These antique shops are bound to have something of use."

It wasn't a horrible idea, so I agreed on the condition that we hurried. The girls left to check into a hotel where McKenzie and Grace would stay, while Noah and I scoured the few shops still open. There was no doubt an array of artifacts and old weaponry from my own time and beyond, but finding some in usable condition was the trick.

In the last store we searched, my eyes scanned the wall of old, ravaged rifles and muskets, rusted swords and remnants of flintlocks. And then I saw it. A harpoon. Marked with signs of obvious use, but still intact and still sturdy. The spearhead was solid. I could sharpen it on the way.

"You thinking what I'm thinking?" Noah glanced over at me, noticing my fixation on the harpoon. Not five minutes later we left the store with our new harpoon, wrapped to appear as an oar or something less dangerous, and met the others back in the city square.

With a few more heartfelt goodbyes and well-wishes for safety, we parted ways, McKenzie, Noah, and Grace agreeing to linger in a nearby hotel in San Juan. Katrina and I trudged back to the shore, now bathed in moonlight and the glow of the city above it. We waded in, climbed aboard the jet ski, harpoon in hand, and zipped back to the yacht bobbing in the distance, onto a voyage more daunting than any I'd ever faced as a pirate.

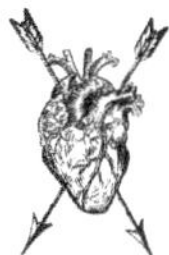

I helped Katrina aboard, still silent in my anger at our encounter with Bastian.

"I know you like holding grudges," Katrina grumbled, "but if we want to have a chance at surviving this thing, you should probably talk to me."

"Why? So you can do the exact bloody opposite of what I say?" I snarled, working the anchor up while Katrina reached for a tank of fuel. "You'll do whatever you decide in the end, with or without me."

"Why are you being like this, Bellamy? You said yourself we don't have time!"

"We don't! But it doesn't matter, because in the end you're going to do something stupid and get yourself killed regardless of what I say! You're just like her! You're reckless and headstrong and you don't listen and it's going to be the death of you! I won't live here on this shitty earth alone without you, too!" I slammed my fist against the hull, sure I would later regret the bruise it would leave on my knuckles.

I didn't even register the words coming out of my own mouth. I was losing myself to my thoughts of Serena as they flashed before my mind's eye. This all felt too familiar. Too repetitive to be real...

"This isn't about me, is it?" Katrina's voice softened, and I knew she knew.

"You're part of it," I grumbled. "But no...it's really not about you. Feel free to take the helm." I walked away and retreated to my room. The floor became my focus as I slipped away into the start of a memory...

I watched her from the back curtain, entranced as any song-struck sailor as she flitted through the water, turning and spinning and dancing in the bubbles behind the glass. She waved at the audience before blowing a kiss. Her hair flowed around her like ribbons in a breeze, and her eyes sparkled with a magic even real sirens didn't possess. Dancing joyfully from the confines of the massive display tank, she was a vision of herself in her truest form. In the water was where her spirit came alive. Anyone could see it.

After her performance, I snuck backstage, past the next act of dolphins and sea lions doing tricks for their trainers. The moment I saw her, seated at her dresser, already out of her tail and wrapped in a towel, I ran to greet her, planting kisses on her cheek and lips. She was carrying on about how she missed a cue to blow bubbles during the music because she couldn't hear it well under the water.

"They loved you. You were amazing," I breathed into her still damp hair as she rubbed her eyes.

"I was afraid you weren't going to make it." She turned to me, nuzzling her adorable nose against my jaw.

"Well, being on time is hard when the ocean controls your schedule," I teased, making her giggle. "But of course, I'd be here, just like I promised. I wish you had more night shows."

"I don't," she stood up, tossing her towel aside and throwing on a sheer white dress to cover her bikini. "I don't want to be here at night when the best swimming is out there." She tilted her head, and I could already tell she was dreaming of dipping into the waves beneath the moonlight, as she so often did. It was such a dangerous habit for anyone else, but for her it was life-giving.

She took my hand, a beaming smile across her face as she looked to the back door. "Let's go."

Katrina showed up soon enough, knocking till her knuckles would break by the sound of it. "We have to settle this. I'm not sailing across the sea like this."

I popped the door open just a crack. "Then swim." When I tried to close the door, Katrina stopped it with her foot.

"You said I'm like her," she said. Katrina had moved closer to me.. "Like her," She repeated. "You mean Serena, don't you?" She pushed the door open a bit wider. I let her and stepped outside as she continued. "I'll make sure you don't lose me, too. I won't leave you alone in the world."

"How can you promise something like that?" I groaned.

"Because...because we need each other. We always have." She reached forward and placed her arms around me, in a warm, comforting embrace. I couldn't remember the last time I'd felt something like it. The strength in it. The reassurance. No one had given me that before.

She was right. There was some unbreakable bond between she and I, and ultimately, all three of us. I had to face the doubt clouding my soul. Some sailors would stop sailing in a fog and wait it out. But I was always known to sail through it till I broke through to the other side. And that's what I had to do now. Even if things still weren't the same, and never would be again. Milo still needed us both.

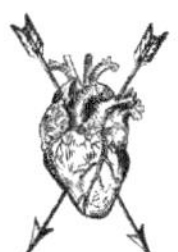

We'd only been at sea a couple of hours before I began to feel the sinking feeling creeping up on me. The rapid countdown of time running out. I hadn't mentioned to Katrina that it would take a month to reach the waters where the Kraken roamed, maybe a little under three weeks at best if Katrina could miraculously carry us on a current again without stopping. But that would drain her. So I was busy trying to calculate how many more years that would mean for Milo.

When Katrina came bouncing over excitedly, I felt hopeful for a second. "This spyglass Bastian gave me," she said, holding up the tool, looking through it. "He said it would help us find the Kraken. Look!"

I took the bronze tube from her hand, raising it to my eye to take a peek. I nearly stumbled backward at the sight. Instead of seeing the horizon in front of me magnified, I was met with the closeup of a growling sea creature underwater eyeing me like prey, as if I was swimming face to face with it.

"It shows us the Kraken!"

"If only it could take us to it," I muttered, still trying to collect myself from the startling sight I saw through the lens. "Seriously...why would he give us this? It's not like he's known for making his deals easy."

"Unless he's really *that* confident we'll die trying." Katrina scoffed. I released a stiff laugh.

"Ha. Or unless he just *really* wants this Kraken dead. For what, I don't know. Maybe he's just *that* bored with his collection." I turned the spyglass in my hand, looking it over, guessing that somehow it probably had some dark enchantment about it that allowed Bastian to watch us through it.

But then I turned the outer tube, adjusting it with a slight twist to focus the lens, and suddenly a pulse of energy emitted from it into the sea around us. For a moment nothing else happened, and Katrina looked at me with concern and confusion. Despite the absence of wind, I noticed a slow-rolling wave cresting far in the distance.

"What's happening?" Katrina asked.

"I don't know," I stammered, wondering the same thing. The wave rolling in grew fast, more than doubling in size every second. I tucked the spyglass in my belt and raced to the helm, Katrina in tow. It was too late to outrun it, but I had to at least position the boat head-on to take a hit from a wave like that. "It's a rogue wave," I shouted as it sped toward us, now at least 70 feet high. "Brace!"

Katrina had no time to run for cover, so she gripped the railing and ducked down, squatting in the floor by my feet. The yacht rose up as the wave crawled up underneath us, lifting us to an angle that left me holding onto the steering wheel for dear life as we barreled just over the crest of the ever-growing wave. Sea spray as thick and blinding as a blizzard engulfed us, and water crashed over the sides of our boat. Katrina screamed, and I braced my leg against her in my best effort to hold her in place as our ship became airborne momentarily.

We rolled back down the other side, sliding down the great slope of water in a slurry of wind and salt. The ship nosedived, crashing bow-first into the sea as the rest of it slapped the surface of the water below, rattling our bones. I couldn't hold on any longer, and Katrina and I both toppled to the slippery wet floor. Sea foam sloshed and spilled off the sides of the deck as the yacht righted itself. Once the ship finished tossing us around, I helped Katrina to her feet.

It was only then that the bitter chill of ice seized my skin and I realized the heavy heat dome of the Caribbean was gone. Katrina shivered, soaked from head to toe in frigid water the same as me. Our breath came out as white puffs in the suddenly wintry air around us.

"Get inside," I chattered. "We'll freeze out here."

We hurried to the cabin, where we dried off quickly and wrapped ourselves in blankets from the beds, though there were few clothing items aboard the yacht fit for cold weather. We sat at a small table by a window to take in our surroundings without freezing our asses off. I didn't care if the boat drifted for a minute. The sky outside was a heavy gray, but it did little to dampen the bright teal blue of the water around us. This was certainly no Caribbean Sea.

"The wave. The spyglass." I rubbed my hands together, still not fully warmed. I hated being cold. "It somehow brought us here. See those cliffs far off in the distance. This looks like the Mediterranean."

"I don't know why I imagined it a bit brighter...and warmer," Katrina huffed, hugging herself tightly after taking a sip of some hot chocolate we'd found in the ship's kitchen.

"Not in January." I tapped my fingers on the table, looking out at the blue water beneath the dreary sky.

"Bastian helped us." Katrina shuddered. "Why?"

"This wasn't just a deal for him. It was a mission. He needs this thing dead for some reason."

"Well then so do I, if it means getting that crown."

"Hmph," I pressed my lips together with a sarcastic tone. "Then I guess you need to get your fish arse in this freezing water and lure it up here." I grinned. "I've heard mermaids happen to be the Kraken's favorite snack...and I'm sure it's been a while since he's tasted one."

21

Eye of the Storm

Milo

The heat of the blood gushing down my arm was nearly enough to distract me from the pain of the blade carving into it. Nearly.

I bit down on the cloth between my teeth, gnashing my jaws as the knife sunk into my skin and peeled the top layer from my muscle. The ink stained down deep. Likely to the bone. I had to stop for a moment to catch my breath.

Clara appeared at the top of the forecastle, looming over where I sat on the steps under the cover of night. "Need some help with that?"

I didn't turn my head. "Deck swabbers don't intrude on the captain's private affairs."

"Then say I'm not a deck swabber fer now. Say I'm just a human watching another human fightin' his demons." She stooped down to meet me, kneeling by my side and taking the bloody knife from my hand.

"Fighting my demons or succumbing to them, I can't tell which anymore," I groaned. She jabbed the knife back in. I winced in agony as she sliced beneath the skin, prying flesh from flesh. Like filleting a fish, she worked the blade underneath the width of the tattoo I'd worked so hard to memorize over the past month at sea. With another month ahead of us, the map was stored clearly in my head now, and I no longer needed this damn seal of Bastian's marking me as his slave.

"There," Clara said, pouring a bottle of rum over the gaping wound in my forearm. I thought my teeth would shatter from how hard I bit down on the rag as the burning seared through my veins. But just as a small sliver of relief began to wash over me that I was at least free of being tracked, the torn open flesh reformed right before our eyes. Sinew and skin appeared as if by magic, reconnecting itself to seal up my arm with a new jagged and scarred version of the tattoo.

"Fucking hell!" I slammed my fist into the edge of the steps, scraping my skin against the salt-worn wood.

"Don't fret about it so," Clara reassured, wiping her bloody hands with the rag that was just in my mouth. "You agreed to do this. Now see it through."

"How do you know anything about what I've agreed to?" I snarled.

"I was watchin' you in the tavern that night, you know. I don't know why you did it or what yer lookin' for. But I know you made a deal and I can see now that you regret it."

"No," I grunted. "I don't regret it. It's what I had to do, but..." I caught myself. So desperate to share the burden on my mind and heart, I nearly gave away everything. I barely knew Clara. I hadn't told a soul on board this ship of what ailed me night and day. And I wouldn't ruin that here. She, like everyone else aboard, needed to know nothing. "I don't regret anything."

"Suit yerself, Cap'n. But just know yer not the only one out here lamenting what you wish you hadn't lost."

I lifted an eyebrow, curious as to what she meant by that, but knowing it was far better not to wonder.

"Thank you for your...assistance." I said, looking at the bloody mess on the deck. "I'll clean this up. You go get some sleep, Clara."

I expected her to protest, but she only turned and walked away without a word, the last bit of her flaming red hair fading into the heavy darkness. I cleaned the blood quietly, left alone with my thoughts once again. I watched the sharks swarming the water below as I dumped the bucket of red water overboard. Scavengers, just waiting for their chance to catch something worthwhile. Weren't we all?

As I left the deck, low thunder growled in the distance, heralding a line of storms looming miles away to the west of us. It was a slow-moving monster, and I expected we'd miss it based on our direction and its speed. We were traveling steady and slow, just to ensure we didn't get too close to it overnight. If it was still out there in the morning, we'd just have to sail around it. I preferred not to stop and wait it out. Time was too valuable to waste.

That night in my quarters I dreamed of her.

She walked to me on the beach, a vision calling out to me with her song. I ran to her, but the sand of the shore grew longer, farther, stretching to create a path I could never outrun. Finally I took a wrong step in the sand, crashing forward into the surf to find myself hitting cold stone. I was back on the lighthouse where I first brought Katrina to show her the stars. Everything felt right here.

She met me at the top, her call soothing my aching soul as she emerged like a queen from the stairs. Like the night I saw her in that glittering dress and lost my breath at the sight of her. As if dancing across the air, she came to me, kissing me with her melody still on her lips, wasting no time driving her tongue into mine, and tangling her fingers in my hair. I felt every inch of her, my hands trickling down her dress to find the slit halfway up her thigh. She guided me underneath, like a song she was singing with her hands, placing mine between the warmth of her legs. I traced the delicate parts of her, up, down, inside and out, yearning to join our bodies once and for all so that time and distance could never separate us again.

I kissed her slow and steady as my fingers moved in her. She released a blissful moan that carried on the sea wind and wrapped me further into her. But then her voice turned dark and cold. "I told you not to become like them."

I opened my eyes to see myself face to face with eyes as blue as the depths of the ocean, staring at me with the narrowed pupils of a predator. I tore myself away from her, my heart breaking as she followed me, no longer in desire but in bloodthirst. Her sweet song became an echo, rattling in my head as she stalked toward me in a state I could not break through. I called her name, begging her to recognize me…but ignoring it all, she placed her hands on my shoulders and shoved me off the lighthouse, following me down into the raging water below.

I awoke with a start as my body hit the wooden floor below my bed. Small bits of sunlight already poured through my stained-glass window along the walls. It was just after dawn.

"What the hell do I make of that?" I muttered, disturbed by the dream as I rubbed the spot where my head made impact with the floor. "Had to be the rum."

I'd downed a good amount last night to dull the pain of my self-attempted tattoo removal, though it hadn't helped much. I glanced down at my scarred arm, the tattoo still perfect despite the skin beneath and around it having been mutilated just hours ago.

I heard a muffled cry from up top. It sounded like Keegan from the crow's nest. He must've spotted something. I rushed to throw on my shirt and boots, grabbing swords and slinging my pistol holster over my shoulder, then hurried out on deck. An eerie morning mist covered the waters and severely limited my view.

"What is it?" I shouted for my first mate. "Felix!" Felix came running up before I'd barely finished saying his name.

"Red flagship spotted, Capitán. We saw it all too late because of the fog. It's close." His heavy Spanish accent coated his words, but he was the most reliable communication on board, making him my choice of first mate. I trusted him, and he was loyal enough to my commands and decisions. However, on a personal level, even after all these months, we hardly knew a thing about each other. Just as I preferred it.

I reached for my spyglass, focusing on the ship in the distance. It was close enough for me to easily make out the flowing red flag atop its mast even without the spyglass once my eyesight adjusted to the fog. Carl Thane's ship. A massive galleon, no doubt laden with cannons and guns far heavier than most pirate vessels. He'd traded speed for strength.

"The bastard never gives up," I said smugly, handing the spyglass to Felix. There was no mistaking the vessel for Thane's. Though I'd lost track of him after the showdown with Bellamy's ship and the warship, I knew it was far from my last encounter with him. I knew he'd turn back up eventually to continue hunting me down once he got back on his feet. I didn't mind though. His retribution was long overdue for when he kidnapped Katrina and left her scarred. I anticipated when he'd come for me again so I could ensure he got what he was owed before I found my way out of this life.

But that would have to be in due time. Not yet. Though I relished at the thought of facing him to enact my revenge, I couldn't allow myself to get distracted now. Not when I was so close to what I believed could be the start of the missing piece of Bastian's map. I couldn't risk my ship. For now, I'd have to outrun him. Give him something to chase a bit longer.

"Increase our speed, lads! Let's catch as much wind as we can!" Felix and I trudged to the helm. Thunder rumbled in the distance, making sure we didn't forget about the presence of the giant storm ahead. We'd be sailing right toward it, but a bit of shaking up from wind and rain would still be better than getting battered by cannons from a warship twice the size of my frigate. But the damn fog had hidden him long enough to keep us from getting a good head start.

My crew set themselves to quick work adjusting sails and securing rigging as we caught the wind and soared onward. The storm winds sucked us right in, pulling us toward it with ease.

I caught glimpse of Clara rushing among the men, nearly shoving them out of her way as she worked faster than any of the others. Her position was a deckhand, but here she was handling the rigging and setting up the mainmast more masterfully than I'd seen any men aboard this ship manage. Later I'd decide whether to chide her or promote her for it.

I looked back to see that Thane's ship had opened full sail, too, emerging from the mist and closing the already too-short distance between us. Even with a ship his size, the winds were favorable enough to give him just enough of a boost to catch up quickly. A clap of thunder struck as lightning cracked in the distant sky like a whip. The storms were probably just a bit over thirty minutes away. They were crawling away from us, but we were moving much faster right into them. I'd rather not be caught up in the line, though it certainly wouldn't be the first torrent we'd braved at sea in the *Falcon*. But a heavy storm might just be the thing to put some distance between Thane and me for now. I doubt he would take the chance of losing another ship.

But to my surprise, Thane didn't slow. He followed us, probably desperate to land a blow despite the stupidity of it in these conditions. I left Felix at the helm to walk the deck, checking our ammunition as men loaded cartridges and prepared the cannons. I silently yearned for this battle, but I also knew that even with my thirst for seeing Thane's head roll, a fierce storm and a massive warship at our backs wasn't setting up for the best outcome. But if he insisted on being stubborn, so would I. Stubborn, or perhaps stupid, it was all the same to me.

Minutes passed, and the foggy morning skies began to darken. The wind strengthened with the scent of coming rain. I resumed my place at the wheel, Felix at my side as we sailed carefully. Thane's ship was close enough within range now that if he were to open fire, he might just be able to reach us if he had a front bow chaser cannon, which would be likely on a gunship like his. But he was much farther than he should be if he hoped for any kind of precision. I wouldn't waste my ammunition at this distance. I wouldn't open fire on him till I knew I was close enough to sink his rig and take him on with my bare hands. And that day wasn't today, unfortunately.

Suddenly, a burst of wind sent us forward, towing us just out of reach and within the storm's suction. Thane must've known he was losing ground. His ship, barely in range, sent a small wave of cannonballs sweeping across the ocean's surface. Most of them arched and crashed into the water behind us, just a few inches from the *Falcon's* stern. But a couple did make impact, slamming the hull and one even grazing a spar on the mainmast. The cracking wood made my stomach sink and my senses heighten. The wooden pole splintered, falling with a bit of sail still attached to it. But at least it wasn't the mast itself.

I asked Felix to tell the crew to hold off the cannons and start taking down the sails and securing ballasts before we reached the storm. He rushed to the forecastle deck to yell the orders. We didn't have time to turn and line up our guns, but I wouldn't leave Thane with nothing to show for his efforts. I rushed to a swivel cannon at the stern, where I released fire at his ship, taking out part of the foremast. That would slow him down considerably. As my men cheered, their voices were drowned out by the sound of one more front cannon blast from Thane. A chain shot. It whirled over the railing just far enough to clip Felix's head.

He dropped like a bag of sand. My gaze flicked from his bloody skull to Thane's ship. It was turning now, retreating.

"Damn coward." I muttered. It was only fitting of him to try his luck at one shot before running away from the storm like the piece of shite he was. And luck had been on his side to take out my first mate. I rushed back to the helm and gripped the wheel, Felix's blood pooling and trickling along the woodgrain to the soles of my boots. I shifted the rudder, taking back control against the choppy water and wind. I ordered some deckhands to move Felix's body somewhere safe until we could give him a proper burial at sea.

"Batten down the hatches and brace for rough seas ahead!" I called out, eyeing the dark clouds and curtain of rain right in front of us. There was no way to pull out of it now. And I prayed our damaged mast would hold up as we headed for the eye of the storm.

22

Any Port

Milo

The *Falcon* fared well in the storm. She rocked and slammed against the waves, but she was sturdy. With most of the crew riding it out belowdecks, a handful stayed up at my command to help secure a few more loose items and repair any immediate damage caused by the storm. Clara was one of them, even though I didn't ask her to.

The blinding rain and wind whipped my face, and my muscles strained against the wheel threatening to be pulled from my grip by the waves. But I could see the clearing just up ahead. Without our sails we couldn't hurry through to the other side, but just the sight of a blue sky gave me enough motivation to weather through it.

After an hour of lashing wind and waves, the sun welcomed us, and quickly brought its heat to make us forget the bite of the storm. The crew emerged, likely as hungry as I was. Rodrigo, the cook set to working, bringing each man his ration of breakfast—a porridge sweetened with butter and rum water. To my empty stomach it was a delicacy, and the nourishment helped to clear my head.

I studied the horizon, nearly calling Felix to help chart out our course, out of habit, but realizing he wouldn't be answering my call, I stopped myself. The storm had long washed away his blood, but I stared at the spot where he fell and called the men to bring him up. For a moment, I regretted that I never learned more about him than what I knew. One minute he was here. A whole life. And the next, in an instant, gone from this world. Not that I was unacquainted with death, but this one felt an awful lot like my fault.

Gathered at the stern with my crew, I laid his sword and pistol across him in the most ornate manner I could manage before we wrapped him in a shroud fashioned from his hammock. I read a rite from the ship's common prayer book, and then nodded to the crew to proceed with committing his body to the deep. He slid into the water and then sank slowly from the weights tied to him.

A somber quiet fell over my crew. Many of them had known Felix longer than I had, except the men I recruited on my own after taking this ship. I wondered how many of them secretly resented me for killing their captain and claiming the crew. I wondered if any of them actually cared. That was the price of being captain. I never knew who'd stayed out of loyalty, out of fear, or the desire for revenge. Except Felix. He was loyal to the sea and this ship, and I admired that about him.

Now I needed a new first mate.

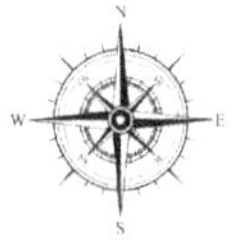

I reworked our course, adjusting based on how much the storm tossed us off course. It hadn't caused us to drift too far, so it would only take an extra afternoon to pick up where we left off. I charted our location, noticing an island just up ahead, a random lush formation in the middle of the Atlantic, but had no name or significance according to my maps. I intended to head toward it so we could stop for the evening and replace the broken mast spar. It was of the utmost importance to get it repaired so that we could resume our normal sailing speed and outmaneuver Thane if—and when—he returned.

By late afternoon, we'd docked as close as possible. The island looked uninhabited but was large enough to sustain life easily. When we disembarked and explored, it didn't take long to appreciate how lush and resource-filled this island was. Like an oasis in a desert, it boasted fresh springs of clear water and fruit trees in abundance. I encouraged my crew to take their fill and gather as much water and food as we could to replenish our own supply before night fell. We even took some extra timber from the dense forest of trees hiding the other half of the island.

As we worked to repair the mast spar by the light of torches and bonfires, I hummed a shanty to lift the crew's spirits. It wasn't long before the rest of them joined in. Clara's voice carried over the men's, a shrill note of power in a chorus of brutes. She half-grinned at me from her spot on the deck handing up tools to those of us perched on the mast, hammering the new spar into place and redoing the sail rigging. I had offered to let her climb up and help, but she insisted she was afraid of heights.

When the work was done, I wiped the sweat from my forehead and climbed down the rope webbing back to the deck. After a month of sailing, I figured my crew might appreciate a night on land, even if it was just an empty island with no taverns. I'd been pushing them so hard these recent weeks, desperate to find what I sought as fast as possible. Katrina was my mission. My reason for all of this. But these men were my crew and I owed them some rest.

With their cheers of relief filling the air, the men indulged themselves in our rum reserves and laid out cots to sleep in the sand under the open sky instead of the stuffy belowdecks. Finlay had even managed to capture a wild boar earlier that we roasted and stuffed ourselves with until we were sick. I suppose that redeemed him somewhat for his gambling addiction.

After I'd eaten my fill, I snuck away, longing for a bit of privacy to think. As if I didn't do enough of that alone in my quarters. But this would be different. This was finally a place without bustling taverns and crowded docks. This was a place I could sit beneath the stars in the sand and just let my mind wander in peace.

"Where ya off to, Cap'n?" Clara's voice called as she noticed me leaving the group.

"Nowhere in particular," I uttered over my shoulder. "Don't concern yourself. I'll be back."

I left her behind and wove my way through the tangled trees and lush leaves coating the lower half of the forest. For a moment, it reminded me of the night I led Katrina back to a safe spot on the shore back in Florida. The second night I saw her, and the first night I realized I wanted her. I fought to admit that to myself for so long. I swore to myself it must've been the necklace drawing me to her. Why else would I have been thinking of her even through my torment at the bottom of the ocean? Why did she—even when I hardly knew her—feel like the missing piece to my broken soul? Why did it seem as though long before time the stars had destined us to meet on that lonely island shore, much like this one?

All for me to end up back here, captaining a crew as the pirate I swore I'd never be. But maybe that was it? Maybe I was meant to stay here. Maybe it was the only way to truly protect Katrina. Her siren side would only grow stronger, and she needed someone without their own dark side to help her fight off hers. What if I couldn't?

Years at sea do strange things to a man's mind.

I pondered these things as I stood in a glade, not even realizing my feet had stopped moving. I stared up at the night sky through a break in the treetops, but I couldn't find my North Star for the trees.

Footsteps rustled in the leafy brush around me before a bright pop of red hair burst forth from the shadows. Clara looked up, her face cleaner than I'd seen it in weeks from washing up here on the island.

"I thought it'd be obvious I came all the way out here to be alone."

"Aye, Cap'n, maybe you aren't the only one in need of a bit of solitude away from those rank men." She shook her head. "Turns out we just happened to have the same idea. Don't worry. I'll be going that way and hopefully we won't cross each other again till it's time to board." She turned away, heading off into the dark forest perpendicular to the way she came.

"Wait," I said, my heart suddenly sinking as I realized I'd left Clara alone with thirty-plus men. "Did any of the crew...did they...?"

"Stop yer worryin', God in heaven, *no*. And if they tried I'd cut their hands clean off before they could lay a finger on me."

I couldn't hold back a small smile as Clara's fiery reply relieved me. Of course I should've known better than to be concerned about her. Twice now I'd seen her bite Finley's head off for looking at her too long.

"Well, I'll be seeing you then, Cap'n. Enjoy your brooding and I'll enjoy mine—feckin hell, what's this?" Her voice changed swiftly, as torchlight closed in on the both of us from seemingly nowhere, illuminating the circle of strange people encircling us.

I tensed, whipping my head to all sides to take in my new surroundings. Tall, sturdy, warrior-strong men and fiercely elegant women stood around us, a scrutinizing look in their eyes as they held us in place with their silent gaze. A woman stepped forward, the torchlight setting her dark tan skin aglow. She was old, with likely the same number of wrinkles as paths she'd trodden in life. She watched me with dark indigo eyes set deep and above the white paint markings on her cheekbones, clothed in woven palm fibers and a blanket of animal skin draped around her. Her graying hair poked through strands of black and strings of shells woven throughout.

She approached me. Clara drew her dagger in haste, but I stilled her with a motion of my hand. I kept my hands where the woman and her tribe could easily see them, to show them I meant no harm. But if I was trespassing on their island, perhaps I'd already done more harm than I realized.

She looked me over, a single word crawling from her lips as if she was tasting a bitter drink.

"Hidden," she lifted her chin, "How?" She asked, her eyes glistening but still sharp as steel.

"What does she mean?" Clara snapped, ready to pounce at any minute. A tall man who had been standing next to the woman stepped forward. His light brown skin was mottled in scars up his arms and across his back and shoulders.

"She means, we are a hidden people. An island hidden from mortal eyes." I was startled at the perfect English he spoke. "She asks how you found this place."

I stood startled, unsure how to answer, still processing the sudden change around me as well as his impossible question. Hidden island? I'd seen it clear as day as I sailed right for it.

"I don't know. I just saw it. I needed to find a place for my men to rest and repair our ship. We'll be leaving soon." I spoke clearly, though I felt myself rushing a bit.

The scarred man spoke to the elder woman in a language I didn't recognize, not taking his eyes off me. She answered him with the same and they nodded. His eyes narrowed as he addressed me again, his voice sure and unwavering. "Men like you never leave without taking something. You will destroy this island and the last of these people like all the others."

"I—I intend to take nothing. I'm no explorer, I'm not—"

"Even if you leave, you will tell others of this land. They will come. And do what they've done best for decades." He glanced at his scars, almost seeming like he hadn't meant to, and then quickly refocused.

"How..." I stammered, "How do you speak English so well if you've been hiding from the outside world?"

"I was not born of this tribe by blood. I was taken from my home. By men like you on a ship like yours. I spent many years among the Spanish and English-speaking people. I learned your languages because with mine I had no voice..." My eyes fell as a feeling of guilt lanced through me. Could my father have played a part in this man's capture, I wondered? A sick feeling refused to settle in my stomach as the man went on. "Thank the sea gods I was brought along for one voyage in particular. A voyage my captor and his family did not survive. They shipwrecked near this island. I washed up here, and was welcomed by these people. I told them what happened to me. I warned them to hide this refuge of theirs. So they blessed this island with their ancient power, by the stars and moon and sun, so that none can see it from afar."

I stood, still taking in everything he told me, searching the depths of my racing thoughts for a worthy-enough response. Stopping here for the night was a foolish decision. I should've known better. I'd wasted time and possibly put us all in danger. "I...I'm sorry for what happened to you. I won't reveal this island. To anyone...I swear it. I'll board my ship and command my crew to leave now."

But they didn't seem willing to negotiate. I waited as the man translated to the elder woman. She looked me up and down, then at Clara, with suspicious movements. The group around her stood unmoving, their torches still flickering as they awaited her next statement. Then one more commandment flew from her lips.

23

Island of the Sun

Milo

"She asks that you remove your shirt," the man said. I hesitated, but slowly moved to pull off my tunic as he urged me to hurry.

The old woman neared me, looking my body over as she circled, her regal frame seemingly gliding over the forest floor. I held my breath. Every moment my own heartbeat grew louder in my ears until she stopped, fixated on the tattoo on my arm. As she explained something in her language to the man, she tensed her jaw.

"The Star you bear grants you mercy." I followed the woman's gaze to my North Star tattoo as the man spoke. "But you also have a dark power on you, she says. A dark enchantment that opposes ours and draws darkness to our island." He pointed to my arm with Bastian's mark.

"I had no choice but to accept this. It's just a tattoo. I have no dark power." I dared not move as I tried to explain myself, eyeing the tribe around me watching my every flinch.

"Come," the old woman said sternly. I was startled by her sudden utterance of a word I understood. I shifted toward her, slowly, intrigued. She looked to the man to translate as I gave Clara a nod of reassurance.

"We have a legend here, that the sun and the moon were once mortals, trapped in a cave and both forged as a result of enduring the same darkness."

"What does that have to do with me?"

"You, too, must not be overtaken by the shadows that bind you. The dark one who marked you can see us now. Even if we kill you, you've already revealed our existence. Soon the ships will come and the men will take what is not theirs. We must break the connection you share with your dark master so that we remain untraceable."

"You can do that?"

"Only enough to blur the tether you hold to the darkness. And then you must leave immediately, so that you're no longer a beacon for our location."

The thought of muddling the connection Bastian held over me sounded like a deal far too great to be true, no matter what it entailed. I leaned in, desperate to know more, and wondering what it would require of me. It didn't quite seem I would have a choice in the matter either way.

The man and elder woman spoke together, conversing back and forth before the elder addressed the tribe around her. Some shook their heads in disagreement, but others seemed to support what she was saying. Though they stood divided, the woman appeared to have made her decision.

"Sun," she said simply.

The translator straightened his shoulders. "You will bear the sign of our sun to drown out the dark power in you. It will sustain you as long as you seek the light. But if you choose the darkness...if you give in to the tempest raging in your heart...it will fade and give you over to your own destruction."

"You're giving me a choice?"

"No, you give yourself a choice. To choose darkness or light. Already you're tempted or you wouldn't ask. You are willing to do whatever you have to do to find that which you seek. And you've let it consume you and define you. Let the sun's light guide you. I will keep you from hardening your heart to the realities of those around you and from bringing harm to others in pursuit of freedom from your own pain."

Her words pierced something in me. There was no more room for doubting. I was meant to find the fountain. To reunite with Katrina. And my only path there right now was through doing as these people demanded.

"I'll take your symbol. I don't seek to harm you. I just want to get home." I offered a slight tilt of my head.

The woman spoke a word the man didn't bother to translate. In an instant, one man and one woman from the circle surrounding us lunged forward and grabbed Clara, each of them holding an arm in restraint as Clara shouted obscenities in surprise. I flinched, but didn't dare draw my weapon. I knew better than to leap to combat in defense. They weren't hurting her, and I knew she'd be fine. I couldn't risk losing any merit I sought to gain with the islanders.

A sharp point dug into my back. A knife or spear tip, I presumed. The man in front of me never took his harsh eyes from mine. "Remove all your weapons," he ordered. "The Elder wants to speak to you alone first."

I obliged, sliding my swords from their sheaths and laying my pistol at his feet. I couldn't explain the feeling I had, but somehow I believed with my whole heart I would come out of this alive. Perhaps it was delusion or drunkenness, but my fear had subsided.

The man before me and the member at my back forced me along a break in the circle encompassing us, leading me down a well-worn path behind the elder woman. With my agreement made known, the elder woman led me away to a place where the forest grew thicker and the sound of trickling water became clearer.

When we were far enough away, the old woman turned to face me. I noticed she'd led me to a stream that snaked through the rich soil of this island, its trickling sound like delicate clattering cymbals amongst the night song of insects. When the woman broke the silence with her speech, I looked up, listening and intrigued as to why she brought me here.

She dipped a withered hand into the clear water, guiding my gaze to the stream bed below. Inlaid with veins of gold, it certainly caught my attention. No doubt this island would be ravaged for this gold if anyone knew of its existence.

I inched closer to take a better look. The woman motioned for me to sit down on the ground. I knelt beside the stream, the elder woman seated regally with hands now folded in her lap. She began to speak and the man stood over us, translating each phrase.

"When you take this mark, remember our legend. Both trapped by darkness in a cave, the sun fought it, and his light grew stronger. But the moon embraced it, so much that she was able to trick the darkness into letting them go. So when they escaped, the sun was devoted to her for the rest of time. They both escaped their prison, but the moon forever harbored a dark side that only the sun could keep at bay. That's why we see her change each night. Her strength over the shadow waxes and wanes, but the sun's light sustains her until one day when she will grow strong enough to overcome it."

I let my gaze drift to the shimmering gold lines traced along the bottom of the crystal stream. The woman's hand, gentle but firm, touched my face to turn my head back to her as she continued.

"I understand the sun's power is great here. And you believe it protects your island." I said, hoping to move this process along.

"Yes. So be like the sun." The woman said this, instead of the man having to translate. She almost smiled with her eyes, though the rest of her face remained tight and emotionless.

"Now give her your arm." The man's voice boomed from above.

I slowly reached my arm forward, the woman began a low chant, humming to herself as she placed the tip of her finger in the water. The golden threads in the sediment began to glow, like warm light from the sun itself. It became like liquid, dribbling out from the cracks in which it rested and floating up in the water to meet the woman's fingertip. She lifted her finger, taking the stream of floating molten gold with it, directing it like swirling smoke.

She guided it to my arm, hovering over the tattoo from Bastian, and then the molten gold took form, searing itself into my skin in the symbol of a sun. I expected it to burn immensely, but there was little more than a mild sting. It settled into my flesh, creating an inlay of gold that became just barely visible once it settled.

"This will keep him from being able to find me as easily?"

"Yes." The man nodded. "It will serve as a veil between you and the dark one who marked you. And more importantly, he will not be able to see that you were here."

I breathed a sigh of relief as the man continued.

"As long as you leave at sunrise."

"You have my word. I'll have my ship repaired and gone before the first light of dawn." I nodded. "And Clara can be released now?" I asked.

The man raised an eyebrow. "The girl? She's unharmed. Go back to her now and tell no one of our existence or this island. Swear it by the stars."

"I swear it." With a solemn nod of understanding, I hastened my steps back toward Clara. When I turned, the woman and man were gone, not a trace of them left behind. Before I could reach the area where we'd been surrounded, Clara came bounding through the brush.

"Thank God, there ya are," she sputtered between hurried breaths. "They let me go and just vanished, they did. What did they do to you?"

"They swore me to secrecy. And made me promise to leave before sunrise."

"Why not kill us and get it over with? Ensure their safety." Clara looked around, seemingly still paranoid of their presence.

"Because they know better than to take a life lightly," I uttered. "But the same can't be said of those who would come here if they knew what treasures lay here. Come on." I motioned, moving forward onto the trail. "Let's get my things and head back to the crew."

I regathered my weapons and shirt, keeping silent as I reflected on the things I'd just experienced. The islanders were here and gone, barely ghosts in my memory and yet they'd left me with such a heavy weight in my heart. The guilt of lives I'd taken for gold, not for greed, but to buy the mere chance to see the girl I loved again, was a burden I'd bear forever. But the true weight was the terrifying thought that she'd never look at me the same. These hands would always be bloody, and it didn't seem right to hold her with them. Maybe this strange sun mark would help me find my way again. Maybe if Bastian's darkness wasn't the only darkness it could drive out...

Clara walked to my side as I turned over the thoughts in my head. Her voice tearing through the calm sounds of night. "What's still gnawing away at ya? I've been around you long enough to see on your face when you're frettin'."

"If the island is truly hidden, I don't understand why I was able to see it." I brushed a branch aside for us to pass through.

"Didn't those people go on about the power of sun and stars or something another? Maybe deep down ya already had a little ray of sunlight in there somewhere."

"Maybe." I glanced down at my North Star tattoo, thinking of Katrina and my path back to her. "Or starlight."

"So what exactly is it that you're looking for so desperately, Cap'n? I'm no fool and I know yer not just sailing this way in such a hurry hoping to find more gold or riches."

"If I told you, you'd never believe me." I didn't want her asking more questions, but it was clear she was catching on.

"I don't think you give me much credit, Cap'n." Clara paused to spit on the ground as we walked. "These past months I've watched you loot and plunder like a greedy dog. Hell I saw you shoot a man point blank for the key to his quarters. But ya never look pleased with what we take. No matter how valuable our prizes. You watch the ships we sink with a scowl while your men cheer in victory. You're richer than most any pirate captain I've sailed amongst, yet you live like you've the weight of the world on your shoulders. Like it's never ever enough. Whatever you're after has to be something beyond what this mortal world can offer."

"You're too smart for your own good, Reid. I can't imagine the trouble you've gotten yourself into...and out of."

"Don't try flattery to make me forget. I've watched ya sell your soul to the devil and agree to do his bidding for something. And I've done nothing but help you try to reverse it. So don't I deserve to know what exactly I'm helping my captain accomplish when I'm puttin' my neck on the line with yours?"

I breathed in a heavy sigh, looking ahead at the dying glow of the crew's fires in the distance. Their silence told me they'd likely long succumbed to their drink and merrymaking. So I'd let them sleep it off for a few more hours. But we'd be back on the water before first light.

"I never asked for your help with any of those things," I grumbled.

"True. But ya never ordered me to leave you alone either."

She was right. I'd never quite found it in me to turn her away, truth be told. I was just as curious about her as she was about me, but I didn't have time to pursue her secrets.

"Tell me where you came from and what it is you want with a life of sailing with a bunch of salty jackasses, and I'll tell you what it is I'm after."

Clara hesitated, surprise at my request clear in her eyes.

"You've been just as secretive as me, so don't act so shocked." I added.

"Fine," Clara crossed her arms. "It's not as daring and noble as you think, Harrington." Her eyes fell downward, focused on our boots in the damp earth below. "I was the daughter of a wealthy family. Always creating mischief where I couldn't find it. And when my mother tried marrying me off, I ran away, joining the first boat I could manage to sneak aboard. But adventurous as I was, I was naïve. My luck ran out soon enough and they found me..."

I wasn't sure if she was going to continue, and I didn't want to press her after the way she looked as her voice tapered off. But she went on, lip quivering for just a split second.

"The devils violated me and marooned me on an island. Said they couldn't have a woman aboard bringing the devil's curses. I was found by some traders, and they dumped me in Nassau, where I met a man I *thought* I loved. I joined his crew, and then I met her...a jewel of the seas. Just like me, she was. She knew all about scraping by and surviving this shite-hole of a man's world. We had a good run, she and I." Clara stared out into the blackness in the distance and smiled, as though reminiscing some cherished memory. "Until the Royal Navy found her...her and most the crew...hanged 'em all for piracy, they did. I escaped—by nothing but pure luck and a too drunk jailer who forgot to lock my cell. I sailed on my own long enough to end up in Madagascar, where ya found me. After that, I swore I'd never trust another captain. And I'd never let another—man or woman—hold my heart again."

"Did you ever trust me?" I asked her, scratching my neck as I awaited her answer in the silence.

"No. But I'm not afraid of ya, either, and that's the difference. I see the way you stare into the sea sometimes, with eyes like a lost daydreamin' lover, and the way you smile just a bit to yourself when you think no one sees ya. So I'll ask once more. What—or who—are you tryin' to find out here, Cap'n?"

I felt my face heating as I thought of Clara observing me so closely. She was too good at reading me. And for whatever reason, I was strangely fond of her fiery, abrasive spirit. I breathed in a heavy sigh, motioning for her to walk alongside me as we emerged from the forest and followed the shoreline.

"There's a lass who has my whole heart out there. But time has separated us. We are centuries apart. She's far into the future, and I'm trapped here. All because of some twisted siren magic. I left her a clue how to bring me back to her, not thinking of the danger it would put her in." I breathed out, thinking of Katrina and wishing that with the next breath I'd draw in, I'd breathe in her sweet scent of apricot and honeysuckle, and hating myself again for getting her mixed up with Bastian. "But if I can live forever...I can reunite with her, even if she doesn't succeed...I can wait for her, however long it takes until our timelines meet again."

Clara stared up at me with a twinkle in her eye, and the corner of her mouth twitched as though she might laugh. I would've expected no less.

"All that for a girl, mate?" She laughed. "I understand bein' lovesick as much as the next bastard but come on now. Say ya just stay here and settle down with a nice lass somewhere, forget that one. Not worth the heartache."

"She's worth every heartache. She's worth dying a thousand times for the chance to live one day with her. It's funny," I huffed with a forced laugh. "I once spent so long looking for a way to die, and now I'm searching the ends of the earth for a way to live forever just to see her again."

"Aye, so you're lookin' for the Fountain of Youth!" She exclaimed.

I half-nodded, but mostly I just looked away, unable to admit to her claim. She went on before my next thought even had time to form. "That's exactly the kind of thing that makes me know you're different from the rest." She grinned with a sideways glance. "Any man who's loose in the head enough to take the mark of Davy Jones just so he has a slim chance of waitin' out eternity to meet his woman...that's a Cap'n worth sailin' with."

I shrugged, not sure of what more to say. A small glimmer of hope rose within me, reassuring me that perhaps I hadn't completely damned myself and this plan.

"Is it, though? Knowing I'd sacrifice anyone and do anything to see her again. Anyone. Be that you or my crew if it came down to it."

Clara tilted her head back. "Everyone has somethin' they'd burn down the world for. Yours just happens to be a bit more decent than most."

"Thank you," I uttered. "And thank you for how you've helped aboard my ship. Your last crew were fools to treat you the way they did. God knows you're better than the lot of mine." I scanned the landscape filled with my snoring men, strewn across the sand lying lifeless as bonfires smoked their last piles of smoldering embers and the waves lapping filled the silence. I thought of Felix, and how he would've been the only one of them to have kept his head this night and not sentenced himself to a brutal hangover the next morning. But he was gone, and I was still down a good first mate.

I looked at Clara, watching her take care of where she stepped as we left the jungle behind and entered the sprawling shore where my ship waited in the distance.

"Don't ogle me like that, Cap'n. It gives me a feeling I don't like. And like I said, my sails don't quite catch the wind that way." She snapped.

"It's not like that," I reassured. "On the contrary...I just...I have a proposition for you." I hesitated, hoping I wasn't about to make a grave mistake. Clara cocked her head, squinting her eyes at me.

"How would you like the position of first mate?" I asked, holding my breath as the words rushed out of my mouth so I wouldn't have time to regret the offer.

Clara's lips twisted into a wickedly mischievous grin. "As much as a dog loves its filth."

"Good," I smirked with a gesture to my ship. "Then let's chart our course and wake up these fools. We've got a fountain to find."

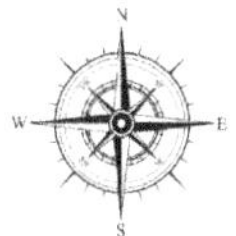

With my crew barely awake and my mast repaired, we hoisted anchor in the faint light of twilight. Clara took her place on the forecastle deck, yelling orders down below as some of the crew grumbled under their new authority. As I looked back at the island that had rested us well, I caught a glimpse of the elder woman and her people watching approvingly from the tree line. And as the distance between my ship and the shore grew, the island suddenly vanished from sight, replaced by nothing but the same ocean horizon surrounding us on every other side.

24

Release the Kraken

Katrina

I really hoped Bellamy was joking about Kraken's eating mermaids. If anything, I prayed that maybe the opposite was true. Maybe we weren't natural enemies like humans were. Maybe I could reason with it somehow in my siren form.

"You just made that up!" I shot Bellamy a playful look of scorn, hitting his arm where the heart and arrow tattoo just peeked out through his sleeve. I'd caught him looking at it more than once, lost in thought—or memory, of adding each arrow as he lost those he loved. I wouldn't be his third arrow, I promised myself. And I'd make sure I ended Bastian's link to him by completing this mission.

"Aye, don't worry. I'm just pulling your ropes. But either way I'm sure the beastie will be more than surprised to see us. I almost feel for it. Once a leviathan of the seas, now hiding in the dark depths lost to time, now being asked to surface again and face a whole new world that no longer has room for it. I can relate."

"Oh stop," I uttered. "You're making *me* feel sorry for it."

"Don't worry," Bellamy stood, stretching an arm behind his head. "I'm sure it won't take long for it to change your mind."

I sighed, glancing at the clock on the wall that reminded me yet again how time-sensitive this assignment was. I didn't know how long it would take to kill a Kraken. "The sooner the better," I removed my outerwear and marched up to the deck.

"Don't look," I said, stepping out of my shoes and pants. The Mediterranean winter winds grazed my face with a chilly whisper of encouragement or doom, I couldn't tell which. I took a deep breath, mesmerized by the clear blue surface of the water that I could see straight through down to where they gave way to the blackest depths below. I almost felt my old fears coming back to haunt me, but this time it wasn't a fear of the water...just what was lurking beneath it.

I turned back to see Bellamy, harpoon in hand and hunting rifle strapped to his back. Thankfully the yacht's armory was stocked with at least that. I stepped up onto the edge of the hull and climbed over, holding onto the rim while I leaned over the water's surface. I was about to dive in, bracing myself for the brief sting in my lungs right before I transformed. But a hand steadied my shoulder. I glanced back at Bellamy, whose forehead was creased with a worry I knew he'd rather not show. "Be careful down there, lass. Don't get too close to that thing."

I gave a firm nod, and then let go, dropping forward and leaning headfirst into the water. Its icy pierce swallowed me whole, and I fought my way through the chill of my body, forcing myself to ignore it until my other side gained control. Once in that form, I no longer felt the glacial temperature of the water on my skin. Everything was as it should be. Me, immersed, one with the water and sinking deeper, deeper...

I forced myself to stay focused and keep the siren voice at bay. Though I wondered if I might need some of her brash fierceness to face this creature of the deep. If I ever found it, that is. I searched, looking for any sign of the sea monster's presence. But as I dove the depths, sea life became more and more scarce.

It was only when I spotted a large school of fish swimming frantically upwards that I guessed they might be a clue to my next direction. With a powerful flick of my tail, I surged forward through the water to where the fish had just passed, and then I turned downward to make my descent to the depths.

As I swam, heavy groans echoed from the ocean floor, creating rippling vibrations strong enough to rattle my bones. Any human would have long succumbed to the pressure. I had to be miles down by now, but there was still no sign of the Kraken. I suddenly feared if I went deep enough to find it, I wouldn't stand a chance against it in its own territory. I had to bring it to the surface.

I wished I had my siren song, because it seemed it might've been the perfect tool for summoning a sea beast. But at least I still had my other power. I wondered if I could create some sort of commotion, maybe I could get its attention. I'd never quite controlled the water from underneath like this. I wasn't sure if it was even possible. But to me it made sense. If my tears connected my power to the ocean's, how much more would it work when I was already submerged in it?

I blinked back the ache behind my eyes. My siren didn't like to cry, of course, but Katrina had mastered the art of feeling her broken heart enough to draw out some sorrows. And if I couldn't find sadness, there always seemed to be some burning anger readily available in this form. I bit down on my lip until it bled, a tiny drop of red blossoming into the dark water around me, only visible to my inhuman eyes this deep. The bit of pain made me wince, and even underwater I could feel the sting in my eyes drawing out a tear from reaction.

Suddenly I felt the water swirl at my fingertips, like energy flowing from me and to me both at the same time. I spun the water around me, creating light currents the same way I might glide a paintbrush along a canvas. Careful, but freeing movements, up, then down. I drew the water around me like a cloak, sending it whirring around in streams of bubbles, and then channeling it all back down.

Another groan reverberated up through the water. It had to be close. It had to be seeing and feeling all this. I twisted more water around me, bending it in ribbons that flowed like paint trails down paper. I dove just a bit lower, sending a few more powerful currents down to the bottom, where I waited, staring into the black abyss that became even too dark for me to see into.

I waited, letting the water around me settle a moment. The silence down here was almost tangible, and once the last few bubbles popped and faded, there was nothing left to fill it. Suspended in the water by my tail, I watched the depths below, my heart now pounding in my ears. The siren in me told me—begged me to swim up, to escape and preserve myself. But none of this was about myself.

When a massive tentacle shot upwards from the darkness, I found myself right in its path. I whipped my tail sideways and darted out of the way, but the tentacle seemed adamant that I was its target. It retreated for a moment, only briefly, before a low quaking sent me swimming back up. I had awoken the Kraken.

The ascent was a blur, as my determination to reach the surface blocked out the memory of the tentacles shooting up around me like weeds. I broke through the water, a desperate gasp on my lips to warn Bellamy of the creature right on my tail.

"It's behind me! Get ready!" I called.

Bellamy rushed to the edge of the boat, leaning as far over as he could, waiting to see the monster we were about to face. For a moment it was quiet, and only a lone bubble surfaced. I dove back down for a quick look, but all signs of the Kraken had disappeared. As I resurfaced, before I could say a word to Bellamy, something broke forth out of the water on the other side of the boat. With a crash that sent the yacht reeling, the great sea beast showed itself in all its glory.

The tips of its tentacles that had attacked me were nothing compared to the entire thing. Each one must've been at least one hundred feet long, the width of massive columns that could easily snap a boat in half. The purplish gray hue of its body shone glossy white in the light as it emerged partly from the water, revealing its brutish form. An octopus-like creature of colossal proportions, it dwarfed our yacht, making it look as fragile as a toy sailboat in a child's bathtub.

The creature raised up from the water. With a deafening roar, it revealed rings of razor teeth waiting to suck down its next victim with ease. I gasped, a sense of fear washing over me at the thought of being trapped in the water with this thing. But I doubted legs would do me any more good than fins. I glanced at Bellamy, who was at the mercy of the beast sizing up our boat. Suddenly tentacles flew up around the sides of the boat, climbing up like vines and taking hold of the hull.

"She'll snap this thing in two and pull it under!" Bellamy called, pulling out the rifle on his sling and firing. The Kraken growled in anguish or surprise at the hot bullet lodging itself in her tentacle. I wondered how Bellamy had any way of possibly knowing it was a "she," but I went along with it. She recoiled, her tentacles sliding down the boat's edges in a momentary retreat. Bellamy aimed at the water below, using the scope to help him hone in on his target. He fired once more, this time into the animal's head. But a bullet from a rifle was probably no more than an ant bite to this creature. She merely reared back as if to attack, unfazed by the pebble-sized chunk taken from her flesh.

"I think you're just making her mad!" I yelled to Bellamy. As if on cue, the Kraken pulled her grip from the boat. She turned her attention to me, lifting a colossal tentacle and sending it crashing back down like a falling building. I dodged it by ducking under the water and using my tail as a rudder to help me dart off to the side. I gathered my courage and swam underneath the monster, looking desperately for any sort of weak spot or injury I could use to my advantage.

Dammit. Nothing.

I summoned some water and balled it up into an orb of energy, sending it hurtling toward the belly of the beast. It was enough to make her take pause and lurch up as the force made impact with her body. But she no more than rocked back into position with ease and continued her attack on the yacht. The boat's shadow moved off, and a trail of bubbles churned out quickly from the propeller. Bellamy circled the yacht around her, and I watched from beneath, still trying to think of how I could weaken her with her own element.

I swam back up to the surface, desperate. Bellamy reeled the boat around the backside of the Kraken. Her size certainly made her slow, which seemed to be the only advantage we had. He left the helm and rushed to the side of the boat, shooting the thing with a flare gun and then a few rounds of the rifle. The flare seemed to stun her, and it allowed for him to get a few shots in, but the bullets nearly bounced off her skin. Nothing was working.

"Still feel sorry for it?" Bellamy shouted over the roar of water splashing and the sea beast groaning. I rolled my eyes, then dove back under to look once more for weak spots.

As I swam, I began to question everything. Could we really kill this thing? No wonder Bellamy was so mad at me when I accepted Bastian's deal to do this. What if he was right? What if this really was a suicide mission. If I couldn't bring Milo back, that was one thing, but I should never have asked this of Bellamy.

Crackling reverberated through the dense water as the monster reached for the boat once more. Her tentacles squeezed it like an eggshell. It would either break in half or be pulled down in seconds. I motioned for the water and created a swell big enough to push her off the boat, but I couldn't hold it for long.

Letting go of the wave, I burst back up to the surface, my eyes meeting a panicked Bellamy's. "The harpoon!" I shouted. I knew Bellamy was saving that for a one-and-only shot, but I was beginning to think it might be time to take the chance. With the Kraken right up on the boat, he would at least have an easy shot.

He rushed to the creature, fighting the swaying of the boat as the tentacles secured their grip around it once more like a spider going for the kill. With a grunt, he stabbed the side of the monstrous thing, right by its massive beady eye. It shrieked in pain, a shrill sound deafening to the ears.

"We need more harpoons! It would probably take hundreds of them!" Bellamy screamed over the animal's agonizing roar.

My thoughts raced. Even with more harpoons, her underside was armored by the thickest hide I'd ever seen, probably impossible to pierce with anything that wasn't...magic. Then an idea struck me. I recalled the icy bite of this water when I was human. The sharp stab of cold water was worse than any blade. Ice.

I had no idea if my power could manage such a feat, but now was as good as any time to find out. I painted scenes of frozen water in my mind, dreaming of how I'd shape the crisp, sharp form of ice in hues of white and blue. I felt the water around me, forming crystals at my fingertips and drawing the water to me in a way I'd never before. It hardened, forming a staff of ice shards with a tip sharper than a sword—ice harpoons. I formed a dozen or so of them, and with every ounce of concentration in me, I harnessed the small army of ice spikes surrounding me in the water, turning them on the Kraken and sending them forward with all the speed and force possible. They shot forward, their icy tips driving into various spots on the beast. She wailed in pain and dipped down into the water to face me. Her blood stained the water around her, creating an eerie sight of cool blue and swirling scarlet. She lunged at me, showing that terrifying ring of teeth and sending her tentacles at me. Instinctively, I put up my hand, inadvertently forming an ice shield between us. Her tentacle hit the clear ice wall, cracking it before it dissolved into the rest of the water.

Ice was the answer. At least for now. I could slow her down enough with it while Bellamy used the ice harpoons. We could do this. I swam back up to the surface, an artillery of ice spikes forming alongside me as I emerged.

"Use these!" I cried, sending a wave up and over the yacht's edge to carry the harpoons to Bellamy. He grabbed one, not even pausing to question it, and launched it toward the roaring beast before us. It released another roar and lunged forward, going for the boat, but I caught the water just in time and blocked her with an icy wave. I wasn't strong enough to freeze large amounts of water at once, so my ice walls were thin, and shattered like glass when the

Kraken so much as touched them. But it was a decent distraction while Bellamy bloodied the creature with his skillful precision.

I couldn't believe we'd gotten this far. Weakening the Kraken was one thing. But taking her down would still prove to be another. I frantically swam to the boat's edge creating more ice harpoons from the water around me and sending them shooting upwards at the Kraken all at once. Some of them pierced her skin and stayed there until they melted from the heat of her blood. A small few of the rest shattered on impact with her body.

She ducked below the surface in an effort to escape the ice spike barrage. I dove under, watching her speed toward the boat from underneath. Thinking on my feet—or rather my fins—I shot a hand forward to move the yacht forward with a current from underneath, fast enough to push it right out of her path as she burst forth above the water, angered by missing her target. She plunged back down, and this time her attention wasn't on the boat. Her black eyes darted back and forth, and her tentacles swirled around her chaotically. She was looking for me.

I did my best to swim amongst the shadows, but the clear water made it difficult to hide. When she saw me, she swatted at me with those massive trunk-like tentacles. She could move much more quickly down here, and the force of her limb swooping past me caught me in an undertow even I could hardly manage to swim out of. I tumbled and swirled in the water, fighting to regain my equilibrium. She overshadowed me, trapping me beneath her as her razor teeth closed in. I swam for my life, and she snatched me with a tentacle, wrapping me in her grip like a python. She carried me along as she refocused on the boat above. I could hear Bellamy screaming my name from above, no doubt wondering what kind of underwater battle was ensuing.

As I squirmed in her grasp, she squeezed my waist and hips so hard I thought I might faint. My tail was immobilized, but one hand was free. As she charged back up to attack the boat, I gave one last ditch effort to call on the water, begging it to crystallize fast and create a barrier between the Kraken and the yacht. But in her unstoppable rage, the beast crashed up through a thin sheet of ice I'd just barely started to form, slamming the whole of her body into the yacht. It nearly tipped, and Bellamy was soaked as he held on for dear life. Reaching for the rifle, he fired more shots, but the unfazed Kraken moved into the bullets like they were no more than snowflakes.

She slid a tentacle into the water, wrapping it around the underside of the boat.

"Bellamy! Look out!" I shouted in warning. Her grip tightened on me and subsequently the yacht. Creaking split the air for a few seconds, and just as Bellamy leapt overboard, the hull snapped in half from the pressure of the Kraken's squeeze. She submerged herself again, taking me with her as she sought out Bellamy drifting in the water. He was fighting the suction of the sinking boat pieces, nearing the surface when she grabbed him with another tentacle. My eyes widened in horror as she dragged him along, heading downward into the depths with both of us in her clutches.

25

Drowning

Bellamy

Diving into that chilled water felt like a kick in the gut, but I hardly had time to register it as the slime of that monster slid across my body. It dragged me down, suction cups holding me in place as I fought to preserve the last breath I took before leaping off the boat. Under here, I couldn't see Katrina's face, but I knew despite my blurry vision she could see me perfectly. I could feel her watching me, and I knew she was hating herself right then.

Some part of me did wish I could have one more moment on the surface with her just for the satisfaction of being right. I wasn't above being the type to say "I told you so, lass." But I knew she didn't need me to say it. And for that, I was sorry.

I didn't blame her for any of it. Hell, I'd almost killed her before because I wanted to bring back Serena so badly. I wasn't one to talk. But when you're drowning in the clutches of a Kraken, maybe it wasn't abnormal to feel some resentment. But even then, I knew what I was risking by trying to bring back Milo—my brother at sea. And some time back I had already decided that if he would be lost at sea, it was only fair that I should be, too. So, this was fine. I'd die...again. At least this time it was sort of worth something.

26

A Mermaid's Kiss

Katrina

I should've listened to Bellamy. Killing the Kraken truly *was* an impossible task. I could only imagine what he might've been thinking if he wasn't struggling to breathe right now. I couldn't blame him for hating me. I didn't care if trying to save Milo meant being eaten by the Kraken. But Bellamy shouldn't have been facing the same fate. I couldn't bear to live with myself as I watched him drown. I wished there was some way—any way—I could at least save him.

I watched him struggle against the tentacles binding him, knowing he wouldn't last much longer submerged as we were pulled to the depths. Down, down, darker and colder. It was too deep for a human. The pressure and the cold would be too much, if he hadn't drowned already. I couldn't bear it, and I cried underwater. I cried so much that I fought the Kraken with all the strength in my tears. I found the might to push back against her, trying to sweep us back up to the surface with the water I controlled. But even I couldn't hold back a Kraken. And finally, I saw the light dim from Bellamy's bright blue eyes as his head rolled back in the water. Like a rag doll, the monstrous creature carried him, and I wondered what fate awaited us when she finally reached the bottom.

The Kraken sank to a sandy floor with a thud, where a dark cove awaited in the shadows. She'd take us there and chew us up with that garbage disposal of a mouth I was sure. Along the ocean floor she slunk, sliding along by her tentacles, which grew tighter and tighter around us. I'd given up my voice for this.

I'm sorry, Milo. Maybe I'll find you again in death.

As I braced myself to become a meal, I was startled at the impossible sound of a voice, clear as a bell, ringing out from the dark cave.

"Cala, finish them off! Show them what happens to those mortals who defy their place on land. Show them what happens to those who try to hurt us."

I blinked, trying to recognize whose voice I was hearing. It reached my ears like cool velvet, a strange power and beauty in it, almost like a siren's, but less soft and seductive...it was stronger to the ear and drenched with authority. It had come from the ominous shadows of the cave.

The Kraken groaned softly, drawing a limp Bellamy and me closer and opening its terrifying jaws wide. At least Bellamy would be unconscious for this part. I recoiled at the sight of the teeth so close to shredding me open as it pulled me near to its mouth. I wriggled my tail with the last of my strength, to no avail.

Just as I closed my eyes, preparing myself for the pain of those knife-like teeth to tear into my skin, the voice called out again, this time with an urgency I might've even mistaken for panic.

"Wait!"

The Kraken froze, still carefully restraining us in its clutches.

The great beast lowered Bellamy down, still holding me tight as I watched onward. His body drifted to the sand below and I couldn't help but notice the peace in his face. I almost envied him. I still searched for the voice. Then I saw her. Somehow in this darkness beneath the sea, I could see her clearly, as if some light radiated from her and illuminated this bit of sea floor. My gaze followed the flow of a current swirling towards a womanly figure, wrapping her in a dress made from the very water around her. Like a veil, the current obscured her face as she walked with slow steps on the sand. She was no siren or mermaid. She moved as though she was one with the water, but her body looked fully human. I couldn't die like this, without my curiosity quenched. I had to know who she was and how she walked down here, commanding deadly giant squids with just her words.

The ocean woman neared Bellamy, and I couldn't keep from calling out to her. "Please don't hurt him! Can you send him back to the surface? Kill me, but give him a chance to live! It was my idea to come here, not his!"

She ignored me, seeming completely fixated on Bellamy's lifeless body. I wished I could see her face, but the water kept a blurry shield whirling around her. I could make out her movements with ease, though. She knelt down to him; touched his hair with her fingers. She felt his face and neck and chest, as if she'd never seen another human before. And then, she leaned over, putting her face to his as the glassy wall of water surrounded them both. I couldn't tell for sure, but it looked like she kissed him on the lips.

As she pulled her mouth away from his, I watched in confusion as the water veil faded away, leaving me with a clear view of her now, even in these dark depths. She looked my direction and I gasped at the vision of her beauty and power. But beyond that, the shock of recognizing her left me paralyzed. In an instant, my mind flashed back to the old newspaper clippings Russell showed me and photos from Mrs. Gutierrez' album. It was impossible, yet undeniable. Here down at the bottom of the ocean, I was staring right at Serena. And she was staring back.

"S...Serena?" I uttered, the name stuck on my lips.

Her dark eyes narrowed at me, piercing through the water between us like one of my ice spears. She ignored my question, and turned her attention back to Bellamy, who was somehow beginning to stir. The Kraken still held me tight, but it was no longer crushing me with its grip.

I watched Bellamy as he shook his head slowly, squinting here and there as though slowly rousing from a nightmare. He brought his hands to his head. Then he opened his eyes and sat up, seemingly unaffected by the fact that he was underwater. He glanced around, startled at the sight of the beast towering over him and eyes wide when he looked forward at Serena.

"How is he alive down here? How are *you* alive down here? And how did you do that?" I asked. I didn't expect an answer from Serena, and she didn't give one.

But Bellamy, still steadying himself as he propped himself up by his hands in the sand, took a deep, satisfying breath that reassured me he was miraculously fine. "A mermaid's kiss..." he said, his eyes fixed on Serena. "...is said to grant the ability to breathe underwater."

He spoke while transfixed on Serena, and she nodded to her Kraken a command to release me. I watched from my distance, unsure if I moved how the animal would react. So, I stayed in place, watching a scene so tense and quiet. Serena leveled herself with Bellamy, reaching forward to touch his chin as she held his gaze with hers. She spoke to him, not me. "A mermaid's kiss indeed. And if it can do that, what do you think a kiss from a sea goddess can do?"

27

THE SEA QUEEN

BELLAMY

As my vision settled and Serena's face came into focus, I thought I had finally died and found my way to her. But it didn't take long before I noticed the entrapment of the water around me and the slimy squid beast at my back. I was still very much alive. Somehow, here on the ocean floor, and somehow I was staring at a woman I'd watched drown with her heart cut out nearly half a century ago.

But none of those unanswered questions mattered. Nothing mattered. Not the water, not the Kraken, and not the sea salt stinging my open wounds from my battle with it. I didn't care if I'd been damned to Davy Jones Locker, if it meant Serena was here.

But I couldn't let myself believe it. This couldn't really be her. I refused to trust that this vision before me, walking underwater as naturally as on land and shrouded in an ethereal glow, was really Serena. I'd hallucinated her before. On my father's ship, in the brig, I'd even sworn Katrina was her, only to be snapped out of my delusion and faced with heartbreak every time.

But this time, she didn't fade away. Her deep skin shone with an almost iridescent sheen down here, like the purest pearl, as dark braids of black and even blue drifted around her amongst loose strands and pieces woven into gold. Her dress was like white sea foam forming an ever-flowing wrap around her, trailing off at her feet as it flowed into the water around her. Her voice held its same unmistakable lure as it did the night she stepped onto the shore in front of me. It was her. But it couldn't be real.

"Serena," I uttered, my hands shaking and lips trembling with disbelief. She looked at me for a moment that felt like it stretched into hours. Her eyes flickered from my face to my body and back up again.

"That is the name by which you know me. Yes, it's me." she smiled. "Good to see you again, my love."

Ignoring the questions bombarding my mind, I pushed them aside, not caring that I was underwater, not concerned that I should technically be drowning, and barely even aware that Katrina was off to the side watching this insanity unfold.

I lunged forward and plunged my lips into hers, drowning in her as if to prove to myself one more time she was real. She guided my hands to grasp her, sliding her own down my sides as she deepened our embrace. When she pulled away, I stood dumbfounded, still trying to make sense of it all.

She smiled that wickedly seductive smile of hers and brushed her fingers along my pierced ear. "Stop trying to figure it out, sweet Bellamy. It took me dozens of lives to finally understand."

Suddenly I felt weak. *My* father had killed her and somehow damned her to this pit. I led her right to him by loving her. I didn't stay away. It was my fault. And now I had to face her. I had to remind her that I killed her.

"I'm sorry." I choked, still half-convinced I was speaking to her in the afterlife. "I should've protected you better...I should've..."

She placed a finger to my lips and shushed me gently, as if reading my mind. "You did not send me here. You could not have protected me. It was meant to be this way. It was always meant to be this way."

"Wha—what do you mean? No, you weren't meant to die. You had a whole life ahead of you."

She took my hand and gently guided me to her, the water passing between us like swirling magic. "I've had more lives than I can count. If your father didn't kill me, I'd still be trapped."

"Trapped? Trapped in what? Serena, please tell me what's going on." I begged, gripping her gently with my fingers in her hair, afraid to let go of her in case she vanished before my face.

Serena closed her eyes and looked down, her hair drifting in thick, heavy tendrils all around her. "You don't remember," she whispered. "Because you're not meant to. But you and I have been bound since the beginning of time. Since I fell in love with you at the start of the earth. When I was called by another name—Atargatis."

The blood drained from my face, leaving me with an icy stabbing in my chest. I thought back to Bastian when he told us about the sea crown and Atargatis.

The first sea queen. The ancient mother of sirens. A divinely beautiful woman who fell in love with a mortal man.

"You fell in love with a man and killed him? That's how you became this?"

"I fell in love with *you*. It was you then, and still now. It's been you all along. You have always been drawn to the sea as your first love. Because I am the sea, and you've been seeking me your whole life without realizing it. I've lived many lives, because my power—my crown—was taken from me. To lose their power is a god's greatest curse. It traps us in a form opposite our nature. But we still cannot truly die at the hands of mankind, so we just keep returning as someone new. I've been a human for so many reincarnations, unable to return to the sea, forced to live and die on land. But when your father cut out my heart and cast it into the sea, he returned me to my true place — the water. But I'm bound here without my power, guarded by—well—her." She pointed to the Kraken, who purred out a low, threatening growl.

I dug deep for words, but they failed to come right away. How long had my heart yearned for her without even knowing it? Before I met her in 1989, did I know her before? What did it matter? I had her here in front of me now and that was enough. "What is she protecting you from? You don't have to hide anymore. Come with me and we can be together."

"I want to do that more than anything," Serena looked down. "But without my power, I cannot risk it. The one who took my crown still seeks to kill me once and for all. And without my power, I cannot stop him. Once an ordinary man, but now he draws power from the dark lord of the seas, so he has the ability to kill a goddess. He's been long jealous of you, my lover, because I refused him and chose you—so he killed you.

"I thought the legend says that Atargatis accidentally killed her lover herself. So...if you're her...and I'm your lover...then it wasn't you who killed me. It was him?"

"Yes, he killed you." Serena bowed her head. "And when I tried to follow you in death, Poseidon was moved to turn me into a sea goddess so that my beauty would never die. Bastian lied to deceive you, as he always does. I didn't kill you, my love. *He* did."

"How did Bastian...?" I rubbed my temple. "He wasn't always immortal. He was just a man. That's why he wanted a siren heart. How has he been part of this all this time?"

"Yours, mine, and Bastian's destinies are intertwined. When Poseidon realized what he had done, he sentenced him to an eternity of lifetime after lifetime, rebirth after rebirth, until his wrong could be made right. But Bastian has been dark-hearted in every lifetime, and it was during one lifetime soon after he finally found a way to end his own cycle of death and rebirth—he bound himself to Davy Jones for shadow power and immortality—a way to cheat himself out of the curse. But soon enough he realized that with Jones' power came a duty to the souls of those lost at sea. So he sought another source of eternal life—a way to keep his dark power, but no longer be indebted to Jones. Potions, spells, the Fountain of Youth, siren hearts—he's tried them all to no avail. And since I have still refused to love him all this time...and since he knows I want my revenge...he wants me dead."

It all made sense. That's why Bastian wanted the Kraken gone so badly. He knew it was guarding her. And with it out of the way, he could finally kill her.

Well done. A snake-like voice in my mind hissed. *What a mystery-solver you are.*

I feared Bastian would know I was here with her. He would know we didn't kill the Kraken. He would come for all of us...and he would come fast.

I glanced over at Katrina, suddenly remembering she was here, too. She watched us both, her eyes wide, glancing between the two of us. The Kraken groaned behind her in the shadows, waiting to restrain us again at a moment's notice.

"Bellamy, are you okay?" Katrina asked. "What's happening?"

I hesitated, trying to find a response that could encapsulate everything that I'd just learned. But there was no time. I couldn't reiterate it all here.

"Who is your friend?" Serena asked, her eyes shifting. "I thought all sirens were dead."

"My mom and I are the only ones left," Katrina said boldly, her tail straightening as she puffed out her chest and shoulders.

"Then I'm sorry that you are no longer blessed with my protection," Serena said softly, but without emotion. "I created sirens and when I have full reign of my power, none can harm you."

"But you've lost your power, right?" Katrina asked, swimming toward us. "I heard you tell Bellamy you're the goddess we've been looking for. We need your help."

"I'll help you if I can, but without my power, I'm limited. And if I leave this cove and the protection of the Kraken, Bastian will hunt me."

"We'll protect you," Katrina said. "We won't let him hurt you, right Bellamy?" The way she glanced at me almost made me sick. I couldn't promise Serena protection like that. I couldn't even protect her from my father, much less a man channeling Davy Jones' power. But I did want to restore her.

"You sound just as confident as you did about killing the Kraken," I uttered, "And we see how that turned out."

Katrina glared at me with a look I'd forgotten she was capable of. "Then we go back and get that crown and bring it here."

"We'll never get that crown if we didn't fulfill our end of the bargain. We'll have to find another way." I shifted, only just then noticing how I somehow didn't produce bubbles when I spoke. I still was still partially sure this was a dream of some kind.

Serena stepped forward, the sand swirling like flowing glitter at her feet with each step. She moved gracefully to Katrina, touching her on the arm. "Dear young siren," she said. "What is it that you so desperately came seeking help for?"

"It's a long story, but someone I love was sent back in time by the Trident's power, and you're the only thing strong enough to bring him back. Can you even do that? Can you alter time?"

Serena's eyes softened, and she tilted her head as if trying to find a way to relay bad news in the gentlest way possible. "I can't do that, even in my full form, I don't hold power over time."

Katrina's face twisted and her forehead creased. She blinked several times with a look of bewilderment before speaking again. "Wh—what? No...Then why...why would Milo tell us to find you?" She looked past Serena's shoulder, meeting her eyes with mine with disappointment. "Why would he tell us...?"

I hesitated, just as lost for an answer as she was. But regardless of what she could or couldn't do for Milo, there was no way in hell I was going to leave Serena down here. Even though it seemed impossible, I had to find a way to get that crown back for her.

"It doesn't matter," I stepped up to Serena, taking her hand with a bit of trepidation. I'd be lying to say it wasn't a bit nerve-racking to take a goddess' hand in mine. "I'm going to save you this time. Whatever it takes."

"You'd have to kill Bastian to get that crown back. And you can't kill him."

"Already found that out the hard way," I grunted.

"He's probably grown so powerful by now," Serena's eyes flicked sideways with worry.

I glanced at Katrina, who still seemed too distressed to speak, suspended in the water by slow flicks of her tail. I couldn't imagine the disappointment she must be feeling. Her only hope just told her there was no hope. I wanted to feel as bad about it as she did, but my heart was torn in so many directions. It was crushing to think that there might not be a way to bring Milo back after all. I would always carry the weight of failing him and letting Katrina down. But at the same time, I'd been reunited with Serena, and for that, I didn't believe there was a price too high. So as I watched Katrina staring into the void with absolute emptiness in her eyes, I ached for her.

"Serena." She finally spoke, her voice hollow and stiff. "You're sure there's nothing I can do? Please...there has to be something."

Serena paused for a minute that felt like hours, twisting a strand of her braids with her finger as if thinking over Katrina's question. "I'm sorry, but there's no power I have that can do what you ask."

"Then come with us," I said. "Come with us and we'll keep looking for a way. And we can finally be together."

"It's not that I don't want to," she said, "but...it's not safe for either of us." She looked at me, her hand still in mine.

"What do you mean? No, I swear to you I'll free you, Serena. And if I can't, I'll join you down here forever."

"Bellamy, no." She shook her head, but I took her face in my hands with sudden boldness. "No, no! I don't want you to get hurt. Please don't."

"Yes. Either way we'll be together," I breathed, pressing my forehead to hers.

She started to argue, but then stopped herself with a deep breath and shrug of her shoulders. "I would never let you stay in this bottomless pit, Bellamy. I've been safe here for years. And I'll stay safe with Cala. Go on and live your life. I can't let you do this."

"My life is with you. And if you won't let me stay, then you have to come with us," I kissed her gently on the lips. "Because we're not leaving you here either."

Serena's eyes shone with tears as she shook her head over and over. "No...no. This is not right. How is it that you come down here with the boldness to command a goddess?"

"Because I think we've earned the privilege after your pet tried to kill us." I winked as the Kraken hissed behind me.

"Bellamy, please. Do not go after that crown. Don't let Bastian have the chance to hurt you again. Let knowing that I am alive be enough."

I tensed up at her words. How could she ask this of me? We couldn't help Katrina, and now she wouldn't let me help her? "No, it's not enough. I'm going back whether you want me to or not. If you think I'm not going to free you from this pit then you're out of your mind. I failed you once and I'm not doing it again."

"I wish I could stop you," she pleaded with a break in her voice. "But I know how stubborn you are. So I'll go with you. Because I can't stay here knowing you're going to go face Bastian alone."

I should've been glad to hear it. I should've been relieved. But the heartbreak on her face made me feel otherwise. We both wanted to protect each other. But she didn't seem to realize this was our chance to finally be together. Maybe this was how we were supposed to right Bastian's wrong. And we couldn't do that while she was damned to hide in this cave in the ocean.

Serena sighed, seemingly lost in thought for a moment before suddenly addressing Katrina, who perked up at her words. "And as for you, little siren, I think I may just have had an idea for how to help your loved one."

Before either of us could respond, she gave a tilt of her chin, and we were swept upward in a swift current that swirled around us like a gentle cyclone that carried us back to where the sky meets the sea. And I still wasn't sure any of it was real.

28

Meet Me in Eternity

Katrina

"Our boat is destroyed," I noted as we surfaced to see a deserted ocean all around us. I was trying hard to hide the worry in my mind as I selfishly ruminated on how the hell we could get to Milo in time. The sweet relief of Bellamy not drowning was still fresh and reassuring, but though I was happy to see him reunited with Serena, I was still eaten up with the lack of progress we'd made in getting Milo back before time ran out. And now we had no way to travel. But I tried to calm myself with a deep breath and a reminder to keep my head. Maybe there was hope yet.

"Whatever your idea is, please tell me you have a way of getting us out of here," I said, a slight bitterness in my voice that I fought hard to hide. "What is your plan anyway?"

"Little siren...Katrina, was it?" When she said my name, I felt a sudden timidness, as though I shouldn't have dared speak to her with such casualness. I almost felt anger toward her for a moment, wondering why, if she really was the one who created sirens, why did she withhold a soul from us? Why did she make our very existence a contrasting battle between self and siren? But then I remembered not all sirens were half human. Regardless, I couldn't waste time dwelling on it right now. I had to hear her plan as we bobbed in the water at the mercy of the sea.

"I may not have all my power," she spoke, "but I'm not rendered completely useless. Water is a medium, and it can be used to channel power, as you know from your tears." She nodded in my direction approvingly. "I can still do small things. I can at least let you see the one you love. Tell me his name, and if you have anything belonging to him, that will make it all the easier to find him."

"Milo. His name is Milo Harrington." I frantically thought of what I could give her, and suddenly remembered the ring Milo had given me, still secure on my finger. I quickly slid it off, not easily, and handed it to her. "Can you use this?" I asked. Serena nodded.

She closed her eyes, focusing with the ring tucked away in her closed fist above the water, and the droplets that trickled from her hand formed ripples in the sea that localized around us. I could see the faintest outline of a man, with Milo's physique. It was fuzzy, like looking through a stained-glass window, but I could see his blurry form amongst others, on what looked to be a ship. He spoke to someone with deep red hair beside him, but their voices were muffled as though underwater.

"What do you see?" The questions leapt from my lips. "Where is he? Is that him right now? How much time has passed?"

Serena didn't answer me for a minute as she seemed to concentrate with her eyes shut tightly. Finally, she opened her hand, the water droplets stopped, and the ripples disappeared as they faded away into faint rings melding into the waves.

"He's on his way to the Fountain of Youth. And he's very close."

"He wants to keep himself alive long enough to find you again," Bellamy shuddered as the cold water lapped up against him. "What a clever bastard."

"No," Serena snapped. "Not clever at all. The Fountain of Youth is a place meant only for the souls of the dead. It's where those souls collected at sea by Davy Jones are meant to be sent. It is not a source of eternal life as believed, but rather a passageway to eternity. And there is no clear way out. Those who have sought its power have all become lost in between here and there, trapped in a nothingness that will never end. I fear that will be his fate."

My hair stood on end, and my heart dropped in my chest. "How close is he?" I turned to Serena, nearly grabbing her shoulders in desperation but thinking better of it. "We have to stop him."

"We can't get my crown back in time to stop him," she said calmly.

"Then—then let's get the Trident back. You can get it back, can't you?" I no longer cared what I was saying, or if it made sense. My mind was racing in a desperate panic in search of solutions.

"That power is gone now, destroyed and hidden where it belongs, thanks to you." Serena said.

"I only buried it. Maybe it could still be used." I looked down, still tempted by the call of the siren to go find that buried, broken trident and unearth it from underneath the sea floor. But I knew it would no longer be Katrina who wielded its power if I did that, and my siren would have much different plans for its use than I.

"Yes, and it was the wisest thing you could've done," Serena said. "A siren was never meant to harness power like that. Even I wouldn't dare touch Poseidon's Trident. It would destroy us all in the end."

"Then what the hell do we do?" I nearly screamed the question, feeling time slipping away like the water whisking through my fingers and along the flares of my fluke. "If you can't alter time, and you can't use the Trident, and you can't bring him back, what *can* you do?"

"I can help you meet him there."

"What do you mean?" I begged, glancing at Bellamy as if there was something he could add to this.

"I mean I can take you to the Fountain, and you can find him in eternity, and hopefully, we can lead him out."

Bellamy's confused expression did little to reassure me, but trusting Serena's plan was my only choice. I looked around at the desolate sea surrounding us on all sides, knowing our yacht was at the bottom of it

"Then let's go," I said, feeling the siren in me riling up. "We can't waste any more time. We have to find a ship. Which way is land? If we can find a harbor nearby..."

Bellamy pointed north, and without hesitation, I summoned the water to carry us in that direction. As we rode the current, Serena neared me.

"Not many sirens ever realize their power," she said. "You had to open your heart enough to allow it to be broken to learn to do this. Most are too stubborn to shed their tears."

"I know. But most sirens also don't have a human side." I grumbled. "Why? Why did you create us this way? As selfish, evil creatures incapable of real love."

"To protect you," she said. "Love is what got me killed. In every lifetime. It will kill you if you're not always looking out for yourself."

"Is that why you didn't give us a soul then? So, we can just live out these selfish, long lives without a conscience, just to die in the end and turn to sea foam?"

Serena lifted her chin haughtily in response. "Everything I did was to make you all strong."

I sighed, keeping my gaze ahead. "I'm strongest when I'm willing to break for those I care about. Living with a broken heart is the only reason I can use my power." Serena was quiet. It was strange to look at her, just a girl like me—not even twenty—and to think that she was the reincarnation of an ancient goddess.

Just then, a small wooden sailboat came into view as we approached the coasts of some landmass in the Mediterranean. I didn't bother to ask Bellamy where we were, because it didn't matter. All we needed was a boat, and as luck would have it, a small fishing harbor separated us from the rocky cliffs in the distance.

"Let's take that one," I said, swimming faster than the current toward the vessel in the distance. It looked empty, and being a simple sailboat, we wouldn't need a key to work the engine.

"Katrina, wait." Bellamy called, but I was already on the move. I dove in toward the handful of boats moored around the coastline and darted toward the single sailboat I'd made my target. It looked empty, but if there had been anyone on board, I'd have had no qualms with sending a wave to knock them overboard. It was nothing like our yacht, but it had a small enough cabin for sleeping and a bit of privacy if needed. It would do.

I waited for Bellamy and Serena to near, and then sent a swell to lift us up to the hull. I impatiently waited for myself to dry as Bellamy found a blanket to wrap around me. Bellamy and Serena checked the boat, working quickly to avoid being spotted stealing it in broad daylight. I noticed the way Bellamy's eyes hardly left Serena, as if he was scared she'd be gone if he looked away too long. I couldn't blame him. It's not every day you find out the woman you loved and watched die is a reincarnated goddess and has been fated to you since the beginning of time.

But even with a goddess on our side, I couldn't fathom how we were supposed to get out of here in time and make it to the Fountain before Milo in his timeline. But then I remembered the spyglass that brought us here.

"Bellamy, did you drop the spyglass when the ship sank?"

"Come on now, love." He tilted his head with a condescending smirk, "You should know me better than that. This isn't my first shipwreck."

He pulled the spyglass from his jacket pocket and tossed it to me. I waited till we had caught the wind and drifted out far enough from the harbor. As I held the lens to my eye, I tried looking to see something I didn't even know existed just a few moments ago. I concentrated, thinking only of that damn fountain, and slowly a vision began forming in the tube. A cavern with a glowing pool, water glistening and surreal...an undiscovered secret untouched by time. With my target locked, I twisted the spyglass and out rippled a force across the waves, summoning a rogue wave that would carry us to the Fountain of Youth.

29

A Song to Save You

Katrina

The wave spat us out just next to a mangled nest of islands and cliffs jutting from the water in a part of the sea I didn't quite recognize.

"Well where is it?" Bellamy asked, standing on the deck with Serena.

Serena chuckled and took his hand in hers as she gestured out to the ocean. "Below," she said softly, her voice like smooth velvet.

"Then let's go." I was already taking my shoes off in preparation to dive in. "Every second that passes here is like another day for Milo."

Bellamy secured our anchor, and I scurried to the side of the boat, dropping into the water where I wriggled out of my clothes and awaited my transformation, though I kept them tucked under my arm in case I needed to not be a topless siren at some point. Once my tail appeared, I glanced upward to see

Bellamy and Serena enter the water in a barrage of bubbles. As long as Bellamy stayed with Serena, he could breathe under here just as easily as we could. I followed Serena as she led us to the base of one of the cliffs. Towering up from the sand, there was a small opening that even I would have overlooked blindingly if I hadn't known it was there.

Serena swam in, effortlessly whisking between the tiny entrance in the dark rock. Bellamy gestured for me to go in next, and he trailed behind me. It was a dark canal, almost pitch black, but Serena's subtle aura shone more prevalent down here and helped guide the way.

After a few minutes, we emerged, somehow breaking through the water to a dry cavern. A trickling waterfall and glimmering pool of water filled the farthest corner. I lifted myself out of the water and willed my skin and scales to dry quickly, changing back into my clothing as fast as possible. I glanced at Serena, who stepped out of the water with the grace of stepping out of a silk robe.

"Do you ever have a tail? If...if you wanted, I mean?" I couldn't help but ask. She'd always had legs when we were underwater. But it was only natural that the mother of sirens could become a siren herself if she so pleased. At least, that's what I would expect.

Serena's eyes crinkled with a giggle as she nodded. "Yes, little siren. I can be any form I wish. But my tail is a bit different than yours. It's quite dramatic, so I tend to save it only for special occasions." She winked at me. I wondered what exactly that was supposed to mean, but right now learning about Serena's mermaid anatomy was not my biggest priority. Milo was.

"Okay, how do we use this thing to pull Milo from the past?" Bellamy asked, dipping a finger into the ethereal silver pool. It rippled, but not like liquid. It rolled with the texture more like that of melted metal. "I'm guessing this fountain isn't for drinking?" I looked at the water trickling from the rock, thinking back to the Fountain of Youth tourist attraction back in St. Augustine where people would pay to get a paper cup and sip from some stale old water fountain. This certainly was no attraction. This was the real deal.

"No," Serena said, kneeling and touching the water with her fingertips. "This is the doorway to eternity. And your Milo has already entered, like so many souls before him. He's been trapped there a while."

"A while?" I rushed forward. "How do we guide him out?"

"Use your voice. Your siren song. If he's truly bound to your heart, he'll hear you even across time."

A weight dropped in my chest like a hammer. I fidgeted with the siren scale I wore on my wrist. "My song..." I choked. "I gave it to Bastian in a deal."

Serena's brows creased and her lips tightened. "You what? A siren's song is the most precious thing she possesses. How could you think that was a good idea?"

"I know, I know," I looked down, the scale on my wrist glowing ever so faintly. "That's strange. It only does that when I use my song." I paused as the last word left my lips. Perhaps I'd regained my voice somehow since we didn't fulfill the deal.

I didn't wait to ask. A hopeful hum rose in my throat. I was going to try.

The scale on my bracelet glowed brighter, and my song became stronger. It was clear to me now that, for whatever reason, my song had returned. I didn't know why. I didn't understand how. But I didn't care.

I stood before the portal of water. With a silent prayer pleading this would work, I began to sing, my haunting melody reaching out like an outstretched hand. I sang the second verse of the song that had tethered us together since the beginning. The one that seemed the most fitting.

"Lost out at sea
Do you dream of me?
By the call of the waves
I hear you and seek you
Till again the roaming sea
Brings you back to me."

When nothing happened, I looked at Serena, who urged me to keep going with an encouraging gesture and nod of her head. I sang again, my aria filling the empty cavern. And when that didn't work, I sang again, losing hope but trying to remember Milo would be fighting his way through eternity. I had no idea how long that could take. So I'd sing forever if I had to, because if I stopped too soon I'd lose him to the abyss.

When minutes turned to an hour, I felt myself tiring, and worry shrouded my thoughts. I couldn't lose him. Not after all this. I rushed forward, slid to my knees and leaned into the portal. I heard Serena and Bellamy gasp as they grabbed my arms to hold me back, but they couldn't stop me entirely. I pushed my shoulders through the water portal, singing with every bit of strength left in me. In here, it was a chamber of nothingness. Nothingness made of something like starlight. There was no end and no beginning, and the longer I spent looking at it, the sicker I felt. But I closed my eyes and sang, with Bellamy and Serena holding me back to keep me from falling in entirely.

I sang and sang, for however long—I couldn't tell anymore. Even with a magic song, my lungs felt like they would give out. My vocal cords ached with each note that left my lips. But I kept singing. And then, I finally heard a voice echoing somewhere in the distance faintly. And the voice was desperately calling my name.

30

Leviathan

Milo

We steered ahead, the morning sun at our backs. Another few months at sea had taken their toll on my men and me. They were starting to complain, and they'd caught on that I was seeking something more than what I was telling them.

I'd been up for days, charting the stars at night and calculating a logical path to the Fountain. I wasn't sure what I was looking for, but some hopefulness ensured me I'd know when I found it. But something told me we were close. Perhaps it was the strange siren song I kept hearing in my head since we'd left the island, echoing faintly, like it was guiding me along. I hadn't told anyone about it, not even Clara, but something in me made me believe it was leading me on all these weeks.

"Tell me, Cap'n." Clara stared out at a pod of dolphins racing alongside us as the *Falcon* sliced through the smooth waters with ease. "You ever think anymore about just abandoning this goose chase and making the most of yer time here? I know ya love her, but you've gained so much here. You ever think maybe...maybe it's just fate."

"And despite what it may look like, I've gained nothing here."

Clara shifted her elbow on the side of the ship. "Oh come on. I know ya love her, but you ever think maybe...maybe you bein' here and becomin' this powerful captain...maybe it's just fate."

"I once thought like that. I once believed our destinies were set. Unchangeable. But not anymore. Now I think a man can choose his destiny, even change it, if he's willing."

"Exactly, Harrington." Clara's smirk faded into a look more solemn and serious than I'd ever seen in her eyes. "And that's why I'm asking you...are you sure you've chosen yours?"

I tore my eyes from the water and looked down at my boots. She knew. She could see right through me. I was breaking these past few weeks. I still hated myself, and I feared what Katrina might think if and when I saw her again. And if her siren had grown more powerful, she was sure to have no use for me once that voice in her convinced her of my terribleness. It haunted me like a ghost, and drove me mad at times to imagine finding her again and losing her in a different way. I worried I would hurt her more by coming back into her life than staying out of it. My greatest fear was that I couldn't be her sun.

But then that siren call in my head would sing out again, calling me to her, urging me once more to keep going. Her voice was my compass, and her song was reassuring me...I was almost there. I was supposed to be there.

"All the glory and glitter of the sea isn't worth losing her. I think, though we can choose our own paths, some part of us will always be calling us where we're supposed to be. And I imagine it's awfully hard to ignore."

I paused, running my calloused, fingers along a small chip in the ship's hull. "What about you? You've had long enough here to figure out what you want. Have you?"

Clara pressed her lips together and looked back out at the horizon. "I just want this, Cap'n. A life on a vessel fast enough to carry me far away from my troubles." She drew in a sigh as the wind picked up. "I just wish that was enough for you, too."

I grunted with a nod, and we both watched in silence. Pointing to the horizon northwest, I finally spoke again, changing the subject. "If my charts are correct, the Fountain lies ahead that way."

"I've heard that before, Cap'n," Clara rolled her eyes.

"No, this time, I'm sure of it." I thought of the siren voice in my head, and how it grew louder and louder the farther I sailed this way.

Suddenly, Keegan's voice rang out from above, a dire warning signal of oncoming ships to the south of us. I glanced back, able to make out the blooded sails from here without needing my spyglass. Thane had been tailing me for a while now. I expected him to catch up sooner or later, so it was no surprise. But it was a bit of an inconvenience. "What was that you were saying about getting away from your troubles?" I teased Clara as I swung over the stair railing and went up to take charge of the helm.

The siren song in my head sang softly, calling me onward to a small series of islands just a few leagues ahead—the same network of islands where I believed the Fountain to be. I could trap Thane there and outmaneuver him easily in the *Falcon.* Thane's new ship, *Leviathan*, was a beast, but mine was fast. I'd get that mammoth of a ship lined up just right, in a place he couldn't wriggle it out of, and then blast him to hell with cannon fire and mortar.

"Full sail!" I gripped the wheel and maneuvered us toward the islands. To Thane, it would appear I was running from him. And he'd never turn down an opportunity for a good chase.

For now, I guided the *Falcon* toward the islands, careful to steer clear of the hidden sandbars lining the waterways. If I could catch Thane's big ship on one of them...I smirked at the thought.

We slowed as we neared the island cluster. The sight of Thane's red-flagged ship hurtling toward us was just what I hoped to see. He was taking the bait. And he wouldn't be able to slow that massive galleon of his in time to steady itself through the islands.

Clara threw her weight into managing the crew as they adjusted sails and readied cannons. I reached for the pistol and swords hanging on their holsters, if for nothing more than just the mere feel of them in my hands. I reached up to touch my scarred eye. And then I thought of Katrina, held hostage and terrified at Thane's hand. I replayed the moment he sliced his knife across her delicate face, and the rage I felt then boiled in my blood just as strongly now. Finding the fountain could wait until I'd cut Thane open and watched him bleed out like the filthy bastard he is. I waited, clutching the hilt of my blade as we wove through the stony islands with the *Leviathan* lurking on our tail.

31

THE FOUNTAIN OF YOUTH

MILO

The bow of my ship nearly crashed into the passageway of the rocky cliffs, but we could turn just in time to keep some sort of momentum. Thane's ship eased its way in, desperate to reach me, but forced to nearly halt at the entrance of the cliff maze. I shouted for the crew to let fire, aiming from the rear cannons to get a direct shot. I could tell Thane was trying to ready his own fire, but I wouldn't give him a second more. The cannons erupted at my command and shook the *Lark* before hitting Thane's ship with a force to be proud of. Thane fired back, as I expected, but I doubted he knew what I had in store for him.

Clara glanced at me worriedly as the *Leviathan's* retaliation shot pounded our hull. I gave her a nod, and she screamed out the orders. It was time to send Thane to hell.

The mortar shot was one I'd been waiting so long to use, and I'd been saving it just for Thane. With a fiery burst, the shot launched forth from our deck and soared—an eerie and beautiful sight all at once as fire arced across the water and lit the enemy ship ablaze. In seconds, Thane's vessel went up in flames, black smoke billowing into the air as the sails and masts became engulfed.

The sound of shouting men filled the air, along with an acrid stench of burning wood and tar, as bodies leapt overboard from the burning ship. I reached for my spyglass, locating Thane as he maneuvered around the deck of his vessel. Through the smog, I spotted him, and I watched the gears turning in his head as he decided on his next move.

"Come on, you bastard," I muttered beneath my breath. "That's it. It's about time you come to me for a fight." I couldn't help it when my lip curved into a small grin at the sight of him meeting my gaze and gritting his teeth at me in rage. He made a gesture indicating he would kill me and marched forward before dropping into a jolly boat below. If he thought I would try to keep sailing away, he was wrong. I wanted this. I wanted Thane to climb up the side of my ship so I could finish him once and for all.

But the siren song in my head, it grew louder all of a sudden. I clapped my palm over my ear, trying to escape the deafening sound ringing like a bell in my mind.

"Cap'n?" Clara's voice barely cut through the sound of the chaos. "Cap'n! Are ya' alright?"

I folded over, nearly knocked to my knees by the haunting melody echoing in my head. It was calling me, drawing me, demanding that I jump overboard. The Fountain was close. Right underneath me, it said.

Underneath?

But I fought the sound of her call long enough to focus on Thane approaching me in his skiff. Clara kept calling to me, asking if I wanted her to shoot him. Somewhere in that mangled mess of noise in my head, amidst the smoking cannons, shouting men and wailing of a creaking ship drifting against the cliffs, I managed to scrounge my thoughts together. "No." I growled. "He's mine."

I gripped a sword in each hand, glad I'd spent some time sharpening them the day before. I held my gaze on Thane as he approached, and I walked forward to meet him as he neared the hull. When he came up, I planned to thoroughly show him why he should have never so much as looked at Katrina.

But then that damn song took over again, forcing me to look down...down into the water. In its strange language, it told me to jump. No. It made no sense. The Fountain couldn't be underwater. My jaw ached from clenching it in attempt to resist the call. I couldn't let this stupid song ruin my chance to end Thane here. The Fountain could wait just a few moments more.

But at the last minute, just as Thane was mere feet from me, the siren call became too strong to ignore. As if I was bewitched, it took hold of me, somehow infiltrating my mind so strongly that I had no strength left to fight it. And no choice but to obey it.

Jump.

Tucking my blades into their sheaths, I dove off the ship, leaving behind the distant sound of both Clara and Thane shouting curses. I swam under, cursing silently on my own as I followed the lead of the siren song. Perhaps it was leading me to my death. Perhaps this was all a trap of some sort from the sirens of old that lured men to the depths. Perhaps.

But I couldn't stop myself from following her voice. There might have been a tether wrapped around me, pulling me by her invisible cord. She led me to a cavern. A chill swept down my spine as she compelled me to maneuver myself through the small, dark entrance. Seeing underwater was already difficult enough, given my limited sight. My scarred eye was even more useless down here than on land.

A light startled me, glowing just enough to light the space around me. A golden glow bringing warmth to this pitch-black space, growing from the sun marking from the island tribe.

I glanced down, realizing that Bastian's mark was also changing. Not with light, but a shift in the pattern. The rest of the map formed before my eyes, completing itself on my skin with the stinging pain of sliced flesh. I'd found the Fountain. And now Bastian would, too.

By the faint light of my markings, I saw that the cavern ended, and at the beckoning of the siren call, I looked up, seeing the familiar ripples of those created by an underwater air pocket. I swam up, desperate and grateful, on my last few seconds of air. When I broke through the surface, the breath that hit my lungs tasted crisp and strangely cold. It was unusual. Normally these pockets were filled with old, musty air.

I glanced around. This was no ordinary air pocket. This was an entire grotto, with a stream of water flowing to a small pool meters from me, sourced from a heavy trickle of water toppling down the stony sides of the cave. My eyes followed the water's path. It appeared to gush out of the rocks themselves. Like magic.

The siren song echoed clearly here, still in my head but somehow louder, as if she was hiding right in this very place. I paddled forward to the edge of the pool from which I'd surfaced. Just as I placed my hands on the cold stone to pull myself out, a firm and sharp grasp on my boot yanked me back. I slid down into the water, kicking out at the attacker I could not see. The heel of my boot collided with something hard and bony, and in the dimly lit cave, I could see the shape of a man underwater, reaching for me. I was glad to see Thane, but I was worried my chance to end him was dwindling.

I hoisted myself out of the water, and Thane emerged seconds later. The cave reverberated with his taunting voice as he shook the salt water from his eyes.

The voices in my head screamed, and I couldn't decide which to follow. The siren said keep going and stop for nothing. But my own said turn around and destroy Thane.

I took a step toward the clear, glistening pool on the other side of the cave, each note of the siren guiding my feet. But Thane's voice kept cutting through hers.

"You seem to like burning my ships almost as much as I enjoyed hearing that little bitch of yours scream," he hissed. I clenched my jaw, feeling like it might shatter. "I was so hoping to find her aboard your ship all this time. What did you do with her? Traded her out for the loud-mouthed redhead?"

I heard him emerge from the water. I couldn't stay like this—with my back to him. I gripped my weapons and turned to face him. "She's gone. Some place and time where you'll never find her. Safe from you."

"Oh, she'll never be safe from me, Harrington. Not after what I did to her." Thane shook his head, his evil smile growing wide as water dripped down his hair and through his scraggly beard. "I left far too great of a scar on her memory. One that won't fade quite as easily as the one on her pretty face."

No.

"Come on...Didn't she ever tell you all the things I did to her? All the fun we had together right before you found us in that alley? How my men held her while I stuffed myself down her throat until she cried?" He reached down and touched his belt with a sickening groan.

I stopped in my tracks, using every bit of my mental strength to shut out that damn song haunting my brain. The siren *would* wait. This man would die.

I lunged at him, screaming out my anger as I slashed my sword across his shoulder. Blood spattered across his face and he laughed, looking up at me through wild eyes as he licked away his own scarlet droplets from his chin.

"That's right, Harrington. Just face me already. I know you're dying to do what you should've done a long time ago."

"You followed me here. You won't be making it back out." I growled. The hilt of my cutlass felt light in my hand, and I was itching to send it whipping across this man's throat.

I didn't wait another second, and I whipped out my second blade, twirling it in my hand as he drew his own sword. I charged first, meeting his cutlass with my cross blades. He pushed back, the sound of metal grating as our swords sparked. I spun to escape the gridlock, giving him a split second to take the next swing.

I ducked to avoid his reach, and whirled my sword across his knee. He stumbled with a grunt of pain, and I didn't waste a second taking the opportunity to kick him in the same joint I'd just cut open, feeling the bones crunch against the force of my boot.

With a cry that sounded sweet to my ears, he toppled backward. I threw myself at him, my blade ready to plunge straight through his windpipe. He managed to deflect me with his cutlass, knocking my sword from my right hand. Without a second thought, I ripped my flintlock pistol from the holster at my chest and slammed the weapon across his face.

For the first time, I could actually sense fear in Thane. The way he fought against me shifted, and his attempts to hold me back became truly desperate. And it made me fight him harder.

He managed to turn the gun on me, and I headbutted him just as he pulled the trigger, but to my luck, nothing came out but a hollow click.

"Wet powder," I grinned, leaping over him as his disorientation gave me an opening to grab my other sword.

Thane tossed the gun across the cave. Even with his injured knee, he came for me fast, still able to maneuver enough to charge with his own sword drawn. I whipped around just at the last second to come down on his raised arm, slicing through his arm at the elbow.

He shrieked in agony, a sound that shook me only because I never expected to hear it from someone as unhinged as him. He normally reveled in pain, even his own. But he held the severed end of his arm as thick blood streamed down and pooled at his feet like syrup.

The siren song in my head battled for control once more. Leave him and dive into the Fountain pool, it said. But I wasn't finished here. I wanted to see Thane dead. And I would.

I pulled back my cutlass, ramming the tip of the blade just up under his rib, where I twisted it back and forth as it ground through his flesh. Blood blossomed onto his tunic. By now he was barely recognizable as a man. He was barely more than a body, covered in bruises and blood so thick it distorted his features.

Suddenly, I could hear Katrina all over again, just as clearly as the day I killed Thane's crewmen in the streets.

"Don't become like them."

Since that day, I often heard it right before I killed someone in battle at sea. And sometimes it was enough to stop me. Most times it was. But it wouldn't be enough to stop me now.

The siren in my head begged me to hurry back to the pool, that I was wasting time. But I didn't move. I jutted the sword further forward, drawing a hazy whimper from Thane's lips.

"Enjoy killing me, Harrington. You certainly earned it." He smiled through the blood in his teeth.

Katrina's voice mixed with the siren call, becoming one. Suddenly, I knew it was her. It was her. She was calling me. And begging me not to take this life. Not for her. But for my own conscience.

The sword dropped from my hand with a cold clang against the cave floor. I stepped back, leaving Thane to crumble to his knees in his own puddle of blood. I jumped when I heard Clara's voice reverberating through the chamber. Soaking wet she stood at the entrance, heaving and wringing the water from her hair.

"You found it." She said coldly, glancing from me to Thane to the trickling water along the rock wall.

"Aye, I found it." I nodded, breathing hard as I stood over the battered man at my feet. "But I can't leave this piece of shit here knowing where it is too."

"So kill him. Looks like he needs to be put out of his misery." Clara stepped forward, studying Thane without so much as a hint of empathy in her eyes. He refused to meet her gaze, keeping his own fixated on the ground below.

"She won't let me," I muttered, worry creeping into my mind at the prospect of Thane having access to a fountain that would keep him young forever. I hated the siren for holding me back.

When Clara cocked her head at me in confusion, I didn't elaborate. How was I to explain the siren song in my head without making her think I was delusional? It was too much to explain right now.

"Wait," Clara said, her focus shifting entirely as she knelt and yanked back Thane's matted bloody hair to see his face more clearly. "I know this bastard."

She nearly stumbled back, but I noticed how she fought to keep her footing as her voice shook. "You lied to me. You tricked me. You and yer despicable men violated me. You took everything from me. And you ran while the rest of us paid for your mistake. And if you'd fought like a man back then instead of abandoning us, maybe you wouldn't be dying here like a dog for the same reason."

My eyes widened at the realization that this was the same man who'd done all those horrible things Clara had told me before. And I fumed, realizing why the siren wouldn't let me kill him. Because he wasn't mine to kill. And this wasn't where I belonged.

"He's at your mercy now," I said, walking to Clara and placing my captain's hat on her head. "Captain Reid."

"What are you doing?" Clara stammered.

"I'm following my North Star," I said. "As you must follow yours. The *Falcon* and the crew are yours. I couldn't leave them in better hands."

Clara gave me a knowing nod. It was the first time I'd ever seen her speechless, but I knew she was thanking me in her own way. With tears in her eyes, she shakily touched the hat on her head.

"Thank you, Harrington," she whispered.

With one last gesture, I touched Clara's shoulder with my blessing, then turned and walked to the Fountain.

Legend said he who dipped in the pool would have eternal life. But that's all it was—a legend. Who knew what would become of me once I truly immersed myself in the glistening water before me? Something told me it wasn't quite that simple. But I had no way of knowing what would happen once my body touched the water. I only knew somehow, some strange way, Katrina was calling me to her, wherever that was. And the only way to her was through the Fountain.

With my back to the past, I stood over the pool filled by the fountain, its swirling silvery nature tempting me with its unnatural draw. My reflection was as clear as a mirror in its surface.

Come in.

The siren song took hold now, leaving me no choice but to let myself fall into the magical waters below in order to follow it. The last sound I heard was the shrill slice of a sword being unsheathed, and I knew Clara would take excellent care of Thane.

32

Across Time

Milo

I dropped into the water. From above it appeared no deeper than a crystal puddle, but once within, I found there was no end to its depth. I couldn't see here. My good eye was only so useful here, but I doubted even with working vision in both, it wouldn't have saved me from the blinding white that filled my surroundings. Every direction I turned weighed on my muscles like swimming through tar, but I could see nothing around me. It was a void, with no east or west, no up or down.

In a moment of panic, I fought to escape, but realized the pool surface behind me no longer existed...or if it did, I couldn't see it. I couldn't see anything. Somehow I could breathe, but that was all the luxury this place of nothingness afforded me. I felt around in my blindness, half-swimming, half-walking through this muddled abyss. The Fountain of Youth was certainly a myth. This was something else entirely. I only prayed Clara wouldn't follow me and trap herself here too. But deep in my chest I knew she was smarter than that.

Visions of Katrina filled the dark blindness before me. I would never make it back to her. Even if I managed to escape this place, it would be too late. And even if she managed to find Bastian and the Crown, he'd never let her win. He was too powerful. And I'd played her right into his hands.

As I stumbled blind through whatever this was...I stopped, dropping to my knees as the hopelessness set in. I couldn't give it anymore. The ocean had certainly spoken its authority over my fate. I thought back to the night I stayed with Katrina in her room for the first time. How I'd fought to resist the pull she held over me, knowing it was never meant to work. But I gave in. And now here we both were, separated by oceans of time forever.

I remembered the night I told her that fate had decided against us. And though I thought maybe I'd proved it all wrong, now I realized I was the one who was wrong. Katrina and I were never meant to meet. I was never meant to live long enough to meet her. Finding her once was a blessing enough. But I was always meant to die without her.

As I resigned myself to this void of emptiness, a faint sound rose through the silence, chiming like a bell in the distance. The melody grew louder with each passing second, but it still sounded distant. It was the siren song, but no longer in my head. It was here—truly here somewhere in this hollow void. The sound of it washed over me like some last drop of warmth, urging me one last time to rise.

With tears burning the backs of my eyes as they threatened to fall, I waded through the nothingness, desperate to follow the singing. Completely blind, I clung to my only map—a sound. Her song continued, a voice filling the silence with a frail thread of hope I fought to grasp before it was gone. The melody surrounded me, like a blanket of reassurance in my darkest hour, holding me as I trembled in fear of never escaping this place.

I might have wandered an hour or a day. There was nothing resembling the passing of time. Nothing here granted me a semblance of humanity. For a moment I even question if I was still alive or I had already died, and this might be the holding place for my unworthy soul.

But then, after however long it was that I followed the voice, I found it right in front of me, clear and so loud it sounded mere inches from my ears. My feet stopped on instinct, and I stood, listening to her aria as I stretched out a hand before me into the blank space before me. I nearly leapt backwards when my fingers touched something—a hand.

I took the hand, the song still calling, and stepped forward. Arms wrapped around me. I heard my name from various voices. And then I heard hers...Katrina.

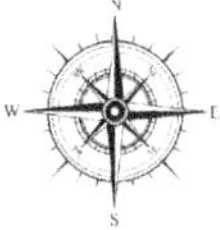

"Milo," she sang softly. "I'm here. You've made it."

My eyes fluttered as they adjusted from whatever magic hold I'd just stepped out from. The light hit, and I could finally focus on those blue eyes that drew me to them with their song. And then I breathed a sigh of relief as they faded back into beautiful brown ones staring back at me. The song had stopped. And it was no longer Katrina's siren who spoke to me. It was her.

Both of us without words, I fell into her arms, clutching her like she was the only solid harbor in a storm. She pulled me into her and held me as I toppled forward from a combination of exhaustion and disbelief. Pressed against her chest, I drowned in the sound of her heartbeat and breathed in her sweet scent.

"You found me," she whispered with trembling in her words. "You heard me all the way across time."

I pulled back to look in her face, brushing back her loose strands of hair behind her ear. "I swore I'd always find you, my North Star." The lump in my throat burned as I swallowed it down, unable to tear my gaze from her.

She placed a hand on my face, her thumb gently sweeping along my beard, across my jaw, and finally over the big scar over my left eye.

"You're...older," she stammered, staring into my eyes. "How long?"

"Some two years." I uttered.

She pressed her head against my shoulder. "I'm sorry."

"No, shhh," I kissed her head, as I took her face in my hands. I pressed my lips to hers and kissed her for what could never have felt long enough. "It might as well have been a minute. Every moment of every day of those years, there wasn't a day I didn't think of you."

I glanced across her shining eyes to her lips, a quick glimpse catching the faded scar along her cheek. It was hardly noticeable now, but I'd always remember the reason it was there. My embrace around her tightened protectively as the sickening things Thane had said replayed in my head. "When Thane caught you back in Nassau...did he...did he hurt you beyond this...before I found you?"

Katrina looked confused by the question, but shook her head. "No, no, he had just grabbed me right before you came. Why?"

I drew in a sigh of relief. "No reason." I pressed myself against her once more and stroked her hair. "I just want to know I did everything to protect you."

"You always have," she rested her head on my shoulder. "And now...now we're free to start again."

I glanced down at the tattoo on my arm, feeling the ink snaking its way across my skin. The map had formed and was complete now. But I doubted Bastian would want the Fountain once he discovered what it really was. I turned to look back at the strange upright wall I'd just walked through, like a mirror made of water, a doorway to something inhuman.

"How did you know I was looking for this place?" I asked, looking back around at her. "How did you know to come here?"

"It's a long story. But I had a little help." She turned to look back at two figures in the shadows of the cove in which we stood. Bellamy and—though I swore my vision deceived me—Serena.

I searched for the words to thank them, but I was as speechless as the stone surrounding us. I watched them both in baffled silence before Bellamy stepped forward. He slapped a hand on my shoulder and leaned in beside me.

"Glad to have you back, mate," he grinned. "Now maybe you can keep this lass of yours under control because I've certainly had my run of it."

I laughed. For the first time in I didn't even know how long, I truly laughed. And not a laugh of humor, but a laugh born out of true, pure joy. Everything I cared about stood here in this cove, paling in comparison to all the gold a thousand ships could carry. And I smiled, knowing Clara would make a fine captain. My men would be taken care of. And my destiny stood right before me.

I pulled Katrina to me once more and kissed her, my blood running hot with the desire to make up for the years I'd longed for her. I couldn't wait to be alone with her, to lie next to her and listen to every word she must've been dying to tell me.

"I don't know how you're here, alive again, but I'm glad you are," I addressed Bellamy. "Thank you for keeping her safe all this time. I feared what might happen if she went to face Bastian alone."

"Don't thank me yet." Bellamy gritted his teeth and his eyes shifted. "We're not quite out from under his thumb."

"What do you mean?" I asked, my concern growing. "What do you owe him?"

Suddenly a rumble shook the walls of the cave, just strong enough to dust us with small rocky debris from above. When the rumble settled, the prominent sound of footsteps filled the cavern, without a doubt the tap of heavy boots with thick leather soles.

A voice that didn't belong here revealed itself as the figure walking in became visible. With a sly smile, he stepped into the dim light of the cove. Bastian Drake himself, of course, looking at Katrina and Bellamy with a hunter's eye, and then at me. "They owe me everything."

33

Off the Hook

Katrina

Bastian loomed there, a menacing look in his eye, and a sly hint of mischief that made my knees feel weak. Whatever he had up his sleeve, I could sense it wasn't good. Bellamy shifted uneasily and put a protective arm across Serena.

"My tattoo," Milo said, glancing at his arm and then at all of us. "It must've led him here. I'm so sorry."

"You know, Harrington," he laughed, stepping forward and glancing over all of us. "Looks like you did finally fulfill your end of the bargain...300 years later," he laughed. "But actually no. You didn't lead me here, thanks to that dreadful sun tribe you found who made it awfully hard to follow you. No, no. You didn't lead me here. Bellamy did."

Everyone's gaze shifted to Bellamy, including Bastian's.

"His father's broken bargain still stands. And so does the mark I left on Bellamy. But even without it, he and I are forever linked by a bit of history and myth. Isn't that right, lover of Atargatis?"

Bellamy didn't respond, shielding Serena with himself as he faced Bastian like a dog ready to be unleashed for the hunt.

"But don't worry, Harrington, you're off the hook thanks to your little island friends. But no matter, because as you well know, the Fountain isn't what I needed after all. I've no interest in sending anyone's soul there, neither yours nor mine. No, that's dear old Davy's job." Bastian pretended to study his knuckles as he walked to Milo. "You're quite the lucky man. The only man to ever truly cheat death with the heart of a siren. If only we'd known back then that all we had to do was fuck 'em instead of kill them. Would've been a whole lot more fun." Bastian's eyes slid over to me with a grin that made my skin crawl. "Speaking of which...Katrina, our little mermaid. Don't you wonder how you got that pretty voice back?"

I straightened my shoulders, daring to appear as confident as possible, though I was terrified of being trapped in this cave with a madman like Bastian. "Our deal is broken. My voice returned to me because I didn't do my part."

"Tsk, tsk, tsk..." he pretended to look at his fingernails as he brought a curled fist to his face. "The laws of my bargains are not quite that easy. You're not off the hook, little fish. Your voice was meant to be a pawn to ensure you would do what I asked. But since you didn't, it became mine to use or bargain with. And bargain with it, I did."

"Wh—what do you mean?" I felt my courageous stance failing, the uncertainty coming through in my voice.

He snapped his fingers and a circle of shadow appeared, forming a floating frame beside him. In it, as I stepped forward to see more clearly, an image of a mermaid trapped in a tank back in his lair appeared, looking desperately out of the glass. It was my mom.

"Mom!" I nearly stumbled backward. "What have you done to her?"

"I only did what she asked," he crooned. "She came to me and offered herself in exchange for your safety and your voice to be returned to you. I couldn't argue with a deal like that. My very own siren at my command? A hell of a bargain, I'd say."

"What about our friends?" Panic stabbed my chest as I thought of McKenzie and Noah. I was still working to process everything he'd just said about Mom.

"Oh, don't worry, they're fine. They were completely supportive of her decision. Your mother can be quite persuasive. Very gifted with her voice. They've no choice but to listen to her and stay behind while she came and found me."

"Let her go. Tell me what you want from me," I growled, my fists clenching so hard I thought I'd tear through my palms with my fingernails.

"Ah, it was a fair trade. She knew full well what she was agreeing to." He strode over to where Bellamy and Serena stood, a smug look on his face. "But I'd certainly trade my mermaid for a powerless goddess."

Bellamy lunged forward, still guarding Serena. "You won't touch her!"

"Perhaps not." Bastian stepped backwards as smoothly as if he were walking on a glass surface. "But now you and your little friends have a choice to make. Mommy Dearest." He gestured to the floating image of my trapped mother, and then back to a wide-eyed Serena. "Or Atargatis." He walked briskly back to the opening of the cave, the spyglass appearing in his hand in a cloud of smoke. "And I'll be taking this back. You failed to fulfill your end of the deal. The Kraken still lives, so you don't get to keep using this little trinket for your personal side quests. When you come to your senses and decide to trade the goddess for your mother, you know where to find me." With that, a shadow consumed him and a wind whisked through the cavern.

Bellamy lunged forward in attempt to stop him, but he was too late. He grappled at the air with empty hands, bewildered at the sight of smoke where Bastian once stood seconds earlier. The silence between the four of us was thick enough to swim in. What was I to say? I couldn't ask Serena to give herself up for my mom. But I didn't know what else to do. My hands had never been so tied.

Milo placed a reassuring hand on my shoulder, but it did little to ease the burning rage in me. "That piece of shit has my mom."

"We're not giving him Serena," Bellamy's voice came out like a deep, low growl. "I've lost her once. I'm not losing her again."

"I know. But we need her if we're going to stop him. You even said yourself you'd do anything to get her crown back. This isn't just for my mom. This is for her. This is for all of us."

Serena buried her face in her hands. "He can kill me without my crown. He knows how to kill me for good. I never should have come with you! I told you!"

"I won't put you in danger. I made that mistake once. But I also can't let you live in a prison at the bottom of the ocean." Bellamy's words came out rushed. I'd never heard him so desperate. "You won't die again because of my stupidity."

"It was never your fault, Bellamy. It was always destiny. Just like my crown being stolen was foretold on the altar of Atargatis. Our love and deaths have been written in the stars since the beginning of time. And whatever lies ahead is the same. You can't tame the sea. And you can't tame me. I'm going back."

"No! Destiny or not, I won't let you. I'll fight for you, Serena." Bellamy looked at me, holding Serena in his grasp. The look in his eyes reminded me of the time he pinned himself against me in a rage back in the brig of the *Siren*. "I'll help try to save your mom, but not at the risk of losing her. It's still about that crown for me, now."

His words unsettled me, but I understood. Still, it didn't tame my emotion in the moment. But something Serena said had stuck in my head.

"Serena, what did you say about the altar of Atargatis? What is that?"

"It's ancient. I don't know what has become of it. But centuries back it was a rock on the coastline where broken-hearted lovers often left tokens for their loved ones lost at sea, hoping I'd spare them as I was spared. Eventually it was carved into a round slab, painted to tell the story of my legend."

"Whatever the case, we need to get moving. Bellamy, we have to work together. 'm going after my mom with or without you. Either way, looks like our only choice is taking down Bastian."

I could tell Bellamy struggled to choose his path. But he spent a minute in thought and glancing between Milo and I and Serena. Finally, rubbing his head, he stepped forward. "I'll sail back with you, lass, because ironically, the only way you're getting your mom back is if we kill Bastian, and the only one here who can do that is Serena...*when* we get her crown back and her power is restored."

I glanced over at Serena, who stayed oddly silent and looked as though she was about to cry. For a goddess bound and powerless, I found it strange how much she seemed to resist the idea of getting her crown back. But that wasn't my concern. Whatever could be so bad about restoring her power couldn't possibly be worse than losing my mom to a deranged immortal pirate lord.

"Fine." I stuck out my chin. "Then we get the crown. Whatever it takes."

Bellamy's eyes narrowed. "Whatever it takes."

34

Sea Shanties

Bellamy

We made our way out of that damn cavern, with Serena's beautiful glow to guide us. I found I could still breathe beneath the water from her kiss, so while I swam, I had plenty of time to think.

I wouldn't use Serena as a bartering piece. I wanted to see her power restored. I wanted her to be free once and for all. I knew she wanted that, too, despite how she pleaded against it. She had to be. So why the hell was she so set on staying in that cave with that disgusting squid? There had to be something more she wasn't letting on. Maybe she was just scared after all that time alone. Maybe. Or maybe she was right. Maybe it was too dangerous for both of us. Had I not learned my lesson by now?

Maybe we didn't have to go back. Maybe I could convince her to run. Somewhere Bastian could never find her. We could run together, and I'd protect her from whatever followed. It would mean turning my back on Katrina, though. I couldn't just leave her to Bastian by herself. But then again...maybe it was the answer. Katrina was strong and far more clever than me. If anyone could figure out how to deal with him, it'd be her. She didn't need me. Sure, I loved Katrina, but not the way I loved Serena, and I couldn't risk losing Serena for *anyone*. But if I didn't ensure Bastian was gone, he'd never stop looking for Serena. And I couldn't risk that either.

When we surfaced, dark skies greeted us. The wind was picking up, and the water had grown choppy. Wild lightning split the sky as the smell of rain and salt stirred in my nostrils. "We can't sail in this. Sorry Katrina but even you can't make a way around this one." I glanced over at Katrina, who watched the storm clouds with worried eyes.

"He's right," Milo interjected. "A storm like that would take a heavy toll on the sturdiest galleon, let alone that little sailboat."

I looked at our boat bobbing where we'd anchored. It wouldn't stand a chance. "Our best shot is to at least get away from these rocks. We can sail downwind for a bit to put some distance between us and them. Then we'll have to ride it out and hope for a miracle."

We all nodded in agreement and started swimming back to the boat. I grabbed Serena's arm as we fought the rugged waters and boarded the sailboat. "Serena, I need you to go back and wait for me. Wait for me with your kraken, and I'll come back once I have your crown and Bastian's dead."

"Bellamy, you know I am the only one who can kill Bastian," she groaned. "You can't do it alone."

"Please," I begged. "Let me try."

"I'll go back on one condition," Serena said as I hung on her every word. "You forget me, Bastian and my crown, and you leave things as they are."

"What?" I threw up my hands. "No! Why the hell are you making this so difficult? Don't you want to end this damn cycle you're trapped in? Don't you want your power back?"

"Of course I do, but..."

"But what?"

"I...have fears. Fears I cannot say, but you must trust me. And if you won't leave me and promise not to go back to Bastian, then I'm coming with you. Because I am the only chance you and your friends stand against him." She didn't allow me the chance to argue. She turned on her heel and walked away with a sigh, sitting on the other side of the boat and leaving me with less clarity than before. What fears was she talking about? And why did she have to be so stubborn? The constant back and forth tore my mind to shreds. But one thing was certain. Someone was going to be disappointed no matter what I did. No surprise there.

The thunder rolling in the distance reminded me to move fast. I dropped the sails as Milo worked the helm, catching the winds from the tempest, and we surged forward, outrunning the storm. Katrina and Serena stood at the starboard side, watching the waves. I knew Katrina must have been stressed about her mom, but this was her best chance of making it back to her alive. And Serena...she was watching the raging sea like a proud parent watches a child.

About twenty minutes later, the clouds were catching up to us, and giant rain droplets smacked the top of my head. "We should probably go ahead and drop anchor," I said. Milo gave me a nod and we sent the anchor down, waiting for it to snag. When we felt the tautness of the boat against the line, Milo gave me a thumbs up and we both headed for the cabin, calling for Katrina and Serena to get their asses away from the hull and join us.

We waited out the storm, a few lanterns our only light. The cabin was small, but comfortable enough for us all to sit facing each other in the glow of the lowlight. We took turns passing around a Mediterranean beer that we'd found in the cabin, except for Katrina, who understandably opted out.

"Try not to worry," I said, noticing Katrina's downcast face. "Bastian isn't going to do anything to your mom before we get there. She'll be fine."

"She has a fish tail, Bellamy!" Katrina snapped.

"And she's alive. That's what matters right now."

Milo rubbed his hands together. Our damp clothes were cold against our skin. "He's right. Your mom is his bargaining piece, and he's not going to do anything to hinder his chances of getting what he wants."

All eyes flickered to Serena, who took a swig of beer and passed it off to Milo. "You are all about to find yourself in hot water."

"Hot water sounds lovely right about now," Milo shivered. I laughed.

The storm outside began to strengthen. The rain pelting the deck sounded like an avalanche above our heads. We fought to keep our balance as the boat tipped and teetered back and forth, waves crashing against all sides.

"Enough about Bastian. I'm sick of his name." Serena said. "Let's sing a song."

I was surprised to see Katrina smile at the idea. "A mermaid and a siren queen want to sing to us. What could go wrong?" I chuckled.

"Oh, that's true. I guess things could get out of hand." Serena smirked. "Then how about *you* sing to us?"

Katrina's smile grew wider as Milo and I protested. "Come on, boys. The crew could use a morale boost. Sing for us."

"Us singing is really not something that will boost morale, lass, I promise you that." I stretched my arms behind my head.

"Oh, I think it would," Katrina laughed, and grabbed Milo's shoulder. "Come on, teach us a shanty or something."

Milo rolled his eyes and pressed his forehead against hers. "I think I'd rather go ride out the storm on deck. Wouldn't you, Bellamy?"

"Aye, man. "We're not drunk enough for this."

"Oh, come on," Serena pleaded. "You weren't a pirate in your first life. I want to hear a shanty."

I sighed, resigned to my fate. "Fine, love. For you. Just this once."

The girls clapped and cheered with giggles as Milo and I turned to each other. "Which one should we do? 'Drunken Sailor?'"

Milo scoffed. "God, no. If I have to hear that one again, I'll lose it. What about 'Santiana?'"

"Maybe if I remembered the words. It's been a hell of a while for me. Best I can do is 'Leave Her Johnny.'" I shrugged.

"Aye, yeah, that's a good one. Allright." Milo straightened his shoulders and smacked his fist against the wood of the cabin bunks to create the beat and we threw out the lyrics to our shanty. I'd only get so many words in before laughing and fumbling with the whole thing, but of course kiss-ass Milo would leave me hanging and keep going. I caught up and then we sang the chorus as the girls laughed at our god-awful voices.

They applauded as we finished. "See? That was amazing." Katrina laughed, pulling her hair off her shoulders. "One more!"

"I was hoping the thunder outside would drown us out." Milo chuckled, tossing the bottle cap into the floor.

The girls begged again relentlessly. Maybe they used their siren powers to control us, because I agreed to another one.

"Allright, fine, but only if I get to pick the next song and it's not a shanty." I laid out my conditions with a grin. "Milo, I don't know if you'll recognize this one."

Silence fell as Milo gave me a curious look and the girls leaned in. I wiped my mouth after a mouthful of beer and began my serenade. I'd only gotten a couple of lines in when a huge smile spread across Katrina's face. "Oh my gosh...Please tell me where you learned 'Carry on Wayward Son!'"

"The ship radio and lots of hours at the wheel." I stomped my feet, continuing the song and dragging Milo into the next chorus with a nudge. He always picked up lyrics fast. Something about that weird memory of his served more purpose than just navigation. As we belted out the words, I added in the stomp of my boot. The sea tossed us around, but we kept singing, and before long the girls joined in, all of us arm-in-arm in our small circle on the floor.

By the time we'd finished the song, the sounds of the storm outside were raging, the waves clawing at the sides of the ship like vicious monsters.

I looked up, my tone turned serious. "I'd say there's another hour and a half of this at least."

"This little thing isn't meant to be in winds like this." Milo uttered. "I hope she holds out."

"You and me both." Katrina shuddered and closed a blanket around her and Milo.

And then a crash sent us tumbling to the floor. The lanterns toppled over, getting snuffed out, and chaos broke loose as we were slammed around every which way in the cabin. I reached for Serena, holding onto her as best I could and shielding her head. A crack of thunder shook the cabin and then all the movement stopped. I shook myself off and then felt around in the dark, calling out the names of my friends.

"We're here." Katrina said. I followed her voice, and we huddled together in the dark.

"I think she's capsized," Milo said.

"But we're not moving." Serena added.

I felt around for the hatch. It wasn't above us, and when I found the handle on the wall, I knew we'd been tipped over. "Right here." I ushered them over, opening the hatch to the sight of an empty shore, the storm still overhead. But we were ran aground. Sideways.

"Shitty anchor." I climbed out the hatch and examined the damage. Milo followed, and we looked at each other as the rain whipped our faces. We'd at least crashed on a small isle, with a small line of trees helping to barricade us from the wind.

"She doesn't look too damaged. We can tip her back over once the skies clear!" He shouted over the gusts and thunder.

We nodded, and then reentered the boat cabin. I didn't realize quite how tired I was. As I sat with Serena to the sound of the rain through the open hatch, my eyes found themselves heavy.

35

Until the End

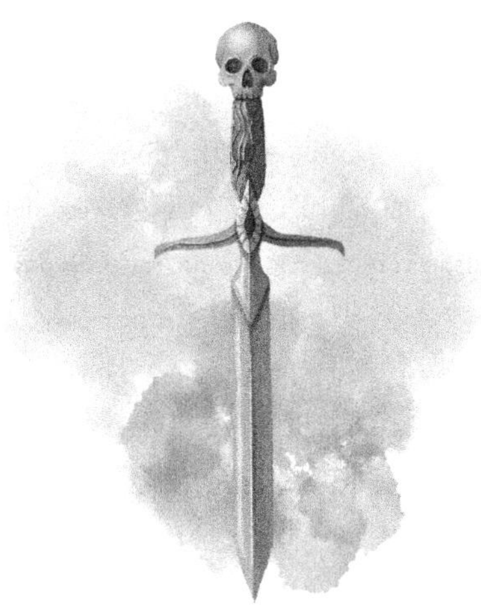

Bellamy

Serena's voice gently woke me. "The storm is gone."

"Fantastic." I muttered, rubbing my eyes. "How long was I asleep?"

"A couple of hours. I didn't want to wake you. You looked like you needed the rest."

The cabin was aglow now, lit up the color of fire as the light of sunset beamed in through the hatch against the cabin's cherry wood stain. "Where are Katrina and Milo?"

"They went to find food. They won't be gone long."

I tousled my hands through my hair. "They're finally getting some alone time after Milo spent two years at sea. They'll be gone a while."

Serena cocked her head and smirked. "Then maybe we should be grateful for some alone time, too." She touched my face. "Did you dream of me?"

"I've been dreaming of you since the day I lost you."

"Oh, you're full of it, pirate. Good thing you're so handsome." She shook her head, turning away, but I touched her chin and turned her back to me.

"No, I mean it. In the way the winds guided my sails as I outran the horizon. In every moment of peace on calm clear waters. In every rolling wave caressing my skin. In every storm raging at sea. When I'd lie down on my ship, you were the waves rocking me to sleep. In the way the ocean called my name as I set my hand to the wheel. It was always you. You were every dream between me and the sea. You've been etched in my memory and my heart since the dawn of time, and the sea has been reminding me of you every day since." I paused, hesitating before asking a question, my lips hovering over the skin of her neck. "If we'd never found you, would you have stayed trapped at the bottom of the sea with the Kraken forever?"

Serena turned away and crawled out the hatch, leaving my question unanswered. I was getting tired of that. I followed her, chasing her down across the sand as she walked along the surf. "Would you stop doing that? Stop being so stubborn for one damn bloody minute and talk to me!"

She whipped around as I neared. "What choice did I have but to hide with the Kraken? I woke up in that pit after your father killed my human form and put my heart back in the sea! Davy Jones basically rules the seas without my power to keep him in check. It was too dangerous to leave. The sea loses its magic more and more each day. The sea gods' power is nothing more than a fingerprint left behind in myth and lore. The wonder of the ocean is just a shell of what it once was. And so am I." A tear shimmered in the corner of her eyelash, and I wiped it away gently with my thumb before it could fall.

"No. You're everything. With or without your power." It pained me to see how much she yearned to get her power back. Especially when I knew it might mean letting her put herself in harm's way. If only she'd just let me do it for her. To make up for the way I failed her before. It almost seemed like...like maybe the harder I tried to fight it, the worse things got. But I couldn't fully convince myself of that yet.

She turned away again to face the tide, and I reached around her waist from behind. I nuzzled her ear. "Let's forget our differences of interest for a while." She spun in my arms, turning to face me and gazing up at me with those hopeful caramel eyes. I slid my hand down. "All the past lives of loving you haven't been enough." I wished she'd listen to me. I wished there was something I could say to keep her from endangering herself.

"You've always been persuasive, Bellamy." Serena breathed with a hint of laughter. "But in the end, you can only decide what *you* will do. You don't get to decide what I do."

I smirked, amazed but also somewhat unsettled at her ability to practically read my thoughts. But it made sense. "Then I decide that right now, I forget all this for a moment, and spend this night worshipping the goddess I'm fated to love."

Her tropical scent intoxicated me. I ran my lips along the curves of her shoulder, and my hands slid down the small of her back. She sighed softly, touching me back in all the right places. I quickly glanced around, looking at the set of double footprints in the sand leading away from the boat to ensure Katrina and Milo weren't around.

"Don't worry about them. Like you said, they're probably off having just as much fun as we are." Serena assured me with a grin. She glowed like the moon as the sun dipped below the horizon. "Just be with me," she whispered, pulling my face to hers. She bit my lip, playing with my mouth along hers as she teased the skin beneath my shirt.

The sunset's orange glare reflected on the rolling tide like a stained-glass window, lighting up the sky around us with a red haze. Serena tugged at each piece of my clothing until she had removed them all, and I returned the favor by sliding off the dress that enrobed her so beautifully. But not as beautiful as how she looked without it. The delicate silk slid between my fingers like liquid as it dropped to the floor. I took in the sight of her—a sight I thought I'd never see again. She was everything a goddess should be, the broken sunlight hitting her flawless skin to cast a glow as warm as the gold she wore.

We danced to the sound of the water swirling around, our bodies pressed together as my fingers worked their way along the smoothness of her thigh. I kissed her deeply, savoring her tongue against mine. Heat roiled in my core down to my pounding lower half. I brought my lips to her breasts, feeling the way they perked up at my touch and relishing the scorch of her skin.

The blood rush in my veins felt like a song in my soul as I indulged in the feeling of her—something I'd been so cruelly deprived of the last time we'd been together in this way. Every touch, every lick, every stroke, every drop of sweat and desperate breath that escaped our bodies felt like the first. What an absolute wild blessing and curse, I thought.

She tried to turn back around in my arms, as she pushed the lower half of herself against me. But I gripped her shoulder, spinning her to face me again. I gently laid her down, pinning her to the sand, kissing her still. "No," I groaned. "I want to look into your eyes as we reclaim each other." I reached beneath her, feeling her slick heat, desperate to fill the need I knew she had. Her soft moans made my muscles tight and hard. It was unbearable. But I was gentle with her, placing myself wherever she needed until I felt her body riot with sensation and heard her gasp with breathlessness.

"Very well," she smirked, opening herself to me fully. I plunged forward, diving into her like the raging sea she was.

The water around us cast a glow of dusk that reflected the very fire I felt in every inch of my body as I joined mine with hers. All I could think about was how I'd never let her go again—and how delightful every part of her felt. Like quenching a thirst I'd been craving, like a cool rush of wind on a hot day, like a burst of sunlight in the darkness. She was all of it, and with each thought, my body grew hotter, faster, and tenser, until I lost myself to a rush of release.

"Serena. Atargatis. Damn, you could be Aphrodite. Whatever your name is, whatever title you hold, I only have one for you. *Mine.*"

"Always yours." She sighed, stroking my hair. She held my head close to her breast as we both rested against the sand. "Since the beginning and until the end."

I whispered with a smile. "From North to West."

36

Fight the Current

Milo

"Looks like maybe we should stay gone a bit longer." Katrina mumbled with a chuckle at the sight of Serena and Bellamy lying in the sand as we stumbled back through the trees to the sailboat.

I set down the crab net and coconuts we'd gathered, taking Katrina in my arms. "I'm alright with that."

She kissed me, dropping the papayas she held and grabbing my face. Even though just a short while before we had been lying sprawled in the sand ourselves, her body beneath mine in a long-overdue reunion, it wasn't enough. I wanted her more every moment. And I'd happily entwine myself with her again here and now.

"Do you know what this place reminds me of?" I said.

"What's that?"

"The first time I met you. When you came to the island of Valdez's shipwreck and sat down next to me without a clue."

"I still don't know how I didn't notice you sitting there on the shore." She twisted her lips into a sideways smirk.

"Maybe because I didn't want to be seen."

"But you talked to me first," she said with suspicion.

"I did. And I'm glad. Because I couldn't resist you then. And I still can't. Something pulled me to you like...like water. And I know better than to fight the current." I leaned in to kiss her between words.

As night fell, I noticed Bellamy and Serena were stirring. "Come on," I said, scooping the food back up. "We should get back and start a fire. I'm sure I'm not the only one who's starving."

We walked out to our friends on the shore, where we presented our gathering of crab and fruit. Bellamy worked to get the fire going, and we sat around it, cooking the crab meat and downing the coconut water like it was the most divine thing we'd ever tasted.

"The boat isn't seriously damaged. A good flipping over and she should be ready to sail." I explained, cracking a crab claw between my thumbs.

"So we could leave tonight?" Katrina asked.

"If you want to. It's your call when we leave." I took a bite, glancing at Bellamy across the flames of the bonfire. "Right Bellamy?"

He shook himself free of the dazed, empty look on his face and straightened. "Yeah."

Katrina leaned forward, her gaze meeting each of our tired faces. "Of course I want to get back to my mom...but I think we all need the rest. We can leave at daybreak."

"All right then." Bellamy tossed a stick into the fire, his voice hollow. "We leave at daybreak."

37

WHERE'S THE RUM?

BELLAMY

We readied the boat at dawn while the girls slept a bit longer. Milo and I set to work rigging the sails and double checking the hull. Thankfully the masts had survived the crash. The skies were perfect for sailing, the winds in our favor. We didn't have far to go.

"It's about a two day's journey, I'd say," I called to Milo.

"I'll take that over two years," he chuckled.

I replied with a half-laugh, walking over to him as I tied the last bit of rigging. "We've missed you, mate, you know that?"

"You? Miss me?" He shook his head. "No hard feelings over the necklace?"

"You know that was a weird time," I grumbled with a hint of fake laughter. "We were all desperate and half-mad."

"I'm just joking." He jabbed me with his elbow. "I know it was all that seawater finally getting to you. Don't worry, I understand."

"Hey now. Who showed you the ropes of pirating? You'd have been long dead on my father's crew without me."

"I'll admit, I might've picked up a few things from you. But don't pretend I didn't help you with that God-awful sense of navigation." He raised an eyebrow with a grin as he tightened a knot.

We both laughed as I shook my head, thinking back to how Milo, a scrawny fifteen year old, would dare correct me on star patterns and my map drawings, right in front of my father, at that. "Okay, fair enough there. Maybe there really was some useful reason my father wanted you aboard."

"If I'm being honest, I'd rather there hadn't been."

"Well, if you weren't valuable, you'd have been dead, so..." I leaned into the edge of the boat along with Milo, using all my strength to nudge it back into the water.

"Given what we've been through, that doesn't sound like the worst option." Milo tilted his head in my direction. He looked older than me now, with a beard thicker than I'd ever seen it and the scar across his eye. His skin was tanned from his time at sea, and he had a calm but wise look about him that spoke of some hidden strength he didn't have before.

I tapped my fingers along the side of the boat. "Aye, come on, mate, it's not so bad. We're filthy sons of bitches and yet for some reason we've been given more chances than saints."

"Maybe we're supposed to learn something from it," Milo waded in next to me, pushing the boat along out of the shallows. I took a breath, winded and thirsty.

"You didn't happen to bring any rum back with you from the good old days, did you?" I was only half-joking.

To my surprise, he reached into his satchel and produced a flask. He tossed it to me.

"You bastard," I smiled wide, chugging a big mouthful. "Never thought I'd taste that again. It's just not the same here."

We kept on about things as the girls awoke. We watched them on the shore as they chattered and prepared themselves for the day ahead. Then we climbed up onto the boat.

"You can't hold her back, you know. Even when you want to protect her." Milo's voice made me look back over my shoulder at him as I went to pick up a rope. He'd better not be trying to give me some heart-to-heart shit about Serena. Not after all he'd caused with Katrina.

"Shocking words coming from you, mate." I cocked my head, dropping the rigging in my hand. "You of all people know what it's like to lose your lass. Don't tell me you wouldn't do anything to keep that from happening again."

"I would. I did. I tried that. I tried to keep Katrina from Cordelia so she wouldn't get hurt. And the trust I lost in her wasn't worth the false sense of security. I was wrong to try to make that decision for her. And it's the same with Serena. She's going to do what she thinks she must, and it's not our place to try to hold them back." He narrowed his eyes at the two girls chatting yards away as the wind swept through their hair. "They're both as untamable as the sea. And isn't that always what you've loved about the sea?"

For a moment I thought on his words, letting them digest as I stretched my jaw forward to relieve the tension I was holding. "I'm not going to hand her over to Bastian if that's what you mean."

"Of course not. But I mean, if her destiny is to face him once and for all, to get back the power that's rightfully hers, do you think you should try to keep her from that?"

I offered a lewd gesture and an eye roll, because it was the only way I could keep from letting him see how deeply his words sank into my conscience. I knew Serena deserved to be restored to the fullness of her power, but surely she could stand back while I did it for her. Because one thing I was sure as hell of—I wasn't trading her for Katrina's mom in a million years.

I looked for a way to change the subject quickly and my gaze landed on Milo's tattoo. "That's new."

"A little token from Bastian in the past. You still have yours?" Milo asked with a nod.

"It's not going anywhere." I reached up instinctively to feel the skin over my collarbone. The inked sea beast curving along it and around to the nape of my neck tattoo on my body had remained dormant for all these centuries until I'd started hearing Bastian's voice through it again on this goose chase. It was our seal—like how he'd taken Katrina's voice—to prove our bargain. Only the bargain was my father's, and I was the pawn piece between them.

"What about the sun thing around it? Don't recall that one." I noticed his arm marking bordering the intricate map. It seemed less like ink and more like a shining inlay of metal.

"It's a long story. But it was supposed to dampen the effect of Bastian's mark." Milo blew a puff of air through his lips and squinted in the sunlight. "Some legend from an island I found. The sun protects them from inner darkness. And they wanted to keep Bastian's darkness from finding them."

""Did it work?" I raised an eyebrow.

"I certainly hope so." He looked back at Katrina and Serena, who seemed to be finishing up their conversation as they waded into the surf to come aboard. "Anyway, the sails are set for now."

I gave him a nod, watching him stride across the deck to help the girls up, but not before he stopped and turned around once more. "Bellamy."

"Aye?" I called.

"You've covered my arse more times than you should have. Don't think I won't have your back in whatever comes next."

"Savvy, mate. I'll hold you to that." I joked with a finger pointing toward him.

Once the girls were on board, Katrina looked concerned and whispered something to Milo. I watched him follow her to the cabin hatch. Making my way to the helm, I glanced over at Serena, who was eyeing me with a look of seduction or disdain, or maybe both, as she leaned on her elbows over the boat's edge. With a wink, I took the wheel.

38

BURN

MILO

"What did you want to tell me?" I asked Katrina.

"I'd rather talk inside," she said, ushering me into the cabin. There wasn't much room, but we made our way around old fishing gear and nets cluttered around the sink area to the farthest area back, where two little sofa-like cots lined the sides of the cabin walls.

I tripped on a net we stepped over when a lure snagged on my pants. I stumbled and caught myself with a mutter. "My ship would've never been in such disarray."

Katrina laughed. "Already lost your sea legs?"

"Ha, not quite," I smiled, leaning my arm on the wall just above her head. "Just distracted by a pretty mermaid."

She rolled her eyes with a scoff. "All that time and you still managed to hold on to that cheesiness."

"I think you mean charm." I flashed her a playful grin as she shoved against my chest lightly, but left her hand there as her face softened and her gaze turned deep. She slid her hand down my chest, her eyes following her movement.

"I wanted to ask you...What happened after..." her voice trailed away slowly. "...after you sent us back here? What happened to you in those two years?"

My thoughts flashed back to the day I sent Katrina to the present using the Trident. I'd tried so hard to forget the hours that lingered after I killed that captain and commandeered his ship. I hardly slept for three days, and when I finally did, I lied down still covered in the blood of my enemies, drunk on liquor to numb myself to my new reality. It took months for me to come back to my senses. But in the meantime, I was merciless.

"I...I'm ashamed to admit that I turned into the very kind of man I never wanted to be. I was so angry." I turned my face away because I couldn't bear to meet her eye. "I thought I'd never see you again."

"Whatever you did, you can't hold onto." She touched my jaw, stroking my beard with her thumb as she turned my head back to her. "Just like your time in Valdez' crew. It's in the past. You did what you had to do to survive."

"This time it was different, Katrina. On Valdez's ship I had no choice. But on my own, I had every choice. To take lives or spare them. And I rarely chose the latter. Because if I did, I'd have been found weak on the seas. I spent weeks hunting down Bastian's fleets in search of the map to the Fountain. Until I finally squeezed out some information from one of his cowards of a captain who told me where I could find him. I tore down anyone who got in my way and sunk more ships than I could count. I set the seas on fire looking for a way back to you."

"You have to forgive yourself."

"Forgive? That's the thing that scares me. I don't regret any of it. I'd do it all again for you. But now I fear I don't deserve you."

"Funny you say that." She took my hands, her breath shaky. "I didn't just want to ask you what happened back there. I...I need to tell you something."

I was confused, but I urged her to continue with a look.

"When I guided you to me through the Fountain...when I sang to you...it wasn't fully me." She took a deep breath. "I started the song, but then my siren took over, and she was luring you. It worked to guide you out, but the song you heard was a death trap. If I hadn't regained control at the last second, she would've...*I would've* killed you. And that terrified me, but I didn't want to let anyone know. Not even you. Because I'd worked all this time to find you, to save you, only to realize I'm the real danger to you. And I don't know what to do about it."

I was quiet for a moment as I chose my words carefully. If she only knew how I'd dreaded this day. From what I'd seen of sirens, I knew even Katrina would eventually succumb to hers. They were powerful creatures, and while Katrina could somewhat control that side of her for now, I feared one day that may no longer be the case. "I've already known this would happen eventually. I just didn't know when. I would be well deserving of a death at the hands of a siren. I certainly played my part in their demise, willingly or not. And if that siren is you...well, then...there's no greater end I could imagine."

Katrina blinked hard. "No, no. Don't even say that. Do you honestly think I could live with myself if I were to do something to you?"

"Katrina," I sighed. "I wish you could understand how truly despicable I am. While we're being honest, I want you to know that I want you now more than ever. But I'm so afraid I'll ruin you." I couldn't believe I was admitting this out loud to her. But she had to know what was eating me alive every moment.

She shook her head, sending loose waves of hair dancing around her shoulders. "*You* ruin *me*? You're not the one with an evil voice in your head. You're not the one who might snap one day and kill me and not even remember it! I can't love you without hurting you. And the more I think about that..." she paused with a heavy sigh, "...the more I wonder what kind of future we can even have."

"The only future I want." I grabbed both of her hands in mine almost as though they might drift away if I didn't do it fast enough.

She swallowed with her head hung low. "The dreams you once told me about. Moving away from all this. Having a normal life and settling down...You can't have that with me."

"Of course I can, and even if I couldn't, those dreams don't matter anymore. You're my only dream now."

Katrina looked off to the side for a moment, those brown eyes swimming in a sea of thoughts before finding my desperate gaze again. "Do you know what these past few days have made me realize? It's made me realize there's no escape. And there never will be."

"No, you don't mean that," I pleaded. Maybe this was what I deserved, but it still felt like a gutting with an iron-hot blade.

Katrina looked up, as if wishing she could say something to make this conversation dissolve, starting and stopping again as she warred with her words. "When I look at my mom, and realize she's just as trapped by the siren blood in our veins as I am, I realize it's never going away. Never. If it wasn't the nightmares destroying our lives, it's this. It'll just keep passing down like it always has. I can't do that to a family of my own. I didn't break my curse. I just traded it out for a different one. So if I can't end the curse, I have to end the family. Which means I can't have one with you. I can't be your dream, because I'm a nightmare. There is no happy ending for us."

"What are you saying, then?" I squeezed her hands, the tension in my body like a tightrope. I knew I couldn't protect her from herself. But I would gladly die trying.

"I don't know, Milo. I don't know." She dropped her head against my shoulder, leaving it there as we stood in a silent embrace for minutes. Until she finally shattered the silence.

"You once told me you did terrible things. I never thought I'd be the one saying it to you."

I huffed out a breath. "We can be each other's sun."

"What?" Katrina pulled away gently.

"It's a legend. As long as the moon has the sun, it'll never be overtaken by the darkness. I'll be your sun, Katrina, even if that means I burn." I lifted her chin to meet my eyes.

She stared at me, her eyes flickering back and forth between mine. She reached up slowly and touched my scarred eye, then with her other hand, guided mine to the scar along the side of her face. She held us that way for a long time, neither of us saying a word. I thought I understood. I hoped I did.

"And tonight?" She whispered. "Maybe tomorrow it'll all make sense. Or maybe it won't, and it'll be worse and we'll realize I was right. But for tonight, let's imagine I'm wrong. If we're gonna burn, let's burn together."

She crashed her mouth into mine, the taste of her tongue like sweet wine. With her hand slipping beneath my shirt, she unraveled me. I almost wondered if it was her siren side taking control, but even if it was, I couldn't say I would've stopped her. I'd been insatiable for her for far, far too long.

I pressed her to me, our lips joining deeper like the tide joins the shoreline. We stumbled back as a flurry of hands and clothing flashed between desperate glimpses. I would've gazed at her body longer if I'd had the chance, but we moved with such urgency, such passion, that I found myself looking into her eyes. But that didn't stop me from feeling her to the fullest. Her skin scorched beneath my fingers stroking her, defining the alluring shape of her curves. I slid my hands across her breasts down to her hips as she pressed her fingers into my shoulder muscles, tracing my tattoos from my back to my upper arms. I groaned as she reached for me, teasing the flame below. My groin tightened with an ache as my craving for her grew stronger than I could endure. I squeezed her thighs and ran my hand along the perfection in between them. Her panting sighs in my ear drove me mad as she pulled me down onto one of the cots against the wall. I climbed over her, and she kissed me as I leaned down. There was little time for more before I found myself anchored in her, wondering if the sound of waves lapping the side was enough to cover the sounds of our gasps.

Each time before had been slow and gentle, but this was furious and unrestrained. Her fingers tangled through my hair as I shackled her wrists with my grip, our entwined bodies slippery with sweat. She pulled me into her like she might die if she couldn't feel me deep enough. My blazing pulse throbbed through every inch of me. When I heard her moan my name in delirious bliss, I gave myself permission to follow in a rush of heat and rapture. If this was what burning felt like, I'd let her take me straight to hell.

I didn't care what tomorrow brought, or all the tomorrows to come. As we slowly fell asleep in each other's arms, I resolved that whatever darkness Katrina felt she couldn't defeat could take me with it, too.

I kissed her forehead gently as I watched her eyes drift closed. "Whether you're right or wrong, we burn together."

39

Parting Waters

Bellamy

As night fell, Serena came up to me, finally, after driving me to insanity with her sideways glances from across the deck. She planted a kiss on my cheek with a wink as she slid her hand along mine. "Do you know we were married in our first life?"

"I wish I could remember that life I had with you. I hope to hell it wasn't as complicated as this one."

"It wasn't. Not at first." Serena sighed.

"Was I the same back then?" I asked as she leaned against my shoulder while my other hand steadied the wheel.

"You were. You looked the same. You sounded the same. And you were just as cocky and stubborn then, too." Her nose crinkled with a laugh.

"Good, at least there'll be no surprises for you then." I pushed back a loose braid over her shoulder. "Do you remember your life when I met you in 1989? Do you remember your families?"

"Some of them I do. Of course, I didn't know who—or what I was—at the time. But I remember some of them. Like my father in my most recent life. He had the gentlest spirit."

"Ha. He hated me, though. He thought I killed you." I leaned back. "Thankfully Katrina proved otherwise to him, but still. He went almost thirty years believing that."

"We seem to have a knack for getting each other killed." Serena laughed, turning her head to look at the stars.

A wave of guilt flooded over me as I thought of something going wrong when we went to face Bastian. "Not this next time. What if we just run and start a new life somewhere else? What if you stay like this?"

She shook her head. "We can't run from this, Bellamy. Not without making your life terrible. And we would always be in danger. We'd never truly have peace. And then when we die eventually we'll just be reborn again, always subconsciously trying to find each other."

Suddenly Bastian's voice crept up in my head, taunting me in whispers.

And if you run with her, I'll always know where to find her.

No. You fucking bastard.

It was then that I realized. Bastian could still see us. All along, he saw and heard everything. And that's how he'd known about Katrina's mom, and leaving McKenzie and Noah behind. He knew the whole time, even before Katrina and I made the deal. And that's why he made us go alone. The closer I was with Serena, the easier it'd be for him to kill her. He was watching us. We were feeding right into his trap. He would know exactly when and where we planned to come and confront him. And even beyond that, if we didn't put an end to him, he would always have access to the people I cared about through me...forever. It would never truly end. He could clearly activate his markings whenever he wanted, and we could do nothing to stop it.

I swallowed hard as I accepted the realization that the only way to keep Katrina and Serena safe was to stay away from them. I released the wheel, nearly toppling over as I fought the sway of the boat.

"Where are you going?" Serena asked, startled.

"I can't tell you. Because he's listening." Without explaining anything further, I rushed to find Milo. He was asleep next to Katrina in the cabin, and I silently shook him awake.

"Dammit man, what are you doing?" He whispered, wiping the sleep from his eyes.

I kept my voice low, careful not to wake Katrina. "My mark is still traceable. I don't have your little sun voodoo trick to help me out. He's going to know when we come to face him. We can't let him have that advantage."

"Hmmm. You're right. But what are you suggesting?" He groaned under his breath.

"I'm saying—" I stopped myself. Whatever I thought or said Bastian might hear. Instead I looked around for paper and pencil, and hurriedly scribbled what I wanted to say.

The girls aren't safe with me. I need to travel separately.

Milo studied the paper in the dim light, then looked up at me with an understanding in his eyes that assured me he agreed. I was surprised, as I half expected him to object. But he didn't hesitate to nod and wake Katrina.

"I'll explain it to her." Turning back to me, he paused. "Who's steering the ship?"

I tilted my head with a shrug and gritted teeth.

"Well go do that then!" He punched me in the arm a little too hard. I retreated, leaving Milo to sort out the situation with Katrina.

Back out on deck, I made my way to the wheel, in no rush at all. Serena rushed to greet me, still confused as to why I'd suddenly left her moments before.

"You aren't safe," I told her. "Not as long as he can track you through me."

Her eyes darkened as she looked me up and down. "What are you asking?"

I reached forward to reassure her with a touch on the shoulders. I bit my tongue, careful not to say too much in case Bastian was tuned in. I pulled out the paper I'd used earlier and resorted to writing again, when Serena placed a hand over mine to stop me.

"I know what you want." she said. "And I agree it's the safest way."

A bit taken aback, I didn't question how she knew. I focused on keeping my thoughts bland and locked down, still paranoid of Bastian's unrestricted access to them. It was everything I could do to help keep the girls from being lured into a trap. Bastian might've wanted us to believe he was patiently waiting for Katrina to waltz in ready to make a trade for her mom, but I didn't trust him to do even that fairly.

I was surprised to see the look on her face—almost beaming with excitement as she looked out at the starry sky over the sea. "We'll travel my favorite way. You boys can have the boat." She grinned.

I hadn't quite thought of *how* we were going to travel separately in my frantic rush, but now that my thoughts were settling, I thought I might have an idea, and I didn't necessarily like it.

As if perfectly timed, Katrina emerged from the cabin, wiping sleep from her eyes. She hurried to us. "What's going on?" She asked through a yawn.

Serena looked at her with a sly smile and led her away to the boat's edge, I assumed explaining the plan to her. Judging by Katrina's startled expression, I think I assumed correctly.

Milo joined us up on deck, taking up a spot next to me. "How exactly do we do this?" he asked. "I'd be lying if I said I didn't feel a bit uneasy about this."

"Same, mate." I crossed my arms. "But only two of the four of us need a boat to travel through water. So what do you think?"

"I get it. But this is exactly what I meant earlier. If I've learned one thing, it's that we have to trust them, even when it feels like we're the only ones who can protect them...because usually trusting them is *how* we protect them."

I chewed on his words for a moment, despite the funny feeling rising in my stomach. Separating from Serena was the last thing I wanted, but if it kept her safe, I'd do whatever I had to.

"Alright, boys," A grin spread across Serena's face as she and Katrina both turned to face us. "We'll see you there." Then she dove overboard.

Katrina turned to Milo and with a long kiss and embrace, assured him she'd be alright. "I'll always find you, remember? This won't be for long."

"Not another two years, I hope," Milo teased, but there was a heaviness in his voice. He had to be fighting every urge in himself to want to stop this. I didn't blame him.

Katrina climbed over the hull and leapt into the water below. Both Milo and I rushed to look overboard, only to see the two girls fully transformed as sirens, glistening tails splashing up and down in and out of the water. I stood in awe, looking at Serena in her breathtaking siren form. It was unlike Katrina's, which sparkled simple bluish silver with a single fluke. Serena's tail was longer, grander, and the scales reflected every possible color of the spectrum, with dorsal fins and long, trailing caudal fins that danced like a cascade of ribbons among the waves surrounding her double flukes. It was truly a tail fit for a goddess.

"Be careful," I uttered. "If you need us to slow down, let us know."

"Don't worry," she smirked. "It's you who might have a hard time keeping up with us."

With that, she dove beneath the water. Katrina offered one last glance back at us before doing the same.

40

When Stars Speak

Katrina

"I've never swam this far before. What if I get tired?" I asked, flicking my tail to keep up with Serena in the water. I'd never spoken underwater before, but it was somehow possible here with her. Our voices carried through the water as clearly as on land.

"That just tells me you've never truly tested out your abilities. You won't tire that easily." Serena looked back at me with a twinkle in her eyes.

With a surge forward, I caught up to her with ease, determined not to look weak as I swam by her side. "Well I haven't exactly been a mermaid for all that long."

Not that you knew, at least. She smiled, speaking to me through my mind. *You've always been one. It's who you are.*

I felt a weight close in around my chest, and not just from the surprise of Serena's voice in my head. The idea of being a siren my whole life sat with me like a sack of bricks. I wondered what my life might've been like if my mother and I hadn't been cursed with this nature. And then the thought that had come up once before came rising to the surface once more—the thought that I would just continue to pass on this twisted legacy if I were to ever continue this bloodline. The thought that I could never have a normal life.

Serena... I stuttered out her name, finding it strangely natural to communicate my thoughts to her. This inner voice connection felt as easy as speaking. But knowing it was just another extension of my siren nature made me uncomfortable. *Is there any way for me to gain a soul? Or my mom? Can she?*

The mischievous look she wore faded at my question. I was startled when she answered me using her voice. "No siren has ever asked me that. Why would you want one of those over the long life you have?"

"Because," I paused, watching our mythical-shaped shadows along the sand below as we passed over a shallow part of the ocean. "Because what good is a long life if none of the people you care about can share it with you? Or if half of you wants to kill them. Being half siren is harder than being a full siren. Because my two halves hate each other. I don't like it. And I don't want to end up as just seafoam. I want to be...more. In this life and the next."

Serena shook her head just a touch, her eyebrows furrowing as she listened to my words. "You're the last living mermaid, Katrina. You and your mother. How could you wish to give that up?"

I sighed. "This power, these abilities. None of this means anything to me. I never asked for any of it. If anything, it's made my life harder. I'm always fighting two sides of myself." My words came out more bitterly than I intended. But I couldn't help it. This burden was something I silently bore each day, and it felt freeing to finally hear myself admit out loud that I didn't want it. Though I could tell my siren side didn't quite feel the same. Of course she didn't. She wanted me to shut up.

"I didn't ask for my fate either," Serena said sternly, still swimming shoulder to shoulder with me. "But destiny doesn't often let us choose."

I opened myself to the freeing sensation of the water around me. Taking in the silky feel of the current, the bubbles from our movements, and the waves rolling above. There was something magical and haunting about knowing I was the last of my kind, swimming this vast ocean like a solitary needle in a very large haystack. And I couldn't quite tell which side of me was in charge. Like saltwater mixed with freshwater, my personas could never truly be separated now that they'd merged.

I finally spoke again, still working to keep up alongside the goddess. "But you want your power, don't you?"

Serena slowed her pace, and looked over at me with a tilt of her head. "I do. It is who I was meant to be. Without it...well, you saw what had become of me."

I paused, wondering what would be next on this journey. I thought more about what Serena said about fate not letting us choose. It reminded me of something Milo had said when he stayed with me through the night for the first time.

Fate has decided against us...

But how wrong he turned out to be. We were able to overcome the boundaries of time to be together. So if we could do *that*, maybe that wasn't the only destiny we could change.

"Then why do you fight against it so much when Bellamy wants to get the Crown for you? Why do you hide from your power if you think you were meant to have it?"

Serena refused to look at me, and for a moment, I thought she wouldn't answer me either. But then she muttered something more subtle than a sea breeze. "Because his destiny is not mine. My loss of power is not his burden. That's all I will say."

"You have to get it back," I said, thinking of how she was my only hope of saving my mom. "Even if fate or destiny or whatever you call it says things have to be one way, sometimes it can be changed."

Serena's eyes softened as she gave me a sideways glance. "You're not wrong, little mermaid. But sometimes you do need a little help from the stars. They're what guided you and Milo to each other. When the stars speak, destiny must listen. You must have a star speaking on your behalf."

I had a hunch which star it might be. As I thought of whatever celestial powers might lie above, I watched in awe at the ones beneath me. We were in shallow waters, and the light reflected along the coral reefs peeking up from below, shimmering their curtain of ripples in between the rainbow of colors beneath. Plants, corals, and animals of every shape and movement, wriggling, darting, and drifting through the water with the ease of a bird in flight. Life down here was peaceful, and certainly something magical, but it wasn't the life I wanted. Not at the price it demanded.

I wondered what came next. What would await us once we got back to Bastian? And what kind of bargaining tool would he use my mother for? It was as if the cold water around me could suddenly pierce my skin as the thought settled. We'd have to rescue my mother, at whatever cost. I'd do what I had to save her. Even if it meant returning to the darkest part of me like I had to do to defeat Cordelia. Whatever it took, I'd do it. I'd get my mom back.

41

Calamari

Bellamy

I glared at the sea, forcing down the worry raging in my chest as I thought about Katrina and Serena out there alone. I knew it was for the best, but still it tortured me. To keep my mind distracted, I pushed away from the side of the ship, turning around to find Milo standing behind me adjusting some rigging.

"They'll be all right. Keep your shirt on," he said.

"Aye." I let out a huff of breath. "I know they could kill us both if they wanted to. And honestly, not sure how I feel about that either, but it's just hard to let them go when you just got them back."

Milo wiped his brow with the back of his arm. "This is how we keep them safe. So let's put our heads down and get this crown for your lass."

I crossed my arms with a chuckle. "Well look who declared himself captain," I pretended to salute. "Want me to swab the deck as well?"

"Don't get like that." Milo smirked. "I thought we settled this back on the *Siren*, remember?"

"Oh, you still haven't let that go, have you?" I spat with a roll of my eyes.

"What? Thought I'd forget when I bested you at the Captain's Duel? Not a chance," Milo bared a row of white teeth with a raised eyebrow.

"Right, because it was the only time it ever happened."

"Because you were too scared to face me again." The half-laugh Milo did stirred up memories I didn't even realize I still had. I'd almost forgotten just how damn cocky he could be. Suddenly I felt like I was talking to the Milo I grew up alongside, the naïve merchant's son who found his footing as a pirate way too quickly for his own good. The one who looked up to me when my father was too harsh on him—which was often. Sometimes I wished some of that goodie-goodie charm had rubbed off on me instead of the other way around, but there was no room for that kind of golden-heartedness aboard my father's ship. I made sure that tender-hearted boy quickly learned that.

"Well, here we are, the two of us sailing the seas without a captain. What do you say we settle who we're sailing under here and now? Who'll be Captain of the..." I paused. I didn't even know if this shoddy splintering toothpick beneath us had a name. I sauntered over to the side to see if she did. Sure enough, painted in some fading lettering chipping through the cracks in the wood, the word "*Calamari*."

"The *Calamari*."

"Ah, just what every pirate dreams. To be hailed as the feared captain of *The Calamari*." Milo swung around the ropes, a mocking smile stretched wide across his face.

"A captain's a captain." I shrugged. "If you forfeit the title, that leaves it to me, I suppose."

"Not a chance." Milo's eyes narrowed. "Letting you call the shots has never worked out quite too well."

"So then let's prove it. Remember I taught you everything you know." I remarked with a lewd gesture of my hand.

Milo paused and disappeared for a moment into the cabin. He emerged with two swords, the ones he'd been wearing when he came through the Fountain of Youth. I opened a hand and reached forward, gesturing for Milo to toss me one of the swords.

"Not everything," Milo slung a sword my way. The hilt hit my hand like some kind of magic reuniting with its rightful owner. Before I could even adjust my grip, Milo swung at me full force, meeting my defense with a burst of sparks and steel.

Suddenly I was back on the deck of the *Siren's Scorn*, wielding my blade against a young buccaneer far too eager to earn the mark of a skilled swordsman.

We'd just come off of a battle with a warship, not a week after my father had forced the merchant boy aboard. I'd mostly made it a point to avoid him, knowing any kind of compassion I showed him would be frowned upon and possibly even punished. It didn't matter that I was his son. My father wouldn't spare me the scourge of the sea—not even for his own flesh and blood. I'd learned that the hard way long before this kid's age. I could still feel every sting of the whip, every deep dig into my skin as the gnarled leather tore across my back, at my father's hand no less. Or the pangs of hunger and burn of parched lips as the blinding sun beat down on me for days shackled to the mast. So when I looked at that broken boy's eyes and saw the cold hopelessness there, I had to force myself to look away, pretending it didn't bother me. He'd toughen up in time, as I had.

But I couldn't ignore him when he found me after a cannon swap and raid—an event during which he usually hid belowdecks. It was still raining lightly, washing fresh blood across the deck. I watched the red water run between my boots and was startled by a blade thrown down at my feet.

"Can you teach me to fight the way you all do?" A voice shuddered. The boy came stepping up, across the bloody mess on the floor, wringing and picking at his hands, face unsure. I might've almost guessed he'd rehearsed this.

"You mean all that time spent sailing with your father and he never taught you to swing a sword?" I spoke down to him, holding my ground so as not to soften.

He shifted nervously from one foot to the other. "I...he taught me some. But mostly to navigate. He wanted me in charge of charts and maps."

"Funny," I chewed on the inner part of my cheek. "You'd think any good merchant worth his salt would want to make sure his son was adequately equipped to deal with dangers out on the sea like...oh, I don't know...pirates." I flashed a wicked grin his way. He was barely fifteen, but he wasn't too much shorter than me. He was fit, but not as strong as he could be. He'd make a good swordsman if he really wanted to learn.

I glanced around at the ship, where the crew had already begun dumping the enemy bodies overboard, cleaning out the bloody crevices of the deck, and rolling the cannons back into place for storage. It was hardly a scene where anyone would notice a little extra chaos thrown in. The unmanned helm in particular caught my eye as my line of sight followed a sailor passing by. I smirked with an idea. If this boy wanted to learn to fight like a pirate, I'd be more than happy to teach him.

"Allright...Milo, is it?" I picked up the cutlass he'd dropped at my feet, running my forefinger and thumb along the blade as I inspected it. "Surely you know a small thing or two. I refuse to believe you're as incompetent as you look. Show me what you know."

I threw the cutlass back to him, and he caught it with a look of surprise. Before he could say anything, I drew my own sword and swung high, near his head. I laughed with surprise when he blocked my blade—sloppily as hell—but better than I expected.

"I see there may be something to work with after all." I grumbled beneath my mocking grin. "Fix your footwork, lad. Like this," I gestured, repeating the move with more force and precision, giving him only a second to observe my correction.

"Like what? That was too fast," he whined. "I couldn't—"

"When you cross your enemy, they're not going to wait for you to figure it out. And neither am I." I swung again, the tip of my sword cutting closer to the stomach this time. I yanked it back, barely tapping the edge of his shirt.

"I'd have killed you just now, lad" I tipped my head with a gesture. Ignoring the pinched expression pressed on his face, I handed him the sword, and told him to go practice on the other side of the deck.He tried to protest, but I shut him up quick with another nudge of my sword and a few more choice words. "Get over there and practice. Now." I demanded, pointing to the open area near the stern.

Little did he know of the fun I had in store for him. When he finally accepted defeat, he moved to go that direction. Just as he passed by a certain section of the ship, I quickly hurried to the helm and gave the wheel a good spin, tilting the ship. The wind tugged on a sail on one of the lower masts and sent the boom whirling around, dropping just above the deck floor—enough to swing down and cut off Milo right where he walked and scoop him up like a limp doll.

I roared with laughter as the boom pole swung to the outside, dangling the boy over the water as he clung to the pole with desperate pleas. A couple of crewmen passing on the deck nudged me as they passed, commending me on the prank as they chuckled. Proudly I watched my helpless mentee struggle as I left him there to dangle just a few moments more.

"You're a pirate now, lad. Always expect what you wouldn't expect." I crooned.

"I'm no pirate." He hissed.

I turned the wheel once more and sent him flying back around on the boom. He dropped to the deck floor immediately as it swung around. My shadow loomed over him as I stepped over to where he fumbled to get to his feet.

"Deny it all you want," I said, "but you're a pirate now, and you'll never change that."

I turned away, leaving him there on the deck floor. Little did I know, the next time I tried to teach that kid to fight, he'd prove himself an opponent more skilled and gritty than I could have imagined. And one day years from now he'd beat me at my father's favorite swordsmanship challenge as my father sat back and watched. And he'd do it again on the shores of St. Augustine, fighting over a necklace and the girl who wore it.

Back on the *Calamari*, the tiny sailboat dipped side to side as we dueled. I no longer noticed the cool air on my skin as sweat beaded on my forehead. Milo was efficient with a blade, and a hell of a lot faster than I remembered, but I definitely had the upper hand on footwork and maneuvering. My blade met his as he taunted me through a boyish grin.

"I'd say this is hardly fair," I spat. "You've had much more practice recently than I have."

"Is that a problem?" Milo joked. "I'm older, too. We're almost the same age now. Makes it a fair fight." He jabbed his sword at me, and I parried it with ease, backing up just enough to dodge the hit, then I leapt forward and to the side.

"No pirate fights fair. And you're somehow good at finding loopholes in reality." I whipped my sword across his knee, with just enough contact to tear through the fabric of his pants. "But it makes no difference here."

Milo looked up at me through a disheveled mess of hair. "I don't need loopholes to beat you."

Hopping up on the hull, I swung around the ropes attached to the sails to take another swing. Milo pulled on the rigging, climbing it to reach me as our blades clashed. At this point, our fight was a game of chase, and I had to hold back a laugh a couple of times at the absurdity of it. Milo grazed my shoulder with the edge of his sword, ripping through my shirt.

"I'll be taking that title of captain now," he grinned.

I glanced at my shoulder in absolute surprise. "Over that? Bloody hell, that wasn't enough to even disarm me! What about when I could've taken out your knee?"

"A shoulder blow is more detrimental." He argued.

I tilted my jaw and pressed my eyebrows together. "In what world? I could've crippled you!" As I stood there, I noticed the loose grip Milo held on his sword, and I took full advantage of the moment to whip my sword at it, knocking it from his hand and into the ocean with a plop.

"Looks like you're the first mate, *mate*." I smirked, watching his shocked expression as he looked overboard.

"That doesn't count." Milo grumbled.

"Like I said, no pirate fights fair." I crossed my arms with a wink.

Milo rolled his eyes and shrugged. "Fine. Take your prized ship. If it makes you feel better."

With a laugh, I turned away, stopped only by Milo adding one more jab. "My ship would've easily outrun yours back in the day. Just know that."

I didn't immediately answer, but stepped up to the helm of the sailboat. "We'll never really know, will we, mate? But for now, I'm the only one here with a ship. Even if it is shite." I looked out at the horizon. "Now go make yourself useful on deck."

With one last drop of his shoulders, Milo sauntered away to do whatever he planned next, playfully muttering under his breath as the sun above gleamed down on us both. "Whatever you say, 'Captain' Calamari."

With my hand on the wheel and full sail ahead, I turned my back to Milo and the sun above. And for a moment I forgot the dark troubles that awaited us and the piercing anxiety I felt about returning to Bastian. And I smiled.

42

Sailing Through Fog

Katrina

Serena and I arrived at the coasts of Puerto Rico before Bellamy and Milo, so we waited on the rocks by the shore, staying hidden until it was time to go after Bastian. I stared, my mind heavy trying to figure out exactly how I was going to get my mom away from him and keep everyone safe. I really wasn't so sure there was a way to do both.

"Think of this paradise. Spending all day basking in the Caribbean sun on the rocks. How can you be ungrateful for this?" Serena asked, breaking my concentration as she dipped her tail in the crystal waters and splashed.

I leaned back on my hands, stretching out to feel the warmth of the sunshine. "I'm not ungrateful," I sighed. "I'll admit this is one of the better perks of being a mermaid. But the ratio of battling sea monsters or facing certain death to basking on rocks so far is like 100:1."

Serena chuckled. I suddenly remembered Russell and Mrs. Gutierrez describing her and the way she laughed. I wondered if she at all missed them.

"What would you say to Russell if you could see him again?" I asked. Serena paused, her laugh quickly fading, and her brown eyes fell on me, fixated.

"I'd thank him," she said, looking away and back out at the coastline of San Juan. "And I'd reassure him that the things that happened to me were never his fault. It was just meant to be." She drew in a breath and slouched. "I hope he's found some happiness."

"Maybe you'll have the chance to tell him that yourself," I said softly, watching the horizon for any sign of Milo and Bellamy.

Serena only hummed a soft sound and nodded in response. After a moment, she turned to me. "What about your mother? How do you plan to get her back without trading my life in exchange for hers?"

The question caught me off guard. I wasn't one-hundred percent sure how I was going to go about that, but I didn't want to say that out loud. So I said the only thing I could say. The only real hope I had. "We get your crown back. With your power, you can free her, right?"

"I can. A goddess' power is greater than that of Davy Jones." Serena leaned forward, elbows in her scaled lap, propping herself up with her hands. "But remember, I can't face him without it. Without my power, he can kill me. And that's what he wants."

"Then we'll have to face him for you. Somehow." I watched the water bubbling as it crashed against the rocks on which we sat. Guilt bubbled in me much the same way, because my siren side was adamant that I use Serena as a bargaining piece . Take down the goddess and get my mom back all in one move. And though my human side fought hard against that idea, there was a small part that was just desperate enough to be tempted to make the trade. I knew it wasn't the real me who had those thoughts, but I felt remorse for not having the will to even fight them harder.

To my surprise, Serena reached over and took my hand. She didn't say anything for a moment, but just sat with me in silence. Though she looked and seemed similar in age, she had some mature, motherly air about her. This was one of those moments in which I felt nurtured by her ancient nature.

"All will be made right," she said. "But not without sacrifice."

Her words sent a chill down my spine. Did she mean one of us would die? I asked her to explain what she meant, but she simply shook her head. "I can't tell you everything. I don't even know what exactly is to come. But I know that this won't be easy, and I sense that something must be given to gain what was lost. Rarely do these things come without a cost."

"Is that why you didn't want to come here?" I asked.

She offered a slight move of her head, barely slight enough to be considered a nod.

My shoulders dropped like the sun beyond the line where the sun and sky met. I was no stranger to sacrifice. "Seems to be a recurring theme."

Serena huffed out a laugh tinged with sarcasm. She seemed like she was about to say more, but just then, she paused, her eyes narrowing as she focused on the horizon.

"They'll be here soon." She uttered. I didn't ask how she knew that, but I certainly believed her.

I wished I had my cell phone to call McKenzie and ask her what happened and how Bastian had even found my mom in the first place, but part of me thought it might be for the better. I still didn't know exactly what happened to my friends or where they were, and it was eating at me in the back of my mind. I had to find them.

"How soon?" I asked.

"Maybe another hour or two."

I closed my fist. "Then I'm going ashore to see if McKenzie and Noah are still all right. If they know what's going on, too, it can only help. We need all the manpower we can get."

I expected Serena to protest and argue with me, but she stayed perfectly silent, a strange look in her eye that suddenly made me feel judged and just plain stupid for suggesting such a thing. "I'll be back in just a bit. I promise."

I slipped down into the water, my focus on the city coast. "You don't happen to have enough power left to make me some clothes, do you?" I asked, looking up at Serena who still sat elegantly on the rocks. I'd gotten used to being naked every time I transformed from mermaid to human, but it would surely create some issues for me if I tried to walk ashore in the nude.

"I'm afraid not," she laughed with a shake of her head.

I groaned and dipped deeper into the water, assuming clothes were one more thing I'd figure out along the way. My tail propelled me to the shoreline, leaving Serena behind. I waited below, lurking by the beaches, looking for an opportunity to snag some clothing.

The thought of using my siren powers for something so trivial stirred up waves of guilt in my conscience. I'd really compromised everything I swore not to be on this journey so far. But then again, hiding naked in the coves of Puerto Rico while your mom was kidnapped by some lunatic was hardly a trivial matter. I *really* needed clothes. Maybe this wasn't such a trivial situation after all.

A young couple playing in a private area caught my eye, soaked in their bathing suits stealing kisses by the palm trees—next to beach chairs and a bag lying close to them that looked like it contained their clothing.

The girl was close enough to my size and build that I felt whatever outfit was in that bag would be more than adequate. Careful not to let them spot me, I swam close, singing my song as my scales lit up and their eyes fogged over. They waited for their commands, entranced by my tune. My siren side elicited a smile from me, pleased at my growing strength. This was the first time I'd controlled multiple people at once. And I liked the way it felt.

I guided the girl to the bag, where she dug in, pulling out a pair of jean shorts, some underwear, and a one-shoulder loose shirt. Under my command, she marched to the shore and tossed them in, where I waited to pull them under with me. I snatched the clothes, then dove under as I released them from my spell. Swimming fast, I returned to the old city area, where I pulled myself up on the crags of coastline dotting the city's border. With a mental pulse of power in my mind, I willed the water on my lower half to dry up, and in milliseconds, I had slender, tan legs again. Then I dried the clothes by draining out their water, casting it out and back to the sea.

Getting dressed frantically in the shadows, I rushed to the hotel where I'd left my friends and mom days ago, but something told me they weren't going to be there. But I had to start somewhere. I ran to their room, knocking on the door furiously only to be met with silence. And I didn't have a key card to enter. I rushed back down to the lobby and asked the receptionist if she'd seen or heard from them.

"Actually," she said, sorting through some papers in front of her on the desk. "They did tell me to leave you a message if you came. Here." She handed me a folded up note, and with my heart pounding in my ears, I unfolded it to read.

> *Katrina, He found us. He knew about your mom. About everything. If you read this, we're probably outside the club trying to figure out what to do and watching for any sign of your mom. I'm so sorry.*

Without another word to the receptionist, I darted out of the building, rushing through the cobblestone streets back to Bastian's club. It was just starting to open, given the time of day, and I rushed inside, pushing past the bouncers that I enchanted with my song to let me pass.

Once inside, I found no sign of McKenzie or Noah, so I rushed back through to the secret passageway leading to Bastian's lair. But when I got there, it was empty. Even Bastian's massive collection wasn't there. My mom was gone. And so were my friends. The only thing that remained was the desk and the shattered jar from the heart I'd broken before. I rummaged through the desk, looking for a clue. For anything. But I only came up empty handed.

"No!" I groaned, my voice echoing through the empty chamber. I searched frantically for another way out, different from how I came in. There had to be some kind of passageway. How else could all these things be moved so easily in such a short time? How else could he transport my mom—a mermaid in a tank—to wherever he was hiding? And where the hell were McKenzie and Noah?

I started to turn around, but just then I heard footsteps coming from a dark corner I hadn't noticed before. It was behind a now empty display case, shoved to the side, well designed to stay inconspicuous no matter what angle someone stood in the room. Faint voices followed the steps, getting closer.

I ducked behind the desk, shaking. As I braced myself to encounter God knows what or who, I saw shadows nearing, and I peeked out to be absolutely relieved beyond belief when McKenzie emerged from the passageway. I stood up, and she rushed to me with arms wide open.

"Oh my god, I'm so glad to see you!" She cried, squeezing me tight. I wrapped my arms around her in response. "I'm so so sorry about your mom! We tried to stop him! And we tried to stop her from making his deal, but she wouldn't listen!"

"No, no, it's not your fault," I said, "I'm so glad you're okay! You shouldn't be down here, especially alone." I tried to keep my voice low, just in case we had company I didn't know about.

She released me from her embrace, pulling back to look over her shoulder. "I'm not alone." Noah appeared to her right and behind him trailed someone I would never have expected to see here of all places. The extra figure's eyes focused on mine and his withered hands were tucked firmly in his pockets, as usual. I was too stunned to speak, but I finally found the ability to utter one question as he and Noah stepped into the main room with us.

"Is that...Russell?" I stammered.

Noah's eyes hardened as he looked dead on into mine. "I didn't know who else to call. He's the only one besides us who knows about this world."

Russell hobbled forward. It was strange to see him in anything but his maintenance uniform from the school. But here he was in a sturdy pair of denims and loose button down work-shirt.

"Noah said you all needed help. I took the first flight to San Juan. I'm not sure what I can do, but I figure an old fisherman who believes in ghost stories is still an extra pair of hands."

I stood, unsure of what to say. Ultimately, I decided he wasn't wrong. The more bodies, the better, for rescuing my mom. But I had no idea what to tell him first. And what would he say when he saw Serena? How would he take it? It didn't matter, I decided. For now I didn't have to explain all that. I just needed to make sure we were ready to face Bastian Drake.

43

Decoy

Katrina

"I worried when you didn't come back this semester," Russell said, his old familiar voice bringing some strange sense of security.

"I had to save someone I love," I uttered.

A knowing twinkle appeared in Russell's eye. "I would do the same."

"Well now you might just have the chance," I said, yearning to tell him that his daughter he thought dead was just a few miles away sitting on the beach. But at the same time, I realized it was more important than ever to see that we won back Serena's crown. I couldn't bear to think of Russell having to relive losing her again if we failed. Which we wouldn't.

"What do you mean?" Russell tilted his head.

"I mean..." I couldn't get the words out. It just didn't feel right to tell him yet. Not here. It was too much at once. "I mean we need your help, but I don't want you to get hurt."

"Noah explained everything to me already. I'm not afraid of something happening to me. Not if it means helping you get your mother back."

I couldn't believe this was the same man who hysterically warned me to stay away from the pirates at all costs. Now here he was, ready to face a man marked by Davy Jones.

"I begged Noah to come home. But he wouldn't listen to me, not for nothing. So if he wasn't going to leave, I had to come to him. It's all I can do to keep him safe." Russell spoke as if he could read my thoughts. He looked at Noah, who offered him a subtle scowl.

"Well, I'm glad you're here either way," I said with my best attempt at a reassuring smile. "But I don't want to put anyone in harm's way. We can't just show up and attack Bastian when we find him. We've got to come up with a plan. Bastian will only let my mom go if we trade the sea goddess for her."

"You found her, too?" McKenzie beamed with wonder in her eyes.

"Yes, but we can't trade her. She's not strong enough to defeat Bastian without the Crown." My gaze bounced between Noah and McKenzie and then down the dark walkway that loomed behind them. "Where does this lead?"

McKenzie took a breath. "We followed it until we found where Bastian went...Don't worry, he didn't see us. We've been mapping out this tunnel system for the past couple of days. But the place he went...it looked like the inside of some old castle or something."

"Right, but it's easy to get lost in there. There are so many passages going in all sorts of directions. Not sure if it was an old irrigation system or a secret part of the fort. But it's a labyrinth." Noah looked around the corridor as if checking once more just to be sure. "I'd highly recommend a compass." He smirked, pulling out Milo's compass and displaying the face so that we could see the needle clearly pointing North.

"So where did Bastian go? Where does it lead?" I asked.

"All the tunnels we tracked were dead ends to the ocean. Except this one." McKenzie pulled up a map of San Juan on her phone, zooming in to show our location and followed the north path upward to a landmark directly above—a section of the old fort that jutted out from a corner into the edge of the ocean.

"Garita del Diablo," I uttered, focusing on the map. I recognized the little stone section that I'd heard legend of thanks to my dad and his Caribbean folklore that he'd randomly share with me as a kid. It was known for the mysterious disappearance of a guard posted there ages ago and other spooky occurrences. Noah and McKenzie watched me as if waiting for me to continue. "The Devil's Watchtower," I explained. "It's closed off to the public."

"Which would make it the perfect cover for another underground hideout," Noah crossed his arms.

I nodded, the significance of how this could help us slowly settling in. With the other tunnels leading out to the ocean, they could've been just what we needed. Bellamy and Milo could enter through those while we used the main tunnel, still allowing us to keep Bastian blind to our moves. But how I would communicate that to the boys was another challenge of its own.

"I have to let Bellamy and Milo know." I clenched a fist.

"You got Milo back?" Noah asked, the concern in his voice obvious despite his attempt to conceal it.

With a nod, I went on, careful to recount details as I remembered them. "He's back. But Bastian knows where Bellamy is at all times. And Milo is with him. He's tracking them to find S—," I cut myself off, looking at Russell before I accidentally let Serena's name slip from my lips. "He's tracking them to find the goddess, which is why I had to come here on my own."

Russell, McKenzie, and Noah all exchanged worried looks before Russell spoke. "Sounds like we're going to need to come up with a plan."

"Don't worry about it, grandpa, we've got this figured out," Noah held up a hand and shook his hand.

"Hey, you called me, remember?" Russell snapped. The tension between them was unbearable, and their backhanded bickering was the last thing I needed. "All I'm saying is, from what it sounds like, this guy is not one to be taking chances with, so you better make sure the one chance you got is as foolproof as possible."

"He's right," I said, earning a sour stare from Noah. "Bastian more than likely knows Bellamy and Milo are on their way here. But he doesn't know that I'm here with..." my words caught in my throat, and I looked away from Russell before finishing. "...with the goddess. Someone who needs to get the Crown back just as much as we do. If Bellamy and Milo serve as enough of a distraction, maybe it can buy us some time to figure out where he's keeping the Crown."

"And then what? Isn't this guy like indestructible?" Noah slapped his arms by his sides.

"Not if we get that crown. And that's what I'm thinking...We go in pretending to make the trade and get my mom, but we draw it out long enough to see if a few of us can find the Crown and get it to the goddess. Then hopefully Bellamy and Milo would arrive to stave off Bastian while we get the Crown and run."

McKenzie nodded the entire time I spoke, her orange waves bouncing like silk around her shoulders. "That sounds way easier said than done. And if the goddess is the one we trade, how do we get the Crown to her?"

I looked at her closely, an idea forming in my head as all three of them hung on my every word. "What if we create a decoy? Let him think we're agreeing to his deal...but really the goddess would be with us the whole time."

"So like a stand-in for the goddess?" Noah leaned forward, his impatience obvious by the tight jaw he clenched. My eyes swept over him and McKenzie and then fell on Russell. I wanted to say it. I knew I'd have to sooner or later. But I couldn't say her name just yet. All in good time. "Does Bastian know what she looks like?"

"I'm pretty sure he does." I cringed, thinking of the clear physical differences between Serena and me. "But maybe we could use a veil or something. Just long enough to get him to let my mom go. What if I pretend to be her? We can make a disguise, and you all can escort me to Bastian's lair to trade me for my mom and get the Crown."

"He'll find that too suspicious," Noah chimed in. "If you're the one he wants to make the deal with, he's going to expect you to be the one to offer her."

I nodded, biting my lower lip as my thoughts raced and rearranged. I began to worry about leaving Serena unprotected back on the coast and felt the growing need to get back to her rising in my chest. My nerves felt shaky, and my stomach turned at the thought of the plan failing. McKenzie's voice ripped me out of my own head and away from my inner panic.

"I'll do it," she said firmly. "I'll be the decoy."

I blinked, as we all watched her with growing intensity. "No, McKenzie," I voiced my protest with a jolt. "Absolutely not. I'm not putting you in that position."

"I know you're not." Her back straightened and she made a point to address all three of us. "I'm putting myself there. We don't stand a chance if we hand over the only one of us who has magical powers."

The chamber filled with a silence greater than I could stand. Finally, Russell intervened. "How about we take this conversation elsewhere? Probably not the wisest to discuss our plans here."

"You're right. Good call," I muttered, my eyes not leaving McKenzie.

Back outside, we huddled in the main town plaza in an open seating area, careful to keep our voices low.

"There's no way I'm letting you walk in there and handing you over to that lunatic," I placed my hand on the table firmly, feeling my frustration growing. "If something goes wrong..."

"Then why did I come all this way?" McKenzie shot up, her chair nearly toppling over backwards. "Why did I forfeit this semester at ISA? Just to do nothing? I came to help you, and dammit Katrina, for once just let me do more for once than lend you a dress!"

The table was silent. I'd never seen McKenzie so worked up or determined. But the thought of sending her into Bastian's grasp was something I couldn't come to terms with.

"She's right," crooned Russell. "It'll seem suspicious if we go in there without you. He'll want to see *you* bringing this person he's bargaining for."

I watched him, somewhat shocked that he would suggest it, but realizing either way, someone was going to be offered up to Bastian like a stock animal. I opened my mouth to argue against McKenzie being the bait, but McKenzie stopped me before I could get any words out.

"Don't try to change this, Katrina." Her tone with me had never been more harsh. "I'm doing it, and it's going to be fine."

My jaw quivered as I fought not to say something stupid or rash. All three pairs of eyes pressed their gaze onto me, until I dropped my head and uttered a single syllable, laced with my distaste for the idea. "Fine."

"Glad we settled that," McKenzie's sunburnt face gleamed with pride at her win. "Now what about the goddess? Why didn't she come with you?"

"Because I couldn't risk Bastian seeing her and trying to kill her on sight. We have to keep her out of the way and hidden until we know for sure we have the Crown within reach." I stood up, gesturing for the others to do the same. "So we have to go. Now. She's left unguarded right now and I don't think we should push our luck." For all I knew, Bellamy and Milo were nearly here. And somehow I'd need to communicate this plan to them without alerting Bastian.

The trio followed me to the shore, a decent enough walk from town, made a touch more difficult by the sand and stone we trekked through. When we finally reached the coast where Serena awaited, I stopped, hesitating as I wondered what chaos would break loose once they saw her. But I couldn't keep wondering forever. Mom was waiting.

"Wait here," I told them. "I'm going to let her know what's going on first."

"Fair enough," Noah uttered.

With a nod, I turned and dove into the water, tossing my clothes back up at McKenzie from the water. "Hang on to these for me!" Not waiting for the reply, I took off, gliding through the water with ease back to the rock where I left the goddess.

"Took you long enough," Serena's playful yet calming voice was a welcome reassurance as I emerged from the water. "Are your friends all okay?"

"Yes," I looked up at her as water trickled down my soaked hair and neck. "And we came up with a plan to get into Bastian's lair and get your crown. But we have to warn Bellamy and Milo so they know what we're doing.

"Then tell them," Serena pushed at the air with her hand. I watched her, confused, urging her to continue. "Your Milo has the mark of the sun. It dampens Bastian's hold on him. He won't be able to hear you if you tell him."

"What do you mean *if I tell him*?"

"Your siren call. You and I in the water could communicate through the mind. It's because we are already linked to each other by nature, as all sirens are. And a skilled siren can also do that with those who are linked by her heart."

"So you're saying I can call him with my mind?" I blinked, flitting my tail in curiosity.

Serena nodded. "Yes, how do you think you were able to call him home with your song? You've been doing it all along."

Trying my best not to waste time, I hurried and closed my eyes, focusing on the way I sang to Milo at the Fountain's edge to bring him home. I reached for him once more, my voice swirling in my mind as it rose beyond the corners of myself and transcended into a place neither within me nor on the outside of me. I couldn't hold it for long, so I thought up my message as quickly as possible.

Bastian's hideout is beneath Garita del Diablo. We've come up with a plan to trick Bastian into letting my mom go and then...

...then you all will get the Crown. When his voice broke through to me, I nearly jumped at the sound of him in my head. And then I settled into the sound of him, cherishing the connection between us that superseded all others.

Yes, I'll let you know when we're at Bastian's lair. Maybe if he's distracted enough he won't have time to notice you and Bellamy coming. There is supposedly a system of tunnels leading in from the coast under the fort cliff. I wish I could tell you how to get to the hideout from there, but you'll have to figure it out. Noah says it's a total maze. Don't get lost.

Don't worry, Milo reassured with a chuckle. *Navigation is somewhat of a strong point for me. I'll tell Bellamy to sail in circles to throw the bastard off.*

"I take it by that smile that it worked." Serena's voice snatched me from my inner dialogue with Milo.

"Were you eavesdropping?" I asked with a grin, ducking down into the water so that only my head was out of it.

"Don't worry." Serena splashed some water my way with a flick of her tail. "Even I can't interfere with another siren's song-call."

"Hmm," I smirked. "Good to know." After a long pause, I pulled myself up to meet her on the rocks. "Now, you should know the plan."

I explained everything to her, ensuring to include the part about her potential body double.

"This girl is going to pretend to be me?" she raised an eyebrow.

I eyed her dark skin and thick braided hair. It'd be a lie to say I hadn't also wondered exactly how we would make my red-headed pale roommate look anything like her. "Well, she's going to try. I was hoping we could get creative with it."

Serena sighed, "Lucky for you, there are few limits on how creative magic can be." I didn't understand exactly what she meant, but I didn't feel like I had time to ask. I was just glad to have some form of approval from her for the plan. With Serena's blessing, I led her back to where the others waited. But when we neared the shore, I turned around to stop her.

"There's something you should know." I whirled around in the water, stopping Serena before we got too close. "Remember when you talked about Russell? You're about to see him again, and he's probably not going to know what to do when he sees you."

Serena's features tightened, her perfect lips separating to form the smallest inkling of a gasp. Then after a short moment, her look of surprise turned into a small warm smile as she glanced at the shore ahead. "You're full of surprises, little mermaid. You truly are." She dove forward, swimming past me toward the coast in the distance. She didn't even turn around as she called out, "Now let's hope you can save one for this crooked pirate lord."

44

What Does Water Do?

Katrina

When we came ashore, the look on my friends' faces was exactly as I expected as my goddess friend neared. McKenzie stood mouth agape in awe of Serena's inhuman beauty. Noah narrowed his eyes in scrutiny, and Russell—Russell nearly stumbled backwards as his eyes widened in surprise.

"Dammit, who are you?" He called through a quivering chin. "What kind of trick is this?" He whipped his gaze to me, his voice cracking and eyes watery.

I stayed in the water as Serena rose up to the shoreline. Her tail effortlessly became legs once more, and she stepped out, the water following her like smoke, swirling around her waist and forming a flowing dress with each step. I stayed behind, tucked down in the comfort of the water as I gave this moment to them.

Russell still stood unmoving, nearly quaking as he watched this girl he believed to be his daughter walk towards him from the waves.

"Serena..." he choked. "Serena, sweetheart, is it really you?"

McKenzie and Noah stepped to the side as she passed, making her way right up to the man she'd called father in at least one lifetime. Her skin glistened in the sun as she reached forward to touch his face, a gentle brush of her palm sending Russell into full tears.

"It's me, Dad," she said softly.

Russell didn't waste time with words. Instead. He threw his arms around her, this grisly old man suddenly becoming soft right before my eyes.

"I don't understand, but I don't think I want to. All I care about is that you're here, now. Somehow."

Serena pulled back gently from his embrace. "I was bound to land in human form. Valdez returned me to the sea. This is where I've always belonged."

"So...you're the...the goddess Noah talked about?"

Serena nodded. Noah neared her, blinking in disbelief. "Wait," he stammered. "So this means you're like...my aunt?"

"I suppose it does." Serena laughed with a touch of her hand to his shoulder. "Hello, nephew."

Russell reached forward to take Serena's hand in both of his, his jaw clenched as pure resolve and determination settled on his face. "I may not fully understand what's going on, but I'm here to help you, sweetheart. Whatever it takes to keep from someone taking you from me again."

Something in my gut dropped as guilt gripped me again—how I had dragged so many people into this. And I worried that might mean dragging them beneath the waves with me if things went under. But here they stood, minds already made up and ready to face whatever destiny held next. And all I could do was let them. That, and try my hardest not to let them get killed in the process.

"Let's get this started, shall we? Before I change my mind." Serena's regal voice broke through as she turned from Russell and faced me.

I shot a pleading look at all three of them, my hair covering most of the front of me. "You guys...I have to get dressed."

"Oh, right." McKenzie pulled my clothes from the bag she carried and set them on the ground.

They awkwardly turned their backs to me as I climbed out of the water. My legs returned and I scrambled to put on the clothes. "Okay, I'm good now," I announced.

As they each turned back around to face me, Serena spoke, eyeing McKenzie. "All right, now it's time to set things in motion. We can start with my decoy. Because we have a lot of work to do in that area."

"Yeah," Noah chimed in, "How exactly are we supposed to pull off making her look like you? There's no way in hell."

"Maybe not without my help. But remember Katrina and I control water. And what does water do?"

She was met with a barrage of answers, while I kept silent, trying to think of what she was getting at.

"Umm, flows? Floods? Washes?"

"Drips?"

"Splashes? Drowns?"

"It reflects." Serena gently guided McKenzie to the water's edge, where she positioned her with a few nudges and turns. A crystal clear mirror image of both of them appeared on the water's surface. "Without my power, I can't perform this. It requires delicate mastery of the water. Detail and steadiness like a painter's hand." Serena looked at me. "You'll have to do this, Katrina."

"I'll try it, whatever it is. But how will I know what to do?" I asked, stepping near the water.

"Because you already do it by nature. Now it's just a matter of matching the water to the vision it reflects. And making sure it stays that way."

With a few gestures of her hand, she summoned up a bit of water, and up it streamed, like a grand ribbon twirling and twisting as she willed it. It coiled around her from bottom to top, and then snaked over to McKenzie, where it spread itself out thin like a veil and completely encompassed her body. Mere seconds later, an image began to form on the outside of the water cocoon. Broken glimpses of Serena formed like pieces of a shattered mirror, her reflection taking over whatever faint vision of McKenzie remained. As the water swirled gently, it closed in, attaching itself to McKenzie like a body-conforming shield. And on the outside, she was no longer McKenzie.

But then the façade vanished, the water falling into droplets like someone wrung out a soaked towel. And McKenzie was McKenzie again. "You must do that, and keep it like that." Serena said.

"Okay," I held out my hands, a bit nervous to try this new magic skill. But it couldn't be any more challenging than forming an image out of watercolors.

And it wasn't at all. My hands and mind knew what to do. I pulled the water back up, encompassing McKenzie in it once more as I formed each detail to reflect Serena. After a few slips, I realized half the challenge was positioning each water molecule just right in the light, to keep it reflecting the image I demanded—the image of Serena.

Aside from a small height difference, two identical Serena's stood before us, McKenzie only distinguishable by the slight glimmer of sunlight on water that sometimes rippled across her body.

"What just happened?" McKenzie spun around, attempting to see behind her own back as she craned her neck around. Her voice was the only thing about her unchanged.

"You look like me, now." Serena stepped back and looked her up and down as if admiring her work.

"Just don't talk and we should be good." Noah laughed.

We all stared in absolute amazement as the two Serenas, and I glanced over at the real one. "I can't believe that's possible."

"Just a bit of telling the water what to reflect and dispersing it out in all the right places." Serena winked. "Not so different than painting." I didn't even ask how she knew about that. I assumed as the Mother of Sirens she probably had the scoop on all of us.

I smiled softly. Then my focus shifted as Milo's voice called to me through my thoughts.

We've anchored. And we're scoping out the area. You were right. These tunnels are a mess. Don't face Bastian without us near, if you can. Give us one more hour. We don't want to leave you to do this alone.

Will do. I replied, looking back out at the friends surrounding me, and pulling in a deep breath. By the time we made it back down to the tunnels beneath the club and found Bastian's lair, it would be more than an hour. And saving my mom couldn't wait much longer.

"Okay people..." I said boldly. "It's almost time." Everyone huddled in closer as my heart pounded so loud, I figured they could hear it. "Are we ready to make a deal with the devil?"

45

Crosswinds

Milo

We'd left the boat moored as close as we could to the shore. Now we were climbing along the rocky cliff side of the coast where the old stone fort stood. We scaled the sides, looking in each crevice in the rocks for any sign of secret passageway. But nothing stood out as a hidden tunnel system entrance, and the setting sun only made it harder to see.

"Dammit, you gave them an hour. It's been way longer than that now," Bellamy grumbled behind me as we scaled the coastline.

"I couldn't ask her to keep waiting. You know she wouldn't have listened anyway," I snapped. "Calm down. If we don't keep our heads we'll never find this thing."

Bellamy hesitated. "I swear to god if something happens to Serena...I can't believe I let her go on without me. Why the hell did I let her go on without me?"

I whipped around. "If you hadn't, Bastian would've already been here waiting to snatch her up. You're protecting her. Don't forget that."

"If he wanted to kill her, why didn't he take her at the Fountain? I just don't get it." Bellamy scanned the area of the cliff we'd searched ten times over now, looking for this hidden entrance that eluded us.

I truly wondered the same, but the least I could do was to try putting Bellamy at ease about it. Little good wondering about it would do us here and now. "Maybe he can't kill her that easily. Maybe he couldn't truly fight us all at once to get to her. Maybe it's not as simple as we think. Whatever the reason, this is the only chance we have to end him for good."

Bellamy agreed with a grunt, his foot slipping and kicking a loose piece of rocks into the water below. My eyes followed the rocks, and I watched the waves at the foot of the cliff for a moment. I noticed a subtle suction of the water when the waves pulled back, different from the rest around it. "Look there!" I pointed. "The water's getting sucked down somewhere."

"That could be it. I'll check it out." Bellamy didn't hesitate a single second before sliding into the water below.

"Hurry," I said, "We don't have much light left."

He dove under, all of him disappearing beneath the waves except the hand holding onto the rock by the area where the water suctioned. Even though I wasn't the one underwater, I held my breath, eager to see if we'd found the tunnel.

Bellamy shot up, shaking the water from his eyes and hair. "There's definitely a passage there. But once we go in, there's no going back. It's tight. If we run out of air, we're screwed. I don't know if the whole 'mermaid's kiss' rule applies indefinitely."

My thoughts shuffled. "We have to find out somehow."

"I'll go check it out. If I don't come out in five minutes, don't follow me."

"I'm not agreeing to that."

"Of course you won't, golden boy." Bellamy mocked. "But if both of us are dead then who will be there for the girls? Do what I say. I'm the captain, remember?"

"Alright, fine, Calamari." I shook my head.

Bellamy vanished beneath the seawater once more, and I began the count-down. Like hell I wasn't going to go in after him if he didn't resurface. I counted the minutes down to the second, uneasiness rattling my nerves like the waves rattled the loose rocks around my feet. When Bellamy didn't come back up at the four minute mark, I refused to wait any longer. I went in after him.

The water shocked my system as I plunged down, taking a giant gulp of air with me. I found the tunnel entrance rather easily, though it was clearly eroded far from what it was originally meant to be. Claustrophobia gripped at me as I squeezed through, but I bit the inside of my cheek to keep myself calm and focused. This place kept out all light, and the pitch blackness smothered me as much as the flowing water around me.

Of course I didn't see Bellamy. He would've been much farther ahead by now. But the passage was so narrow, I wasn't even sure what ahead could've looked like. I squirmed my way through the small tunnel, jagged rock surfaces scraping against my skin as I wedged between them. The way ahead was dark as night, and the burning feeling rising in my lungs was a constant reminder of my time ticking away. And a reminder that a mermaid's kiss only worked for a little while. And I didn't have any recent refills.

I bumped into something, hoping it was Bellamy, but the feeling of human bone in my hand told me otherwise. With a shudder, I kept squeezing through, unsettled by the nothingness around me and the growing fear that I was going to stumble across Bellamy's lifeless body jammed in between some rocks. But then I felt the rock edges curve upwards. There was no more going backward. I wouldn't be able to make it out in time. My only hope was to follow the path. I crawled up, pulling myself up along the stone walls as they closed in on me further. I just wished I could see an inch in front of me.

My hands ran along the stone, and I felt where the opening curved above me, and there was air. I just had to find the strength to pull myself up. But the water was crashing around me every time a wave crested and filled the space. If I could just wait until the next swell, I could reach up and pull myself over. But as my lungs protested in pain, I didn't think I had quite that long.

I reached up, and a hand clasped over my arm, dragging me up just enough to get me out of the water and into the tiny crawl space higher than the rest. My feet scrambled as much as they could to boost me up the rest of the way where I caught glimpse of Bellamy pulling me up. My neck and shoulders scraped the top of a stone ceiling as I worked my way through the cramped nook. I breathed out my relief with a handful of coughs mixed in.

With just a bit more wiggling, I worked myself out the other side, where the tiny space dropped off into a full size tunnel, plenty tall and wide enough for standing. Bellamy stood with his arms crossed. "I told you not to follow me."

"After all this time I thought you'd know me better than that," I flashed a half-grin, pushing back my wet hair out of my eyes. The space was lit by a torch in Bellamy's hand, casting our shadows along the tunnel walls.

"Well now I've saved both you and your lass from drowning at some point or another. So you owe me." Bellamy turned around, shining the torch light down the black abyss of a path.

"How about I'll make it up to you by getting us out of here," I said, stepping forward, compass in hand. "Because God knows you're not going to be the one to do it."

"Would you shut up?" Bellamy groaned as I took up stride beside him. "Let's hurry before Katrina and Serena walk right into Bastian's hands."

"Don't worry," I said. "They know what they're doing." I did my best to put him at ease, knowing it frustrated him to not be able to know the girls' plan. We'd both agreed that it was for the best that I didn't share it with him in case Bastian was listening. But I knew that didn't make it any easier for him.

"I'll get us there." I looked ahead, merging the map in my head of the watchtower's location from the outside and the direction of the compass needle. "It won't be quick, but I'll get us there."

We stepped forward into the darkness, our path barely illuminated by the glow of Bellamy's torch. Of course I'd never tell him, but I was aching to find Bastian and the worry was beginning to set in. Even if Bastian fell for the girls' plan, I didn't imagine it would take him long to realize it. I knew we didn't stand a chance at killing him. But we sure as hell could go down fighting to slow him down. And if that's what it took to get Katrina out alive, it was good enough for me.

46

FALSE GODDESS

KATRINA

We crept forward, sneaking our way back through the tunnels that my friends had already mapped out, using our cell phones for light. I still hadn't gotten used to the fact that we were walking with two versions of Serena, and I tried not to think about it too hard. From down here, the glimmering sheen of water over McKenzie was no longer visible without the sunlight, making them the perfect spitting image of each other.

"McKenzie, when you found the hideout, could you see the Crown?" I asked, running over the plan in my head a million times over and then some.

"No," she sighed. "But he was sitting in a big chair surrounded by all kinds of things, like ocean knickknacks and just weird stuff. He has your mom in a tank behind the chair. The Crown has got to be somewhere in that collection."

"Why does he always have a big chair?" I groaned.

"It's his own personal throne where he can guard his toys," Serena rolled her eyes. "His ego's got to have somewhere to sit."

We neared a section where the tunnel widened, signaling our nearing of Bastian's new hideout. We came upon stone steps that spiraled upward, much like a tall tower of old—a watchtower. Between the watchtower entrance and the corridor we'd just come from, a door stood in plain sight, though it was more of a stone slab.

"This is it," Noah uttered, shoving the stone out of his way with all his might. I tried to look for a quick exit, some way we could leave without subjecting ourselves to being trapped down here. But I knew we wouldn't have that luxury in this winding system of tunnels and stone corridors.

"I'm staying with Serena," Russell said, directing his posture to Noah. "But don't you dare get hurt, Noah. I'm not losing either of you today."

"Give it a rest, grandpa," Noah groaned. "You don't have to keep acting worried about me." I watched the sunken look on Russell's face grow darker, his eyes downcast as his weary spirit. I understood Noah's resentment for the years lost all too well, but it was harder to see this way. Now as an onlooker to someone else's struggle, I saw the bitterness in myself I had to overcome with my own mom, and I hoped Noah could figure out how to do that for Russell.

We left Serena behind with Russell, hoping it'd be enough to keep Bastian blind to her whereabouts while still keeping her close enough to get the Crown to her. I pushed the doorway open, my chest full from a big breath of air I was too afraid to release. We were greeted by a gust of cool air and dim torchlight.

With a massive dome-shaped ceiling, this place really did look like a castle. Cracks in stone streaked like veins through the floors and ceiling. The walls glimmered with an array of items, some likely magic, some not—rare shells, golden statues, rare jewels and tribal masks, body parts in jars. I had to wonder how he'd managed to move all these things from his other hideaway spot in such a short time. Of course, it was likely magic. And in the center of the room, where the dome peaked with a hole through which the moonlight shone, there stood an eerily beautiful stone table with intricate paintings around it, but the images were faded and cracked. A short path of curved stairs led up to it, seeming more for decorative flair than function.

The dim chamber echoed with the taps of our footsteps as we worked around drips of blackened water that left a trail from the door to the front of the room. Bastian was nowhere in sight, but his throne certainly was. It sat empty, its velvet cushion seat nestled in a chair of bronze and gold, a puddle of more dark water pooling in the floor beside it. The Crown was nowhere to be seen, but my mother was.

Imprisoned in her tank, my mom swam to the glass, placing a hand against the glass, her face twisted in fear. I took a step forward to run to her, but the dark water on the floor converged into one mass and blocked my steps. I watched in horror and intrigue as the onyx black water rose up as if it had a life of its own. It grew to my height, then taller, until it towered over me and formed itself into the outline of a human. Bastian. It became Bastian.

"Hello, lovely Katrina," he grinned, the black water still dripping off his face like ink. "I see you did as I asked. Smart girl." His snake-like eyes flicked to McKenzie turned-Serena, who stood near the entrance with Noah. He pretended to hold her arm as though we'd forced her to come here.

"I did. I brought you Atargatis. Now let my mom go," I demanded, my fists balling up without me meaning for them to.

"Patience, little mermaid," he growled in my ear. "I make the rules, remember?"

"And the rule was that you take her and give me my mother. You made the offer. Now I'm taking you up on it."

Bastian let out a low laugh. "I bet dear Bellamy wasn't too thrilled with that decision. I'm guessing that's why you came without him. Poor fellow. He's been stabbed in the back so many times in life, and here you are adding your knife to the tally." He smiled, inky black lining his teeth. "And your beloved sailor. What of him? Did he side with his brother at sea?"

"Don't pretend you don't know where Bellamy is." I said, hoping to keep him distracted as long as possible while I scanned the room.

"Of course I do. If I cared to keep track of pirate scum. But I have no use for his whereabouts without the goddess. And fortunately for him, she's right where I want her." Bastian eyed McKenzie in her Serena form.

I called to Milo. *The Crown isn't anywhere we can see it. We'll have to find it. So when you get here, be careful. But we could certainly use your help. Bastian seems...stranger than before.*

*Of course. We're in the tunnels. *You* be careful.* Milo's voice was my only reassurance in this cold, hopeless place, and I clung to it like a buoy in a storm. My eyes studied the room, desperate for any hint at where the Crown might be, but I couldn't stop looking over at my mom in the tank. I was still grappling with the shock of seeing her with a tail, but then I wondered...since she was a siren, maybe I could communicate with her, too, the way I communicated with Serena underwater.

I called to her, throwing the voice in my head out to her, hoping for her to catch on to my words.

Mom, I'm here. We're going to free you.

I hoped she got the message, but I didn't have time to wait for a response as I stood before an impatient Bastian. "Bring the goddess forward," I motioned to Noah. He followed, hesitating in a way that looked so convincing I couldn't tell if he was truly afraid or just acting.

Noah stepped up beside me, pretending to drag McKenzie along as she put a convincing pull against him on display. They now stood beside me facing Bastian, whose shoes were still oozing in a puddle with the ink-water as it slowly ran down the sides of him.

He reached out to touch McKenzie's arm, but I lunged forward and blocked him.

"Let my mom go first," I demanded once more.

"Very well. After all, it's not like you could escape now." He straightened his shoulders, turned around, and then shattered the tank that held mom with a blast of black water from his hand. Mom flopped to the floor amongst the broken glass, her tail writhing. I ran to her and dropped down at her side.

"Are you okay, Mom?" I worked hard to control my breathing. I couldn't let Bastian sense my fear, especially now that I'd just handed over my roommate and best friend to him.

"I'm not hurt." Mom panted. "Just...just a little in shock. This...what is this? *How* is this?" She touched a trembling hand to her waist where her skin gave way to pearly scales.

"I know," I said. "You'll get used to it. But why did you do this? Why the hell would you do this, Mom?"

Her brown wet hair fell over her face as she leaned forward and hugged herself from the chill. Her chin quivered, distorting her words. "Your whole life I've never done anything to help you. This was me being a better mother. I made him promise he wouldn't harm you in exchange. I did this to help you."

Squeezing my eyes shut was the only way to stall the tears burning behind my sockets. I didn't know what to say. I wanted to be mad at her. And I was, but it would be useless to let her know that. And if things went awry and we didn't make it out of here, the last thing I wanted was for Mom to think I hated her. She'd had enough of that.

Suddenly her voice startled me, because I was looking right at her but her mouth wasn't moving.

Just so you know, I could hear you.

I sat upright, the jolt of her voice rattling me. I hadn't expected it.

Shhh! Listen, the Crown isn't here. But I heard him say he needs the Crown to complete the ritual. So it can't be far.

"What? What ritual?" I didn't mean to blurt out my surprise out loud, but it was an uncontrollable reaction.

She reached up and pulled my face to her so that I had no choice but to pull it together and focus. Her eyes pleaded with me as she went on.

To kill this goddess he's talking about. Katrina, He isn't human. He can transform into some type of...water shadow thing. I don't know. But he's made of that dark water. He controls it..

I should have known he would know better than to leave the Crown anywhere we would be able to see it. But if McKenzie could keep him distracted long enough, and Milo and Bellamy could show up to buy us more time, we just might have a chance at finding it.

I glanced over my shoulder to see Bastian taking McKenzie from Noah, leading her away to the base of the steps leading to the stone altar table. McKenzie stayed silent so that her voice wouldn't give her away, but I knew that she had to be terrified. They began to ascend the stairs. I had to think fast.

I quickly communicated to Milo what my mom just told me, and he responded just as surprised as I was. But he assured me that he and Bellamy weren't far. For now, I had to find a way to stall Bastian from harming McKenzie—or worse.

"Sit, dear Atargatis," Bastian breathed over McKenzie, trailing her collarbone with his finger. She obliged, probably unsure of what else to do. "Funny. I expected you to put up more of a fight. You certainly did all those years ago the first time I offered you my affections."

McKenzie stared at him through hardened eyes, and Noah watched them like a starving tiger waiting to pounce in an instant. His gaze whipped over to me for a second, and I could feel the desperation to intervene raging in him just from his expression and tense body alone. But I shook my head. Not yet. Bellamy and Milo should be here any moment...

"It seems our guests have overstayed their welcome," Bastian's voice cut through the cold stone space, even as he addressed McKenzie. He turned in my direction, leaving her sitting on the altar. "I believe you're no longer needed. Your mother's clothes are by the door. You can all leave now."

We stood, our eyes never leaving him. Things weren't supposed to get this far. We weren't supposed to have actually handed McKenzie over to him. Her purpose was to be a distraction, not a complete replacement. I couldn't let

Bastian actually hurt her. So I braced, thoughts rushing through my head like an unhindered waterfall of what I could possibly do to stop him.

I bit my tongue so that a tear welled up, and I started to draw up the water that had spilled out from my mom's tank, slowly, so that Bastian wouldn't notice. It was difficult working with water so spread out across the stone floor, trying to find all the droplets and molecules and draw them back together. I wanted to call to Milo once more, but I found my mind could only manage to be occupied by one thing at a time. I hid my controlling hand behind my back, and kept talking to hold Bastian's attention.

"What are you going to do to her?" I spat. Any minute now Bellamy and Milo would be here...Any minute now.

"I think you know," he hissed, drawing up his hand to reveal the serpent symbol inked onto his hand. From it, more thick droplets of dark water formed, creating a stream, defying gravity and snaking its way across the open air to Noah, me, and my mom. It wrapped around us, its strength unimaginable, and forced us backwards. Everywhere it touched felt like burning oil on my skin. My head shook with pain as it slammed us against the wall, pinning us there to face the scene of Bastian and his false goddess. "But since you insist on specifics, Atargatis cannot be killed like a mortal. At least, not permanently. Valdez's foolishness proved that and simply returned her to her element. God knows she'll just keep on coming back in the next life. No. She must be destroyed once and for all with the power granted her by the gods, the same way it was given." He reached down and touched McKenzie's head, trailing down her tresses and coiling a lock around his finger. "The Crown? Check. The tail...we're getting to that. The things that made you a goddess must be destroyed together for you to become fully mortal..and fully killable."

A wave of relief flooded over me. At least he wouldn't try killing McKenzie where she stood—yet. Without a tail, she wouldn't quite be the piece he needed. That would buy us some more time as I focused on drawing the drying water on the floor to me. It was the only weapon I could think to make.

"It's a good thing your friends stayed after all. It'll be exciting to have an audience." He grinned, his eyes flashing with madness. With that, he commanded his dark water energy to crawl up my legs, slowly suctioning itself onto my leg. It crept upward, stinging my skin. As it worked its way up, the stinging became unbearable agony, burning like hot coal. "Now transform, Atargatis! Or watch your dear lover suffer."

A roaring sound of water filled the chamber, as shadow water flooded down the corridor, spilling in through the doorway and gushing into the room with us, carrying Milo and Bellamy within. As they choked and sputtered, I cried out. I couldn't break my focus, though. I gathered my emotions and forced myself to find the will to keep drawing the water together from my mom's tank. It was beginning to dry, so I had to work quickly before it was gone.

The rushing black water trapped them, pushing them with a force so hard against the wall, I winced at the sound of their backs hitting the rock. The water began to take its own form, filling up the space around them, as if suspending them in an invisible tank. As the water rose, lifting them higher off the ground, they gasped, struggling to breathe against the gushing rapids pounding over them.

"Let's find out if a siren's kiss helps them survive that!" Bastian laughed.

"No! Stop it!" I screamed.

"What? You really thought they could sneak up on me?" Bastian crooned. "It was a brave attempt, I'll give you that. But when you came alone, I knew better. Your lovesick sailors would never leave you to face me alone. And Bellamy? Thinking writing down his plans and sneaking around would keep me from knowing? I know his thoughts. His feelings. His every intention probably before he even knows it himself."

I felt so stupid, so gullible. We'd tried so hard to avoid this very thing and yet we had played right into Bastian's clutches. No matter what we could possibly think to try, his advantage was always too powerful.

The setback stole my focus, and I lost control of the water I was pulling from the ground. Did I really even think I could fight Bastian with it? His dark water would likely overpower mine with ease. And if it did, then what? My thoughts raced as I felt the water slipping from my mind's grip. I had to at least try.

"Noah," I said, still locked onto Bastian, "Take my mom and get out of here."

I drowned out the sound of my mother's protest as Noah rushed to cover her with his jacket and rushed her to the exit. The water around me pooled at my feet, siphoning to me through my sheer willpower. All around me, distractions screamed for my attention. Bastian grabbed McKenzie by the shoulders and shook her, shouting at her to change form as he threatened all of us with horrible deaths if she didn't. Mom's wailing faded in the background as Noah dragged her out of the room. And the water around Milo and Bellamy sloshed with a strange, looming sound as their muffled voices fought to break through it. And I was still supposed to be looking for the Crown.

I closed my eyes, trying to find solace in the sound of water trickling through my veins, the beat of my heart timing to the waves outside. As I concentrated, the water came to me all at once, the droplets combining to create a solid stream that wove around me like a lasso. And just as I prepared myself to send it lashing toward Bastian, a voice at the door stopped everything.

"Stop!" Serena's voice rose through the air like a queen's command. My eyes widened at the unexpected sight of her, standing tall and unmoving at the door, her water gown flowing around her and the gold woven in her hair glinting.

The silence was immediate, except for the soft swoosh of water. Bellamy and Milo dropped to the ground, released from their watery prison. I quickly eased my hold on the water I was conjuring, to keep Bastian unaware. Bastian turned to face the real Serena, the moonlight hitting half his face from the skylight above the stone table and illuminating his golden glowing eyes. His stone gaze flickered from the Serena in his grip and the one standing at the door, separated only by me standing in the gap between them.

"Well, now," he spat. "I'll admit, that's rather well-played of you. I certainly never expected a look-alike. But I don't see what benefit this brings you." His voice rose with agitation, and a strange crack that made it obvious he was trying to hide it.

"Your quarrel is not with them," Serena said, sticking out her chin. "Release them all and take me. Fulfill your dark destiny if you must. I can ignore the call of fate no longer."

An audible gasp escaped my lips as she stepped forward. Bellamy scrambled to his feet and chased after her. Milo leapt up to follow, but they were both met with a force as Bastian shielded her with a sheet of shadow water that they could not break through. "It's clear that this is what must be done." She stopped to look at Bellamy, only for a moment. "I'm sorry, my love."

"No it's not!" I cried. "What about all that stuff you told me about aligning the stars to form your own destiny? What about that?"

She kept walking, her eyes locked with Bastian's. "Serena!" I screamed. "If you do this, he'll have power over the seas and everything in it! He'll have power over *me*!"

"What else am I supposed to do, little mermaid?" She paused to look at me. "He's already won. I can't let him hurt you all, too. This is what is meant to happen. It's marked in stone."

"What?" I wanted her to explain. Where was this foretold? Why was she so willing to give up suddenly when all this time she'd been so stubborn?

Suddenly, Russell burst in, running after her as a defeated Noah stood behind him as the man tore from his grip. "No! Serena, no! I won't lose you again!"

"Grandpa, don't! You can't stop him! He can't be killed!" Noah called after him. I was relieved my mom was nowhere to be seen, assuming Noah had taken her somewhere safe for the time being.

Serena continued her walk to Bastian, trodding up the stairs to him like a princess about to be crowned. Only, she was heading to a chopping block.

Bastian snatched McKenzie by the arms and tossed her to the side, sending her tumbling down the old stone steps. Noah rushed to her as I called her name. I expected her reflection disguise to fade, but it didn't, and she remained in her form as Serena. I'd figure out how to undo that later, but right now it didn't matter. As Noah tended to her, I gritted my teeth in anger. I summoned my water once again, and sent it twisting and raging to Bastian, who deflected it with his black water with ease. “Nice try,” he grinned. “But you don’t possess half the power you need to fight me.”

Serena was almost to the top of the steps, and Bastian was waiting with a literal open hand. She placed her hand in his. Russell ran up behind her screaming her name, arms grasping frantically as he reached for her. But Bastian sent a black wave to knock him back, pummeling him into the floor as Serena escaped his grasp.

The scene was set. The six of us watched in horror as Bastian took Serena’s hand, guiding her to the altar on which he planned to kill her. “By the moon and sea you were created, and by the same you must end.” A stream of moonlight poured down into the chamber from the opening in the ceiling above. As the white light encircled the stone like a spotlight, I remembered how Cordelia once said we draw our power from the moon. This was how Bastian intended to send it back. And I couldn’t help but wonder, if the Mother of Sirens or her power didn’t exist, would I?

Serena didn’t struggle at all as she daintily sat herself on the table and leaned back. “All this because I would not love you.”

“No, Atargatis. All this because the gods favored you and gave you the sea—something that should have been rightfully mine.”

I looked around, frantic as the moonlight poured in. I strained to hear Serena and Bastian’s exchange of words as Bastian pulled out an ancient-looking dagger with a skull mounted on the hilt. He touched the tip of the knife to his finger and twirled the hilt in his hand back and forth.

“At least let me see it,” Serena begged. “One last time. Let me see what I’ve lost.”

Bastian laughed, holding his knife to lift her chin. “I think I could honor that pitiful request. For a price.”

“For a kiss, then?” Serena’s words sung heavy and clear as she made the offer, hardly a question.

“Fair enough, lovely. Looks like we’ll both be getting a taste of what we could’ve had.” I felt a small gag tickle the back of my throat. Bastian wasn’t only evil and manipulative...he had way too much fun with it. And it ignited a fury in my bones. But maybe Serena was onto something. If she could just get him to reveal where the Crown was...

Bastian snickered, his sharp eyes piercing right through her as he lowered his face to hers. "A kiss for a crown." He placed his lips on hers, forcing her head to him as he gripped the back of her neck. When he pulled away, Serena appeared struck by lightning, her body stiffening and jolting upright. With her head tilted back, she stared straight up, as if watching something above her intently. When the force holding her in place released her, her head fell forward and she gasped as though she'd been holding her breath. "Or rather, a glimpse of it. It's as close as you'll ever get." Bastian sneered.

A vision. Bastian had only shown her a vision of the Crown. Of course she should've known there was no way he would produce the actual crown in front of her. His deals always had a catch. This one was no different. What did that gain her? It was too late now.

So I was left with my jaw on the floor and my body charged, ready to react, but then Serena, up at the stone altar beside Bastian, frantically started yelling to McKenzie below. But the way she moved, screamed, and elbowed Bastian away to buy her just one extra second...it didn't seem like Serena. In fact, the more I watched her, the more clear it became that maybe it wasn't Serena at all.

"The Crown is in the West tunnel! In the floor beneath a half-heart shaped stone!" She cried.

The Serena beside Noah stood to her feet and shoved past him. She whipped past like a blur as she took off running back toward the way we came, disappearing into the stone tunnels that led back to Bastian's lair beneath the club.

It was so much to process that my mind was spinning trying to keep up. I glanced at Bellamy and Milo, who looked just as confused as I felt, but their eyes were fixated back on Bastian and the Serena he was about to sacrifice. Only this Serena was now transforming as a watery sheen ran down her body, peeling away into a puddle that revealed a pale, ginger-haired girl instead of the dark-skinned goddess that she had been just seconds before. It was McKenzie, and a heavy sensation dropped in my gut when I realized it'd been her up there all along.

47

Black Water

Katrina

"Conniving bitch!" Bastian struck McKenzie hard enough to send her toppling down the altar steps, where she rolled lifelessly past me. Noah and I ran to her, kneeling down and cupping her face in my hands. Noah shook her and I begged her to open her eyes.

"McKenzie!" Noah repeated, hovering over her body just as closely as I was, if not more. When she quickly came to, I breathed a sigh of relief.

Milo rushed to hold off Bastian before he could follow after the real Serena, while Bellamy ran after her as he called her name. One glance was all it took to see the disaster unfolding before us. The cave was beginning to groan and echo, tiny sandy bits of ceiling sprinkling us below. Something was beginning to crumble.

"You swapped places without telling us?" I asked, suppressing the slight feeling of betrayal I felt at McKenzie and Serena's secret plan.

"The fewer people who knew, the less chance to mess it up. It had to be believable." McKenzie raised an eyebrow as she sat up, holding the side of her face where Bastian struck. "It worked, didn't it?"

"You could've been killed. And how did you have Serena's voice?" My eyes drilled into her.

"Bastian's not the only one who can keep voices in his jewelry." She moved her hair away to reveal the necklace Serena normally wore—a white and blue piece of sea glass set in gold. "Looks like that acting class I took for an elective paid off."

I hesitated, debating whether to express my anger or save it for another day. I chose the latter. At the sight of Bastian knocking Milo back with his dark magic, I stuffed away my feelings about the secret plan and summoned my water back. This time it came to me fast, rushing like the blood pulsing in my veins. I drew it upright, and sent a cyclone at my command twisting toward Bastian like a raging cobra.

It only held him back for a moment as he met its force with his own shield of shadow and water, but I summoned all the water I could sense in this place and created an impenetrable wave that I sent rushing toward Bastian. I had to keep him away from Serena as long as possible. If she could find the Crown, this would be all over, I told myself as sweat formed on my brow from the effort. Bastian's power was strong, and it clashed against mine in an explosion of black and blue as he fought to break through

"Keep at it!" Milo shouted, charging toward Bastian. He tackled him with enough force to break his dark water hold on mine. With nothing holding it back, the water flowing from my hands shot forth, blasting Bastian across the room

In an uncomfortable silence, with only the sound of water dripping, I paused, watching a sopping wet Bastian groan as he stood slowly. The water in my hands felt like a weight, tangible, alive, and ready to be summoned again at a moment's notice as I drew back the water I'd just used. I couldn't afford to lose the strength of even a drop.

"Remember," Bastian licked a tiny drop of black liquid —either water or blood— from his curling lips. "You can't kill me. But I can certainly kill you."

"I don't need to kill you," I spat. "I just need to keep you away from the one who can."

Milo rushed to my side, and together we blocked the door through which Serena had escaped. Bastian growled, an unhinged rage in his breaths that came fast and hard. The black liquid streaming from his mouth grew heavier, dripping in thick clots. His shadow on the floor began to shift, forming into shapes and curves that didn't quite match Bastian himself.

Milo and I backed up as much as space would allow, our eyes fixated on the horrific transformation happening before us. Bastian grew larger, at least three feet taller and the rest of him in proportion as he shifted into a half-man half-monster before us. Wraith-like shadows curved from his back, writhing like snakes dripping with the same black venom as the liquid on the floor and from his mouth.

His already snake-like eyes began to glow like yellow pits of fire through the sludge of black water drenching his entire body. His voice morphed into a deep, growling version of something supernatural beyond recognition. After everything I'd seen, I thought I couldn't come across anything that truly scared me anymore. But this—this shadowy sea demon in front of me—left me frozen in place, short of breath as I tried to find the strength in my legs to keep from buckling.

"Good luck keeping me anywhere!" Bastian roared, his devilish voice grating against my ears as it shook the ground. He raised himself, lifting himself off the floor with nothing but black smoke and water beneath him. Hovering over us, he reached forward, his dark water reaching for me like a giant arm. Milo leapt in front of me, yelling for me to leave.

Just as the shadowy water struck, a burst of bright golden light sparked from Milo and sent Bastian's shadows flying back with a crackle. Bastian screamed in anger or pain, I couldn't tell which, as Milo stood staring up at him in shock, visibly shaken from what just happened. I noticed his sleeve had been torn off in the clash.

"Milo, your arm!" I pointed to the glowing sun tattoo on his arm. Yellow light lined the marking like golden, sacred veins—the same light that had deflected Bastian.

Milo gripped the marking with his other hand. "The sun. The Island. The light overcomes the dark." He spoke as if trying to remember something or rehearsing a line to himself.

"What?" I asked.

"It's protection. Protection from darkness—from the dark lord of the seas. Protection from Davy Jones." His eyes slowly shifted from his glowing tattoo up to a fuming Bastian. "Katrina, he isn't just controlled by Davy Jones..."

"He *is* Davy Jones," I muttered. It occurred to me all at once. The legend behind the strange cruelty of the seas. The one sailors feared for hundreds of years. The one who collected the souls of the dead at sea...

The Collector, I relayed my thoughts to Milo with my song call. *The things in his collection aren't just things. They're souls.*

Trapped souls. Milo reiterated.

"I am he!" Bastian boomed, stepping closer and closer with the inky sludge of his shadows cloaking him. "The dark lord of the seas. Cursed to this human form by Poseidon himself, but more powerful than any man."

"Poseidon cursed you once. What do you think he'll do to you if you kill her?" I spat.

"The gods of old are long gone. Without her, I'll be the last supreme being of the seas...as it could have been all along if she had chosen me instead of that useless mortal." Bastian snarled, sharpened teeth showing through the black water continually trickling down his face. "You may have the mark of the sun to shield you, but you're not the one I'm after." He struck the wall beside us with a burst of shadow and water from his hand, sending it crumbling to the floor and shaking the remaining walls.

"He'll collapse the whole fort." I watched the stony residue and pebbles dropping down on us from the ceiling.

"I don't think he's concerned about that." Milo uttered. Together we watched dumbfounded and completely baffled as he crashed through the wall and the shadows around him slithered across the floor, carrying him toward his destination—Serena and Bellamy.

48

Written In Stone

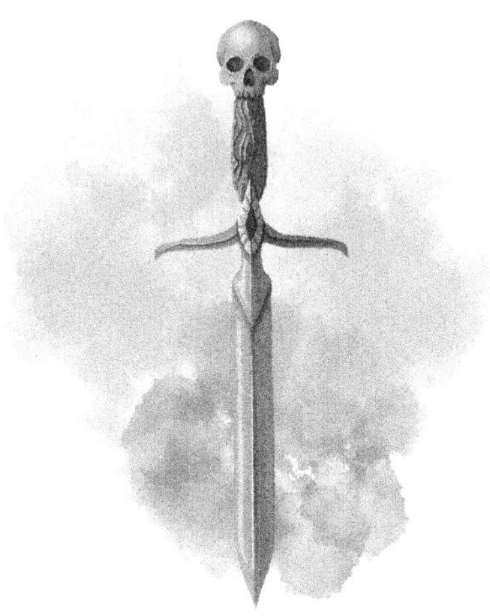

Bellamy

I couldn't think of a time when I'd run as fast as I did then, chasing after Serena—except maybe the night my father killed her and I ran to the pier, trying to save her...and failed.

"Serena!" I screamed, my voice echoing down the dark halls. There were passages snaking all throughout, leading to pitch black tunnels of nothing. I could barely see, as the torch I took from the wall was near to dying. "Serena!"

I called out her name again, stumbling my way through blindly, turning at every entrance and trying to decide which one I should follow. I finally chose a path and wandered into the dark, chasing an end I didn't even know existed and praying to a God I didn't believe in to help me find her. But the passageways around me kept multiplying, and each time I chose one, more would appear.

I spun, surrounded by corridors that taunted me and spun alongside me, my vision blurring at the sight of the dark halls surrounding me. I no longer knew which way was left or right, north or south.

I wasn't one to panic, but in that moment, I felt my heart speeding up in a way that made my chest tighten. And the loud boom in the distance didn't do much to settle that feeling when I heard the sound of stone crumbling and the feeling of an earthquake beneath my feet. The chamber had become some strange illusion of tunnels, a maze that I didn't remember my way out of. Whatever Bastian was doing to my head, I wanted him out.

Find her, that's right. Lead me right to her. He laughed in the recesses of my mind, taunting me with the fact that the closer I got to her, so did he. *Poor Bellamy. The more you try to help her, the more you hurt her. It's always been that way. In this lifetime and the last. Yet you just can't stay away.*

"Shut up!" I screamed into the emptiness. "Shut up and go to hell!"

He didn't shut up. He kept on, making my head ache. I leaned against the wall, agonizing over every word, reaching up to my neck and digging in my fingernails in attempt to claw away his mark on my collarbone. The skin tore, burning at my desperate scratches, but it wasn't enough. I reached for a knife in my pocket and raised it to my neck.

Suddenly a hand caught my arm. "What the hell are you doing, boy?" I glanced up, my vision settling. There were no longer hundreds of tunnels. Just the two passages I was trying to choose between. And the person holding my arm was Russell.

"Nothing," I panted, trying to catch my breath in an attempt to look less insane. "Where's Serena?"

The look in his eyes told me he knew. "She found the Crown."

"She did?" I asked, a smile starting to form. "She's got her power back?"

Russell looked away, a heaviness overtaking his appearance. "Get out of this corner and come and see for yourself."

I followed him down one of the passages, a glowing in the distance as we approached.

"The West tunnel," I muttered, noting that the altar room was stark North of where I stood. "Damn. From North to West." I connected Serena's clue once again, baffled at how they'd been there all along, as Russell led me to the end of the passageway. It was a chamber, somehow inexplicably lit, showcasing even more of the thousands of Bastian's collected items lining the walls like a hidden treasure cove. And there in the center of the room was Serena, kneeling in front of a broken heart shaped opening in the floor from the stone that she'd pulled up, staring at the Crown in her hands with tears in her eyes.

"You got it!" I shouted, rushing to her side. "Wait, what's wrong?" I noticed her tears weren't from joy, but sorrow.

"I got it," Her voice squeaked, placing the Crown on her head. "But it didn't work. I'm still the same."

I didn't know what I expected would happen when she got that crown back. Maybe she would put it on her head and light would shoot out every which way, or maybe she would levitate and shine like the sun. I had no idea. But nothing even close to that was happening. And she made it clear that wasn't how it was supposed to be.

"What? No! Maybe it's a fake. Bastian probably switched the real one or—"

"I assure you, it's the real one." Bastian's voice interrupted me. He stepped into the room, a strange calm about him, though he was soaked completely with his dark water. Something seemed...different, more sinister...about him. He looked relieved as he watched Serena holding the Crown. He spoke so calmly it made me nervous. "So you see...you cannot stop this."

Katrina and Milo appeared behind him, but they didn't approach. They stood, just as mesmerized by the scene as the rest of us, waiting to see a goddess re-crowned. Bastian kept his distance, but he kept talking. "What now, Atargatis?"

"Very well," she said softly. "It's written in stone. How could I think I could defy that?"

"What's written in stone? What do you mean?" I took her hand, pleading for her to make sense.

"The altar is painted with pictures of my legend. The first, a weeping woman by her dead lover. The second, she's walking into the sea. The third, she emerges with a tail. And the fourth is meant to be the last. Her end. My end. I'm destined for this ending."

"The last picture is faded! I saw the altar. You don't know the ending!" Katrina screamed from where she stood.

"She's right!" I screamed. "You're going to let some damn pictures tell you what's supposed to happen to you?" I shuddered as I heard another boom in the distance, wondering what was happening, knowing it was just a matter of time before Bastian got tired of playing cat and mouse with us and made his next move.

"It's my destiny."

"No, Serena. No. You're *my* destiny! So what does that mean? We just give up?"

"What does it take to restore a goddess?" Bastian snickered. "Apparently more than it took to ruin her. Now come with me. Back to the altar, dear."

Something about the way Bastian said the words triggered a clue in my brain. And I carefully sorted through the thoughts in my head, almost afraid to think them because I knew he would be listening. But I couldn't help it. The thought came and I couldn't get it to leave. But I couldn't help but think maybe there was something more about that altar than we knew.

Stop trying. You'll only make this hurt worse.

With eyes clenched shut, I shook his voice away. I wanted to run, run far away from the hold he had on me. It wasn't fair that he could just appear any time and invade my thoughts. And all these years—had he been in my head the whole time? It made me sick that I couldn't escape it.

I'll always know. I'll always follow you. And when you fail once again to do what you failed to do before, I'll be chasing you, ready to remind you. No one has ever kept me out.

I fought like hell to get him out, closing my eyes to help me blockade my mind. But as he spoke into my thoughts, something he said made me finally believe him. He was right. I could never keep him out. No one ever had. So what happened if I stopped trying? What would happen if I just let him in? What if I played his game right back? What the hell did I have to lose?

Go right ahead, mate. Make yourself fucking comfortable. As I spoke back, I could almost feel the hesitation and utter surprise in Bastian's awkward response.

You're going to just open yourself up to me like that? How very bold of you.

Might as well surrender. It seems the only logical option, wouldn't you agree?

When there was no answer from Bastian, I knew that I had him. I was now in his head, as he was in mine, and if he insisted we share a highway between our thoughts, I was going to find out what his were. I was done running.

When I opened my eyes, I saw Bastian, looming with a clenched jaw and anger flashing in his gaze. Serena stood in the center of the collector's lair, facing a grim version of Bastian that I'd never before seen until now. He was taller than humanly possible, and black writhing shadows sprouted from all around him. He controlled some blackened water that burned to the touch, and he sent waves of it forward to wash us all back, separating us all from the one he wanted.

Serena screamed. I grunted with frustration, trying to break through the wall of black water he'd entrapped us in. Though it looked cold, it boiled like molten lava to the touch. Burn marks ate their way through my clothing and onto my arms from trying to break through the barrier. I screamed alongside a desperate Russell, who rammed the wall alongside me as Bastian dragged Serena away in his inky, shadowy clutches.

As Bastian swept her away and dragged her back toward the chamber with the stone altar, I stopped fighting the unbreakable water wall. I couldn't catch him. And I certainly couldn't stop him like this. Desperate and out of solutions, I looked inward again, reaching into my mind for an answer—or rather, reaching into his.

Why don't you just kill her right here? Why the need to keep dragging her back? Are you not strong enough? If I could figure out his secret—why he seemed to need her in that chamber so badly to kill her—maybe it would lead to an idea.

He fought me hard, closing off his thoughts as best he could without losing me entirely. I could feel it. His pride wouldn't let him give up the hold he had on me. Even if it meant I had access to him, however fleeting.

His thoughts flashed before me as I fought the mental battle to stay in his head and see what I could. I could only manage to see broken, fragmented, and fuzzy blurs of thoughts, but they were something. As he carried Serena, he was thinking about how he'd kill her. With a dagger he planned to stab through her...no, he planned to cut off her tail..to give...to give it back...to the gods?

What was given here must also be taken.

He had to kill her on the altar. He couldn't do it otherwise. Some kind of magical god rule, I'm sure. But wait...

On the throne of Atargatis must be her blood... To kill her once and for good.

Throne. Throne.

I reached for Bastian's memories. I knew I wasn't strong enough to be choosy. But I think the fact that we were now sharing a mind-link made him panic. I saw flashes, glimpses of what could have been bits of Bastian's life. I saw faces of the poor unfortunate souls he tricked into his deals. I saw pirate captains and kings. I saw glittering horizons and stormy seas. I saw love and loss, hate and war. And there I caught a glimpse—not even a second—of my life through his eyes. He watched us with envy. Serena and I, and the life we built millennia past.

She was mortal, but still just as beautiful. An ordinary girl with ordinary dreams. In a village built from stones and mud, at the earliest dawning of civilization. And there I was with her, in a life I didn't remember—a man clearly used to hard work and toil, rugged and dirt-covered, greeting her with a kiss as I entered our humble house. All this Bastian had watched, longing to be in my place.

And then I saw what he did to her. What he did to us.

He drove a dagger into my chest while I slept, and left the bloody knife in her hands. When she woke next to my body, holding the blade, she thought she'd lost her mind, and ran to the cliff by her village where she threw herself to the sea.

Centuries later he found her again, no longer a woman, but a goddess, a sea queen, rivaling his own power with her curse-turned-blessing. And he lured her to him, promising a power even she didn't hold—bringing me back in exchange for her crown. In a ritual under the full moon's light, he took her crown, sentencing her to a mortal rebirth, forever searching for the man she traded her power to bring back.

I shook away the visions of Bastian's memories. My legs threatened to buckle as I processed what I'd seen and learned in a matter of moments. What had passed as a lifetime in my mind was only a few seconds here in the real world. I'd hung on to every image. And I remembered the stone altar where Bastian ripped the Crown from Serena's head in exchange for restoring my life. It wasn't an altar. It was a throne. And thrones were used for coronations. We had to crown Serena on her throne. And I had to die to do it.

49

To Crown A Queen

Bellamy

If you crown her, you break my deal with her, and I take back what I'm owed—your life.

Bastian spoke to me even now, and I could sense the wicked smile on his disgusting face from his words alone. My blood turned to ice. I didn't mind dying. I'd already done it once. But losing a lifetime with Serena again...

No. I owed her this. I failed her before. Not again. I wouldn't do this for anyone but her. For her I'd rip out my own barely beating heart. And if I was the cost of her power, so be it. At least my death would be worth something this time.

I turned to my friends, all trapped here with me. "Help me get out of here. I know what to do to get Serena's power back. But I have to be the one to do it. Do you understand?"

As Katrina started to object, I repeated myself before she could finish. "Do you bloody understand?" I choked, my words coming out harsher than I meant them to.

"What are you planning, mate?" Milo stepped forward, a concerned look about him.

I stared at him. I wasn't going to share any of what I'd learned. I'd keep that all with me till the grave. No one else needed to be bothered with all that.

"You just need to know that I have to get to that throne room."

Katrina and Milo hesitated. I knew they cared, but right then I didn't want them to care. I wanted them to shut up and get me out of here. So I couldn't believe I'm admitting to this, but I was incredibly grateful when Russell stepped in.

"Just get him out." Russell blurted. "Katrina, you can do it. It's water, isn't it? Control it!"

Katrina sent a sideways glance my way. "It's dark water. It's different. I've never—"

"Try!" I screamed, my voice raking against the air.

Hesitating, she held out her hands, tears very clearly forming in her eyes. She groaned, sending forth her strongest effort to tame the black water swirling around us. As she fought to control it, her hands shook, but the wall of dark water remained untouched.

"Wait." Milo put his hands over hers. "Don't sirens draw their power from the moon? Let's try something."

She looked at him through heavy, shining eyes that had lost all hope as he guided her hand to the sun star marking on his arm. "Use me as a shield for your power."

Russell and I watched them, tense and hopeful, and terrified all at the same time. The clock was ticking. For all I knew Bastian had already killed her. I had to tell myself to breathe.

A golden light shone from Milo, culminating at the marking on his arm. Katrina held onto him, combining their power so that a golden light began to surround her. She reached forward and touched the dark water, Milo still at her side. Where her fingers met the water, it separated, a golden rim slicing through it as she created a small opening.

"The sun and moon must face the same darkness," Milo whispered beneath his breath. I would've asked him what he meant, but I was too busy rushing towards the growing hole in the water wall.

I went to escape, but stopped at the realization that Bastian would know my plan. He would know that I intended to kill myself for Serena and he wouldn't let me do it. Someone else would have to do it, at a time when he least expected.

My thoughts rushed like the water swirling around us. I turned to Milo and spoke low but urgent enough. "When I get in there...listen...when Serena is crowned, you have to kill me."

"What?" Milo's eyes flashed.

I gripped his shoulders. "I'm asking you this because it's the only way. My life for her power, that was the deal she made. I have to save her. You have to kill me. Do you understand? Kill me."

"I...I can't do what you're asking, Bellamy." Milo turned his head.

"Then I'm not asking. And I'm the captain, remember?" I breathed, my heart pounding.

"Bellamy, I—"

"Don't give me that golden boy shit right now. I already died once for Katrina. You think I won't do it again that much more for Serena?"

"That was different," Milo argued. "You didn't have a choice. We were cursed to hell. We were going to die anyway."

"Well my life's hell without her." I spat, meeting Milo's gaze with my own hardened stare. "I thought you of all people would understand. I thought you of all people would have my back on this. You said you'd have my back...on whatever came next."

He was silent, and I could tell I wasn't changing his mind. I couldn't waste any more time trying to convince him.

"To fucking hell with you, then, Milo. Don't forget to take your knife out of my back when I leave." I shoved him out of my way and ran to the water opening as Milo called for Katrina to close it.

She tried, but she wasn't fast enough. I leapt through, the edges of the water still managing to splash and singe my skin, but I didn't stop to notice. As fast as my feet would carry me, I ran to the Crown lying on the ground and scooped it up in my arms. Then I set off down those dark, empty tunnels, my fate literally in my own hands as I ran to crown my queen.

The walls blurred as I passed. The sounds in the distance became hollow wails that faded from my ears like the remnants of a ghost. I felt water in my eyes as I squeezed them shut to blink it back. I wouldn't let myself mourn this life, dammit. I finally knew what I was meant to do. I finally understood why I was here. And it was to save Serena, once and for all. Milo or not, I'd figure out how.

"Why the hell am I always dying?" I joked to myself. It was the only way to dull the sting of Milo's refusal to help me. I still couldn't believe he'd turned his back on me. I couldn't believe the coward he was.

As I entered the throne room, I heard footsteps behind me. I turned to see Russell, his arms splotched with burns just like mine, only worse. Of course he would've leapt through that opening right behind me. It couldn't have at least been Katrina or Noah, or hell, I would've even taken McKenzie. But Russell was the one standing in front of me, not them. I'd make it work.

"Good timing, old man," I said, scanning the layout of the room one more time. It was becoming clear to me that this would be a two-person job, since I would be dying at some point. I ducked low behind a stone pillar and motioned for Russell to do the same. Bastian was carrying Serena in his arms, shielded by the dripping veil of his dark power as he took her up the steps. She wasn't even fighting him anymore, and her body moved limp as a satin scarf as he laid her across the throne altar.

He ran forward, but I held out an arm to stop him. "Don't do anything stupid," I said. "We have to do this one way, with one chance to get it right. But he's going to know I'm coming because he's in my head."

I couldn't let myself think. Bastian was distracted with Serena at the moment but that didn't mean he was completely oblivious to me. I couldn't think. My only option was to act and act fast.

I placed the Crown in Russell's hands. "I'm going for Bastian. Make sure this gets back to her, no matter what. You go up there and you put it on her head as soon as you see me attack him. I have to let him kill me. It's the only way she's coming out of this alive."

I darted off before Russell could ask questions or say something useless to try to slow me down. But, by God, he'd better do what I said. At least, I thought, there was no one else here who wanted to save Serena as much as I did. Maybe, just maybe, it was for the best that Russell was the one who'd made it here with me. He might've been the only one who loved Serena enough to understand how to complete a mission I couldn't fully explain to him. Not if I wanted to keep Bastian unaware of it. Russell had no reason to give a shit about me, so he was likely the perfect one of the bunch to do this.

The chamber around me faded, becoming a mere haze to line the path before me. My focus homed in on Bastian and Serena. They were all I could see as I drew nearer, my footfalls speeding up with each frantic beat of my heart. I could make out the details now—the white terror in Serena's glistening eyes; the beading sweat above Bastian's brow as he lifted the skull-hilted dagger to kill her. I recognized it from the memory as the same one he'd used to kill me in my first life. And the same dagger my father gifted me. Knowing my next move, I couldn't help but realize it was once and forever intended for me.

With the moonlight pouring in from above, I nearly tumbled down the cracking stone steps as I climbed them. Bastian turned to me just as I ran up on him. He knew I planned to attack him. Of course he knew. I expected that. We were linked, and always would be, no matter how much I wanted to escape that. But did he know what the rest of the plan was? I'd fought so hard to separate it from my mind, to deny my own thoughts, hoping I could somehow hide my true intentions from him. I only had seconds to do it...

He whipped around to face me as I tackled him. Serena screamed.

"Bellamy, stop! Let him do this! Forget about me, please!" She begged through the tears flowing down her cheeks. I ignored her.

Bastian fought me with inhuman strength. My muscles groaned as I took a hit from him hard enough to crack a rib. I struck back, but my hits resulted in little damage. His skin was like armor, and his grip like iron shackles. He pinned me against the steps, the jagged corners of the stone bruising my spine. Perfect.

Mustering all the strength I could, I grabbed the wrist of the hand in which he held the dagger, fully intent on making him think I actually had some self-preservation left. His fingers loosened on the hilt, and I fought not to show my hope dwindling. He knew what I was trying to do. But I couldn't let him drop that knife. My tired arms ached as I inched my hands up over his, forcing each finger back down to keep the dagger in his grasp.

"I won't kill you, Bellamy. I know that's what you want." He laughed as his snake-eyes flashed gold. "But I'll certainly let you watch as I kill *her*." He gestured to the table, where Serena pleaded with me, begging me to leave.

Any minute now, Russell. Put the damn crown on her head.

"He can crown her all he likes, but it won't do any good."

"I know," I struggled to speak, my body shaking from fatigue as I fought to keep Bastian's hand closed around the dagger. "But this will."

I caught a glimpse of Russell, as he climbed up the other side of the altar with the Crown in his hands. He lunged forward, just barely reaching Serena as he secured the Crown onto her head. The moonlight struck the Crown, casting rays of its reflection across the room from the moment it touched the golden pearls and glimmering seashells lining the edge.

That moonlight was supposed to be the last image I would see. I was supposed to close my eyes forever to the sigh of Serena glowing with her restored power. But instead, I was still trembling with fatigue as I fought to pull the dagger closer to myself. Bastian resisted with ease, the supernatural strength in him enabling him to overpower me no matter what I did. I glanced over across the stone altar, where Russell pushed Serena aside as he scrambled to us. There was a determined look in his old eyes that made me hopeful he realized what I needed him to do. He practically jumped down the steps, colliding with Bastian's back and reaching over him to add his hand to the dagger we both gripped. With his strength and mine combined, I began to feel the knife lower. Bastian was weakening, and his shaking arm confirmed it.

I grunted from the sting as sweat dripped into my eyes. Bastian's breath tightened as he struggled against the two of us. The dead cool of this cavern wasn't enough to fight the burning in my muscles. But we were almost there...Just a few more inches and I'd have the tip of this blade in my chest.

But Serena...she leapt off the altar, still wearing the Crown, and threw herself on Russell. His grip slipped almost completely from the hilt. She wrestled against him, prying his hands finger by finger from the knife, and yanked him down with her as she pulled away.

"Dammit, Serena! Stop it!" I screamed, my dry voice spent.

"I won't let you—" The words hadn't fully escaped from her lips before her shriek tore through the air as I felt a sting between my ribs.

I took one slow, long look down at my chest, where the dagger was buried deep, held in place by a hand on the hilt overpowering Bastian's. A hand and arm with the mark of the sun. My eyes shifted up to Milo, whose eyes softened with a knowing, solemn nod. Bastian caught him with his elbow and flung him off in a rage. He staggered back, cursing us all as a light began to emanate from Serena's crown. I looked at Milo where he crouched on the steps.

"Thanks mate," I managed to utter as my breaths shortened and a scarlet warmth dampened my shirt.

"You're the captain," he said.

Serena's screams faded into muffled silence. Bastian filled the air with a flurry of curses that sounded like jumbled slurs to me. My head felt light, and a cruel chill dominated my body as my blood leaked out. This wasn't at all like dying in that cursed shipwreck. This was unsettling and slow. My eyes were too weak to move. I kept my focus on Milo. His eyes were full with budding tears, and they were the last thing I saw before the darkness swallowed me whole.

50

Call of the Ocean

Katrina

I'd just made it into the altar room as I screamed at the sight of Bellamy lying dead on the steps to the stone slab. Milo said he wouldn't do it. How could he do it?

"Bellamy!" I screamed. But it was too late. Bellamy was gone. I saw the knife in his chest and his lifeless body slumped across the steps. And behind him, Serena rose up, tears soaking her face and neck, reflecting a glistening light that showered her from the Crown on her head. The frame of the Crown grew downward, spiraling and weaving itself into her hair, joining the Crown to her as if it were a part of her. Her hair flowed, bits of blue intertwining with the rest of her full, dark locks. Bellamy was dead. And Serena was a goddess again.

I glanced at Bastian, who looked a lot like a man who knew his time was up. He quickly turned and summoned his shadow water, and it shot up from the ground, cloaking him in flowing midnight before it twisted into a cyclone that he drove into the walls. The whole place shook violently and sent chunks of stone raining down. I dodged them just barely, running to meet Milo as he worked to salvage Bellamy's body amidst the chaos. As he lifted him, the steps cracked between them, pulling apart and ripping Bellamy out of his reach. Milo's half gave way, and the only thing he could do to avoid falling to the churning water below was to throw himself to the only piece of solid floor left—the same piece on which I stood. He stumbled off the quaking steps toward me just as they collapsed behind him.

Serena knelt on the altar, face in her hands as she groaned Bellamy's name in agony. Through her tears, she paused long enough to catch Bellamy's body with a wave before he slid into the sea. The wave cradled him in place, holding his limp figure safely out of reach of the torrent. Serena cried his name, and drew it back to her, where she pulled him from the water and held him in her arms as everything around her toppled to pieces.

The squeal of McKenzie drew my attention from behind. I whipped around to see her with Noah, running as he tried to shield them both from the crumbling ceiling. The floor was giving way and pieces of it sloughed off into the ocean below the cliff it was built on.

"Both of you get out of here NOW!" I screamed.

"We're not leaving you!" McKenzie screamed.

"Yes you are!" I summoned water from the sea behind me and sent forth a blast that whisked them both away and back to safe, dry ground. I just hoped my mom had stayed put at least wherever Noah had taken her.

I'm okay. Don't worry, Trina.

I didn't expect to hear her voice in my head right then, but I couldn't have been more glad of it.

Good. I'll see you soon. I called back to her. *Just stay away from the sea right now.*

There was an unusually long pause.

I'm afraid I can't do that, Trina.

"Mom, what is that supposed to mean?" I blurted out loud. She never answered me.

Milo finally reached me and urged me to the exit back to the tunnel. "You need to go...What? What's wrong?" He panted, taking notice of the twisted look of confusion on my face.

"Nothing," I lied, shaking away the thoughts of Mom for a moment. "But I can't leave! Bastian's getting away."

"Serena will take care of him! It's not your fight anymore."

"Oh yeah? Where is she then?" I screamed, realizing she was no longer up on the altar. And neither was Bellamy's body. As I glanced up, the altar still somehow intact despite the rest of the fort having crumbled to pieces around it.

The watchtower above us had long fallen, leaving an open night sky above us and the sea before us. Milo and I stood on the open ledge, searching desperately for any sign of Serena or Bastian.

"I don't see them. What if Serena's too heartbroken to stop Bastian?" The ocean wind whipped my hair across my face, and I spat out the wild-blowing strands as I tried to talk through them.

"Surely she wouldn't let Bellamy die for nothing!" Milo screamed over the roar of the water that seemed to be crashing up against the cliff more and more loudly by the second.

There was a bubbling in the ocean, marked by a heavy darkness rising up from the bottom. It bloomed into a bubbling fountain of black, and the waves around it churned, parting to reveal the top of a charred mast. The water continued swirling, and the wind grew stronger as it lifted a ship from the depths. But this ship was in pieces, with wooden slats missing and broken mast poles and torn sails. It was coated in an inky black, similar to the dark matter around Bastian...almost like tar. And Bastian himself was at the helm, a vision of his true self. No longer an eccentric, vibrant club-owning collector, but a dark sea captain dripping with power and the decay of the souls he kept captive.

"His ship." Milo muttered, his eyes wide as he watched the ship rising up before him. "He's trying to run."

My eyes scanned the waters, and I remembered what my mom said. Was she down there? And more importantly, if she was, why would she be?

I suddenly felt a call to jump in as well. The sea tugged at my soul and my siren side was immediately in control. I resisted, though it was like trying to ignore an all-you-can-eat buffet on an empty stomach. Painful, tempting, and hard as hell.

Suddenly something burst forth from the water, glowing with a light that illuminated the crystal waters around it for meters. It was Serena, wearing the sea as a flowing gown, and no longer the size of a human. She was now a giant—at least two or three times the size of her normal height. The Crown on her head dripped with golden droplets, as if the water that touched it melted right into the precious metal.

The call of the ocean grew louder. I stepped forward, ready to let myself drop right in. Milo gripped my arm from behind. "What are you doing?"

"I don't know," I said, turning around to look at him. "I just have to go. I can't stop it."

He looked at me with a long pause. He pressed his lips together and released my arm. "Your eyes are blue. Go on and do what you have to do."

I nodded and with a leap forward, I dove off the cliff into the ocean. I'd never fallen from such a height before, but the need to be in the water below overrode the fear of the drop. Crashing into the waves, my lower half quickly morphed into a tail and all at once, I was at home.

51

SEAFOAM

KATRINA

Some strange instinct called me to it, drawing me to a force I didn't quite recognize, but couldn't resist. I didn't know where I was going, but I swam there with foreign confidence. As I followed the draw, I searched for my mom in the water without luck. Still I pressed on, following some innate primal instinct in me that I didn't know I had.

Chunks of stone from the old fort came floating down around me as they continued dropping into the water from above. I thought of Bellamy and shivered at the notion that he might just be lost in all this, cold and alone, drifting in the chaos. He deserved so much better. Milo once said life had always been unfair to him. He was right. I choked back some tears in sadness and anger, and

I couldn't help but think to myself that if Serena didn't bring down justice on Bastian after that, I'd do it myself.

But Bastian was on a demon ship, sailing away to save his pathetic ass. And here I was, flipping my tail through some mystical pathway to answer a call only I could feel, unable to fight it. And through the ocean I swam, until I saw a light in the distance under the water. As I neared, the elegant shape of another mermaid welcomed me—my mom.

Mom, how did you get here, too? Where are we?

My mom tilted her head. She looked so rejuvenated in this form, as though she was still herself, but herself with an inhuman beauty about her. Especially here, suspended in the open ocean. Her brown hair framed her face that had been softened with an ethereal touch. Her eyes held some strange, feline charm that was never there before, and right now they were the same ocean blue hue as mine. It was almost hard to look away. Was that how I looked to others in my siren form?

*I don't know. I just...came here, s*he said.

Great. So neither of us understood why we were drawn here.

Above us the water rippled, and a whirlpool formed, with the funnel's wide part at the surface. It spun and trailed down right before us, then whisked back up to reveal Serena in its place. She was in her mermaid form, her glorious tail nearly reaching the seabed, but this Serena wore a warrior queen's expression. Beneath a furrowed, tense brow, her sharp eyes flicked back and forth between my mom and me.

I've called all the sirens in the sea, and only you two remain. I prayed it wasn't so, but I had to know for sure.

Of course that made sense. We were drawn to Serena, our queen. She was the Mother of Sirens. It was impossible to resist her call. Whatever she asked of us, we would do.

I need you to protect him while I face Bastian. Take care of him and get him somewhere safe so that I can focus on destroying that bastard.

She waved a hand, revealing Bellamy secured in a giant bubble. His eyes closed, that black hair contrasting harshly against his deathly white face, and the dark red bloodstain across his chest, all untouched by the water around him—it was an image I didn't want to see. But we were charged with guarding him, and that was something I didn't need a siren queen's command to do.

My mother and I swam to Bellamy's body, taking up either side of him with knowing nods. Serena said nothing more but fixed her gaze on the dark shadow looming above on the water's surface in the distance. Bastian's ship I presumed. Serena took off toward it, but stopped to look back at us one last time as she entrusted us entirely with the body of her beloved.

I wasted no time telling Mom to help me carry Bellamy back to the surface. There was no safer place for him I could think of than with Milo. I used my song-call to tell Milo what was happening, and he planned to meet us at the shore.

We swam with Bellamy between us, one arm in each of ours, careful not to disturb his peaceful appearance. Up on the shore, Milo waited for us, and he'd managed to reunite with Noah and McKenzie. We passed Bellamy up to them, and together they laid him on the sand.

We were careful to stay out of sight, as the entire side of the fort crashing into the sea had obviously drawn attention of the locals and authorities. Nestled in a corner away from the flashing blue lights and police tape in the distance, we ensured no one saw the two mermaids with a dead body meeting their friends ashore.

"I can't just stay here," I said, unable to tear my eyes away from Bellamy. I couldn't make myself believe that I'd never hear that snarky accent or see that stupid, cocky smirk again. I'd just healed up from my grief from losing Milo. And now a new wound was created. Ripping at the still-healing seams of my heart.

I clenched my fists and closed my eyes as I allowed the reality of it all to set in. Losing Bellamy the first time was unfortunate, sad even. But I'd barely known the real him then. But now, now was different. We'd crossed oceans together. We'd stood by each other in pursuit of things others would call impossible. We'd watched each other's heart break and heal again. Losing him after all we'd been through together, even if it was technically his choice, just didn't seem fair. The tears burning behind my eyes reminded me how I first learned to control water aboard his ship. And the way he found me a blubbering mess on the pier in the twilight, mourning. And the way he faced Bastian even when he didn't want to, just for me to have the chance to get Milo back. He'd said it was a death sentence. I didn't think this was what he meant. And something told me he didn't either, at the time.

I opened my eyes and let them follow the ripple created from the tear that fell. A thirst for vengeance rose in me, and I wasn't sure if it was me or the siren, but I didn't try to resist it. "I've got to make sure I see Bastian pay for this."

We watched as in the distance a ship's silhouette flashed against a midnight sky, lights of gold and white bursting like fireworks around the masts. Explosions of water and light leapt forth from the sea as Serena and Bastian battled. From here, it almost just looked like an ordinary storm out at sea, instead of a duel between two oceanic immortals. It was probably a good thing, given the attention the crumbling fort was drawing.

Ignoring Milo and my friends' pleas against it, I dove down into the water and flipped my tail as swiftly as I could manage toward the ship in the distance. I couldn't help but wonder what was taking so long. Serena was supposed to be able to kill Bastian when she regained her power. Whatever this battle between them was, and however long it was supposed to last, I didn't have the patience for it. Bellamy deserved his justice now. And Serena had better truly be powerful enough to overthrow him or I'd try my hand at overthrowing them both. No—that was the siren talking.

My siren vision allowed me to see perfectly in the dark, so I could easily make out the scene of Serena, in her grand goddess power, held high as the ship's masts by the hand of the waves enrobing her from the waist down, fending off Bastian's attacks with her own. In a vortex of water I assumed was controlled by her, the ship bobbed in place, tilting and tipping as the water kept it from sailing out of Serena's reach. The sails in the masts strained against her hold, and the ship groaned with agonizing creaks as it drifted about.

In a clash of Bastian's black water against her golden waves, the forces of their waters raged on, turning the sea around them into a choppy, ominous abyss. Supernatural lightning struck between them each time their power collided, and the moon dripped its glow down upon it all as I neared. I was in awe at how easily Serena wielded her power, holding back Bastian's ship with the tide while striking him with magic waves streaked with golden lightning.

"I told you to guard Bellamy!" Without even turning around, Serena immediately knew of my presence, even as she dueled with Bastian from her post above the water.

"He's safe!" I shouted over the roar of the churning water around us and the creaking of Bastian's ship. "I came to help!"

"Your human side allows you to defy me." She shook her head, stopping just long enough to turn and make her point clear. "I don't need you, little mermaid! You possess no power that I don't already have tenfold."

As she spoke, a blast of darkness collided with her, knocking her into the water with me. As she resurfaced, she turned to me with a cold threat in her eyes that pierced me like harpoons. "You're distracting me! Leave now!"

A spout of black water came spinning toward me, but Serena launched it away with a burst of golden light from her hands. "If I have to waste time to protect you, you aren't helping!" She hissed.

"What's the matter, Atargatis?" Bastian's voice echoed around us in a cloud of shadow on the water. We looked to see him walking to the edge of his ship.

He cocked his head and pretended to think. "Can't get your pet to behave? Perhaps if you'd spent more time protecting your mermaids in the first place they wouldn't all be extinct now would they?"

Serena flushed red that I could see burning in her cheeks even through her dark skin. Her eyes flashed with rage and panic, and she stilled in a way that made me nervous.

"That's right," Bastian went on, standing on the hull with his hand on the rigging. "Don't pretend you're better than me. We both fail to accomplish the tasks bestowed on us. You were willing to risk all your sirens, giving up the only thing you had to protect them, all for a man that still ended up dead anyway."

It was then that I realized Bastian not only took Serena's crown to take away her power, but to take away her army as well. It made sense that he took it in a time when pirates and greed ruled the seas. He was as responsible for the downfall of all mermaids as Cordelia was.

"Giving up my power for love is different than keeping souls captive for your sick collection." Serena shot back. "And you know it. That's why you're running. It's your only chance."

"I'll give you that, I thought it was." Bastian mocked. "But now I see you can't even control one testy little siren. So maybe you're not as powerful as I thought."

Serena bared her teeth, a flurry of water shooting up around her. The waves rolled and foamed around her, and the sight of it struck something in my brain. Something Cordelia once told me.

Seafoam.

I called to Serena with our siren connection while still keeping my eyes on Bastian.

She glanced at me with a raised eyebrow and tilted her head to one side, a look of half-aggravation and half-confusion. *What?*

I ran my fingers through the water, emphasizing the bubbles the movement created. *Is it true that when sirens die they become seafoam?*

Serena wrinkled her nose at me and looked away, continuing to send her golden waves toward Bastian. *Yes, but why are you asking me such a question at a time like this?*

"Because I don't think your army is gone." I shouted out loud.

Serena stopped short and her gaze fell on mine. She got it. With a nod she dove down under the water. I looked for her, waiting for her to resurface. An eerie whistle carried on the wind, sweeping in from all directions. The ocean shifted, and the waves reversed, sinking low and drawing down the entire water level with it. A rumble underneath created an endless stream of ripples across the surface, and I half expected a tsunami.

Bastian glanced around, his face white with fear as he realized the only one who could defeat the dark lord of the seas was about to fulfill that duty. I followed his gaze as he watched something in the distance. It was a wave rolling in—a foaming wave consisting not of water, but of the ghostly forms of sirens within the sea foam. Every single siren who'd ever lived and died at the hands of mermaid hunters, one unearthly chorus of their songs echoing in unison across the night air, as if their voices were infused in the sea spray itself. And in the middle of the siren wave, Serena swam amongst them, her magnificent tail flowing through the water like an iridescent rainbow and her crown glittering brighter than the moon.

The wave approached, and so did the sirens' wailing song. It was a sorrowful one, full of lament and mourning, but as it grew nearer, it turned to one of anger. I looked up to see Bastian running from one end of his ship to the other, desperate for a way out. As the wave crashed into his ship, he threw up his hands and shielded himself with a wall of black water, but the foaming siren wave wasn't hindered by it for even a second. It crashed through, engulfing him as the ghostly song grew so strong even I almost covered my ears. The wave took down his ship, specters of thrashing mermaids pulling it down to the depths, creating a whirlpool where Bastian remained. The sirens swept him up in their foaming tide, drawing him into them as they swirled around him like a cyclone, Serena amidst it all as she orchestrated their every move.

The cyclone of sirens spun faster and faster, creating a blur of Bastian behind them. And then, his shadow leaked out from him like ink as they drew it out. He cried out with a desperate scream as the water around him stained black.

"As you dethroned me, I now dethrone you." Serena's voice boomed like a clap of thunder, somehow beautiful and terrifying at the same time. Bastian groaned and cursed Serena as he writhed in the prison of the sirens. They encircled him in a blur, moving so fast as to draw out of him the source of his dark lordship, pulling from him the very spirit of Davy Jones that he'd been joined with all these years. Once more Bastian was a mortal man, stripped of his dark power, and the curse of Davy Jones was once again cast away to roam the seas, looking for its next willing host.

My eyes followed the dark shadow that loomed over the waters, erratic and frantic as the sea soaked it up like a stain. I shuddered to think who might welcome him next. But for now, at least it was no longer Bastian.

At last, the ghostly siren wave slowed, the spinning cyclone slowing as it lowered and pulled Bastian down. Davy Jones' power may have been his curse, but he was still wretched at heart all by himself, with or without the strength of a dark sea lord. And for that, he met his justice at the hands—and fins—of the vengeful mermaids that he'd indirectly slaughtered. They dragged him down with them as they crashed back into the ocean, leaving clouds of billowing sea foam in their wake. I thought at once of Cordelia, and wondered if she had been in there somewhere. She'd wanted to avenge the sirens and redeem herself. And now I guess she had, in a way.

The silence that followed was chilling. The water stilled, and the waves calmed. I drifted there alone, still taking in the fantastical event I'd just witnessed. I could almost still hear the haunting song of those sirens and I replayed their foreboding words in my head.

In future, in past
Our shadow is cast
Torn from the depths
Till nothing was left

One last time we rise

One last lullaby

Sun and moon unite

The wrongs of old made right

Thus ends the the ocean's night

The song echoed long after in my core, awakening my siren fully, and I couldn't shut her up fast enough. *Kill the queen. Take the Crown. Kill the queen. Take the Crown.*

My siren had an idea, and she wasn't polite about it. She insisted. She was clinging to something Serena said. That I was able to defy her, unlike other sirens. So that meant I could challenge her. And if I defeated her, I could become the new siren queen. I could have the powers of a goddess.

My mind was silenced. It screamed no in the back of my head, but it was silenced by the siren's overpowering commands. She was right. Serena didn't deserve the Crown. She didn't wield her power properly. If she had, sirens would still rule the seas.

Find her. Kill her. Take the Crown.

I had to follow. I had to.

I went to dive under, but something caught my arm. I hissed, my head snapping around to face my captor as I thrashed against him. It was Milo, who'd snuck up on me in a dinghy. But his voice and gentle eyes did nothing to calm my fury and power-mad desire. I hardly recognized him. And my siren wanted him out of the way.

52

Sweet Sailor Bold

Katrina

"Katrina...listen to me!" Milo shouted as I ripped my arm from his grasp. He was trying quite desperately to tell me something but everything he said became muddled. Something about the siren magic surge under the moonlight strengthening my siren. But I didn't care why she was suddenly so powerful. I just needed to let her take control. I was tired of him and those mortals ashore holding me back when in reality, I was something so beautifully powerful. How dare I suppress it any longer!

I opened my mouth to sing a song I'd never heard before, but my siren was more than happy to teach me the words. From my lips came an ancient melody, the preferred siren song of old, used to lure sailors to their deaths. It flowed from me as naturally as breathing air into my human lungs. This song, not heard on these seas for centuries, now filled the air and Milo's ears.

"My heart searches for a sweet sailor bold,

Out on these seas and the depths untold,

A sailor who'll love me and follow me down,

A sailor to kiss is a sailor to drown."

Something primal in my blood boiled over, taking complete control. Milo had fallen under my spell. He leaned over the dinghy, his gaze helplessly entranced on me. I placed my hands on either side of his face as if to kiss him, and then, just before my lips touched his, I yanked him down and dragged him into the deep with me.

Finally.

He wriggled and struggled against me, but my strength easily overpowered his as I pushed him deeper and deeper. This was what it meant to be a siren. To commit such an act of irony so fitting on this perfect night of vengeance. I smiled as I thought of it—the last of the sirens, drowning one last worthless man.

But then something stopped me, and a flash of Katrina broke through. Warm lips against mine, and a gentle hand on my face. He was kissing me. He'd stopped fighting me and was kissing me. At first I recoiled, but he embraced me harder and deepened the kiss. And that was the moment I broke free.

This man—this was Milo. I loved him. What was I doing? Oh my god. Immediately I wrapped my arms around him, shooting upwards as fast as my fins would allow, back to the surface. No sooner had we just approached the surface of the water did I feel Milo's eyes on me. I'd expected him to be sputtering and coughing up seawater, but then I remembered the power of a mermaid's kiss.

"Milo, I'm so sorry!" My voice quaked frantically as I released him from my grip. "I didn't mean to—"

"I know," he said calmly as he caught his breath. "That's why I came to warn you. So you didn't just leave us all to disappear into the sea."

"Did you know kissing me would let you breathe underwater?"

"No," Milo's breaths were still short from wrestling against me. "Must've missed that bit of folklore somehow."

"Then why did you kiss me?" I blinked away some salty droplets from my wet lashes.

"Because it was the only way I knew to bring you back to me." He smiled that crooked half smile and I wanted to melt right into the water around me. "I'm just glad it worked."

"Me too," I swam near him and he flinched, making my heart twinge with guilt. "How...how did you know I would lose myself out here?"

Milo's eyes grew heavy and he turned his head away as if searching for his words. "Your mother...she couldn't resist the call of the sea. We tried to stop her but it happened so fast. She swam out and we haven't been able to find her."

"She just found out she was a siren. Of course she wasn't strong enough to fight it." My heart sank as I thought about what I could do to find her. I tried to use my song-call, but she didn't respond to it. She could be anywhere in the open ocean by now. The siren magic influence was too great for her to resist.

Neither of us said anything for a moment. There was too much to say, and too much to think about. I'd just almost killed Milo. My mom was a runaway mermaid. And that stupid siren song still kept ringing in my ears.

It was the last of siren songs I wanted to hear. It was unsettling, and gave me a twisted feeling in my gut. A feeling that reminded me why my siren side was just as much a curse to me as the power of Davy Jones was a curse to Bastian. The difference was, Bastian embraced it. He used it to magnify who he truly was at heart. But mine was a constant conflict. And the more time passed, the more I wasn't sure which side of me was stronger. But what happened tonight had brought an answer to that question once and for all. And I didn't like it.

So there in the dark, as Milo swam back to the dinghy, I stayed for a moment. With nothing but the ocean and me, my thoughts drifted. I'd forever be at war with the voice in my head. A voice that sought strife and destruction. A voice that would always threaten to overpower my own. A voice that could take everything and everyone from me eventually, if I ever lost control for too long. It would always make me choose the sea over anything and anyone else. It would always be a constant reminder of the soul I didn't have.

I made myself admit it out loud. I hated being half-siren. It wasn't an existence that was meant to be shared with a human side. I'd never be happy to walk—or swim—in both worlds. I needed to choose one. And I had one more idea in mind that I hoped Serena would be willing to hear.

53

Daughter of the Sea

Katrina

I followed Milo in the dinghy back to shore where everyone still waited. When we arrived, McKenzie, Noah, and Russell stood around Bellamy's body, their faces still downcast even though we'd technically won the battle for the seas. And I didn't blame them. Not much of it felt like winning when one of us didn't make it out alive and one of us was lost at sea, even if it was by her own accord. I hoped my plan would at least solve one of those problems.

"Where's Serena?" Russell asked, worry etched in his eyes.

"Don't worry," I said. "She'll be back for Bellamy. She wouldn't leave without him."

"How do we just go home after this?" McKenzie's voice sounded weak, and even from where I watched in the water I could see the tear marks on her face.

"It's going to be hard," I swallowed, looking at Bellamy. "But I try to just keep telling myself this is what he wanted."

Suddenly there was a swooshing of water behind me, and a soft light emerged from the surface as Serena lifted from the water. She stepped out, regal and elegant, the dress of seawater trailing behind her with a train like a waterfall. Her skin almost seemed to sparkle beneath her flowing hair tinged with blue. Across her waist, she carried a bag made of velvet and a sword hanging from a sheath.

But her face was dull with heartache. She stood, looking at each of us one at a time. "Thank you all for your help restoring my power. We've paid a great price for it." Her eyes dropped to Bellamy and she hesitated for a moment as we hung on her last words with anticipation. "I must return to the sea now, as there are no sirens left to rule, but there is always darkness to keep at bay. And before I depart, I have something for each of you, as a way to show my gratitude and to honor Bellamy's sacrifice."

First she walked to McKenzie, who she handed the sea glass necklace from around her neck. "A fitting keepsake to remind you of that time you impersonated a sea goddess." She and McKenzie exchanged smiles, and then McKenzie threw herself at Serena and embraced her in a hug, which didn't surprise me. I smiled to myself.

Next, she handed Noah something resembling a rolled up scroll. "A map of the seas, even the secret parts," she winked. "To remind you of the things you once didn't believe in." Noah nodded his thanks.

Next, she silently trudged over to Russell, placed a hand on his cheek, and uttered something just between them. I supposed she was helping him come to terms with the fact that his daughter was really an ocean goddess and maybe to ease the goodbye. Her gift to him, I couldn't see, but I believed that was sort of the point.

Last, she turned to Milo. She reached for the sword at her side and placed it in his hands. "This is—"

"Bellamy's cutlass." Milo cut her off, his voice catching between the words.

"Yes." She blinked. "Who else better to have it than the one he taught to wield it?"

Milo pressed his lips together with a dutiful nod. When Serena turned away, I caught him staring at the sword with hollow eyes. He held onto it for a long time before looking back up at us all.

With everyone on land dealt with, it was my turn. Serena turned around to face me standing with her feet in the surf as she looked down at me. "And you, little siren, what is it that I can give to you?"

I hesitated, my voice seemingly gone. I'd planned to ask Serena for this anyway, but I hoped it wouldn't anger her. Hell, I just hoped it was even possible. "Can...can you take away my siren form?" I spat it out, trembling.

Serena knelt down, her solemn expression unchanging. "Tell me. Why would you want that, Katrina?"

I looked at my friends standing behind her, and I looked for a long time at Milo. "Because of them. And because of my mom. I want to be fully human. I want a soul."

Serena stood back, and I fully expected her to deny me what I asked. I didn't even know if she *could* give me that. So when she spoke, I breathed a sigh of relief. "I can do what you ask, but not without something from you. The ocean demands a covenant of your sincerity for me to fulfill a task so great."

"Whatever you need," I said. "It wouldn't be the first deal I've made."

"It's not a deal," Serena snapped. "But it's the only way to relinquish all your siren qualities—your voice, your power, your strength. Just as Bastian needed to destroy the things that made me a goddess to kill me, the things that make you a siren must be destroyed for you to become fully human. And for you to gain a soul."

"So what is it that you need then?" I flipped my tail with impatience and a bit of nervousness.

Serena gave me a look that cut right through my core. "You must cut off your tail."

Smothering silence fell over us all like a wet blanket as I considered the condition. "Another mermaid before me cut off her tail, and that's what started all this."

"And now it must end with the same. Your great-grandmother did it to place a curse and spare herself. You do it to lift a curse and spare those you love."

"Fine." I sucked in a deep breath. "If that's what it takes, I'll do it."

"Katrina, you sure about this?" McKenzie asked, her face contorted in a grimace.

Once more I recalled all the times my siren had made me do something I regretted, and the answer came easily. Would I sever off a piece of me to rid myself of her influence? "Yes." I eyed Serena, anger rising in me for what she was about to make me do. Whether it was truly a requirement of the ocean laws or simply her own, I couldn't help but almost hate her in that moment. But that wouldn't change anything. My only choice was to get over it and grab a sword.

"Let's go somewhere a bit more...private," Serena looked out toward the sea. She was right. It was only a matter of time before someone noticed us down here. The shore and old town was already filled with commotion from the fort collapse. She turned and looked at me. "There's a small string of sandbars just east of here."

"I'll meet you there," I said firmly. My eyes flicked to Milo for a second, who watched me with a tense gaze and uneasy stance as he shifted from one foot to the other. "Will you come with me?" I asked.

"I was hoping you'd say that." He stepped forward immediately, but Serena stopped him. "She must do this alone."

"Why?" I tossed out the words with disdain and shock. "Why can't he come with me?"

"Because," Serena lifted her chin, "When you are at your weakest moment, and when you think that you can't go on for the pain, when your siren is begging you to stop, you must prove that your human strength truly is greater. I won't allow you to become something less than what you already are. If I remove your sirenhood, it must be because you are more powerful without it. And that, my little mermaid, you must prove."

I chewed my lip and flared my nostrils, unsure of what kind of response I could offer to such a twisted condition. But Serena was an ocean goddess, and like the sea itself, she was unpredictable, powerful, and clearly sometimes even ruthless. But if this was what I had to do to get rid of the side that made me much the same way, I wouldn't be deterred.

"See you at the sandbar," I announced loud enough for everyone to hear before diving under the surface and heading straight for the tiny islands just below the horizon. My siren's voice haunted me the entire way there.

Kill the queen. Take the Crown.

When I arrived, Serena was somehow already there, waiting waist-deep on the shoreline. The moon glittered on the water's surface like a beacon to mark the place where I'd give up half of myself. Behind her, on the island nestled crookedly in the surf was the stone altar, washed up from the collapse, I assumed. I swam up to her slowly. She offered not a word, but handed me a sword. Bellamy's sword.

"Milo thought it might help you," she uttered.

Now's the chance. Kill her with the sword. Kill her!

I took one look at the blade and thought of the bloodshed and combat on the seas it had lived through. How many lives had it taken? I wondered. Had it ever taken the life of a siren before tonight?

I slid myself across the sand and up onto the stone slab. My eyes lingered over the artwork lacing the edges of the altar, each a depiction of the story of how a woman became a siren. But now it would end with the reverse. And I thought how fitting it was that the last image was nearly erased. Because we'd forged our own endings, despite what legend demanded.

Serena followed me to the stone and lowered the sword into my open hands. It all felt very ceremonial and sacred, and it sent shivers down my spine and tail. As a silent sense of doom crept upon me I looked up at the stars for comfort.

Kill the queen.

Seated with my tail hanging down into the water, I stretched it out in front of me, straightening it out the same way I would if it were my legs. I raised the blade, studying the impossible lower half I'd been gifted and cursed with. Scales of silvery blue caught the moonlight and rivaled the stars themselves. It reminded me of the starlight dress I'd worn to the gala the night Milo admitted his love for me. And that was everything I needed to shut up the voice in my head. I wanted to dance with the man I loved beneath the stars and build a life with him. I wanted that night forever. And I never wanted to try to kill him again.

With that vision sustaining me, I raised the sword above my head with both hands, trembling as I squeezed the hilt, now slippery with my sweat and seawater. I looked above at the sky to pinpoint the North Star. When I found it, I fixed my gaze on it and drew in a breath.

What are you doing? Stop! STOP!

I plunged the sword down. I watched that star as I gritted my teeth against the pain so hard I thought my jaw would break. The blade dug in, slowly, shooting agony through my waist. I kept looking at the star.

Stop this, now! You're making a mistake! You're betraying yourself!

The siren screamed within me, begging and pleading, and finally demanding that I stop. The human side of me begged, too, because the searing torment of slicing through my own flesh was almost too much to bear. So much that I stopped halfway through, as the steel of the blade met bone. A shooting pain beyond comprehension paralyzed my body and mind. My tail writhed, and my arms shook in agony and exhaustion. The saltwater on my open flesh stung like the flames of hell as it seeped into every crevice of my raw, open tissue.

"I can't do it!" I screamed, the sword jutting out of me. I hung my head as my body quaked through my ragged breaths.

That's right. Listen to me.

I opened my eyes, drawing on the strength of the stars once more. I had to shut her up. I had to gain my soul.

I tightened my grip and slammed down, digging the blade into my very core, severing the connection between my torso and tail.

No! You fool!

The scream that burst from me might've shaken the depths, but the bleeding wail from my siren pierced my mind like an icepick to the brain. In twisted, cruel torture, I pushed on the hilt with every ounce of power I had left in my quivering, feeble arms until I broke through to the other side. The siren's wail died out as my head spun, and my vision of the stars grew dim. Every part of me tingled with icy numbness until I could no longer feel anything at all. I looked down at the vision of the waves washing up the stone over my waist, washing away the river of blood gushing out as fast as it flowed.

A flash of light blinded me, a prism shooting up from the water at my waist and shining to the heavens. My body felt hollow, and my head felt light and empty as my sight left me. The sound of crashing waves became nothing. I was awake. Barely. My consciousness was slipping away, drowning in the darkness of disorientation.

"Open your eyes, little mermaid." Serena's voice sounded underwater.

My weak eyes fluttered open with timid blinks. The white light died down, leaving behind the sight of the waves washing back to reveal my bare legs in place of where my tail had been.

"Well, you proved your strength. You're fully human now." She stood at my back, where she had been the whole time. I twisted around to look back over my shoulder, my body still wobbly and trembling from the trauma it'd just endured.

"Thank you," I managed to utter. I touched my fingers to my stomach and ran them down to my hips. My waist was smooth, except for a small scar in the shape of a cluster of scales just in front of my hip bone. I glanced at Serena with surprise.

"A little reminder for you. Of what you could've been. I'll be honest, I wasn't sure if you would really do it." She stepped forward, offering her hand to help me up. Getting to my feet was a task in itself, my legs shaking as if they'd never been used before.

I shivered, hugging myself in the night sea breeze. Serena motioned with her hand and summoned the tide. It washed up my legs, spiraling upwards around me until it formed a flowing dress, the top shimmering midnight blue, fading into a gradient silver cascading skirt for the bottom. "You'll always be a daughter of the sea."

To hear those words was a relief, somehow freeing, and yet a small bit of sadness lingered. Regardless of how much I hated it, and even though I'd only known about it for a few months, I'd still just given up a part of myself. There was a weird sort of heartbreak that came with goodbyes of any sort. My body felt regenerated, and though it was back to my normal human form, it was somehow different in a way I couldn't quite identify.

"I...I have a soul now?" I asked with timid breaths.

Serena nodded. "You do. And there's one more thing I think you've earned. A bit of a surprise I have for you." She gestured toward the water, and I squinted out to see a figure on the water, a shadow walking along the surface like a ghost. Finally, I could see the figure was that of a woman, clothed in a similar, more subtle dress than mine. And as she stepped through the night fog, closer to the shoreline, she locked her eyes with mine and I knew them right away.

"Mom!" I took off running on my wobbly legs, each step feeling like the first as my feet kicked up sand behind me. She flung her arms open and I met her embrace with possibly the tightest hug I'd ever given her. "Are you..."

"Fully human," Serena finished. "She asked me for this before you did."

"Is that where you were?" I studied my mother's face. She was still beautiful, still the same. But I noticed now that she had a few creases where she hadn't before. Just a tinge of sagging beneath her eyes held the promise of aging to come. She was aging normally now, as no one in our family line ever had the chance to do. She had a soul.

"I wasn't strong enough to do it, Trina." My mom slid her slender hands over my face, brushing my scar as she spoke in a tender voice that I hadn't heard since I was a child running to her from my nightmares. "But you, beautiful girl, once again, you saved the both of us."

I gulped back a lump in my throat. "No, Mom," I whispered. "You gave up yourself to save all of us. Into a world you only just found out about a few days ago. You were protecting us that whole time. Who knows what Bastian might have done to us if you hadn't?"

My mom pulled back long enough to look at me with a broken smile. The starlight reflected on the tiny teardrops rolling along her eyelashes. "I love you, Trina."

"I love you, Mom." I squeezed her in a tight hug and whatever rift was left between us seemed to drift away in the tide at our feet.

When we pulled away, I noticed Serena was gone. I followed the path of footprints in the sand only to find her a ways off, facing the other side of the shore. Turning, as if she knew I was watching her, she wore a tender smile beneath tired eyes that refused to meet my gaze.

"I like this little shoal," she uttered. "I think Bellamy would, too."

There was a long silence between us before I finally said something. "Let's get the others."

Serena bit her lip and looked away, the breeze catching a few loose unbraided strands of her hair. "Yes," She barely spoke loud enough for me to hear over the lapping of the waves. "Let's get the others."

She cupped her hands and dipped them in a small tide pool, lifting the handful of water to her lips where she whispered a message. She poured the water into the ocean, and it trickled down in droplets of gold and zipped away through the water back towards the mainland shore in a trail of light.

"Now we wait," she said.

54

Burial At Sea

Katrina

I wasn't sure how much time had passed. I'd never been any good at keeping track. But dawn hadn't come yet. My mother and I sat on the shore watching for the others while Serena stood alone, unmoving, some meters away.

A small glow broke through the fog in the distance, burning from a lantern on a glass-clear canoe formed of water as it approached with the others on board. Their faces were somber, with Milo and McKenzie flanking one side of Bellamy's body and Noah and Russell on the other.

They slid ashore, bringing the enchanted boat in, where it dissipated back into the waves once everyone was out. No one uttered a sound. There was only the song of the waves and the patter of footsteps crunching wet sand as Milo and Noah carried Bellamy to Serena and laid him at her feet.

Serena looked down at her lifeless lover. With movements far too graceful for any human, she knelt down and kissed his forehead. We all stood encircling them, honoring this moment as best we knew how.

"A burial at sea, so that he can always be with me." Her whispers carried in the air like ghosts. "To love a siren is always a path to destruction." Then she began singing, a slightly different version of the siren lullaby.

"My heart found a sweet sailor bold,
Out on these seas and the depths untold,
A sailor who loved me and followed me down,
A sailor I kissed is a sailor I drowned."

Her voice cracked at the last word, and a tear rolled off the tip of her nose and fell onto Bellamy's pale cheek. I found myself holding back my own tears, still filled with more anger than I could contain at Bastian. He was long gone, but his damage was done.

Milo stepped forward and placed the sword on Bellamy, gently placing his hands over the hilt as though he was holding it himself. "For the locker, mate." He choked.

I gave him a moment, and then knelt down myself, placing my hand over Bellamy's. The cold stiffness of his fingers forced a sob out of me I didn't realize I'd been working so hard to keep in. With my head hung, I uttered my goodbyes.

Serena straightened her shoulders and summoned a patch of water that swirled nearby and reformed the crystal water jolly boat, this time just big enough for one. Another stream of water washed beneath Bellamy and began to gently lift him, pulling him into the boat. As we braced to send him off, a sudden shift in the wind caught everyone's attention. A harsh breeze blew in from the west, eradicating all the sea mist around us. And following it was a cloud of shadow, whisking right through us all and knocking the sword from Bellamy's hands.

"Davy Jones," Serena uttered with a scowl. "Even now he can't let us rest."

The black shadow moved aggressively, weaving between us and over Bellamy again and again before finally shooting out to sea and plunging in. Where it entered, a ripple of black formed that grew larger and larger until it was a slow-swirling black watery void—just big enough to swallow a small boat whole.

"Leave us!" Serena screamed, her desperate plea scathing my ears. But the shadow pool didn't leave. "I'll burn his body before I let you take him!"

We all looked at one another, not even Serena knowing what to do next. And for a moment, I missed my siren powers, because I felt helpless as the darkness raged off the shore.

55

DARK WATER

MILO

The strange dark whirlpool grumbled with hunger, drawing nearer and nearer to the shore of the sandbar. I ran to grab Bellamy, pulling him away from the waterline. In my struggle, Bellamy's arm shifted, revealing his open palm and a black snake marking on it. And I understood.

I stopped, still clinging to Bellamy as the realization settled into my bones.

"Serena," I called out. The look in her eyes pained me, but she had to know. "He's been chosen. He's the next to be Davy Jones."

"No, no!" She fell across Bellamy's body with her own. "No, he can't have him! I'll protect him. If he's the next chosen, Davy Jones will never stop pursuing him...so I will never stop protecting him." Each word was more frantic than the last. She struck the void with a blast of her golden water, and for a mere second it dwindled and vanished. But seconds later it returned unscathed.

The shadowy vortex continued spinning, sloshing and splashing like a growling lion waiting to devour. We all watched, all seven of us, stealing glances at one another as if perhaps one of us would know the answer to the question before us. Was it right to let Bellamy become Davy Jones, even if it seemed fate would deem it so? Or was Serena truly meant to guard him for eternity?

I looked at Katrina. Her gaze was already on me, and I knew what she was thinking—what we were *both* thinking. I cocked my head as if to make certain, and she replied with a solemn nod. So I spoke up. "The souls. The lost at sea that Bastian trapped. Bellamy could free them."

I expected the verbal lashing that followed as Serena turned red with rage at the very idea. Some of the others gasped or muttered amongst themselves.

"How could you even dare?" Her nostrils flared as she pierced me with a deathly stare. "That you would even suggest—"

"If there's anyone who could handle the power of Davy Jones, it's Bellamy," Katrina blurted out. "There's enough good in him to balance out the darkness. It has to be him. It has to be."

Serena whipped her head around from me to her, her face shining with tears. "No it doesn't!"

"She's right, Serena." I met Serena kneeling on the sand. "If it's not him, Jones might find someone with a truly black heart, maybe worse than Bastian. But Bellamy...Bellamy has enough good in him to balance the power. He'll fulfill the duty the gods gave Jones. He'll send the souls on." I placed Bellamy's lifeless hand in hers, truly believing my own words, and hopeful that it just may be the key to keep from losing Bellamy forever. "And he'll rule the seas with you, instead of against you."

That seemed to spur a reaction from her. She wiped her eyes with the back of her hand as she lowered her gaze to Bellamy's hand in hers. "With me," she sniffed. "With me, forever. He'd never age. Never die...never die." She repeated the words quietly as she stroked his cold skin with her thumb.

She pushed me aside and stood to her feet, facing the roaring black pool of shadows waiting in the water. She watched it for a moment as we hung on the suspense. If any one of us were breathing, it was impossible to tell.

"It's your decision, Serena." I stood up, too, before stepping away to resume my place at Katrina's side. "Do what you think is right."

Her eyes darted back and forth between me, then Bellamy and the whirlpool. Like a clock ticking, it beckoned, urging her to make her choice.

Finally, in one swift, sudden movement, she sent the crystal dinghy out to sea, into the path of the swirling black void. Gasps and screams erupted from our group as her power guided him to the heart of it. Though the water twisted and raged around him, his boat remained steady as though drifting on a calm sea. Ink-like water seeped into the boat, filling it to the brim until it covered Bellamy entirely, and pulled him slowly into its depths. The pool settled, becoming a ripple once more, moving in reverse—inward instead of out. And when it was all gone, nothing remained but a quiet, steady sea.

56

Dead Men Tell Tales After All

Milo

The sobs of Serena echoed in the silence as we waited ashore. McKenzie buried her face in Noah's shoulder, and Katrina and Grace stood huddled hand-in-hand, watching with anticipation. Russell and I glanced at each other, before he went back to wringing his hands and worriedly watching his daughter.

As the stillness lingered, I began to question if it was the right decision. Perhaps I shouldn't have spoken up. Perhaps Serena knew better, and it truly would've been best for her to spend the ages guarding Bellamy. Katrina and I might've made a grave misjudgment...and if we were, could we live with ourselves to see our friend return as a puppet of the sea's darkest force? The doubt gnawed at me, and I swayed uneasily, still watching the water that took Bellamy.

"I'm a fool for listening to you!" Serena wailed before lunging at me. "He's gone because of you! You were wrong!" I didn't stop her as she hit my chest and shoulders with the edge of her fists. I couldn't blame her.

"On the contrary, love, for once he was right." The voice that broke through Serena's rampage brought us all to a standstill. My head snapped to see Bellamy, taking form from a stream of shadow over the sand. He now wore the pirate lord's clothing, a long, black captain's coat and a skull medallion around his neck. His hair was long again, like our early days on the *Siren's Scorn*. He looked restored and rejuvenated in some ominous way, as though he'd been gifted a do-over of a life long past.

The smile that swept across my face was hindered by a gripping fear. I was certain we all had to be wondering the same thing. Bellamy stood before us, but was he still the Bellamy we knew?

He held his arms open wide as Serena ran to him, leaping into his embrace, weeping with joy. He spun her around and placed her down with a kiss. Katrina and I stood back as everyone else rushed to greet him with excitement and relief. He walked to me, to my surprise, and slapped me on the shoulder. "Don't stress yourself mate. I'm not completely evil."

I huffed out a sigh through my grin. "Still the same asshole as before, I see."

"With a few upgrades." He snapped his fingers and black water swirled from his hands and snaked its way around Katrina and me, wrapping around us loosely like a ribbon before Bellamy called it back with a motion of his finger.

"Bellamy!" Katrina stepped forward and threw her arms around him. "I've never been more glad to see you."

"You should know by now I don't stay dead for long, lass," he chuckled, patting her back in a friendly embrace, but then he gave her a protective squeeze, and I knew I could never thank him enough for keeping her safe.

"Thank you...for everything." I pulled his sword from where it hung at my side and offered it to him. "I believe this is yours."

He took a long look at the blade, and for a moment I thought he was at loss for words, as he dropped his guard for just a moment and allowed me to see beneath that aloof and sarcastic exterior. "You keep it, mate. I don't think I'll quite be needing a sword anymore." His eyes flashed silver and shadow swirled around his shoulders.

"You'll free the souls Bastian trapped?" Katrina asked, a hopeful look in her eye.

"If I must," he rolled his eyes with a sigh.

"Yes, you must," Serena stepped in with a chiding smirk. "That's kind of your new job."

"Aye. The deep sea undertaker. Could be worse, I suppose."

Katrina and I chuckled as the others drew in around us.

"So...will we ever see you guys again?" McKenzie asked.

Bellamy and Serena exchanged glances. "Maybe sometimes," Serena said gently. "Like when you come to the ocean just to get lost in the sunrise. When you're alone on the shore as the tide rolls in. When your soul is in true need of a breath of fresh sea air. We'll be there, watching over the ocean and those who've made it their grave. The last remnants of what the sea gods left behind."

"Then this is where we part ways?" I noted the dawn finally breaking over the horizon. Serena nodded.

"We'll miss you, you know." Katrina spoke to both of them, but she was focused on Bellamy. She stepped forward and embraced him in a hug, a burst of brightness clinging to his dark, looming figure. "It won't be the same without you."

"I know, lass." Bellamy said with more softness in his voice than I expected him to let break through. "But as long as you're by the sea, I'm never far away."

"Then you'll come visit us?"

"If Bastian can run an underground club, I'm sure I can squeeze in a visit to my best mates every now and then." They released their embrace, and Bellamy blinked a few times and swallowed. "Just bring along some rum and Dr. Pepper. Not sure they have much of that where I'm going."

Katrina laughed as she wiped a tear and sniffed. "Will do."

Bellamy turned away, leading Serena to the edge of the water. The tide was lowering, and the wet sand was cool with the promise of morning. Just before the dawn's light reached us, Bellamy waved a hand over the water, summoning the dark brigantine ship that had carried Bastian earlier. It rose up, ghostly black sails high, and almost seemed to levitate above the water.

We stood behind, waiting to see them off, but Bellamy turned around one last time and addressed me. "Turns out dead men tell tales after all. And what a tale you have to tell, brother." He went on with a half smile and a shake of his head. "I better not see you for a long while. Try to make it to the end of your life this time."

I nodded his direction and placed my hand on the hilt of his sword. "Aye. Till then, brother."

"Till then, indeed, mate."

With one last nod, he and Serena stepped hand in hand onto the ship, where they vanished with the sunrise in a stunning display of a splash of golden light mixed in a wave of shadows.

57

DAVY JONES

BELLAMY

I stood on the rocks as I watched the souls I'd freed leave the objects imprisoning them, taking the magic with them. On they went, to meet their so-deserved end at the bottom of the sea where they could rest once and for all. And once the last soul had gone, I clapped my hands and watched Bastian's collection shatter as two black waves crashed down on the once-enchanted items and ground them into dust. This was my show now.

What can I say? Becoming the next Davy Jones wasn't exactly in my plans. But somehow things all made sense for once. My father, Cordelia, the curse, Katrina, meeting and losing Serena, all lead to this. As weird and wild as it seemed, being the dark lord of the seas wasn't all that bad of a situation. I could be a captain of my own ship for eternity with my sea queen by my side...I just had to keep track of a few pathetic souls every now and then. How hard could it be?

Never mind that by the legend's design, we were meant to be sworn enemies. But we were making our own rules. Bending the laws of destiny, I like to think. A siren goddess as untamable and unpredictable as the sea spending forever with the ocean's grim reaper—what could go wrong?

Katrina and Milo might've chosen the mortal path, but I hoped they knew we'd always be there, on whatever shore they found themselves on.

"You know what we need?" Serena asked, placing her hand over mine on the helm.

"What's that?" I propped my leg up on the base of the wheel and pulled her onto my knee. She wrinkled her nose and nuzzled it against my cheek. "A pet. And I think I have the perfect one in mind."

I rolled my eyes with a shrug and a smile. "Your Kraken?"

She nodded with a grin and a giggle I once thought I'd never hear again.

I placed my hat on her head. "Captain's orders. Let's go get your beastie."

So we headed into the great horizon, two eternal guardians of the waters on which we sailed.

58

Maybe Someday

Katrina

Puerto Rico shrunk beneath us as the plane lifted, the blue sea so far below. It was foreign to be so separated from the water and not feel the siren call to it. I might not be a mermaid anymore, but my heart would always be drawn to the sea in its own way. Serena was right about that.

As we headed back home, back to Constantine, I hoped the school would let me pick up where I left off. But it could wait until the start of the next semester. For now, I just wanted to rest. Just to sit on the beach like a normal 19-year-old and enjoy the sand and sun. Maybe I would stay at my home again in Arkansas to reset a bit, but I knew in my heart I would always end up back on the coast. I wondered if life could ever be normal again. And if it couldn't, maybe that was okay. Milo placed a gentle hand on my thigh, reminding me that whatever came next, he was there with me. They all were—McKenzie, Noah and finally, Mom. I even had Russell to count on, in a way.

It was hell, but I'd do it all again to know it ends like this.

I jumped with a gasp, startled by Milo's voice in my head. "I could hear you just now!"

His eyes grew wide with surprise as I replied with my thoughts as well. *I guess Serena left one thing after all.* I laid my head on his shoulder.

Milo leaned in and kissed my forehead. *Or maybe she just couldn't take away what's written in the stars, fair lass.*

My elbow met his ribs with a light nudge and a laugh. *If only she took away your cheesiness.*

He chuckled softly.

I reached over to my wrist, feeling for a siren scale bracelet that wasn't there. I could still hardly wrap my head around all the fantastical things that had come as a result of moving to the little town of Constantine. Within the passing of only a few months, I felt as though I had lived a thousand lives. Just a girl from a small town, who liked to paint, discovering she was a mermaid and finding her soulmate in a time-defying pirate. It wasn't exactly what I'd had in mind when I started college at ISA. But if anything had ever confirmed I was right where I was supposed to be, this was it. And I had every intention of returning and finishing what I began. I just hoped relinquishing my siren powers didn't also mean my watercolor abilities had gone with it. But I guess I'd find out soon enough. I already had so many ideas for the next piece I wanted to paint—the missing image that should've been on that last section of the painted stone table—a mermaid queen surrounded by her true power—the ones who crowned her.

I smiled, hearing Russell a few rows over gently teasing Noah about McKenzie and Noah nervously denying his feelings for her.

"No, no, it's not like that," Noah swore.

"Yeah, definitely not like that at all. We're just...really good friends." McKenzie fumbled with her words.

I laughed to myself as Russell pressed them, refusing to accept their obviously fake denials. It was plain as day to everyone except themselves. Maybe the old man poking fun at them might help them finally figure it out.

From the sound of it, Noah and Russell had begun to heal the rift between them, and I hoped Noah would continue to give his grandfather a chance now that he understood everything so much more.

My mom turned around from her seat in front of me, reaching her hand back for me to take. I took her fingers in mine and squeezed.

"So are we telling Dad about any of this?" I raised an eyebrow.

My mom paused, visibly in thought as she turned her face to the window beside her. "I've put him through enough..." She blinked. "But maybe someday."

"Maybe someday sounds good to me." My mouth twitched into a smile. Maybe we'd find a way to explain it all one day in the future, or maybe not. Because all that mattered was that what started as a nightmare had ended as a dream. And the things once torn apart, now mended.

EPILOGUE

MILO

Ten years later...

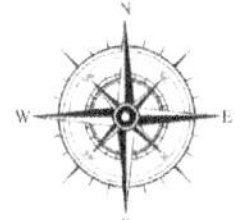

The sun would be setting in an hour, but those two just couldn't get their fill of the ocean. I watched from the beach as they picked up shells on the surf, throwing in the odd splash or two every now and then as the foaming tide rolled in. The beautiful barefoot woman and the starry-eyed child at her side who loved the sea as much as she did. My wife and son. My absolute greatest treasure.

"Katrina! Caspian!" I called from where I watched from the reeds by the boardwalk connecting our home to the beach. "The boat's ready when you are!"

"Five more minutes!" Katrina laughed, the wind sending her hair flowing as she danced in the wet sand with our little boy just shy of two years.

Five more minutes, Starlight. I told her with a warm smile at the sound of their laughter mixed with the crash of waves.

We'd planned a night on the sailboat for stargazing just off the coast, the three of us. I hoped to show Caspian the stars and tell him the tale of the mermaid who loved a pirate, and how they crossed time to find each other. And how the pirate found his greatest wealth in the life he built here by the ocean, where he could be the man he'd wished his own father had been. And years from now, I'd pass down my compass to him, to help guide him when his own storms came.

I reached up and felt the scar over my blind eye, a permanent reminder of my path. But I didn't need sight in both eyes to see I had everything I needed right in front of me here, in my final and most priceless life—one so much more than I deserved—as a port engineer married to a watercolor artist on the coasts of Cape Cod. Of course, we made sure to pay a visit to Constantine every couple of years to visit Noah and Russell, who owned a joint auto shop and boat repair shop, and where Katrina's paintings lined the halls of the school she once feared wouldn't accept her.

As Katrina approached with Caspian in tow, she smiled at me, and I was captivated by those deep brown eyes as much as every time before. I watched them walk back to the house, a trail of saltwater footprints, big and small. And I thought to myself that I'd cross oceans for a mere glimpse of this moment. But I didn't have to. It was mine. Full sail to the days ahead. No more curses. No more pirates and sirens. Just she and I and a lifetime.

"Have you checked the mail today? I'm waiting for a postcard from McKenzie. Last I talked to her she said she's loving London. She says she can't wait to—oh! Everything okay? Are you coming?" Katrina turned around with a grin as she released the hand of a giggling boy who ran to me.

I snapped out of my reverie and went to meet them, lifting Caspian onto my shoulders and kissing Katrina on the way.

"Of course I am." I smiled.

And I packed the Dr. Pepper. Just in case.

Acknowledgments

Thank you to the sea, for inspiring so many legends and mysteries.

But mostly, thank you to everyone who made it this far.

Keep a weathered eye on the horizon for the next adventure.

Follow the Author

Thank you so much for reading. To keep up with my current works and be the first to hear about new releases and special reader opportunities, follow me on social media @authorvalelane or sign up for my newsletter at authorvalelane.c om

Printed in Great Britain
by Amazon

49805058R00202